BUSTED

A CADE RANCH
SPECIAL EDITION
BOOK THREE

Greta Rose West

eBook ISBN: 978-1-955633-02-4
Print ISBN: 978-1-955633-05-5
Special Edition Print ISBN: 978-1-955633-18-5

PRESS

ALSO BY GRETA ROSE WEST

Wild Heart: Welcome to Wisper

Subscribe to the newsletter for this short introduction into the Cade Ranch world and for extra goodies and scenes. Sign up at gretarosewest.com.

THE CADE RANCH SERIES IN ORDER

BURNED

BROKEN

BUSTED

BRAVED

BLINDED

THE WISPER DREAMS SERIES IN ORDER

RIVERS BETWEEN US

STORMS INSIDE US

MOUNTAINS DIVIDE US

LIGHT BETRAYS US

Acknowledgments

This book simply would not exist without many amazing people.

Voor Cece: Heel hartelijk bedankt, mijn vriend. Je bent de beste boekenvriend in de hele wereld, en zeker de beste Nederlandse vriend. Je bent gewoon een geweldige vriend. Ik hou van je. Bedankt dat je het me geleerd hebt. Dit boek zou niet bestaan zonder jou. Ik weet dat toen ik je een bericht stuurde op GR, je waarschijnlijk dacht dat ik gek was, maar bedankt voor lezen. Dit boek is niet over jullie zoon geschreven, maar hij staat op de pagina's. Net als jij. <3 (I apologize for the likely many errors in my translation, but I couldn't email my Dutch guru for corrections since that is you! I put it through the translator, but we all know how accurate those things are. I know cuz you laugh at me often when I use them ;))

Peter, I found you specifically for this book. I don't know what I did to deserve such luck, but thank you for replying to that first email. I bet some days you wish just a little you hadn't. The courage it took to send it is the courage I find in myself every day as I write and publish these stories. For fostering that courage, you are so appreciated. Thank you for being so open with me about your own experiences. You helped me find the confidence I needed to send Kev and Luuk out into the world. And thanks for feeding my MS when we shared custody. He had fun at your house.

Thanks to Joanne for calling me out for my dangling

modifiers and run-on sentences and for not having a coronary every time Luuk said "this" when he should've said "that."

To each and every ARC reader and reviewer, I so appreciate your words and your time, and your willingness to follow me down this path. It's not one many in my genre traverse, and I love that you did!

Damn, GAI. If ever a song could inspire a whole book… "Was I Just Another One"? Good God. In the caves in Tennessee—I wasn't there, I saw it online—but these characters were born from that feeling even before I heard the song. They were born from the beauty in the strings, the weird but sexy space noises, and the *fuck* in your voice when you wailed at the end. Thank you for that. Someday I will hear it for myself.

And my biggest and most beautiful thanks goes out to each and every person in this world who has the courage to live their truth out loud every day, naysayers be damned. You give the rest of us courage, too, and you inspire me every minute I am alive.

To You:
Love is love is love,
and you deserve it.

ONE
KEVIN

I watched from the back of my horse in the front paddock under a gray winter sky (yeah, right, like I was my brothers, all broody and whiny—gimme a break) as a big blue GMC Sierra raced up the lane to stop right smack-dab in front of my house.

My family had been a little on edge, so it was no surprise to me when my older brother, Dean, appeared on our front porch with a shotgun aimed at the driver of the unknown truck as he emerged from the cab.

I was too far away to see or hear what the blond-haired, sexy-bodied man said. Yeah, so maybe I needed glasses, but I still had a pretty good view of the shape of him 'cause he wasn't wearin' a coat. Tall, lean, invitin'—fuckable, if he happened to swing that way, which he wouldn't 'cause this was Wyoming—but he raised his hands in front of his chest and advanced slowly.

After a few seconds, my brother lowered his gun, and his girlfriend, Oly Masterson, emerged from the house in her pink pajamas and snow boots, squealed (I heard that), threw her hands up into the air, and ran down the porch stairs toward the stranger. She jumped into his arms and he hugged her close.

My brother and Oly had just gotten back together after a long time apart, like, literally a couple days ago, so I was a little confused as to why Dean didn't pummel the guy into the snow. To my surprise, the guy released Oly, and she grabbed his hand as they climbed the porch stairs, and all three of 'em went into my house like they were BFFs.

The guy looked hot and I was curious, so I fed Classic some hay, leavin' him happy in his stall, and stalked up the gravel lane leadin' to my house to investigate. I still had an air cast on my right leg from a break three months before, and I had to cover it with a stupid rubber boot and eight damn socks so my toes didn't freeze off, so I hobbled a little like an idiot, but I finally made my way to the porch.

When I pushed the kitchen door open and barreled in like I always did, my whole body was assaulted with the sounds, scents, and sights of my nightmares. Or my dreams.

I couldn't fuckin' decide.

I heard my brother introducin' the guy to my family.

"… and this is Ma." Dean stepped away, and I saw the sexified stranger extendin' his hand to my best friend, my surrogate mama.

"*Hallo, mam.* Pleasure to meet you. Luuk van der Wouden." It sounded kinda like he said Leuk Vandervoouden, like he described himself as lukewarm, but he wasn't. He was hot AF. I hadn't even seen his face yet, but his body… *Good grief.*

Ma held out her small hand and he clasped it gently, givin' it the tiniest of shakes.

This had to be Oly's friend from veterinary school. She'd been expectin' him.

"Luke?"

"No, *mam*, Luuk. Think of it as L-E-U-K, but you can call me whatever you like. My English friends call me LV. Except

Carolina." He turned his perfectly coiffed blond head to the side to smirk at Oly, and I choked on my own spit. Just the side of his face, with his dimple and his full lips—oh my God. And the sound of his voice? Pure fuckin' sex, even with the weird accent.

"Well, aren't you a charmer," Ma cooed, sittin' back in the old brown recliner in the livin' room. "LV? Sounds like Alvie. Maybe that's what I'll call you." She laughed. "Well, Alvie, this is Jay, Dean's youngest brother, and have you met Carey?" She motioned to the two dumbasses sittin' on the floor.

"*Hallo*, good to meet you, Carey. Jay, it's nice to meet you as well."

Jay and Carey stood to shake the guy's long-fingered hand.

"We spoke on the phone," Carey said.

"We did?"

"Yeah, I'm Sheriff Michaels. We talked when you called about Oly's accident the other day."

"Oh, *ja*, of course."

Carey relaxed back on the floor into the ridiculous bean bag chair he'd previously occupied, and the guy smiled, lookin' a little confused, probably at the *super* professional image of the Sheriff of Teton County perched in a bean bag chair. Man, we really needed to invest in some new furniture.

"Good to meet you, Luuk," Jay said. "You hungry? We got enough food to feed an army this mornin'."

"Sure, sure, *ja*. I'm actually starving. I have been on the road all night."

"Luuk, you drove all the way here?" Oly asked. "I thought you flew. That's not a rental?"

"No. I bought it a few weeks ago. Did I forget to tell you? And *ja*, I drove straight here. Carolina, I thought you had been highjacked."

I snorted.

"Carjacked. I tried to call, Lookie Loo. I'm sorry."

Lookie Loo? What a stupid nickname.

"*Ja*, but by then, I was somewhere in the middle of—Where am I?" He laughed, and all the blood in my head rushed to my dick when the silky sound of his voice entered my bloodstream through my ears. "I spoke to your parents, but I lost my cell signal. It's okay. I'm just so relieved you're not hurt."

"So, Alvie, where you from?" Ma asked while Jay walked into the kitchen and looked me up and down, standin' in the middle of the room, frozen, hard, and stupid. What? So maybe I didn't get out much. I couldn't remember the last time I'd seen a guy so hot, though I hoped Jay couldn't tell what I was thinkin'. I sat at the kitchen table, unlacin' my boot and removin' my stupid cast.

"Eh, originally I come from Oudewater, a small farming town, but also we lived in Amsterdam for a short time. In the Netherlands."

"Have a seat, sweetheart," Ma said. "Oh, I bet it's beautiful there. I've always wanted to travel. I just never really had the chance. Do your parents still live there?"

"No, *mam*, they passed when I was fifteen." He sat on the couch next to my almost-sis-in-law, Evvie, and she smiled and patted his leg.

"I'm so sorry. Please forgive me."

"No, no, *mam*, please. It was a long time ago." He smiled a little awkwardly, like maybe he didn't really wanna talk about his family, but he also didn't wanna make Ma uncomfortable.

"Oh, honey. Well, who raised you then? Do you have brothers or sisters?" I could hear Ma adoptin' him in my mind. She kinda tended to do that. Ma—our lady of lost boys.

"No, it's just me. I stayed in boarding school until I graduated. Then I went to university and then to vet school, where I met Carolina."

"Oh, you poor dear," Ma said, and he smiled at her, but somethin' sad flashed across his face, or at least the half of it I could see. "Well, congratulations on your graduation, Alvie. What an accomplishment."

He tilted his head a little. "*Dank je wel, mam.*" He sounded completely taken back by Ma's praise.

Carey asked, "Boardin' school, what was that like?"

"It was pretty boring. I found a lot of trouble. I guess you could say I had a habit of trying to make my own fun."

Carey snickered and Jay laughed, walkin' back into the livin' room. He shoved a huge plate of food into Luuk's hands, and Luuk thanked him. God, that voice. Like a low, relaxin' hum.

I took the opportunity to walk in there to get a better look at the guy, and when he saw me, he choked on his first bite of bacon and eggs! *Hm.* Interestin' development. Did he like what he saw? I sure did.

He was sexy as shit! Blond hair, blue eyes for days, dark eyebrows, and his jawline coulda cut through leather. Shadowy, two-day scruff covered it, framin' a smile to die for. 'Cept, he didn't smile. Somethin' dark and... intense hid behind his eyes. He stared up at me, slack-jawed, and I arched an eyebrow. Oh man.

Catch, *fuck*, and release.

"Luuk, this is Kevin," Oly said, and he glanced at her for half a second before lookin' back at me.

"*Hallo,* nice"—he lifted his arm to cough into it, clearin' his throat—"nice to meet you, Kevin."

I didn't respond. I just stood there like an idiot, lookin' at him. I kinda felt like I was stuck in a trance—I couldn't look away from his aqua-blue eyes.

Finally, Sheriff Dickwad reached over and yanked on my pant leg, and I lost my balance. I tipped over but regained it before fallin' on my face in front of, literally, the sexiest man I'd ever laid eyes on. I pounced on Carey, took his ass down, pulled his arm around his back, and shoved his face against the wood floor.

Rollin' me off him, he sat up. "Quit bein' a jerk. Sit down and join us," he said, grabbin' a ridiculously large bucket of popcorn from the floor, shovelin' a handful in his mouth.

"Fuck you, Sheriff. Did you really get elected, or did the other guy just *die*? And why you eatin' popcorn at nine in the mornin'?"

"Kevin Christian Cade, watch your mouth in front of our guests, or I'll wash it out with soap."

"Yes, ma'am. Sorry." Yeah, okay, I wanted to be cool in front of Dutch Hot Guy, but I couldn't be rude to Ma.

"Nice, Kevin," Jay said, and Carey smacked the back of my head, causin' my hair to fall in my face, and I coulda sworn I saw Luuk, outta the corner of my eye, watch me push it away. He licked his lips.

"We're havin' a movie marathon. We finally talked Evvie into somethin' other than Christmas movies." Carey leaned closer to me. "So fuck you too," he whispered, thinkin' he'd be the one to get away with a little profanity.

"Carey Michaels, you may be the sheriff, but I'll still tan your hide," Ma scolded. "Show a little decorum, would ya? Jeez-o-pete, what's the matter with y'all? Buncha hooligans."

Sexy Luuk chuckled, and I turned away from Carey to face the TV, tryin' to act like the hottest guy on the planet wasn't sittin' right behind me. I felt pretty confident from his physical reactions to me that he thought I was hot, too, and I planned on takin' full fuckin' advantage of that.

Contrary to what my brothers believed, I hadn't had sex with anybody in a *long* time, and by sheer coincidence, I'd just found the guy to break that unlucky streak.

I sat with my back to him, flexin' my shoulders while I pretended to watch whatever stupid movie played. I knew he watched me. I felt it, like he had lasers in his eyes and aimed 'em right between my shoulder blades.

A lotta people liked watchin' me. I'd never had a shortage of admirers. Mostly women, unfortunately, but I knew I looked good, and I still felt his eyes on me as he ate, and everyone else casually asked questions about his life and work while I listened to his every word, plottin' how I might get him on his knees in some dark, secret spot.

"So, you're visiting with Oly for New Year's?" Evvie asked.

"Em, yes. Well, actually, I'm going to work with her at the veterinary clinic. I was supposed to interview with Dr. Prittchard, but now, I will full in to help Carolina while he recovers from his stroke."

"Fill in, dear," Ma corrected him. "Isn't that sweet of you. I'm sure Doc will appreciate the help." She swooned and I rolled my eyes. Dude sounded like a goody-two-shoes to me. A hot-as-fuck goody-two-shoes, but still.

"Seriously, I can't thank you enough, Luuk. You are totally savin' my butt," Oly said. "I have no idea what I would do if you couldn't help me. I've been a vet for five minutes. I can't do this by myself."

"Of course you can, Carolina. But I'm happy to help. Denver was not really working out for me. I much prefer a mixed practice, and the clinic there is strictly small animals. I miss cows and horses."

"You're in the right place then," Jay said, standin' and steppin' toward Luuk. "Here, Luuk, lemme get your plate."

"No, no, please, relax. I need to stretch my legs." The couch creaked, his clothes rustlin' when he stood.

"Alright, well, make yourself at home then. Grab a soda or there's coffee, if you like," Jay said.

"*Dank je wel.* Can I get anything for anyone?" he asked, and finally, I sprang up from the floor in one lithe movement and turned to him.

"Yeah, but I'll get it. Sit, Doc." I took his empty plate from his hands, makin' sure to touch my fingers to his, and looked right into his eyes. He kinda fell back down onto the ugly plaid couch, and I smirked but schooled my expression quick. My brothers didn't know I liked guys, and I wasn't about to broadcast it.

I wondered if everyone in the room could hear my heartbeat. It pounded in my chest like a bass drum while I stared at him, imaginin' chasin' him into the kitchen and takin' him up against the ancient fridge.

Luuk stayed in Oly's little cottage in town, and I didn't see him again till almost a week later, on the night of Jack and Evvie's weddin', New Year's Eve.

I'd been gettin' really annoyed with all the endless weddin' preparations. Somehow, I'd been the one to end up takin' care of all the horses and the barn, and I needed to let out some steam. I wondered, if I showed up there, just knocked on his front door, would he invite me in? If he was— If he liked guys like I did, maybe he'd welcome the opportunity without havin' to go lookin' for the hookup. Or maybe he'd be shy about it.

Fine. Maybe I was shy about it. It wasn't too often the perfect guy showed up on my doorstep though. Not in Wisper. Probably not in Wyoming, period. But one had, and turned out, he didn't seem shy about it at all.

Also turned out I was a gigantic dick. Well, everyone knew that already, but Luuk hadn't.

He was about to find out.

"This stud is magnificent," Luuk said while I stood behind him, starin' at his ass in his fancy jeans while he appraised Mad Max, our gargantuan black stallion, in his stall.

Luuk had shown up to the weddin' in time for the nuptials and stayed after to help clean up and hang out with Dean, Oly, and her parents. I'd gone out to the barn to take care of the horses and close down for the night, and Luuk followed to help. Said he wanted to be useful. I could think of a couple things he might do to be useful to *me*.

"Yeah, that's Mad Max. He's a feisty S.O.B. Jack's the only one can calm him," I said, leanin' back against Hobbs' stall, crossin' one boot over the other.

"He's beautiful. He reminds me of a horse I had when I was a boy. Are you going to breed him?"

"That's the plan. Jack likes his pedigree, thinks he'll bring in some money," I replied as the stupid goofy three-year-old gelding stuck his head over the railin' behind me, rubbin' his slobbery horse lips all over my shoulder.

"I am thinking of five people I could call right now who would love a foal from this horse."

"Yeah? Talk to Jack. He runs the show 'round here."

He turned real slow, lookin' down the aisle and back, his eyes dartin' everywhere but at me, like he was nervous to be alone with me.

"So, em, *welk paard rijd je*?" He clicked his tongue. "Which horse do you ride?"

"Classic." I nodded toward my horse's stall, then headed down in that direction. Luuk followed and stood in the aisle while I stepped in with Classic, my obstinate chestnut gelding with a white star on his forehead.

"He was my dad's horse. He don't really like anybody else to ride him, but I guess I'm just stubborn." I patted Classic's back and whispered to him to get a load of the hot vet behind me. His big horse ears lifted and turned, listenin', and he snorted and stomped his hoof. He probably disapproved of my sexual predilection just like my dad woulda.

Luuk and I worked together, feedin' and waterin' the horses. With the weddin' and all the guests on the ranch all day, supper had been late, and the beasts weren't shy about lettin' us know. We spoke a few times but not about anything too excitin'. I got the feelin' he felt uneasy around me, which was very disappointin' 'cause I was *extremely* drawn to him. He looked at me, though, a lot. I caught him peekin' many times.

He peered in at Mad Max again while I went to put the hose away, and like an idiot, I banged my recently broken and metal-pin-infused leg against the water spigot.

"Fuck!"

When he came joggin' to find me, I sat on the barn floor next to the hose with my eyes closed, clutchin' my right leg and holdin' my breath. I knew he was standin' there. I heard him breathin', but my leg hurt really bad, and I couldn't concentrate on bein' Mr. Cool Guy in the moment. Technically, I shoulda still been wearin' my stupid air cast, but I was a vain motherfucker.

"Kevin? Are you hurt?"

"I'm fine."

"You do not look fine," he argued.

"I'm fine," I said again and tried to stand, but as soon as I put weight on my right foot, pain shot through my leg down to my goddamn toes. "Shit!"

I lost my balance, and he jumped over to give me somethin' to lean against. I threw my arm out and grasped his coat in my fist, steadyin' myself, tryin' not to fall the fuck over.

"Have you hurt your ankle?"

"No, it's an old injury. I banged it against that stupid metal spigot. Just smarts is all. Gimme a minute." I blew out a big breath and inhaled again, holdin' it in and squeezin' my eyes shut against the pain.

"Breathe. It will help. It hurts more if you hold your breath."

I exhaled like he said and he did too. He was breathin' heavy, and I realized I was still touchin' him as I opened my eyes and felt the heat from his body on my hand. He watched my face, my lips, and I had to fight the urge to lick his bottom one. He bit it hard, and the sight of his white teeth tearin' into that plump skin made all the blood in my body travel on a one-way ticket right to my dick. I coulda pounded nails with it.

Well, ow.

Okay, so I coulda pounded *somethin'* with it.

Raisin' his head a little, he released his lip and blew out a slow and steady breath, and his eyes looked right into mine. I was frozen—a mouse in the snake's snare. *Shit. Say something, you idiot. Speak!* But I couldn't. My brain wouldn't work.

He'd caused some kinda short circuit.

He watched me warily as I inched my face closer to him, and closer still, until my mouth hovered a centimeter from his. I felt his breath against my cheek.

I couldn't seem to stop myself.

Lookin' down his body and back up, my eyes raked over his neck as I imagined bitin' and lickin' it, and my fingers unzipped his red, ridiculously overstuffed winter coat so slowly. I had no clue what I was doin', but he didn't stop me when I placed my hand on his ribs over his shirt.

Oh. My. Fuck.

I wanted to dig my fingers into his skin and slam his body to mine.

My hair brushed against his lips as I looked down at my hand inside his coat. He inhaled and his ribs expanded with the breath. It felt a little choppy, which gave me confidence. I was so hard, if he touched me, I'd blow right there in the middle of my family's barn.

Liftin' my head, I looked in his eyes.

What I imagined myself sayin' sounded sexy and irresistible, but what came outta my mouth was: "Want me, Doc?" He didn't answer, but his lips quirked just a little. "I think you do. I saw the way you watched me earlier. You like watchin' my body? Imaginin' me suckin' you off? My lips 'round your cock?"

Breathin' faster and faster, his face was set in deadpan

lust, his eyes blue flames, like one of them blue-green drift-wood fires.

Touchin' my nose to the skin beside his bottom lip, I inhaled, drawin' my breath in slowly and closin' my eyes as the heady scent of his skin overtook my better instincts (well, the one or two I still had left).

I'd never kissed a man. I'd been with plenty of women, kissed 'em tryin' to force myself to enjoy it. And I'd been with guys. Well, I'd fucked 'em or they'd sucked me off. But I'd never kissed 'em. Never let 'em kiss me.

Kissin' Luuk, though? I wanted my tongue in his mouth so damn bad. Even closed, tipped up in a sarcastic, uncertain smirk, with his sexy lips—and *God*, those dimples—his mouth was my own personal haven.

Or I thought, maybe it could be.

I had just been about to growl like an animal and shove my tongue into the wet, hot Dutch cave of my dreams, when I heard my brother, Finn, callin' my name, and I froze. I wanted this man like none I'd ever met, but nobody could know it. The guy was a vet in my town, for a little while at least, and I lived and worked on a horse ranch.

What in the world was I thinkin'?

I stood up tall, backed away, and lied, "I know I look good, and you're welcome to dream, but that's all it's gonna be for you. I ain't a fuckin' fairy." I winced as I said the word but pulled my hand away from him and limped outta the barn.

Shit.

Shit, shit, shit.

Two

LUUK

Die verdomde prick.

I could have strangled Carolina for not warning me. I mean, *mijn* God, she could have at least told me what I would be walking into—*who* I would be walking into—although I think she maybe had not known.

Beautiful, sarcastic, rude Kevin Cade.

Prachtige, sarcastische, onbeleefd Kevin Cade.

"Doc? You in here?" Kevin's brother, Finn, called out, searching for me.

"*Ja. Geef me een moment.*" Damn it. I could not even think with this man around me. "Give me a moment, please."

"Where you at?"

Begging my body to calm, I willed the blood in my groin to flow back through my damn veins so it could take oxygen to my stupid brain so I could think.

I took two deep breaths. "Here, Finn. I am here," I said, stepping around the corner so he could see me.

"You okay? You look a little…"

An almost hysterical laugh escaped me. "*Ja.* No, I'm fine. Yes."

Finn inspected me. "Sure 'bout that?" He did not look convinced.

"Yes. I was just, em, just looking around. Uh, this stud is beautiful." I motioned to the large black stallion, hoping to distract Finn, and took another deep breath.

Finn narrowed his eyes. "Sure. Yeah, Mad Max is somethin' else. Hey, I apologize for my brother. If he said somethin… rude? He can be, um, kind of an a—"

"No, no, it's fine. I was helping him, but we are done now."

"Okay, well, c'mon up to the house. Carey's here. He wants to talk to you."

"To me? Why?"

"To all of us. C'mon."

Oh mijn God. That man! What nerve did he have to get so close to me, put his hands on my body, his mouth? If he hadn't walked away, I might have punched him. Or… something else.

"Doc? Comin'?" Finn asked and looked at me like he thought I might have come unhinged.

I snorted. "*Ja. I'm coming,*" I said and followed him. Maybe I was unhinged. But I could not afford to make a mess. I had to be professional. I was only here to help Carolina. I shook my head. No, no, no, no. No.

Verdomme. No.

"Doc?" Finn stopped walking and turned to me as we climbed the stairs to his front porch.

"What?"

"Did you say somethin'?"

Now I was talking to myself. Out loud?

"Don't listen to me, Finn. Please, continue. I'm coming."

Finn inspected me again, and I shook my head. He pressed his lips together, raised his eyebrows, and turned around to open the kitchen door. Clearly, he thought I had lost my mind.

And then we walked into the house, and the sheriff kicked me right in my aching balls when he told me I had to stay the night at Cade Ranch.

"Fuckingmother." *Shit*. Had I said that out loud too? I looked around, but no one seemed to notice my outburst.

"Sorry, Doc. I'd really appreciate it though, if you don't mind. That way I know where you are. It'll be safer here."

He looked at Evvie and smiled. "I'm sorry to do this on your weddin' night. I planned on comin' back with a big ol' bottle of whiskey to celebrate, but a man's been spotted in Jackson fittin' the description of the thug who harassed Dean and Oly."

"It's okay, Carey," she said. "Just tell us what's going on."

He looked at Jack. "All the guests have gone home?"

Jack nodded.

"Alright, well, the FBI thought this guy would try to pass into Canada, but I just had a feelin' he'd come back here. Seems I was right. I think we need to assume he knows where Oly lives. I think he's the guy who broke into the vet clinic a couple weeks ago, so I have to assume he has her address." Finally, he looked at me. "Which is where you're stayin', Doc."

Jezus. What had I gotten myself into?

"I've already spoken to the feds," he said. "Meanwhile, I've got two uniforms doin' patrols. Keep an eye on your feeds, make sure they're all on."

Stepping behind Carolina, I whispered, "Feeds?"

"Security cameras. They have them outside, all around the house and barn. It's a long story."

"*In* the barn?" I asked as quietly as I could. "Not a fuckin' fairy," my tight ass, but I had a feeling Kevin didn't want anyone to know he was gay or bi, or whatever he was.

"No, I don't think so," she whispered back. "Well, actually, I'm not sure. Why?"

"I will tell you later."

The sheriff walked backward toward the door as we—the Cade brothers, Evvie, Carolina, and I—sat at their kitchen table. He turned his head to the sound of a car we could all hear approaching the house.

"So, um, you ain't gonna like it, but I had my deputy bring your… Daisy here. She's been stayin' in the little apartment over the diner, but I didn't think it'd be a good idea for her to be alone there with this guy lurkin' about."

"Goddammit," Jack grumbled, slumping back in his chair.

"Jack," Evvie pleaded. "She's in danger too. It's just for the night."

I didn't know who this Daisy person was, but it was obvious she wouldn't be a welcome addition to the group. All of the Cade men bristled and stiffened.

Except for the youngest, Jay. "She can have my room," he offered. "I'll sleep on the couch."

"Fine," Jack said through clenched teeth, and a soft knock on the door interrupted the uncomfortable silence.

When the sheriff opened it, a female version of Jack, much shorter of course, appeared. This had to be the Cade brothers' mother. She looked to be in her fifties, maybe. Still very beautiful, but she smiled apprehensively, highlighting age lines around her eyes and mouth.

She looked around the table and whispered to Sheriff Michaels, "This isn't a good idea. Maybe I could just stay the night at the Sheriff's station?"

"Dean," Carolina whispered and elbowed her boyfriend in the ribs, and he stood.

"It's fine," he said. "You'll stay here."

Kevin Cade sat to my left, and I'd angled my chair toward Carolina so I wouldn't be forced to look at him all night. I could feel him staring a hole into the back of my head, but now, the energy radiating from him changed when Daisy entered the kitchen.

He stood abruptly, sending his chair back several feet, and stormed out of the house.

"Where you goin'? Don't leave the ranch," Sheriff Michaels warned Kevin when he knocked past him.

"Just goin' to the fuckin' barn."

"Keep your eyes open."

"No shit," Kevin growled and left the house. He wasn't wearing a coat, and I couldn't stop myself from staring at his ass as he stomped away.

He did not even look at his mother.

"Well, here we go again," Sheriff Michaels said. "This time I don't plan on anybody gettin' the jump on us. I'll be in my cruiser, lookin' for the douchebag. Happy freakin' New Year. Call me if you see anything, even if it's just a damn raccoon." He yanked the door shut behind him, following Kevin.

"Daisy, have you eaten?" Evvie asked. "We have plenty of food. I could heat something up for you."

"No, thank you, Everlea."

"Oh, you can call me Evvie. Everybody does." Hm. So Jack's wife did not know his mother? Kind of weird. I didn't remember seeing her there, but hadn't Jack's mother been at his wedding? Surely, she would have met Evvie then?

"Jay, whiskey," Jack ordered.

When Carolina told me Dean and his brothers were ranchers, this had been exactly what I pictured—muscled, brute, and gruff.

"Good fuckin' idea," Finn said. "I'll get it." Finn, though, was the opposite, funny, silly, and always kind. And gorgeous. He'd grilled me endlessly earlier in the evening while I'd helped clean after Jack and Evvie's wedding about the food in the Netherlands, which, sadly, most people thought was not so great. But I missed it. Lots of *boterhammen met hagelslag*, sandwiches with sprinkles; *snert*, pea soup; and *frites met mayonaise*. My favorite was *boerenkool stamppot*, kale stew.

"Excuse me. I'm gonna go change. I wanna get outta this dress," Carolina said. "Luuk, come with me?" She nodded toward the living room and raised her eyebrows. Oh, *godzij-dank*. I'd never been in a more awkward and unpleasant situation. The woman, Daisy, looked so uncomfortable, and her sons were clearly irritated at her presence.

And Kevin? I didn't want to be anywhere near him when he came back into the house.

"I'll change too," Evvie said, standing and pulling on my shoulder. She was still wearing her wedding dress, and she held the skirt in one hand, holding it up off the floor. "Follow us, Luuk. I'll find you a place to sleep. Oly, I'm borrowing some pj's."

I followed the women upstairs, and Evvie whispered, "Try to be quiet. Ma's asleep." She motioned to a closed bedroom door at the end of the hallway. "Luuk, you can sleep there in Kevin's room. He'll probably stay in the barn tonight. I'll put clean sheets on. I am so sorry. You probably want to run screaming after all that awkward family drama."

I could do nothing but stare at Kevin's door. Was she kidding? Sleep in his bed? I held in another deranged laugh. "I think it would be best if I get a hotel in Jackson, yes? I am in the way—"

"No, Luuk," Carolina whispered, winding her arm through mine. "C'mon, I wanna change, and Evvie and I will fill you in. I'd rather you stay here with us so I know you're safe."

An hour later, after they'd told me a story about the men's mother leaving twenty years ago when they were little boys, and how she'd just come back to town after living in Colombia with the head of a drug cartel, and now, that man's son was after Dean and Carolina, I thought I might have entered some sort of twilight zone.

I dressed for bed in borrowed clothing, Dean's Marines T-shirt and a pair of black joggers that were probably twice as big as I needed. It was like some bizarre teenage sleeping party. I felt really uncomfortable and in the way, and I had just been about to actually run screaming from the ranch when we heard shouting down the hall.

"Movement!"

Carolina threw Dean's bedroom door open, and Jack, Dean, Jay, and Daisy came rushing up the stairs to see what Finn was shouting about.

We all crowded into Finn's—*Oh God. What a mess.* Finn's bedroom looked like that of a sixteen-year-old boy. I tried not to breathe or step on anything… alive.

He pointed to one of many computer screens on a desk in the corner. "There," he said, and Dean pulled his phone from his back pocket.

"I texted Carey. He's on his way back. Dammit. Kevin's in the barn."

Daisy's hand flew up to cover her mouth.

"What's all the shoutin' about?" Ma asked as she appeared in Finn's bedroom door, blinking at the harsh light in her blue sleeping dress with white fluffy slippers on her tiny feet. "What on earth is goin' on?"

"I'm gettin' my rifle," Dean said, and he pushed past us all to go to his bedroom.

I had seen some kind of movement on the screen, but I hadn't seen a person. Maybe what Finn saw had been an animal. It was hard to tell on the grainy video in almost complete darkness outside. There were lights outside the barn, but they were not very bright.

"Kevin's not answerin'," Jack said. "I texted him three damn times."

"Someone tell me what's goin' on."

"Here, Ma, come sit down," Evvie said, and she held Ma's hand, trying to pull her to sit on Finn's bed.

"No. Everlea, tell me. Who is that?" Ma demanded, stepping away from Evvie and further into Finn's room, pointing at the computer screens.

A man had appeared on one screen. He was on foot, and he emerged from behind a tree beside the long drive to the house, right outside of the big red barn.

Kevin stepped out of the barn, holding a shotgun.

Daisy whispered, "Oh no."

"Is that Kevin?" Ma asked, looking around at everyone, fear clear in her quiet voice.

I heard a creaking noise behind me and turned to see Dean pulling a set of folding stairs down from the hallway ceiling. He carried a large rifle slung over his shoulder by a thick strap and climbed up into the attic. I turned back to watch the screen.

It looked as if Kevin was speaking to the man. I could see the sarcastic set of his body and could almost hear the rude words.

The man took two steps toward Kevin and tilted his head back and to the side, as if he were listening for something. But then he lifted his arm, took one more step in Kevin's direction, and fired a gun. I saw the flash from the exchange of the bullet before we heard the sound outside.

Oh no. KC. Kevin Cade.

Ma gasped and I ran.

I barely heard the shouting behind me as I jumped down the stairs and threw the front door open, stopping only to shove my feet into someone's dirty pair of muck boots on the floor next to it.

Racing to the barn, the only thought in my head was to get to Kevin. I didn't remember Dean had been a shooter in the US Military. I didn't think about being shot myself.

I only ran.

Kevin could not have avoided the bullet; it had been aimed straight at his chest.

The man lay on the gravel drive, holding his shin, but he

reached for the handgun lying next to him as I ran past. Dean must've fired a shot from the attic, but I hadn't heard it. I heard it now, though, as he fired another shot, a whizzing sound and a soft thud, and the man howled.

Running faster down the little hill leading to the first barn door, I slid in the snow on my knees, throwing myself at Kevin and grabbing his wrist to check his pulse. He was flat on his back in the snow, shivering.

"What're you doin'? I'm fine. Did I get him?"

"*Ja.* Someone did. Are you hurt? Did he miss?" I looked in his eyes, but he wouldn't look at me. He stared up at the night sky, struggling to take a breath, so I pressed my hand against his abdomen, feeling for the strength of his inhalations.

He tried to sit up, and I felt his core muscles tighten, but he blinked a few times, looked at me, and fell back. His eyes rolled back in his head, and that was when I saw the hole in his shirt, the blood soaking the fabric, and realized there was no pulse in his arm.

Klote!

THREE

KEVIN

"Dean, stop moving the light. *Ik heb de bloeding in mijn vingers.* Just… fuck. Carolina, I need a clamp. Get… just get *something*!"

Wakin' to the sound of Luuk's voice fillin' my head while he shouted orders at my brother and Oly, I could smell him all around me. I didn't think he wore cologne. Was that just how his body smelled? Like, his sweat? Jesus. Openin' my eyes slowly, I saw his face right above me. He was lookin' intently at somethin', his eyebrows pulled down hard in concentration.

"Get him in my truck. It'll be faster than waitin' on an ambulance!" Carey yelled, but I wasn't sure who he was referrin' to. It couldn't be me.

"I'm fine," I said. No need to make such a fuss. But it did kinda hurt to breathe.

"He's awake!" Ma's voice floated around behind me somewhere. "Kevin?"

"S'okay. No biggie. I'm fine. You got the bad guy, right?" I tried to sit up, but hands from every direction pushed me back down in the snow. Luuk looked away from whatever held his attention and got right in my face, lookin' right in my eyes. My soul.

I'd never seen anyone so breathtakin'.

"Do not move. You are shot. The bullet has micked an artery *en je bloed*." He shook his head a little. "You will bleed… very much. I'm holding it in my fingers to stop it," he said in his stupid accent that sometimes made his W's sound like V's and his V's sound like F's. He leaned down closer to my face and whispered, "Please, KC, please do not move your beautiful body, okay?"

"*Nicked* an artery," I corrected him. "Yousmellsogood… mybodysbeautiful?" My words slipped out all jumbled, and I knew I should be embarrassed about havin' this conversation anywhere near my brothers, but I just couldn't stop the ridiculous stream of consciousness comin' outta my mouth.

I thought maybe I was dreamin'. The only thing I saw was Luuk's face. The worried look on it. The beauty of it. His stunnin' blue-green eyes and sexy lips. His hair fell across his forehead, and I wanted to push my fingers through it.

"Here." Oly knelt next to my head, holdin' somethin' shiny out to Luuk, and he glanced at it for a half a second but shook his head and looked back at me.

"*Ik kan niet loslaten.*"

I didn't know what he said, but I smiled. It kinda felt like his words were drugs, and they made me loopy.

From somewhere to my left, I heard Carey's bossy voice, but there was all kindsa stress in it. "Get him in here!"

"This is going to hurt, KC," Luuk whispered. "Please, forgive me."

Casey? Why did he keep callin' me that? Just before he moved away from me, he brushed his lips against my cheek, on the edge of my lip, and whispered, "Do not struggle."

He pulled back, sittin' up straighter, and my brothers' faces appeared in my view as they all converged and lifted me up. Luuk stood, too, and he looked away, back down to whatever he was doin' with his hands on my body, but I wanted his eyes on mine again. I tried to lift my hand to pull his face back, but my arm refused to move.

I heard my mama's voice. She cried and blabbered, and Evvie soothed her, and I thought my head might explode as the whole week came slammin' back into my brain: my mama comin' home after twenty years, my brother gettin' married, the Colombian drug lord shootin' me. Luuk and the disgustin', *desperate*, despicable lie I'd told him in the barn.

"He's gonna be okay, Daisy. Breathe. It's okay," Evvie said softly. She tried to sound reassurin' but she cried too.

"Guys, I'm fine. Everybody... calm the fuck... down," I said, hopin' my usual bluster would ease everybody's tension, but my breath came out raspy, and I kinda had to force the words.

"Take a slow breath, Kev," Dean said carefully from behind my head, so I did, but before I could blow it out, they started walkin' slowly and *fuck*. I clamped my eyes shut and gritted my teeth against the pain.

Holymotherfuckin'shit!

I didn't wanna scream and cry like a little kid and probably didn't have enough air to do it anyway, so I just passed back out.

Leisurely, I woke. My body felt slow and groggy, and I heard a low and steady beepin' sound. When I finally opened my eyes, I saw the dismal gray-beige walls and smelled the cold, sterile air of a hospital room.

Oh shit. I'd been shot!

I hadn't been able to move my left arm, and I'd known I was bleedin'; I'd felt the warm, wet blood soakin' my shirt and flowin' outta me and over my shoulder, down in between my chest and arm.

Luuk had been there tendin' to me. He'd been so serious, so intent on somethin'. I remembered wakin' up in Carey's truck at one point, just lyin' in the back seat, driftin' in and outta my body, listenin' to Luuk as he talked to me in Dutch. I had no clue what he said, but his words and his voice soothed me.

And then I remembered everything else.

The beepin' noise sped up, and I tried to sit, but Luuk was there, gently pushin' me back down and shushin' me.

"Don't get up, KC. Your collarbone is broken, and you have had surgery. Look at me. Everything is okay."

I focused my blurry eyes on his face, and immediately, my heart slowed. I took a deep breath and winced. *Ow.*

"*Wees voorzichtig,*" he said, blinkin' a buncha times, drawin' my eyes to his eyelashes. Jesus. Never before in my life had I noticed anybody's eyelashes. What the hell? "I meant be careful."

"Where is everybody? Are they okay?" I asked when he pressed the button to raise the head of my bed a little. My voice sounded rough, and my mouth was dry as a desert. Luuk held a plastic cup with a straw to my lips, and I watched him as I sucked the water up.

"Careful. Just a small snip."

His eyes surveyed me in a clinical way, checkin' to make sure I was okay, I guessed. His expression was tight, like he worked hard to control it. And even though I knew it was the worst time for it, I imagined suckin' *other* things. I released the straw, and my lips curled up of their own accord.

"Sip," I said and laughed. *Oh, ouch, ouch, ouch.* The whole left side of my torso ached and throbbed.

"Try to relax." He looked at the smirk still fixed on my lips, and his eyes raised to mine. "You are trouble." Yeah, he wasn't too far off the mark. And did he know he rolled his R's?

"Where is everyone?"

"Everyone is okay. Jack is here in the hospital somewhere. Carolina and your brothers took Ma and Daisy back to your house. I'll text them to let them know you are awake." He sat in a chair next to my hospital bed, pullin' his phone from a shirt pocket on the chest of the scrubs he wore.

"No, will you wait a minute? I wanna... talk to you."

He dropped his phone back into his pocket.

"Nice duds," I said as I eyed his green scrub shirt. It was a far cry from the sexy fitted shirts and sweaters I'd seen him wearin', the ones that hugged his body and made my mouth water and my dick hard.

"Duds?"

"Clothes, the scrubs. You look like you're ready for a night on the town."

"Ah, you joke. Yes, eh, my clothes were wet, *vies*—dirty. There was blood."

"Yeah, about that. I'm pretty sure you saved my life last night. Was that just last night?" I asked and scrunched my face up, rememberin'. I was certain only a night had passed, but somehow, it felt like a month.

"*Ja, het was gisteravond.*"

"You know I don't speak Dutch, right?"

"What? Oh. Sorry." He shook his head a little. "Yes, it was last night."

"Right. Luuk, thank you." He looked down, and I dipped my head, tryin' to catch his eye, but he wouldn't meet mine, so I tried again to sit up. It got his attention, and he jerked his head up in alarm, and I pinned him with my stare. "Thank you for savin' my life," I said, relaxin' back onto the bed.

"I thought you will die. I could not— I did not want you to die," he said, and he looked at the floor, exhalin' a big shakin' breath. I couldn't see his eyes with his head down, but I watched his lips as he spoke, and I remembered he'd sorta kissed me.

And I'd sorta liked it.

Fine. No sorta about it.

Other men had put their lips elsewhere on my body but never anywhere near my lips.

My heart drummed in my chest, and I looked around, then out the window next to the big wooden door leadin' to the hallway outside my room, makin' sure we were alone.

"Will you—" He raised his head to look at me again. "You kinda kissed me last night. Will you— Do that again." I swallowed and was sure the whole hospital heard it.

I didn't know if I was askin' or tellin' him to kiss me, but it didn't matter. I knew I wouldn't be sayin' any of this if I hadn't been hopped up on pain meds and groggy from bein' sedated, but I didn't care.

I wanted his lips on my skin. Anywhere, really. I preferred him to kiss my lips, but he coulda kissed my elbow or my thumbnail, and I woulda loved it.

"I don't think this is a good idea."

Oh, right. 'Cause I told him I wasn't a "fuckin' fairy."

"Luuk?"

He raised his eyebrows.

"I'm so sorry for the thing I said in the barn. I-I'm really attracted to you—like, Jesus, I've never felt anything like it—but I, I'm not— No one knows I'm… gay." My breath rushed out, and I sucked in another one. "It's a defense mechanism. I'm sorry."

He stood and leaned over me, placin' his hands on either side of my face, rubbin' my scruffy cheeks with his thumbs, then leaned in closer. He didn't close his eyes and neither did I. I couldn't. I watched with rapt anticipation as he moved closer and closer to my face.

"*Dank je wel voor dat,*" he said, and he touched his lips to mine.

My memory of the previous night wasn't too clear, but I definitely remembered his lips. It was the first time in the whole of my life that someone I *wanted* to kiss me kissed me, and I liked it. I liked it a lot. The connection, the intimacy with another human bein', when they feel so compelled by you that they want their tongue in your mouth, their spit, their breath in your lungs—I wanted it. I was desperate for it. So much, my whole body shook.

I figured my breath had to be pretty rank, so I tried not to breathe and just concentrated on how it felt. Pretty PG as far as kisses go, but an involuntary moan escaped my throat at the soft touch, and he closed his eyes as my whole body turned red, and my fingers curled into fists 'cause I wanted to reach for him.

The heat from his body blanketed me, wrapped around me, and I wanted to throw my arms around him and devour him with my mouth. The damn heart monitor beeped wildly, outin' the storm inside me I'd been tryin' hard to hide, and Luuk leaned back, chucklin'.

Oh my God. Could you fuck a dimple? Oh, I'd figure a way.

"Rest, KC. It has been a long night, and I think you will be angry with me later. You're still medicated. I'm not sure you know what you do."

I cleared my throat and licked his kiss from my lips. "I'm clear headed enough." Cockin' my head to the side, I wondered, "Why you call me that?"

"Call you what?"

"Casey."

"Oh. Eh, I don't know. It's just how I refer to you in my thoughts. KC for Kevin Cade. It's a thing I do to remember names. A mnemonic." He smiled a shy smile at me, and I felt my heart stutter. Heard it too.

He was bein' so kind to me, so open and real. There was no jokin' or uncomfortable silence fillin'. No macho bravado. We were just us, and I felt like shit on shoes for the way I'd treated him.

The door to my hospital room opened, and Evvie rushed in with Jack slowly followin' behind her. "You're awake," she squeaked.

Luuk backed away from my bed silently. Away from me. Jack looked from me to Luuk, then back to me, and I panicked at the thought of my oldest brother seein' us together, but I *really* didn't want him to stop touchin' me.

"How you feelin', brother? You scared us to death last night."

"Yeah, sorry 'bout that," I said as Evvie hugged the right side of my body and kissed my cheek.

"Are you in pain? The nurse said she'll be right in."

"I'm okay, don't worry," I told her, and she smiled.

It seemed funny to me, but I couldn't believe how fast someone could become so embedded into a person's life. There were two people in the room with me I hadn't known much more than three months, one not even a week, but I couldn't imagine my life without either of 'em in it, which was a big problem since I barely knew the one and couldn't seem to do anything about my *serious* attraction to him even though he was the only person on the planet who knew I was gay.

"So who wants to fill me in?" I asked to clear the air, to wipe Luuk's kiss off the slate. "I don't have much memory of last night. I'm fairly sure I got shot and my buddy Luuk here saved my life, but other than that, I'm feelin' clueless. What's wrong with me, and how long do I get outta work?" I laughed, tryin' to cover the desire still coursin' through my body, causin' knives to attack my chest and shoulder. I groaned and Jack laughed at my pained attempt to joke, and I used the distraction to bend my knee and adjust my hips, so my ragin' hard-on was, hopefully, a little less visible under the scratchy bedsheets.

I could feel Luuk close himself off to me. It was a physical shift in the air, like the pressure changin' before a big storm. But that was exactly what I'd just done to him. I'd closed myself off with my dismissal of the private moment we'd been havin' before my brother entered the room.

I busted right through it with my fist.

"You screwed yourself pretty well and good, Kev," Jack said. "You got a broken collarbone, and they had to repair some arteries in your shoulder. You were bleedin'. A lot."

My eyes darted over to Luuk. He looked so proper and polite, standin' there with his arms in front of his body and his hands clasped together.

"That explains the knives in my shoulder when I so much as blink my eyes." I tried desperately to act normal, but I couldn't stop myself from lookin' over at Luuk every three seconds, tryin' to catch his gaze.

But he wouldn't look at me.

"Yeah, so you're facin' a few months' recovery, at least. I dunno how long you get to play hooky. We'll have to ask the docs when they come in." Jack walked across the room and sat on the concrete-like couch under the window, and Evvie squeezed my right hand and patted my head like a kid, then walked over and snuggled up to him.

"You guys okay though? No one else got hurt?"

"Nope, just you, as per usual." Jack rolled his eyes.

"What about that guy? Is he dead?"

"No, he's here in the hospital too," Jack said. "Dean added a few new holes to his orifice count, but the FBI's takin' him into custody. Seems they got a whole list of crimes to charge him with. Apparently, he ain't as good a criminal as his daddy was."

Luuk took another step back. "Please, excuse me. I will

leave you to…" He took one more step back, attemptin' to escape from the room. Maybe he was tryin' to escape me.

"Luuk, please stay. You don't have to go."

"Thank you, Evvie, but I should go. You have family issues to discuss. I need a shower and clean clothing. I just wanted to make sure Kevin was okay. But now, I will go. I have work."

I wanted to beg him to stay, to kiss me again. I wanted to feel his hands on me again. But I didn't. I couldn't. It was obvious he wanted to go—he felt uncomfortable, especially after my "buddy" comment. I couldn't be real with him, about him, with Jack in the room. If I couldn't say out loud that I was gay, that I liked men, how could I show affection, or even just attraction, for one?

I wanted to. I was so fuckin' tired of puttin' on an act. But I lay there, silent anyway. He looked at me one last time, searchin' for somethin', some hint of the pull we'd both felt between us.

I closed my eyes and dropped my head.

I was a coward.

If I hadn't shown him what an asshole I was already, he knew now. He'd go. He *should* go. I would do nothin' but treat him like shit. I'd deny him. I'd deny myself. I already had. I was right now! He seemed like an amazin', beautiful, carin', good man. Courageous. He saved my life. That was courage for ya. What was I?

Nothin'.

A scared little boy.

And I was about to prove it. "Yeah, I don't really feel like hangin' out right now anyway. I'm tired." I rolled over onto my right side, causin' myself enough pain with the movement to make me nearly throw up. Gulpin' down bile, I faced away from all three of 'em, pretendin' I wanted to be alone. Pretendin' not to want him to lie with me, to wrap his body around mine, to kiss me and comfort me and talk to me, to run his fingers through my hair and rub my back. To whisper in my ear.

"Goodbye," Luuk said, and he walked out the door.

I kept my eyes closed. I didn't wanna see him walk away. I didn't wanna see the possibility of him disappear even though I knew I could never act on it. Goddammit, and now I did sound like my whiny, emo, bitch-ass brothers.

"Evvie, why don'tcha go and make sure Luuk finds a lift home since he rode here in the back of Carey's truck while he was savin' my ungrateful brother's life. Call Finn or Oly to come get him if he'd rather not wait for us."

"'Kay," Evvie said softly, and I heard her feet shuffle across the floor.

"There somethin' you wanna talk about?" Jack asked when the door clicked closed behind Evvie. "Some reason you were just so rude to the man who saved your life?"

"Nope. Just tired."

He stood and slowly walked to the end of my bed. "You sure? I mean, if there is..." I didn't need to look at him to know he was crushin' his hat in his hands.

Yeah, like I would just open my mouth and say, "Well, Jack, since you asked, I'm gay. I like fuckin' guys. Would you like me to tell you all the ways?"

I didn't say anything.

He cleared his throat. "If you wanted to tell me somethin', you could... I mean, I'd listen. But Kev, Luuk is— You can't— He's our vet."

"Jesus fuckin' Christ," I gritted through clenched teeth. God, it was torture listenin' to him. "Just stop. What, you think you're my therapist? Fuck you. I'm not—"

Thankfully, before I could flat-out lie to my brother, the door opened and a woman walked in. Outta the corner of my eye, I saw pink scrubs with purple cats on 'em. "Good morning. How are we feeling?"

"Fine," I lied. On *so* many levels.

"He ain't feelin' fine. He's in pain, many different kinds. 'Scuse me. I'll be back for the meetin' with the doctors," Jack said, and I heard his boots hit the floor when he quietly walked outta the room, leavin' me alone just like I'd pretended I wanted.

But it was the very last thing on this earth I wanted.

FOUR

LUUK

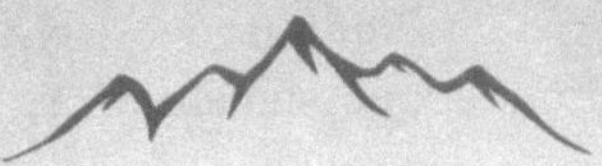

"**D**uck, why're you makin' me do this?" Dean whispered to Carolina as she reached on her toes to adjust his shirt collar.

"Dean!" she whispered back.

"Trust me, you cannot be any more uncomfortable than I am, Dean," I assured him.

He repeated, "So then, why are we doin' this?" but this time louder so I could hear.

"*Ja*, Carolina, why?" I asked, collapsing on the tiny green couch in her living room, hoping desperately my cell phone would ring with a farm emergency so I could avoid our dinner plans.

"Because I promised Brady. He's a great guy. And you were just sayin' you needed a night out, Luuk. Since Doc had his stroke, you and I have been workin' our butts off. We deserve to have some fun."

"Yeah, but why do *I* have to go?" Dean whined.

"Oh my God, you are both such big babies. You can't make conversation with Brady for one evenin'?"

"No," Dean and I recited simultaneously.

Carolina rolled her eyes. "Too bad. Let's go."

While I sulked in the back seat of Dean's truck, Carolina chittered away happily in front of me, telling me again how great this Brady person was—the man she was forcing me to meet—and Dean cringed in the rearview mirror.

Since Brady was most likely the only other gay man in Wisper (at least, the only other one anyone else knew about), *natuurlijk*, she had to set me up with him. I agreed to it because I loved her, and I knew she worried about me being alone, but it was clear to me that we were going to need to have a conversation about stereotypical, even if lovingly meant, setups.

I'd been avoiding this meeting since I'd arrived in Wisper. I knew Carolina thought highly of Brady, and I trusted her opinion, but I didn't want to get involved with anyone.

When I agreed to stay to help Carolina, I'd known Wisper —and probably all of Wyoming for that matter—was not a mecca for gay culture, but I thought I could use my time here to reset. To be alone for a while before I found myself in some man's bed, hungover after I'd fucked all my sadness and anger into him. Again.

And honestly, there had been only one man to occupy my thoughts lately. One overgrown child-man. One rude, cowardly, annoyingly beautiful man. One stupid American cowboy with his stupid wavy hair and stupid sexy body and stupid, endlessly deep navy blue eyes.

I hadn't seen Kevin Cade in more than two months. Since New Year's Eve. This is not true—I'd seen him from afar, occasionally, when I went to Cade Ranch to work on one of their horses. And I'd seen him one other time in town, buying flowers at a flower stand at the farmers market. Probably for a woman—his gay beard. But he never spoke to me, and usually, when I was at his ranch, he was not.

I didn't care. Or I tried not to. And it was probably a good thing anyway.

I'd made a mess that night. The night he almost died.

I hadn't meant to. I hadn't meant to say the things I'd said or do the things I had done in front of his brothers or Ma.

I felt awful about it. It made my stomach hurt to think about it. But there had been so much adrenaline coursing through me, and the situation had been so far out of control, and I just reacted.

He almost died!

I hoped the trauma of being shot had made him forget my words that night when I told him he was beautiful. When I kissed him in front of everyone.

And in the hospital the next day, when he apologized for what he'd said in his barn, it spoke to me. His vulnerability. His apology. I couldn't imagine what it would have been like to grow up as a gay man in this part of the country. His brothers were all strong, traditionally masculine men. That could not have been easy.

But maybe he did not even remember. Maybe it was the reason he hadn't come near me or spoken to me. Maybe I did not occupy his thoughts the way he occupied mine. Maybe he hadn't thought of me once since then.

"You're gonna be nice to Brady, right, Luuk? I wouldn't normally worry about it, but you've kinda been a pill lately," Carolina complained, climbing out of Dean's truck when we parked.

"Carolina, if you thought I'd be unkind to this man, why have you dragged me here? Of course I will be nice to him." I leaned down to whisper in her ear, "But I will not fuck him just because you want me to."

"Luuk!" she shrieked and punched my arm. "Fine, but you're the one who said you needed to get... *laid*," she whispered. "This is what I'm talkin' about. Since when are you so crass?"

"I'm just being honest. I'm Dutch, remember? We cannot say what we don't mean. It's a national trait."

"Pfft. Whatever. Just keep an open mind." She walked

ahead of me, and Dean stepped next to me. I looked at him, and he closed his eyes and shook his head.

Oh *mijn* God. Why had I agreed to this?

When we walked into the trendy warehouse restaurant and microbrewery in Jackson, Wyoming, I saw Brady immediately. I could have picked him out of a "this is your next gay lover" lineup. He was leaning on the bar top, talking to the bartender.

Yes, he was very good-looking. Dark skin, hair, and deep dark eyes, set off by a straight and perfect nose that pointed to his, admittedly, sexy mouth. He smiled when the bartender said something to him, and I tried to imagine him smiling at me. I couldn't. I felt only a mild attraction, probably to his perfectly symmetrical features.

"Brady!" Carolina greeted him, hugging him, and Dean bristled next to me. He did not like this Brady embracing his girlfriend. I wondered why he never seemed to care when Carolina hugged or touched me—she had always been a very demonstrative person, always pulling me around by my hand.

"Hey, Oly. How ya doin'?" Brady looked over her shoulder, right at me, while he hugged her, and his mouth curled a little in a hint of a rapacious almost-smile.

Carolina released him, turning to Dean and me. "Brady, you remember Dean."

"Yeah. Hey, man," he said, extending his hand for Dean to shake. Dean grasped it and grunted, and I had to hold in a laugh. Gruff rancher, indeed.

"And this is Luuk." She smiled up at me like she was my mother showing me off at the first day of school.

"Luke?" he asked, reaching to shake my hand too.

"*Ja.*" I didn't feel in the mood to explain the difference. "It's nice to meet you, Brady."

"Yeah, you too." He smiled, and his dark eyes twinkled in

a very American, "oh yeah, I could totally fuck this guy" way. I tried hard not to scoff and roll my eyes.

It was easy to see what Carolina liked about Brady. He was intelligent, very well-spoken, and just a little endearingly dorky. He seemed nervous. Normally, this would attract me easily. He was nearly exactly my type. Shorter than me, fit, handsome, but not in a boyish way. Very mature. Carolina told me he was a lawyer, so he was successful in his career. But he also seemed reserved, like he followed every rule. He was polite even though I thought it clear from the look in his eyes when he spoke to me that he did not want to be.

He reminded me too much of myself.

And I did not want to date myself.

I wanted bold, unapologetic, sarcastic… rude… *ughhh*.

I wanted Kevin Cade.

"So, Luke, tell us about growin' up in the Netherlands," Brady said in boringly expected fashion as our server cleared our bread plates and refilled our water glasses. Okay, so maybe I was being a bit of a "pill." I hadn't ordered a drink, and clearly, the lack of alcohol in my system affected my cooperation.

"Eh, it was normal."

"You guys talk amongst yourselves," Carolina said suggestively. "Dean and I are gonna go take the brewery tour while we wait for our food." I shot knives out of my eyes at her, but she just smiled and dragged Dean away by the belt loop on his jeans.

"So," Brady said, smiling at me and unfolding and refolding his napkin, then he set it on the table and dropped his hands into his lap. "You're gay."

I nearly spit out my water.

"*Ja*," I said, coughing to clear my throat. I laughed. "I'm gay. Is that not why we are both here?"

"Yeah. Sorry. I told Oly not to set us up, but she didn't listen."

"This I know. She never does."

"You two went to school together?"

"*Ja*, vet school. At Cambridge."

"That's pretty cool. Did you spend any time in London?"

"*Some.*"

"How's the scene there?" he asked. He meant the gay scene.

"It's… abundant," I shrugged, "like any other big city."

"Did you *date* a lot?" Did I fuck a lot.

"*Ja.*"

"I can't imagine what it must seem like to you, comin' from there to Denver to Wisper. You won't find many choices here."

I laughed under my breath. He was pretty forward, not as reserved as I'd thought. "This is okay for me. I'm not, eh, I don't really want to date right now anyway."

"Really? Why not?"

"I just— I could use a break." I didn't know him well enough to explain why—that I used sex to ease my pain, so I didn't go out looking to ease it in other ways. "What about you? Where did you live before you moved back to Wisper?"

"Oh, I was in Boise—"

"You guys gettin' along okay?" Carolina asked as she pulled Dean back to our table. She winced at me. "Sorry, it was a short tour."

"*Ja*," I said as my phone rang, and I quickly pulled it from my pocket. "*Pardon*, this is Yola. I must take this." I almost jumped out of my chair but caught myself and stood slowly, then stepped through a door onto an empty outdoor seating area near our table.

"Hey, Doc. Got a call for you, or you can give it to Oly if you want. I know you guys were goin' out to dinner tonight."

"No, this is okay. She's dressed up. I will take it."

"You sound almost relieved. Date night not goin' so well?"

"Yola," I warned her, "what is the emergency?"

"Okay, okay, I'll get the gossip from Oly tomorrow," my self-appointed, bossy older sister taunted me. This was the best thing about Wisper so far. Everyone treated me like family or friend.

Except one person, one arrogant, beautiful—

"Cal Johnson called. Seems a bear or somethin' attacked his herd. He's got a bull, a pregnant heifer, and a calf needs stitchin' up."

"A bear? Really? Did he see a bear?"

"Naw. It was probably a coyote, but he's all-a-flutter about it. Get your butt over there."

"Thank you, Yola." I hung up and smiled, feeling inappropriately elated to have three injured animals waiting for me, and hurried back to the table.

"I must go. Apologies, but there has been an emergency."

"What is it?" Carolina placed her napkin on her plate and stood.

"No, no. Please, sit. It's not bad. Just three cows needing stitches at the Johnson Farm. I can do it myself. You're right. You deserve a night out. Please stay, enjoy your dinner. Brady, it was nice to meet you. I'm very sorry to run."

"Oh, yeah, no it's— It was nice to meet you too." Disappointment flashed across his face as I searched in my pocket for my keys and realized I did not have my truck. Carolina had packed some of her supplies into Dean's back seat in case of an emergency, but I hadn't thought about the possibility of needing to go on a call by myself. I should have.

"One problem. I do not have my truck."

Brady sat straighter in his chair, and just as I thought he would offer to drive me, Dean spoke (maybe for the first time since we'd entered the restaurant).

"Here, take mine." He tossed me his keys. "Oly's work pack is in there. The ranch is just down the highway from the Johnson's. If you need anything else, give the guys a call.

Brady can drive us back to town after dinner." He smiled victoriously at Brady.

"Uh, yeah, sure," Brady reluctantly agreed, pasting a false smile on his face.

"*Dank je wel*," I thanked Dean a little too enthusiastically, and Carolina pursed her lips, glaring at me as she sat. "Brady, I will see you around, *ja*?"

"Yeah, sure."

"Must go. Goodnight," I said, trying not to seem too happy about the excuse to escape because I knew I would be reprimanded for it later, but I couldn't help my smile.

I grabbed my jacket off the back of my chair, turned, and walked quickly toward the exit but caught our server on the way and paid her three hundred dollars to cover dinner, drinks, and her tip.

To get out of the "here, meet my *other* gay friend" date, it was a bargain.

FIVE

KEVIN

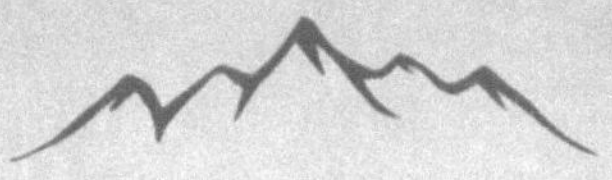

"**W**hat?" I barked into my cell phone when it rang for the fiftieth time. "Christ on a cracker, Finn."

"Jeez, Kevin. Couldn't answer the first two times I called?"

"No, Finn, obviously I couldn't or I would have."

"Whatever, man. Just get home and pick Oly up from the clinic on your way."

"Why, what's goin' on? What's wrong with her truck?"

"She don't have her truck. Just do it, then get home."

My jerk brother hung up on me, and five minutes later, I pulled up outside the Wisper All Animals Veterinary Clinic. Oly was waitin' for me on the stoop outside, and when she saw me, she locked up and climbed into my brother's truck. I'd borrowed it to drive myself to my checkup with the doctor in Jackson and to my physical therapy session.

After almost three months, I was pretty well healed from the gunshot that almost killed me (and my stupid broken leg), though I still had pain in my shoulder, and I still had to go to the damn doctor every other week to get a test done to make sure my blood still flowed through the arteries they'd had to repair. Okay, so that was an exaggeration, but wouldn't I know if my blood wasn't flowin'? Whatever. It got me off the ranch for an afternoon, and I got to drive a little and have some time to myself to think.

The problem was, *all* I could think about was Luuk van der Wouden. Doc V. Alvie. Whatever you wanted to call him. That sexy Dutch motherfucker had become a thorn in my side. I found him on my mind breakfast, lunch, and dinner, coffee and crumpets besides.

I couldn't shake him.

"Hey, Kev. Thanks for pickin' me up."

"Yeah, where's your truck?" I kicked my own ass in my head for the bark in my voice—I wasn't known for havin' a filter—but Oly was too kind to reprimand me.

"Luuk was in an accident, so his is in the shop. He took mine out on farm calls today."

"Accident? What happened?" I asked. I had to work hard to hide the anxiety in my voice.

"Some lady hit him. She was goin' too fast comin' off the highway, T-boned him. He was pinned inside till the fire department got there, but he's okay. He's *so* mad though." Oly giggled. "That truck is practically brand new. He treats it like it's his baby."

"Oh, but he's okay? I mean, he didn't get hurt at all?" I wanted to turn around and drive straight to him, just to check on him. What if he had some sneaky internal injury he didn't know about and he—

"He said he's totally fine." She looked at me, her body turned toward me in the passenger seat of Dean's truck. I could see and feel her starin' at me outta the corner of my eye.

I cleared my throat and changed the subject. "Any idea why our presence was requested at the house?"

"No." She faced forward. "Dean texted, said you were gonna pick me up, and we were all meetin' at the ranch. Wait, you don't think it's Ma, do you? I assumed it was just a family meetin' about the horse therapy project, but it just occurred to me somethin' could be wrong."

Well, damn. I hadn't thought about that either. Pressin' my foot harder on the gas pedal, I worried the rest of the way home about Ma and, completely ridiculously, Luuk.

When we pulled up to the house, Oly stumbled out of the oversized, too-tall truck. I ran around to help her, but she didn't want it. "You okay?"

"Yeah, I'm fine, just tired. It's been a long day," she said as Dean walked out the kitchen door and came to pick her up to carry her inside. Guess she didn't have to worry about expendin' any more precious energy that way. *Jeez.*

When everyone, except Ma and Evvie, had been accounted for and were seated around the dinner table, Jay stood and coughed a little. "So, we heard back from the bank, and the therapists, actually. They gave us their decision."

My baby brother, Jay, was the actual brains of our family (though Finn told everybody it was him). He'd been workin' on a new opportunity for our ranch, and we were about to find out if his idea had any legs to stand on.

"But," he said when Finn and Jack sat up a little straighter in their chairs, "it's not what you're thinkin'—"

"So, they denied us, then. Whatever. It's fine," I said, tryin' to act like I wasn't completely disappointed.

It wasn't fine. I thought it was a good idea, and I'd actually been kinda excited about it. I liked helpin' people, 'specially kids. Cadence Williams, the daughter of a friend of the family who was autistic (and also a tiny little-girl angel), was a prime example of what our horses could do for people. The animals calmed her, and takin' care of 'em gave her a purpose and a way to practice talkin' to people, a way to connect.

We'd also been helpin' my brother's friend, Bigsy, a Marine vet with a physical injury. If someone would give us a shot, we could help a lotta people like Cadence and Bigsy. I'd be proud to be a part of that.

"Whatever," I said again. "Who cares—"

"No, Kev. Well, yes, they did deny our proposal, but only 'cause they came up with a better one."

"What's that mean, 'a better one'?" Finn asked.

I watched Jack while we waited for Jay to explain. He looked really nervous. He hadn't ever been good with change, and he absolutely wasn't good with someone else bein' in control of any part of our ranch.

"Mr. Markham, the guy I pitched to—and Oly's best friend's dad," Jay said, smilin' at Oly, and she winked at him, "he shared our proposal with another man. An extraordinarily rich man. And this man, Theodore Burroughs, offered to fund the whole thing!"

"What? 'Fund the whole thing'? What does that mean *exactly*?" Jack demanded. "That's a lotta money, Jay. Nobody just gives that shit away for free."

"Apparently, this guy does. I mean, it's not *free*. He wants to invest. Provide start-up capital. We'll need to do our own due diligence on him, suss him out, but he's got a lotta money, and he's lookin' for somethin' to do with it.

"He offered to put up what we asked to make additions to the barn and arena, and he offered to pay us a salary. He even offered to pay for vet care. He gave us some time to talk it over, and then he'd like to meet with us so we can discuss the details."

"Wait a minute." Jack argued. "He doesn't know us. He don't know anything about Cade Ranch. Why us?"

"I dunno, brother. We can ask him when we meet with him."

"Sounds too good to be true. I'm gonna call Billie and ask her to do some diggin'," Dean said.

Billie, a black-leather-clad hacker chick, helped us last year when Evvie came to us. She'd been stalked and tortured by some serial killer dude (who, incidentally, also shot me), and

Billie helped us find the guy. I bet she could get all the dirt on this "investor," Theodore Burroughs.

"And what about the therapists?" Jack asked. "You talked to them too?"

"Yep, and they're both on board as soon as we get our shit together. Dr. Ross and her colleague, Dr. Harris, are both in, and then a friend of Harris' from grad school is pretty interested, too, though she's a different kind of therapist. She would like to discuss the possibility of offerin' an adaptive ridin' program in addition to equine therapy. Oh, and Dr. Harris brought up an idea. She thinks we'll need some volunteers, like maybe some high school kids or college kids to help us."

"Help us with what? Since when do we need help?" I asked. We'd been takin' care of the ranch and the horses on our own our whole lives. We didn't need anybody comin' in here, tellin' us how to do our jobs.

"Think about it, Kev," Jay said. "If we have several clients here at one time, there's only four of us. Jack will still be runnin' the breedin' program and the ranch in general, and he needs our help. So we'll need people who know about horses so there's always at least one horse handler with each client. Dependin' on each client's needs, we may need two handlers per client.

"We might need help with the office side of it and with feedin' and general care of the horses. Volunteers are great 'cause they're free, and we can offer some kinda school credit, or, I dunno, somethin'. Win win. It'll all have to be worked out, but in the meantime, let's find out what we can about this Burroughs guy and go from there."

Jay's annoyin' optimism was interrupted by a knock on the kitchen door, and my brothers all scattered while I grumbled, "Don't everybody rush to the door all at once. I'll get it."

"Where's everybody goin'?" Jay asked, followin' Jack into the livin' room. "Shouldn't we celebrate?"

"No, Jay, what the fuck are we celebratin'—"

But that was all I heard 'cause I opened the door to find Luuk standin' on my front porch, lookin' in my eyes. I was dumbstruck by him. My tongue stuck to the roof of my mouth, and I couldn't speak. He raised his eyebrows when I didn't say anything and just stood there, starin' at him.

"*Hallo*, Kevin. I hope you're well. I'm just, ehh—" He glanced behind him to Oly's old Four Runner. "I brought Carolina's truck back."

I nodded, mouth open like an idiot, and opened the door wider. He stepped in, around me, but his shoulder brushed mine (not the one with a hole in it), and it felt like he'd burned it with a brandin' iron. I closed my eyes and silently closed the door.

I hadn't known he was comin' over, and I wasn't prepared for it. I'd only seen him a few times in the last couple months, but every time I did see him, I remembered the two times he'd kissed me, and it took everything in me not to grab him and attack him with my tongue. Maybe that was why I couldn't speak around him—my subconscious locked my tongue in my mouth so it couldn't run wild and make a goddamn mess outta everything.

Break free from your lock. Speak, ya fucker!

"You're okay," I mumbled, and he turned to face me as he walked past, but he stopped and looked at me like I'd lost my ever-lovin' mind.

"Sorry? KC, did you say something?"

I hadn't actually spoken to him since New Year's Day, the day I pretty much dismissed him from my presence 'cause I was too much of a coward to admit to my family who I really was inside. But every day since then, and every single night, I thought about him. Wanted him. But I didn't trust myself not to grab him and never look back.

I didn't trust myself not to hurt him.

"Oly said you were hit. I mean, your truck. Accident." I cleared my throat. "You're okay? You're not hurt?"

He smiled, a small tilt of his lips, but it lit up his eyes and his dimples slayed me. They hid under his dusky stubble, but I saw 'em, and I wanted to touch 'em with my fingertips and, well, my tongue.

"*Ik ben oke.*" He shook his head, and I laughed under my breath. He was always doin' that and it was kinda adorable. "I'm fine, thank you."

"Hey, Doc. How's it goin'?" Finn walked over, releasin' Luuk from the trap I had him in by the door. When he heard Finn's voice, he turned his head, severin' the connection I wanted so desperately. It felt like his body had magnets in it, and they pulled me to him. I had to plant my feet on the floor, and I twisted my bum shoulder so the pain would stop me from walkin' forward.

"I'm well, Finn. How are you?" They shook hands, and Finn pulled Luuk away from me.

"Doin' good, Doc. You hungry? Evvie made burgers."

"Oh, no, thank you, I—"

"Luuk, sit and eat," Oly said. "I'm starvin'. If you don't mind, I'll drive you home after dinner? I feel like I haven't eaten in days." She yawned, and her whole body slumped in her chair.

"Okay, that will be fine. Thank you."

Finn shoved Luuk into a chair at the table. "Have a seat. Relax. Want a drink? We got water, whiskey, beer, and well, whiskey."

"*Ja, water is goed. Bedankt.*"

I stared at him so I noticed when he peeked up at me. He looked away quickly, but I saw it, the desire he always had in his eyes when I was near—he wanted me. I wondered if he could see it in mine too. Did I hide it as well as I tried to? I sat in my usual chair, directly across from him.

"This is Ma's seat. Will she not join us for dinner?" he asked, lookin' at Jack, then Finn, and then me.

I didn't answer. I couldn't. I fought with myself again. Should I answer his question and out myself to my brothers? There was no way they wouldn't notice how I looked at him, the sound of my voice when I talked to him, about him. Or should I ignore him, or pretend to like I usually did, keepin' my cover intact but pushin' the possibility of him further away from me, which was the exact opposite of what I wanted?

Jack saved me from the pathetic mess in my head. "No, Doc, Ma won't be joinin' us. She's havin' a hard day. Evvie's upstairs with her, tryin' to get her to eat."

My heart dropped into my gut, and I closed my eyes. Every time I thought about Ma dyin', my chest *hurt*, and I had a hard time draggin' air into my lungs.

"Doc Whitley thinks it won't be long now," Jay mumbled with so much sadness in his voice that I wanted to hug him. He sat at the table and handed Luuk a plate with a burger, a bun, and all the fixin's.

When I opened my eyes, Luuk looked right in 'em. "I'm sorry to hear this," he said, and the corner of his sexy lip turned up into the saddest smile. He was sorry for me? For my pain? How did he know losin' Ma would kill me? Was killin' me? I'd never told him what she meant to me. I'd never told anyone.

"How were your last two farm calls, Luuk?" Oly asked through a mouthful of potato chips, changin' the subject. "Everything go okay?"

"Uh, *ja*," he said, takin' a deep breath, then looked at her. "Everything was fine. Well, I lost Mr. Kelly's first calf of the season. I wish he would have called in the morning. He waited too long." Hangin' his head, he dropped his hands into his lap. He felt responsible for losin' the calf, even though I was sure he did everything he could to save it. I'd seen him work on our horses, and I knew he'd do anything to save an animal.

Releasin' his breath, he looked back up at Oly. "But then I went up on the mountain to help Philomena Beasley deliver a farrow of piglets. We got twelve of the little stinkers." He smiled when he said it, and I could tell he was proud of what he'd done.

I'd formed the opinion that Luuk was a pretty simple guy. He came off as fancy and worldly 'cause of his accent and sometimes the way he dressed (who wears expensive designer jeans to a horse ranch?), but he seemed happiest when he was gettin' dirty or workin' with animals.

Like I needed one more thing to attract me to him. Jeez.

I'd thought a lot about it. I decided I must've had some kinda hero worship thing goin' on. 'Cause he'd saved my life. And 'cause he was so hot. And 'cause there was somethin' inside him I wanted. I didn't know what it was, but it felt raw and angry and beautiful, and it spoke to the angst inside me. I wanted my hands on it, my dick in it, and my tongue all over it.

But no matter how much I wanted him, I knew it couldn't be. My brothers were all good men, and they loved me, but I'd grown up in probably the most red-blooded place in the world. All my life, I'd heard "boys don't cry," "get over it, you ain't a girl," or "art is for faggots." I didn't think I'd ever heard my brothers say those things, but my dad hadn't been shy about his opinions, and they'd grown up with him as a role model too.

Could they ever accept that I was gay?

What if they couldn't? Since our mama left, my brothers were all I had in the world. And Ma.

We ate and talked. Well, everyone else talked. I sat in a prison of my own fuckin' makin', desperate for Luuk to look at me again, and dreadin' if he did, in case anyone noticed. He didn't. I got the feelin' it was on purpose. He looked down at his hands in his lap a lot or at his plate when he wasn't involved in the conversation. He wasn't a shy person, so maybe he did that for me, so he wouldn't give my secret away.

Evvie came down halfway through dinner. "Hi, Luuk. Good to see you. I thought it was your voice I heard. Ma was asking about you."

"Good to see you too." He wiped his mouth with his napkin and laid it back in his lap. "How is Ma tonight?"

"She's okay. She's been feeling really nauseated and she's tired. She's always tired," Evvie said, sittin' in Jack's lap, and he wrapped his arms around her waist, restin' his chin on her shoulder. Did they have to be physically connected every second of every day? "Actually, when you're done eating, I think she'd like you to go up to see her."

"Me? Really? Why?"

"I think she just wants to say hello. She's stuck in her room a lot these days. She doesn't get to visit with people as much as she'd like."

"Oh, okay. I'll go up now, yes? I have finished eating, and I don't want to make her wait. *Pardon*." He stood, placin' his napkin on his empty plate, and pushed his chair in, and finally, he looked at me again. His eyes lingered on mine for a short few seconds, then they roamed over my face, my neck, my hair. It was like I could physically feel his gaze—everywhere he looked, I burned.

And then he turned and walked away, leavin' me with a racin' heart and no air in my lungs.

SIX

LUUK

Climbing the staircase in the Cade Ranch house, I thought about what an utter mess I'd found myself in, agreeing to stay on at All Animals Clinic until Dr. Prittchard could return to work after his stroke. Thankfully, it had only been a mild event, and he would be returning soon.

I wanted to help Carolina. I liked Wyoming and I loved the work, but I couldn't seem to be in the same room with Kevin Cade and breathe simultaneously. And since Carolina was always with his brother, and he lived on a ranch with horses that often needed veterinary care, I would see him a lot.

It was a problem.

I had never experienced an attraction like this before. I'd been attracted to many men, had a few relationships and plenty of sex, but there was something about Kevin Cade. I thought it must have been because I couldn't have him, like a forbidden fruit. I barely knew him. Why else would I want him so desperately?

And oh, I did.

Pathetically, I thought of him every day. I listened as Carolina talked about Dean, about the Cade Ranch and

Dean's brothers. I listened intently every time for Kevin's name. I thought she must have known what I waited for because she barely said it: Kevin. KC. The name rarely came out of her mouth. And every time, I was disappointed again.

Just like tonight.

He answered the door, and my first thought had been, "Fuck, I want you. Please say yes."

I smacked my forehead. How long had I been standing outside Ma's room, looking at nothing?

"Alvie, is that you? Whatcha doin' out there in the hallway? Come in here."

I took one last breath, forcing a gentle smile on my face, then entered Ma's bedroom, knocking softly on the door before I opened it.

"*Hallo, mam.*" I walked in and shut the door quietly behind me.

"Well, hello, Alvie. I knew it was your voice I heard downstairs. How are ya, sweetheart? You look good. It's been a while, hasn't it?"

"Yes, it has. I'm well. How are you? How are you feeling?"

She smiled, and the thin skin around her eyes crinkled and folded, her soft white poof of hair messy and flat on one side of her head. She tried to act like everything was normal, but there was an air of illness in the bedroom with her, and it made me sad.

"Oh, well, Alvie, now, you know I'm dyin', don'tcha?"

"*Ja, mam.*"

"You were just bein' polite. You're always so polite. Come, sit down here next to me. How was your double date the other night? Oly told me all about it." Patting the edge of her small bed, she sat up against the headboard. She had one of those pillows behind her back, the kind with arms out to the sides, but she looked like she might fall over at any second.

As I sat, I noticed a vase of bright wildflowers on her bedside table. She saw me looking at it, and she reached for my hand, but her grasp was so weak, her hands cold and stiff. I didn't quite know how to respond to her question, but she didn't seem to need my answer to continue.

"Oly also tells me you're stayin' at Mrs. Ellison's boardin' house now that Dean is livin' with her. How is that?"

Looking away from the flowers, I focused on her face. "It's fine. Small, but I don't need a lot of space. I thought they could use a little privacy after their... reunion," I lied and smiled, but I hated that stupid room. It was completely depressing. I'd been more than a little surprised it actually existed. It was like something out of an old American Western movie.

I'd thought many times about looking for my own place, but I wasn't sure if I'd be staying in Wisper long, so I didn't want to deal with a lease or buying a house if I would just end up leaving in a few months. Dr. Prittchard would be back to work in the near future, and I didn't know what that would mean for me.

I wasn't sure if Wisper was where I would stay.

"I think you're bein' polite again. I've seen Mrs. Ellison's place. You must be miserable there." I smiled again and she patted my hand. "Well, now, I have an idea. My house is sittin' empty over on Billings Street. Why don'tcha stay there? I'm not usin' it. Technically, I've given it to the boys, but they're not usin' it either. I've already asked Jack, and he said I should offer it to you. What do you think?"

"Thank you, this is very kind but—"

"Alvie, you need a place of your own. You'll stay there. It'll give you a sense of home, your own space. A place to figure things out. Now, it's small, only two bedrooms. Mr. Mitchum and I never had children of our own, so we didn't need a big house, but it should suit your purposes. It's close to the clinic, so that'll be nice." She patted my hand again, smiling up at me, and I remembered the first time I'd met her. Her kindness and knowing expression had reminded me so much of my *omaatje*. I wanted to throw my arms around her and hold on tight. This woman was the definition of home and family, and just being in the same room with her made me feel loved and comforted.

"Thank you, Ma. I appreciate your generosity." I decided it wouldn't be worth arguing with her, and I really didn't want to pass up the opportunity to get out of that dark closet of a room.

"Good. You go and have a look at the house tonight. There's still some furniture in there. If you don't like it, just move it out to the garage and put some of your own things in. Paint it if you want. The neighbors are nice but not too close, so you'll have some privacy. Kevin will take you." She set her mouth into an immovable smirk.

"Oh, that's okay. It's late. I will go there tomorrow before work. Carolina can take me."

"You'll go tonight. Evvie told me you don't have your truck, so you'll need a ride home anyway. Kevin can take you." She smiled, but in her eyes, I saw something... suspicious.

Uh-oh.

I laughed out loud and shook my head. I knew what she was attempting. I'd heard about Ma's matchmaking endeavors.

"Ma," I looked directly into her eyes, "I think I know what you're into. You're trying to play cupie."

"Cupid, dear, and I don't know what you're talkin' about," she said, smoothing her blanket across her legs.

"Ma, it is not a good idea. He is— He's not, em, he doesn't..." What in hell was I supposed to say to her?

She sighed and dropped her shoulders. "Oh, Alvie, Kevin knows exactly what he wants. He's just scared to admit to it. He grew up around men who thought such things were wrong, so he's always thought about himself that way, but he's comin' around slowly. He sees his brothers happy, and he wants that too. He just hasn't figured out yet that he deserves it."

"Does Kevin know what you think about this? That you know he's gay?"

"Well… no." She looked at her hands. "It's not somethin' we've ever talked about around here. But I've known this about him for a while." Looking up, she grabbed both of my hands, squeezing them as hard as she could, which sadly, was not very hard at all. "So, you'll let him drive you?"

I sighed. "I will let him drive me, but Ma, you cannot force this on him. You understand? He has to decide for himself what he wants. He must be able to admit it to himself before he's ready to—"

"Yes, yes, I know, but you can help him. You can show him it's okay to be who you are, that there's nothin' wrong with it, and that he deserves love too. You show him, Alvie. Please?"

How could I say no to her? I smiled and nodded and kissed her cheek, and she hugged me. I knew I was agreeing to hurt myself. Involving myself further with Kevin Cade would most likely end in disaster, but I saw in her eyes how badly she wanted this for him, how much she loved him, and how desperate she was for KC to have happiness, but… what would *I* find in trying to "help" him?

Klote. What had I just agreed to? Again?

When I left her room, I opened the door and stepped back out into the hallway, right into KC.

"*Het spijt me*—sorry. I didn't see you." He didn't say anything. He just stared at me like he usually did. "Em, Ma wants me to go over to look at her house. She and Jack have offered to rent it to me. I was going to have Carolina take me there, but would y—"

"Oly's asleep. Fell asleep right at the dinner table," he said. "I can take you." He bit the inside of his lip, like he was nervous.

"Okay, *dank je wel*."

"Go 'head, I'll be down in a minute. We'll take Jack's truck. I just wanna say goodnight." He nodded to Ma's bedroom door and cleared his throat, and I left him and went back downstairs to wait.

I wondered what Ma would say to him, how she would explain why she wanted him to spend time with me, or if she even would. I also wondered what these men would do without her, what KC would do. They loved her so much. She was like the sun and they the planets in orbit around her.

I worried for KC; he seemed to be closest to her, and I had a feeling that when she was gone, he would not handle it well. And maybe that was why she was so desperate for him to have someone to love him.

The problem was, I was fairly confident I wasn't the *right* someone. Actually, there were so many problems with this scenario, I didn't even know where to begin.

⌃

"So, what is the house like?"

We drove through the black night in the red truck. It was a cool truck, but really old, so there were many noises coming out of it, and I worried we would find ourselves on the side of the road, waiting for a towing truck. I wondered why KC didn't have a vehicle of his own. He always borrowed his brothers'.

"It's old. And small," he said, staring straight ahead, watching the road so seriously.

Oookay. I tried again to get him talking, "Did you spend a lot of time there as a child?" I smiled to myself, picturing what he must have looked like as a little boy, his sun-kissed brown hair falling into his eyes as it did now.

"Yeah."

Ugh. *So* verbose. I was growing less and less keen on this

idea of Ma's, her "gay is okay" campaign. If this was how things were going to go, I was already dreading it.

"KC, you can just drive me to my place. I can go in the morning to look at Ma's house. I'm sure you have other things you would rather be doing. In fact, I'm fine at the boarding house. I don't need more room. I will just—"

"No," he grunted, and I sighed and slid down a little in the seat, defeated. It felt like forever, but finally, I sensed him looking at me. "You told Ma you'd take a look. She worries about you, and you told her you'd do it. Don't wanna go back on your word now, do ya?"

"No, I—wait a moment." I glared at him. "You're trying to — What's the word? Mm, you know, make me feel… *schuld* me into this."

"What're you accusin' me of?" He laughed. "I'm not doin' anything."

"*Ja*, you are, you're—guilt! That's the word. You're trying to guilt me."

"I dunno what you're talkin' about," he said, pressing his lips together to stop himself from laughing at me. "You don't have to live there if you don't wanna, Doc, but at least take a look. You might like it. It's a nice little house."

"I'm sure I will like it. This is not the issue."

"Then what is?"

"I don't know. I don't want to impose. Your family has been so generous to me already. I feel like I'm taking advantage."

"You're not takin' advantage. Ma wouldn't have offered if she didn't want you to take her up on it. The only imposition will be if you don't stay there. She'll hound us both. Once she makes up her mind about somethin', ain't no talkin' her out of it."

Ja, I was aware.

"You seem very close with Ma, but she is not your grandmother?"

"No, she and my granny were friends. When Granny died, Ma stepped in. We didn't really have any other capable adults in our lives."

"You didn't grow up with your parents?"

"We did, but my mama left when I was little. And my dad, he wasn't what you'd call real emotionally available. So, Ma was there. She's been lookin' out for me my whole life."

"I saw you downtown buying flowers. They were for Ma, yes?"

He peeked at me, blushing. Even in the dark truck, I could see it. "You saw me?"

"*Ja*, at the market. It was a few weeks ago."

"Oh. Um, yeah, Ma loves flowers. Usually, I pick wild ones for her, but in the winter and early spring, I buy 'em."

He didn't say anything more and neither did I. Only three feet of space separated us in the cab of the truck, and my left hand felt like it weighed one hundred pounds. It was all I could think about because I wanted to reach across to touch him. Instead, I watched his hands and his fingers gripping the steering wheel as if they had been glued to it.

A few moments later, we pulled into a short drive in front of a garage, much like Carolina's. The house standing beside it was a small cottage, also like Carolina's but white with a real American white-picket fence in front. It looked quaint. KC killed the truck's engine, and the muffler rattled, then silence surrounded us in the cab.

"So, this is it," he said. "It's small. I said that… G'on, have a look." He opened his door and stepped out into the darkness but waited for me. There was only one streetlamp I could see, but it was further than a block away. I stepped out, too, and walked slowly to the front door.

He followed and stood right behind me. If I had reached back with my hand, I would've touched his stomach. My pulse raced at the thought. Loneliness reared, and I fought the urge to grab him and pull him into the house, to force him onto his knees so he could make me forget.

Pulling the key Jack had given me from my pocket, I inserted it into the lock, but when I turned the knob and pushed, nothing happened. The door wouldn't open.

"Put a little elbow grease into it. It's an old door. It sticks."

"Grease? I don't have any grease. Have you some in the truck?"

He laughed. "Push. Use your muscles."

"Oh," I said and felt my ears turn red. I pushed again and shoved the door with my shoulder. The heavy door stuck to the frame, opening this time but barely, and I grunted. My ribs had been bruised when the SUV hit my truck earlier in the day, and I'd been trying to ignore it, but *verdomme*, it hurt.

"You okay, Doc?"

"Mm, *ja*, I'm fine. I hit the door too hard with my arm," I lied and walked into the house.

It was small. I could see most of the interior of the house from where I stood at the entrance. There was a door in front of me, leading to a closet I assumed, and a hallway to my left. The first door in the hallway led to a bedroom, though no bed was visible through the open door. The living room was to my right, and through that, a small dining area and kitchen. The house had only one other bedroom somewhere, I knew, and it looked like possibly a small back porch, but it would be big enough for me.

The whole thing had been decorated in mild, neutral colors with a lot of pink and yellow knitted accents, with blankets covering the arms of the couch and reclining chair, and those knitted round things under lamps and on an old and battered coffee table. *Doolies?*

Many framed pictures hung on the walls, most of them black and white. Some looked old, but most were modern photographs, which surprised me. The furniture was sparse and a little outdated but in good repair. It was not my aesthetic at all, but it was cozy and warm and would be suitable for me.

KC cleared his throat. "Go 'head, have a look around. The kitchen is through there." He pointed through the living room to the kitchen, and I couldn't see him, but I felt his arm behind my right shoulder.

"*Ja.*" I walked into the living room, and he followed. Looking around, it was difficult to concentrate on what I saw because all I could focus on was KC behind me. He'd stopped walking and was watching me. I sensed it and I felt self-conscious. Pulling the bottom of my sweater down around my waist and straightening the neck, I said, "*Ja, dit komt wel goed.*"

"Do you think in Dutch?"

"Hm?" I turned to look at him. "Oh, sorry, I said this will be fine."

"Sometimes you say 'yes' and other times '*ja.*' When you're nervous, you say things in Dutch but don't seem to notice." He tilted his head to one side. "And sometimes you think for a minute before answerin' a question. I was just wonderin' if you're translatin' whatever it is you wanna say in your head."

Hm. So he had *not* been ignoring me for the last three months. And now, I was really nervous.

"*Soms.*" I laughed at myself and shook my head. "Sorry. I mean to say sometimes. It depends on who I'm talking to or what I'm talking about. I tend to think in English when I'm working because I learned how to be a vet in English. It's usually regular everyday words that I forget."

He didn't say anything else. He just stood there, staring at me again, and I wasn't sure what to say. "So, this is the second bedroom here?" I motioned to a door in the little hallway. When I opened it, I was surprised by a bright, modern bathroom.

"I did some updatin' for Ma. She saw a bathroom in some

magazine and said she loved it, so I fixed it up for her birthday last year."

"You did this?" The bathroom was gorgeous. The shower stall had white subway tiles, with a built-in bench, and the bathroom floor was a ceramic tile made to look like dark wood. Modern light fixtures surrounded an old, oval mirror, which hung above a really cool pedestal sink, and there were heated towel racks mounted on the wall. I was impressed. Now, this was definitely my style. "This is gorgeous, KC."

He shrugged and looked down. "Yeah, so this is the other bedroom here." Taking three steps down the hall, he opened another door, flicking on a light just inside.

The décor was similar to the living room, but then I noticed that the queen-sized bed had been covered with many papers and small tools.

"Oh, shit, I forgot this stuff was in here," he said, leaning over the bed to scoop the papers up. "I'll get it outta your way." A few fell to the floor, and I picked them up to help him, trying to ignore the sharp pain in my side bending caused.

I gasped when I saw what I held in my hands: two large black and white photographs. One was a picture of the magnificent black stallion, Mad Max, standing in a field with a mountain in the background, his head held high and his mane whipping in the wind. He looked wild and regal. The other was a picture of Jack and Evvie gazing into each other's eyes. Both photos were striking, and they looked similar to some of the pictures hanging on the walls of Ma's house.

"Who took these? They're beautiful."

"They're just some pics I shot when I was workin' on a gift for Jack's weddin'. Nothin' special." He swiped the photos from my hands, crushing them and shoving them into a box on the bed.

"No, don't do that. They should be framed." I pulled them

out and tried to straighten the wrinkles he'd made in them. "They're lovely. You're very good."

He made a dismissive noise and turned to leave the bedroom, but I reached for his arm to stop him. "Really, KC, you are an artist. Your photographs are stunning."

Looking down at my hand on his forearm, he whispered, "What're you doin'?" He raised his eyes to mine, looking at me through his dark eyelashes, and turned toward me, stepping closer.

Shit. The look on his face was severe. I'd made a mistake. I should not have touched him. Dropping my hand from his arm, I took a big step back. "Please, forgive me, KC. I only meant—"

But he moved closer.

"Kevin," I breathed his name. I couldn't make my voice any louder.

Taking one more step closer, he looked like he wanted to hit me, his gaze so intense with his eyes locked onto mine, not blinking. I felt like a gazelle and he was a fucking lion. He was the most mesmerizing man I had ever met. But the *way* he looked at me—it twisted my stomach, and I wasn't sure if the feeling was born from desire or fear. I stepped back again and felt the wall behind me.

He had me trapped, and I couldn't look away from his eyes. So blue, *so* intense with the darkest navy rings around the outsides, as if his eyes were so potent, they needed something to contain them, to keep them from unleashing their power.

I lowered my arms—I hadn't realized I held them up in front of me—and placed them flat against the wall behind me, hoping I could keep them there.

Still, he didn't speak. It didn't look as though he breathed.

When he closed the last distance between us, there was nowhere left for me to go. Less than an inch separated our bodies. His eyes lowered to my mouth, and he very slowly brought his arms up beside my head. His hands were open, like he wanted to grab me and maybe bang my head into the wall.

But he didn't.

Instead, his face moved closer to mine one millimeter at a time until there was not even air between us. Our eyes met, and I could hear nothing but my breath forcing its way in and out.

He touched his lips to my open mouth, barely, pressing his chest to mine, barely. His hands were still raised beside my head, and they shook, barely.

Against his lips, I whispered again, "KC."

But he closed his eyes and tilted his head, inhaling my exhale, and slowly, he pressed his tongue inside my mouth. His breath rushed out of him and entered into me, and he moaned.

And then… he kissed the *fuck* out of me.

I was aroused before—just being near him made me hard. I wanted him. But my whole body ached with a need to touch him. I needed it so much, my hands shook too. Tentatively, I placed them on his hips. I didn't want him to stop kissing me, and I feared my touch would startle him. But as soon as I did, it wasn't enough.

My fingers dug into his skin through his jeans, pulling and pushing and seeking more, and I dragged him against my body. Oh *mijn* God. Every part of him strained, as did every part of me.

His tongue and lips were unrelenting and so wet and soft, and he tasted like sin in heaven. I couldn't get enough. He pumped his hips, rubbing his erection against mine twice, and I groaned and grabbed his ass, smashing his body to mine.

It was all so hurried and desperate until, finally, he touched me, and I gasped into his mouth. The pressure from just the tips of his fingers on my face felt so acute, I thought I could identify each crease of each fingerprint.

It was so unlike me to hold back. Normally, I would already have my hand inside his jeans—I would simply take what I wanted. And, God, did I want. But this was different. He was different. He was innocent, and he had ensnared me.

I dropped my hands to my sides and stood there, unable to move, while he dragged his palms over my jaw then, very slowly, over my body. With his lips still connected to mine, he stopped kissing me, drawing a breath in through his teeth as he pushed his fingers through my hair, clutching at my scalp. He breathed into my mouth and moved his fingers, so slowly, down my neck, over my collarbones, my shoulders and chest.

I was so hard, it felt like I had a five-kilo weight attached to my body.

I wanted in him so badly that I struggled to keep an intelligent thought in my head. Specifically, thoughts about why this was *not* a good idea. I was just about to force him down on top of all the photographs on the bed to fuck him senseless when he ran his palms down my ribs, and I grunted and winced, hunching my body and jerking my arm against my side, reflexively protecting my injury.

I'd forgotten about my bruised ribs.

His eyes blinked open, and he became completely still. Without looking away from me, he pulled the left side of my sweater up, exposing my black and purple bruise, and he looked down.

"What the fuck, Doc?"

"It's nothing," I whispered. "Don't stop."

"Are you kiddin'? I think your ribs are broken. I barely touched you. The entire left side of your torso is black and blue."

"It is a contusion only. I'm fine."

He continued to pull my sweater up and leaned down,

inspecting my injury, but then he looked up my body. Oh God. The image of him on his knees, sucking my cock into his mouth while he looked up at me like that, dulled the pain in my ribs.

Breath shuddered out of my mouth.

"This is from your accident earlier?"

I nodded.

"Sit," he said, and he took my hand, leading me to the edge of the bed. As I lowered myself, he stepped back to look at me, eyes landing on the stone-hard bulge in my jeans. He licked his bottom lip and looked up. "Don't move. I'll be right back."

When he left the room, I stayed stuck to the bed. My heart raced and my lungs pumped, which made my rib hurt more. I couldn't stop it. I tried to breathe deeply to slow my pulse, but that made me want to shout.

But I didn't care that I was in pain. I wanted him to kiss me again. I'd never been kissed like *that* before. *Jezus,* just thinking about his lips on mine and his tongue in my mouth, his hands all over me… I sucked in a breath, which caused a sharp stabbing pain in my side, and only that stopped me from *klaarkomen* in my jeans.

KC came back into the bedroom with something in each hand. *Ah,* a cold compress in his right hand, covered with a pink *handdoek*—a towel—and a bottle of some kind of alcohol in his left.

"Here, take a shot of this. A big one." He handed the bottle to me, and I did as he directed.

"Whoo. *Het is sterk.*" Bourbon. It was strong and woody, and the burn as it traveled down my throat did nothing to quench the fire in my body.

"Now lie back and turn toward me." He sat beside me carefully, and I eased myself down.

Now that I was focused on the pain, it began to dominate my thoughts. When I was flat on my right side facing him, he pulled my sweater up again and placed the wrapped cold compress on top of my ribcage.

"*Jezus, kut*! Fuck. Take it off!"

"Okay, that's it. You're goin' to get an X-ray. C'mon, up ya go."

Seven

Kevin

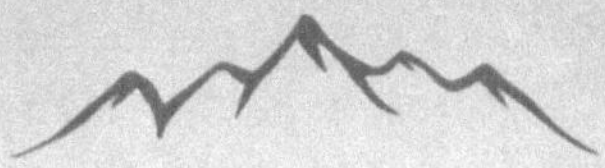

Fuckin' A. I hadn't expected the night to end up at the clinic unless I'd screwed Luuk through a wall, which, if he hadn't been injured, woulda been a definite possibility.

That kiss. I'd never kissed anyone like that. I've never *felt* anything like that. I'd wanted to consume him, body and soul, and only his extreme pain coulda stopped me.

Adjustin' the rock-hard baseball bat in my jeans as we walked through the clinic doors, I punched the button on the wall, alertin' Doc Whitley to somebody in his waitin' room.

Doc's clinic sat square in the center of Wisper in the front of an old house. He and Mrs. Whitley lived in the back. They'd built it up over the years so they could be here, in the heart of town, where people could get to Doc easily. He never turned anyone away, rich or poor, day or night.

The door opened, and Doc stuck his head out. "Kevin, Dr. van der Wouden, what can I do for you?"

"Sorry to bother you, but he needs an X-ray. I think he broke some ribs."

Doc looked at… Doc. *Ha.* Doc looked at Luuk and nodded. "Okay, give me just a few moments to finish up here with another patient."

"Sure thing. Thanks, Doc," I said, and he disappeared back through the door, leavin' Luuk and me standin' there just starin' at each other.

Finally, he spoke. "You know, there is no treatment for a broken rib, yes?"

"Yeah, I've broken a few myself, but he needs to check to make sure you ain't gonna puncture a lung or somethin'."

He didn't argue any further, just kept starin' at me. It turned me on. Now that I knew what he looked like under his sweater, it was all I could see, minus the purple/blue/black of it all. The longer we stood there, the more my breathin' increased and the harder my dick got. I was just about to pin him against the wall and shove my tongue back in his mouth when the door opened again, and my mama walked through it.

I wondered if Doc Whitley would stab my eyes out with a scalpel if I begged him to.

"What're you doin' here?"

"Oh!" She jumped when she heard me. "Hi, um, I-I needed stitches. I cut myself chopping tomatoes for José." She held up her bandaged finger as proof, lookin' back and forth between Luuk and me.

"You're supposed to bend your knuckles when you're choppin' so that don't happen." Didn't everybody know that?

"I know that now." She laughed. It was a sound I recognized; it made me feel warm inside my body, but it pissed me off.

"Are you okay? What's going on? It's Dr. van der Wouden, right?"

"Please, call me Luuk. Yes, everything is fine. I have a contusion on my rib. Not a big deal."

"A *broken* fuckin' rib," I mumbled, "not a damn contusion."

Doc stuck his head through the door again, holdin' it open with his arm. "Dr. van der Wouden, please, come with me."

"It was nice to see you again, Daisy. Kevin—"

"I'll wait, give you a ride home."

"*Dank je*, but you don't have to do that. My place is just down the street."

I was distracted by his mouth when he spoke. His words ran together sometimes, like a sentence was made up of one continuous word, and with his accent, his lips moved differently than other peoples'. I couldn't keep my eyes off his lips.

I raised my eyes back to his and said, "I'll wait."

Glancin' between my mama and me, he nodded once, then followed Doc Whitley back to the exam room.

She waited for the door to shut before she spoke again. "So, he's okay? Luuk?"

"Think so, but just in case."

"How are you feeling? After the—"

"After the gunshot wound that almost killed me?"

"Yes. I'm sorry," she whispered.

"I'm fine. Don't worry 'bout it."

"I do worry, Kevin. I think about you every day."

"Really? Coulda fooled me. We haven't seen hide nor hair of ya since that night."

"I didn't think you wanted to see me. Any of you. JJ stopped by the diner a couple of times but... And Sara said you weren't ready. That I should give you more time."

"Sara? You mean Ma? You been talkin' to Ma? And his name is Jay. No one calls him JJ anymore."

"Oh. Right. I always forget. Yes, I've spoken with her. I wanted to thank her for... for taking care of you. When I didn't."

"What a fuckin' surprise, you forgettin' the names of the people you haven't seen in twenty years." I knew I was bein' a dick unnecessarily, but I was angry. She'd been back for a few months, and still, we hadn't seen her. Maybe I didn't even wanna see her. Maybe I didn't even wanna know her.

And she'd been talkin' to Ma? *My* Ma? And Ma never said a word.

"How's everyone doing? Jack and Evvie? Are they enjoying being married?"

"I don't fuckin' know. Why don'tcha drive over there and ask *them*?"

"Okay, right." She nodded. "I'm sorry. I hope your— I hope Luuk is okay," she said, and she leaned forward, like she was gonna try to hug me or somethin', but I stepped back.

She didn't say anything more. Her lips tipped up into a pitiful smile, and she took a deep breath and walked out the door.

Luuk finished up with Doc Whitley twenty minutes later. Doc gave him a pain shot so he could sleep, so I drove him back to the one-room boardin' house he'd been stayin' in. He had to be miserable there. The place was probably old as Adam, the rooms the size of a broom closet.

He wouldn't let me help him inside, so I sat in my brother's truck, watchin' him walk up the long path to the front door. When he got there, I thought he would turn around to look back at me, and he started to, but then he squared his shoulders and disappeared inside.

It was late, but I didn't wanna go home. I decided to go back to Ma's place to clean my shit up. Luuk would probably move in soon, so he'd need the bed and the dinin' table I'd been usin' for my camera gear and photos.

While I drove there, I remembered my mama sayin', "I hope your— I hope Luuk is okay." What was that? What had she meant to say? My what? Luuk wasn't my anything. What, she thought she was gonna blow back into my life, actin' like she knew me?

She didn't know shit.

I cleaned my stuff outta the dinin' room and removed all the knitted blankets and doilies from the livin' room, foldin' 'em up and packin' 'em away in a box in the back-bedroom closet. There was enough of that junk to roof the house with. Luuk wouldn't like all that stuff lyin' around. He'd really liked the updated bathroom but seemed indifferent to the rest of the house. I could do some renovations—well, not tonight, but if he wanted, I wouldn't mind. I liked doin' that shit. Felt productive. Satisfyin'.

I cleaned the bathroom, scrubbed the toilet and the shower, and went into the bedroom to clear out all my stuff. There were a lot of my unused photos and the stuff to mat 'em with, some extra frames, X-Acto knives and the like.

He liked the pic of Max I'd taken, so I printed another uncrumpled one and used one of the leftover frames, givin' it a good thick mat, and hung it up in the livin' room, behind the couch.

I was gonna strip the sheets and put some fresh ones on, but then I remembered I'd slept in the bed a week ago. I liked thinkin' about him sleepin' on the same sheets I'd slept on. I'd only slept there for a few hours—it wasn't like I jacked off on the fuckin' things.

But then, thinkin' about that made me think about Luuk. His body, what it had been like to touch him. To kiss him. We hadn't gotten very far but...

Standin' from where I sat on the bed, where he'd been sittin' not even two hours before me, I walked over to where I'd pinned him up against the wall. I touched my forehead there, closed my eyes, and tried to imagine he was still with me.

I couldn't. All I could think about was Patrick Kessler, the other kid from my high school who was gay. The only other gay person I'd ever met, till recently.

By ninth or tenth grade, Patrick had become the laughin' stock of our whole school. Kids called him Patty Cake and made fun of everything about him: his hair, his clothes, the way he talked, the way he carried himself. They made fun of his parents. Even some adults around us, teachers, people in town, treated him differently. I couldn't let that happen to me.

To my brothers. They'd already gone through so much.

People had *died* in Wyoming for bein' my kinda different. So, I became someone else. Someone who wasn't gay.

And then I remembered when I'd had Luuk cornered in the barn right before I got shot.

Yeah. The time I told him I wasn't a "fuckin' fairy." The time I treated him just like all those people treated Patrick.

'Cause I was a coward.

I was so ashamed of the way I'd acted. It just mixed in with all the other shame I'd felt my whole life, and all kinds of memories rushed through my head.

"Dammit, boy, put that shit away." I remembered the time my dad threw my photography class project in a pile of manure and stepped on it. "What are ya, some fuckin' faggot? You're wastin' my time with this art bullshit. How's it gonna help the ranch? Get to work!"

I remembered the time he'd caught me drawin' a picture for Ma. "Goddammit. What I tell ya about that crap? This is a workin' ranch. We don't have time to sit around diddlin' our pricks with sissy bullshit. You still *have* a prick? I remember seein' one when your mama used to change your diapers. Or maybe I'm rememberin' it wrong. Is that why she left us? Put it away or I'll throw it away. Go help your brothers, or your hands too soft for that?"

I was eleven.

My dad's fucked up view of what a man should be was the only narrative in my head most of my life.

Now, as an adult, I had no idea what a gay man was supposed to look like. Yeah, I'd seen all the stuff on TV, online. I knew most people around here thought gay men all wore bellbottom jeans and cut-off belly shirts while they sashayed their hips and held their hand up in the air like some lady in an old movie holdin' a cigarette between her fingers. Just 'cause a man didn't go around gruntin' and flexin' his muscles didn't make him less of a man. Just 'cause he liked clothes or gardenin' or… art.

There was so much about gay culture I had no idea about. I could read about it, but till I lived it, I wouldn't know. I wanted to, though. I wanted a connection to other people like me. I didn't just like lookin' at men or screwin' 'em; I wanted to know 'em. And I wanted them to know *me*. I wanted to know their beauty inside.

I already knew their beauty outside.

I loved the way a man's body moved. It was more beautiful to me than any woman's long legs or the curve of her neck. The strength, the hard planes of a man's muscles, large or small, from their necks to their chests, to their stomach. Their backs, strong legs. Hands. Coarse hair. That's what I saw when I thought of beauty.

I wanted to capture it all with my camera.

Why did it have to be wrong? Wasn't it beautiful?

It was to me.

Luuk was. He wasn't effeminate or butch. He was just Luuk. He spoke softly, but he was confident, smart, honest. He told me my photos were beautiful. What other man would say that? They'd say, "Your pics are dope," or "That's tight, man."

Luuk said "beautiful."

EIGHT

LUUK

"**O**rder up!" José, the owner of the diner, called from behind the serving window when I walked in. It was Saturday, so the diner was busy for breakfast. I smiled at Sally Johnson while KC's mother, Daisy, served her breakfast at a booth in the window of the little café.

"*Hallo*, Mrs. Johnson. How are you? How are my three patients?"

"Oh, they're doin' fine, Doc."

"The antibiotics are working?"

"Seem to be. Everybody's doin' well. How 'bout you? I heard you were in an accident."

"You did?" I laughed. "I'm fine. Thank you. How did you hear about this?"

"Fred from the fire house told his wife, who told my sister-in-law, who called me."

"Oh, okay. Yes, I am perfectly fine. My truck needs some work but—"

Daisy held a coffee pot over Mrs. Johnson's mug to refresh her cup, but Mrs. Johnson covered her mug with her hand, giving Daisy a rude look. "No, *thank* you."

Daisy smiled and backed away.

"Have a good day, Mrs. Johnson." I smiled and turned to sit at the counter to order breakfast. Sometimes, small towns were not so friendly.

"Good morning, Luuk. You don't usually come in for breakfast," Daisy said, holding the same pot up in the air. "Coffee?"

"Yes, please. No, eh, my truck is in the shop, so I'm walking to work. They will bring me a rented car later today, but the diner is on my way."

"Oh, the accident."

"*Ja*. How does everyone know about this?"

"It's a small town, sweetheart. They know about *everything*," she said, peeking at Mrs. Johnson. She leaned forward, whispering, "Are you all right? Is that why you were at the clinic last night?"

"*Ja*." I smiled. It wasn't a secret. "I'm okay. I have a small fracture on my rib, but it will heal."

"Was Kevin with you when you were hit?" she asked, looking a bit worried.

I patted her hand on top of the counter. "No, *mam*, I was returning from a farm call. He wasn't with me. He's okay."

"Oh, well, thank God. I mean, I'm sorry you were in an accident, and I'm happy you're okay too." She laughed a little awkwardly.

"I understand. You're his *moeder*, his mom. Of course you worry."

I didn't know all the details of why she'd left Wisper twenty years ago, but I'd seen her with her sons and knew their relationship couldn't be in the best place. But she was still their mother, and I understood her anxiety.

"What can I get for you? Are you hungry? Or just the coffee?"

"I'm very hungry. I would like *pannenkoeken*—eh, pancakes, a veggie omelet, and hash browns, please."

"Comin' up," she chirped, her eyes sparkling. I wondered

if she'd just been happy to have someone to mother a little. I didn't usually eat so much junk, but I was starving. The injection Dr. Whitley had given me for pain knocked me out. I slept like I was a rock, and I could have eaten three omelets.

"*Dank je wel.*"

She smiled at José as she stuck my ticket in the spinning thing in the window, flicking it with her finger to send it to him, and he smiled, pulling the ticket off the spinner and ducking his head. She walked back to clean the area around me while we talked.

"So, where are you from, Luuk? Wait, may I guess?"

"Sure. Shoot it."

"I'll give it my *best shot*," she said and winked, pursing her lips and rubbing her hands together for dramatic effect. "Okay, well, I spent some time in Paris, so I know for sure it's not France. It's definitely not south of France, like Italy or Spain. You're not from a Hispanic country. My top three guesses are, mmm, Belgium, Germany, or... the Netherlands?"

"Very good. I'm from *Nederland*, Oudewater and Amsterdam."

"Outer water?"

"Oud-e-vateer. Have you been there, *Nederland*?"

"No. I flew from the US to Paris and stayed there. I got to see a few rural areas outside of Paris, but I didn't do any country hopping. I did get an opportunity to go to Rome and Barcelona, though, but they were pretty quick trips, so I wasn't able to see a lot outside my hotel."

"No? That's a shame. They are both beautiful cities. Eh, well, maybe someday you will go back."

She smiled but looked down, focusing on wiping the already clean counter, and I thought maybe what I had said made her sad. "So, is your family still back there?" she asked. "How did you end up in Wisper, Wyoming, of all places?"

"No, my parents passed when I was a teenager. I was

actually born in the States, in New York, but my parents took me back to the Netherlands to raise me there. I went to England for vet school. This is where I met Carolina. She asked me to come here to help her a few months ago."

"Oh, you mean Carolyn?"

"Yes, everyone calls her Oly, but ehh, I don't know why, but I have always called her Carolina. It's a knickknack, I guess."

"A nickname?"

"*Ja.*" I laughed at myself.

"I'm sorry to hear about your parents, Luuk."

"Thank you. So, what about you? How have you been? How is your finger?" I asked, nodding to her bandaged and gloved finger.

"Oh, it's fine. I just needed three stitches. I am no chef."

"Order up!"

"Oh, that's your breakfast. Be right back."

As she reached for my breakfast in the window, José called her name, and she bumped the swinging door open with her hip.

"Can you come back here for just a sec?" he asked her.

"Sure."

When she disappeared into the kitchen, I added one teaspoon of sugar and one creamer to my coffee, wishing I could allow myself three more, and checked my phone for messages.

"Hey."

I looked up and right into Brady's dark-brown eyes.

"*Goeiemorgen*, Brady."

"Mind if I sit?"

"Sure, sure. Please."

He sat, flipping an empty coffee mug in front of him on the long counter. "You know, they have way better coffee over at Coffee Shot."

"*Ja*, I know, but I am without my truck today. I'm walking to work."

"Oh yeah, the accident."

"Seriously?" I tossed my hands in the air. "You too?"

"Small town, man. How'd your call go the other night? Everything turn out okay?" he asked as Daisy delivered my breakfast and filled Brady's mug.

"Thank you, Daisy. Oh, em, yes. It was actually Mrs. Johnson's cows." I nodded toward Sally Johnson. "They're fine."

Brady waited until Daisy walked away, then asked, "You wanna get dinner sometime? I know you said you're not datin' right now, but I just thought, might be nice. I kinda miss talkin' to people I have stuff in common with."

I laughed. It wasn't a bad idea. I missed talking to people too. "Sure."

"Cool. We'll go to Jackson, or I dunno, somewhere other than Wisper, or the gossip will roar. Speakin' of gossip." Brady raised his eyebrows, nodding in Daisy's direction as she dismantled one of the coffee machines.

I lowered my voice. "What do you mean?"

"Daisy Cade's name is on everybody's lips lately," Brady said discreetly. "She's the talk of the town, as are her sons."

"Why? I mean, I know why they gossip about Daisy. Why her sons?"

"Oh, it's nothin' bad. They just talk about how they're handlin' her bein' back. About Jack's weddin'. Small town life can be pretty mundane. People gotta find ways to entertain themselves, I guess. I heard someone the other day talkin' about Kevin Cade. Now that Jack's married and Dean and Oly are back together, people seem to think he'll be next."

I snorted. I hadn't meant to. I tried to cover it with a cough.

"Ohhh, that's right, you've already met Kevin Cade." Brady leaned in, whispering, "He's gay, right?"

"I-I— Emm. *Ja, dat is*," I cleared my throat, "eh, not my—"

"I know he's not out. I'd never say anything. It's just, I saw him a while back over at Manny's Bar. I knew the second we made eye contact. I didn't know growin' up, but he was a year or two behind me in school, and back then, I was too busy tryin' to hide my own sexuality. Anyway, I doubt he'll ever be out. I remember their dad. Guy was somethin' else. A real jerk. Kevin's hot as hell though. If he were willing…"

Looking at Brady, I saw someone completely opposite of what I had imagined when I'd first met him. He wasn't nervous or shy at all.

His phone rang, and I thought about KC while Brady spoke to whoever had called. The Cade brothers were all very masculine and virile, but I couldn't imagine any of them treating KC badly just because he happened to be gay.

Brady ended his call as I took a bite of hash browns. I didn't want to be rude, but I couldn't wait any longer. I was starving.

"Sorry. I gotta go. Here, put your number in my phone." He pulled up his contacts and handed me his cell phone. "And, by the way, if *you're* willing…"

I scoffed and shook my head but smiled.

"What?" He tossed a five-dollar bill onto the counter. "I'm stuck in the middle of nowhere, but I'm not dead. I'll text you."

After he left, I ate quickly, said goodbye to Daisy, and got out of there before another person could ask me about my accident, as it seemed like the whole town knew.

I had moved everything I owned into Ma's little house on Billings Street. I didn't have any furniture really, just a book-case and a desk I used for my laptop. And I didn't have any dinnerware or silverware—Ma had given hers to Evvie, but I was a bit excited to go shopping for all of those things. I didn't shop very often, and most things I needed, I bought online, but furniture needed to be tested, which was kind of fun.

With the small inheritance my parents had left me from selling our farm to a large dairy company, I'd been relatively comfortable. It wasn't a large amount, but I had a friend at university whose father was a finance guy, and he showed me how to invest and grow my money, so I hadn't had to worry about finances often.

My parents' money allowed me the chance to travel and to pay for school without having to take out large student loans, and it allowed me to be here in Wisper, to help Carolina. Not many people my age would be able to work for the small amount of money I made at the clinic and to live off of it without the help of family. I was constantly grateful for my parents' foresight and generosity.

I would much rather have had them alive and with me, though.

After bringing the last of my clothes in from my rented truck, I looked around at the meager furnishings left in Ma's little cottage. They weren't to my taste, but they were kind of cool without the knitted coverings everywhere. I thought if I bought some modern pieces and mixed them in, they might look nice.

When I'd first walked into the house to start moving in, I'd noticed KC's photo of Mad Max hanging in the middle of the living room. He'd framed it and hung it on the wall behind Ma's old couch.

I wanted to call him. I'd take any excuse to do it, but maybe it was not a good idea. I hadn't heard from him in a week, not since he'd driven me to the clinic for my rib. I didn't want to push him... but that kiss. It was all I'd been able to think about. But it was just one moment in time.

No. It would be best if I just forgot about Kevin Cade. If Brady was right, and Kevin never came out, how would that even work? I'd been out my whole life. I couldn't go back "in" if I wanted to.

Carolina pulled into my little driveway, and I turned to meet her at the door, but before I could reach it, the door grudgingly allowed itself to be pushed open. "Luuk, you here?" she called. "Oh, hi. You really need to do somethin' about that door. Takes a batterin' ram to open it. You ready?"

"*Ja*, let me get a jacket."

"Okay, I'll be in the truck."

Carolina, Evvie, and I were going to Jackson to look for furniture and to buy paint. Ma said I could paint the walls if I wished, but I hadn't been planning to do it. It felt weird to change too much of her home, but then she phoned to tell me she would hire a painter to do it if I didn't. I couldn't let her do that, and this way, I would be able to choose the color. I grabbed my jacket from my bed and walked out onto the porch, locking my new, old, little house behind me.

"So how do you like Ma's house?" Evvie asked while Carolina drove us to Jackson.

"It's nice. It's the perfect size and the location is good. It's not even a mile to the clinic."

"What kinda furniture do you wanna look for? I know Ma's stuff isn't your thing *at all*," Carolina said, laughing.

"No, well, I did move a few things to the garage, and I took down some of her photographs because they were personal. Actually, maybe you can take them to her? She might want them around her. But I kept the coffee and side tables, and the dining table. So, I guess I'd like a new couch, maybe a chair. I'm thinking I'd like to find modern dining chairs to put with that old table. Except for this, I have no idea. This is what you are for."

"Are you sure you don't want to keep the hutch?"

"No, no, Evvie. Ma said it was part of your Christmas gift from her. It's yours. And also, I don't have anything to put in it. You said Jack will come to get it, yes? But if you're not ready to move it into your house, please just leave it for now. I don't mind."

"No, we are ready. We're pretty much living there now. There's just a few things left to do. We still need to paint the bedrooms, and we have some shopping to do ourselves. I'm keeping my eye open today. I've never bought furniture before." She giggled. "I'll be honest—I rarely ever used furniture."

"What do you mean?" What a weird thing to say.

"I haven't told Luuk your story, Evvie. I didn't think it was my place."

"Oh, well, it's not a big deal. I mean, I don't mind if people know. I guess I figured everybody already did know."

I turned to look at her, forgetting my rib, but the pain was not so bad. It was healing well.

What story? I knew she'd had a hard life. Carolina told me as much, but where does a person live where they wouldn't have the need for furniture? Maybe the jungle?

"Would you like to know?" she asked me.

"I am curious, Evvie. How did you not need furniture?"

"I lived in my car mostly. My parents died when I was eleven, so I was sent to live in a state home. When I turned eighteen and left there, I was… mmm, well, stalked, basically, for nine years. Until last October."

"What? Stalked by who? Why?" What in hell?

I sat in disbelief as Carolina drove, and we listened to Evvie tell her story. When we arrived at the first furniture store, Carolina parked, and we sat silent in the parking lot for a long time while Evvie talked.

"Why'd you pick Wisper?" Carolina asked. "You coulda gone anywhere."

"I don't know. I stayed away from any place I'd ever been to before, so I always chose somewhere new. And I usually stayed in larger cities, but that wasn't working. My money was running out. Big cities are so expensive, you know? So I looked at my map, and when I saw the Tetons, I remembered a book I'd read that had a description of them, and I thought 'that's where I'm going. I want to see that place. Maybe I can be lost in a sea of land instead of a sea of people.' Luuk, you said your parents died when you were a teenager. Were they both sick or…?"

"No, they were in an auto accident. They passed in the hospital two days parted from each other."

"I'm so sorry. That must've been really hard."

"Thank you. It was."

I rarely thought about that time in my life. It was hard. Really hard. I'd been alone without any other family. The social services in the Netherlands had been pretty good, so I had support until I went to university, but still, it was very lonely.

"But then I decided to pursue vet school, and things started coming together for me. And I met Carolina, and my life was completed," I joked, batting my eyelashes in her direction, and Carolina rolled her eyes and reached across the seat to kiss my cheek.

"What made you stay in Wisper, Evvie?" I was curious because maybe I wanted to stay in Wisper too.

"I met Ma," she laughed, "and she took over from there. She pretty much shoved Jack into my life a week later, and the rest is history."

"I need to hug you. I'm comin' back there!" Carolina crawled into the back seat, landing on Evvie, and they giggled and hugged. "I'm so glad you're here now. I can't imagine what the ranch would be like without you."

"You too. Dean's like a different guy since you came back." Evvie laughed. "Luuk, get your butt back here."

"You're going to regret asking me to do that," I warned, and my rib protested a little as I pretended to climb over the seat I so obviously would not fit over. Evvie screeched and laughed more, like a little girl, and I climbed out of the truck and opened the back door. I pulled her across the seat and crushed her to my body, hugging her and holding her up off the pavement. "I am *so sorry* you had to live through that. But I'm glad that you found your Jack and your family, and that I can know you now."

"Thank you, Alvie, but you know you're part of my family, too, don't you?"

"I am?" I asked, setting her on her feet and releasing her.

"Yeah. Ma's the boss, the boys are hers, Oly and I are hers, and she totally adopted you. Didn't you know that?"

She was joking, but still, it was a shock to hear someone say I was a part of their family, that they wanted me to be. I wasn't sure she was right, but it felt nice to hear her say it.

"Evvie, that's not gonna work," Carolina whispered loudly, "'cause that would make Luuk and Kevin brothers, and we can't have *that*."

"Carolina," I growled at her, warning her with my eyes to *houd haar mond*!

"Alvie, I know you like Kevin," Evvie blurted. "He likes you too. You don't have to hide that from me."

"Yes, but it's a little more complicated than that. He is not, he—"

"He's not ready," Evvie offered.

"No. So there's no point in talking over it."

"Don't give up on him. Just look at Oly and me. He'll be worth the wait, all those boys are. They can be a little thick at first, but once they figure out what they want, there's no stopping them. And you will not regret it." She waggled her eyebrows.

"What do you mean 'thick'? You're not talking about his—"

"No! Oh my God. I meant stubborn. They can be *stubborn*."

"Oh my God!" Carolina laughed and bent forward, clutching her stomach.

"You are both preferred. I cannot believe I'm hanging out with you." I scoffed and stomped away from them, pretending to be angry.

"Perverted!" they yelled in unison, laughing more.

We shopped for hours. Fortunately, we didn't get any farm calls, so I was able to find a couch and chair, dining chairs, a console for a television, and a television. Both Carolina and Evvie said I had to have one, if for no other reason than they might want to watch movies at my house. I laughed at that but bought the *verdomde* thing. I had been meaning to binge watch *Game of Thrones* and watching it on a humongous television would be better than squinting at it on my laptop.

I still had the use of Ma's old kitchenware, so I didn't bother to buy any pots and pans. I could get that later or online if I needed to, but I doubted I would. Cooking was not my gift or a desire I possessed.

The girls found blankets, pillows, and small decorations that would accent the new furniture, and then we stopped at the hardware store for paint. They chose a soft gray color and said it would match well with the furniture I'd bought.

It was nearly ten at night when we arrived home. They dropped me at my house, and Carolina called from the truck window. "Take tomorrow off, Lookie Loo. I'll take any calls we get so you can paint. Your furniture will be here Tuesday. You probably won't get another chance to do it before then."

"Are you sure? I can paint between calls."

"Positive. Take the day. I'll call if I need help, but I'm sure I'll be fine. You deserve a day off."

"Okay, thanks."

"But call us when the stuff gets here so we can come decorate. I had so much fun today. I can't wait to do all this for my house."

"I will, Evvie. Thank you for your help."

"Welcome. Have fun tomorrow." They rolled up the window and drove off, giggling, and I shook my head. *Women.*

Lugging my ginormous television inside, I dumped my packages by the door and went straight to bed. I didn't even brush my teeth.

The next morning, I woke feeling *kiplekker.* I felt rested and energized, and I could barely feel my rib anymore. I brushed my teeth first thing—because gross—and went for a short run. I found myself downtown, so I bought an espresso from Coffee Shot, downed it, and jogged back home.

Draping plastic sheeting everywhere to protect any furniture left in the living room, I turned on my favorite heavy metal playlist and got to work. It occurred to me I probably should have waited to take a shower because I would soon be covered in paint. *Eh, tuurlijk joh.*

At 9:07 a.m., there was a knock on my front door. I looked down at myself and laughed. I was already covered in paint and wasn't wearing anything but boxer shorts, so I ran to my bedroom, pulled on my sweaty joggers, and went to open the door.

When I did, Kevin Cade stood in front of it.

Shit.

"Umm. *Wat doe je?* I mean, what are you— Shit, let me grab a shirt. Just, emm, come in. I'll just put over a shirt—"

"Don't you fuckin' dare," he said, and he barged in, slamming the door shut behind him.

Nine
Kevin

I was nervous standin' on Luuk's front porch, waitin' for him to answer the door. Oly had asked me to come help Luuk paint because he was still injured. I jumped on the opportunity. I hadn't seen him since the night of The Kiss, and a thousand times, I imagined doin' exactly what I was currently doin'. My heart tried to strangle me, clawin' its way up my throat, my hands were sweaty, and I couldn't stop tryin' to bite a hole through my lip.

But then Luuk opened the door, and my brain stopped workin'. He wore a thin pair of sweatpants and nothin' else. *Ohhh*. He was all long, lean, hard muscle. Strong. Cut. He was—

"Umm. *Wat doe je*? I mean, what are you— Shit, let me grab a shirt. Just, emm, come in. I'll just put over a shirt—"

I gawked at his body as he said it, probably droolin', and he turned to walk away from me.

"Don't you fuckin' dare."

It just came out! I almost growled it, and he whipped back around to see if I'd lost my damn mind—I couldn't control my brain or my body.

Steppin' over the threshold, I slammed the door shut with

my boot, and he backed up a couple feet. If I hadn't been so turned on, I woulda laughed at the expression on his face. His eyebrows were raised to the ceilin', and there was flat lust—and a little fear—in his eyes.

Wait a minute. Was he listenin' to Anthrax? I heard "Anti-social" playin' somewhere inside the house. No shit? My favorite.

"Can I help you with something? I mean, why did you come here, KC?"

Could he help me with somethin'? Really? Well, as a matter of fact. I grabbed his hand and yanked it right to my dick, holdin' it there with my hand on his, tryin' to feel the heat from his skin through my jeans.

Pushin' him back against the closet door, I leaned in to whisper in his ear. "Can you help me with that?" I bit his earlobe, and he tightened his fingers around my cock, squeezin' hard.

He groaned but then pushed me back against the front door, dislodgin' his hand and separatin' our bodies. "KC, what are you doing?"

Slidin' my arms outta my jacket, I dropped it onto the linoleum floor, then pulled my shirt over my head. I looked down at his sweatpants, to the enormous hard-on under-neath, and back up into his eyes, cockin' an eyebrow.

"Shit," he breathed, and I stepped forward.

I had about two inches on him, so I stood above him a little, and I used it to my advantage. I looked straight into his eyes, trappin' him with my gaze so he wouldn't see what I was doin' with my hands.

Leanin' my face in, I kissed him so, *so* softly, and while his attention was otherwise engaged, I placed my hands on his sweatpants, on his hips, and pushed. I wanted to rip 'em off, but I had to give him the opportunity to say no. He wasn't gonna, but I had to at least act like I wanted him to have the choice.

"KC, *dit is geen goed idee*. Not good." He whispered it against my lips, lookin' into my eyes and shakin' his head. There was a little trepidation there and somethin' else— that barely suppressed emotion I'd seen in him before. Somethin' intense. I still didn't know what it was, but I wanted it.

I wanted him to unleash it on me.

"Not a good idea? You sure?" I penetrated his mouth with my tongue and didn't even try not to drown in it. He closed his eyes, leaned into me, and moaned, groaned, and growled.

He kissed me back, and now, I was the one groanin'. I might've even sobbed a little.

It felt so fuckin' good.

His mouth was everything. His lips were so soft, and he sucked at mine, bitin' 'em a little and lickin' the pinch away. He rolled his tongue against mine, and all I could think about was what it would feel like on every other inch of my body.

My dick was so hard, it ached.

Grabbin' my hair in his hands, holdin' my head immobile as he pulled away from me, he stared at me for an eternity, trappin' me in his own gaze, decidin', I thought, if he would give in to me, then he lowered his head and licked my nipple, sucked it into his mouth. He fuckin' made love to it.

Oh God. The burn inside my body was nearly debilitatin'.

He licked from my nipple to my collarbone, up my neck, over my jaw, stoppin' to nibble there, and back up to my lips, assaultin' my mouth again with his diabolical tongue.

I couldn't take any more or I'd come in my 501s. I pushed him back again with my hands on his chest, then gripped his arm and whipped him around so fast, shovin' him into the bedroom which was, thankfully, only a few feet away from us.

"This is *niet mijn slaapkamer*."

"Who gives a shit." I assumed he meant it wasn't his bedroom, but I didn't care. We coulda been in the middle of Jackson, in the town square, and I still woulda striped him bare and sucked him stupid. Turnin' him and pushin' him down onto the chair in the corner, I kinda expected him to get up to argue, but he stayed down and he devoured my body with his eyes.

"Why are you here?"

"To help you paint. Oly said you needed help 'cause your rib still hurt."

"She lied."

"That matters how?" I unbuckled my belt and unbuttoned and unzipped my jeans, and he licked his bottom lip, scrapin' his teeth on that plump and perfect temptation, then he palmed his cock through his sweatpants. "No. That's mine," I growled.

"Unghhh," he groaned, and his head fell back.

I dropped to my knees on the floor. It was mornin', but the room we were in had dark curtains coverin' the only window, so the light was dim, but I could see a thin sheen of sweat on his chest, and I wanted to taste it.

He lifted his head to look at me, and as I looked back into his eyes, I panicked when I realized he was the first person I'd ever really made eye contact with who I messed around with. In fact, I couldn't stop lookin' in his eyes. I kept gettin' lost in 'em.

What the fuck did *that* mean?

"KC?"

I looked down at my hands on his hips. He was lookin' right into me. He could see everything I didn't want him to see.

Fuck, fuck, fuck.

It scared the shit outta me. He was gonna see all my lies. He would see the truth. He would see that I was nothin', I wasn't worth his trouble, that I didn't deserve him. Anyone. He would see, with me, he could only lose. I would ruin him.

I couldn't let him see that.

"KC, what's wrong?"

"Nothin'. Shut up."

I kept my eyes on his body and pulled at his sweatpants, tryin' to tug 'em down, but my hands shook and I couldn't do it.

"Kevin. Stop." He covered my hands with his own, squeezin' softly. "Please, look at me."

"Don't wanna stop," I said, buryin' my face in his hip, lickin' that sexy fuckin' skin, tryin' to push underneath his sweatpants with my chin. God, he tasted so good. I moved lower, lickin' and rubbin' his cock *through* the damn sweatpants, and my fingers gripped his hips and the hard planes of the muscle above as he flexed 'em, tryin' to sit up.

"Kevin—oh *mijn* God." He moaned and panted when I sucked the head of his cock through the fabric. "Look at me, please?"

My hands were frantic, clawin' at the goddamn sweatpants.

"Kevin. *Stop*." He sat up, and I teetered back on my knees. *Fuck.*

He knew. He'd already seen.

Squeezin' my eyes shut, I stilled my hands and held my breath. There was only one thing left to do. "You wanna fuck or not, Doc?"

"Kevin, can you look at me?"

There was tenderness in his voice, a gentleness. It broke my fuckin' heart 'cause I was about to bust his all to shit.

I looked up into his eyes. "I can. I just don't wanna. I can get this somewhere else with way less hassle. This ain't some fairy-tale fuck. I ain't gonna fall in love with you. Is that what you thought we were doin'?"

Disappointment flashed across his face, and he closed his eyes. He whispered, "Kevin."

There was pity in his voice, and I felt disgust. For myself. I knew he wanted me and not just for sex. He had since we met. He wanted to know me, to be inside me, inside my head. And even though I was desperate for it, I... couldn't allow it.

I looked back down, then stood and zipped my jeans. "Fuck you, Doc. Paint your own walls."

"How'd it go?" Finn asked when I walked into the kitchen eleven hours after I'd left Luuk. I drove till I ran out of gas and Jack's truck died on the side of the road, the whole time thinkin' about how much I hated what I'd just done and said, then I walked three miles to the nearest gas station and the three miles back. I drove some more and finally came home.

"What?"

"Paintin'?" he asked, like I'd forgotten.

"Fuck off."

He nodded real slow. "Okay, man, whatever. Hey, Ma's been askin' for you," he said before he walked out the same door I'd just come through.

Great. What now? Grabbin' the bottle of whiskey off the top of the fridge, I guzzled enough to make the crack in my chest go numb, then stomped up the stairs to knock on Ma's door.

"Come in."

I nudged the door open and stuck my head in. I didn't wanna go all the way in. I didn't want her to see me either. She'd know what I'd done to Luuk just by lookin' at me. She'd see the disgust in my eyes.

"Finn said you need somethin'?"

"I don't need anything, honey. I just wanted to see how you're doin'."

"I'm fine," I lied, backin' away from the door.

"Kevin."

"What?"

"Get in here and sit down."

"I got sh—stuff to do."

"Now."

Fuck.

"Yes, ma'am, but I ain't sittin'." I walked into her room and closed the door behind me, but I couldn't look at her. I just couldn't do it.

"Why not?"

"Don't feel like it." I stood at the end of her bed, lookin' down at the floor.

"Why're you actin' like this?"

"Actin' like what?" *Oh, you mean, why am I bein' such a colossal dick?* "I ain't actin' like nothin'."

"Kevin, you're a grown man. Stop actin' like a child. What's the matter with you? Look at me." I took a deep breath, squared my shoulders, and looked right in her eyes. Her beautiful old face crumpled like she wanted to cry. "Oh, my boy. Why are you doin' this to yourself?"

I didn't say anything. I stood there silent, locked in place, wishin' she had the strength to get up from the bed to beat the fuck outta me.

I wanted her to pummel me. To crack my skull open. It would hurt less than it did to look at her and see the sadness and disappointment in her eyes. I wasn't sure how she knew, but I'd let her down. Again. She had all this love for me, faith in me. She expected shit from me, and every time, I let her down.

"I love you, Kevin. No matter what, I love you."

I scoffed. "I gotta go. And what's this bullshit about you and Daisy with your heads together? What, you're friends now?"

She pursed her lips at my cursin' but didn't scold me. "Your mama wanted to talk to me. She wanted to thank me for lookin' out for you boys. I know you don't wanna hear it, but I think you should talk to—"

"Yeah, right."

I had to get outta there. I was so angry at her. Why? Why would she let that woman back into our lives? And why did she love me? I hadn't ever earned even a goddamn ounce of her love. I never would, and still, she kept givin' it.

Why?!

Every time she gave me more, I felt guiltier and guiltier. Hadn't she learned anything from my mama?

I wasn't fuckin' worth it.

Maybe they could chat about it durin' their weekly book club. Shakin' my head, I walked outta her bedroom, slammin' the door shut behind me.

When I got downstairs, Jay stood in the kitchen, lookin' at some papers he'd spread out on the table.

"Let's go."

He looked up when I said it. "Go where?"

"Just get in the truck. You're drivin'. I'm gettin' plastered." I needed at least one bottle of bourbon. I'd start with that. I threw Jack's truck keys at him. "Manny's. Now."

He looked at me with pity on his face. "Kev, I'm not sure tha—"

Screw his pity.

"No? Okay then, I'll drive myself." I walked over and tried to rip the keys back outta his hand, but he gripped 'em tighter.

"Fine."

Jay drove like an old lady to Manny's Bar, and I sat there, crawlin' outta my skin. I wanted to hurt myself. Punish myself. Suddenly, I had a brilliant idea. I either needed to start a fight or find a woman to fuck. Either would do. I might end up in jail, but I didn't give a shit. Actually, that might work out for me. People got beat up in jail all the time.

We walked into Manny's ten minutes later, and I scanned

my possibilities. There weren't any drunk morons around, so sex with a woman would have to do.

That would hurt just fine.

Ahh, perfect. Vicky Harmon. She'd fuck me. She chased after Dean when he came home from the Marines, and she tried chasin' after Finn too. She didn't give a shit which guy she ended up with so long as his last name was Cade.

"Kevin!" She slithered toward me. She'd already seen me and set her sights.

"Vicky. How are ya? Baby girl, you look *good*."

"Oh, shit," Jay mumbled behind me. He knew what I was aimin' for. It wasn't the first time I'd brought him along. Whatever. It wasn't like I could let him down any more than I already had.

I spent the next half hour suckin' back as much liquor as I could and flirtin' with Vicky, touchin' her here and there, scootin' my body closer to hers an inch at a time. I couldn't have cared less about a thing she said, which made me sound like the monumental asshole I was, but also, all she talked about was herself and how great she was. *She* went to massage school, and *she* finished top of her class. *She* got a new car, and it's nicer than Katie Ambuson's BMW. *She* lost ten pounds while her poor sister put on fifty after she had her twins. Good fuckin' grief. After about three minutes of that bullshit, all I could really hear was the nasal hummin' of her voice, and I couldn't take it anymore.

I'd all but decided to abandon my plan till I saw Oly outta the corner of my eye. What the hell was she doin' at the bar? I looked around for Dean but didn't see him, and that was when I noticed Luuk's head above all the rest. I'd bet he was meetin' Oly for a drink after a farm call.

Probably to talk about me.

Wonderful.

I was fully prepared to give 'em somethin' to really talk about. This was the perfect opportunity.

Could this night have gotten any better? I thought not.

Luuk and Oly hadn't seen me yet in the dim light of the run-down dive bar since I was covered head to toe in Vicky Harmon, so I scooted my chair a little to the right, hopin' it would put me into Luuk's line of sight. When he still didn't notice me, I stood up, pullin' ol' Vicky with me.

"Where you goin', Kevin Cade? I'm not through with you yet." Vicky slurred her words, so I knew screwin' was probably off limits, but I could still get some mileage outta her. I could use her to nail the Luuk coffin shut.

Oly and Luuk were still walkin' toward me, so I pulled Vicky to my side and wrapped myself around her, shovin' my face into her neck. She smelled like old lady perfume, sweat, and onions. I had to actually work not to gag.

Layin' the cowboy on real thick, I kissed her neck. *Ugh.* "Oh, no, baby, I ain't goin' nowhere. I just thought you might like to slow dance a little."

Finally, Luuk's eyes met mine, and so did Oly's, actually, at the same time. They both stopped in their tracks, and Oly made some plea with her face, as if to say "Kevin, don't do this. You're better than this." Or maybe "Seriously? Vicky Harmon? Don'tcha have *any* dignity?"

I didn't.

I locked my eyes onto Luuk's, pulled my head outta Vicky's sweaty neck, and shoved my tongue in her mouth. She moaned and rutted her body against my leg like a rabbit in spring. Jesus. Did *Vicky* have any dignity?

My dick had been hard from the moment Luuk walked into the bar, so Vicky would be convinced of my attraction to her. She was persuaded. She reached her hand down, cuppin' my junk over my jeans, and I watched Luuk's eyes follow the movement.

He laughed and shook his head infinitesimally.

He didn't look amused.

Turnin' his head but not lookin' away, he leaned down to

say somethin' in Oly's ear. She said somethin' back to him, and he turned and walked to the door, and I pulled my tongue outta Vicky Harmon to watch him go.

Right before he opened the door, he looked back at me, flashin' me the most devastatin' smile. It was beautiful, full of sadness, disappointment, and pity.

I burned it into my memory as he walked out the door, and I walked away from Vicky, settin' off the alarm when I punched my way through the emergency exit.

TEN

LUUK

"You're really hot. What's your accent?"

"Dutch."

"Say something."

I leaned in, whispering into his ear, "Something."

"No, I meant say something in— What did you say it was? German?"

"It doesn't matter. I want to fuck your mouth. Come."

I dragged my new "friend" from the entrance of the bar to my rental truck. I'd driven all the way to Pocatello, Idaho to a gay bar, and I'd just spent the last two hours talking and flirting with some man from California. We danced a little and touched, and I couldn't wait any longer. I led him by his tie, and he followed clutching my hips.

When we reached the truck, I turned and pulled him to my mouth, but at the last second, I pushed his head into my neck. I wanted to imagine KC kissing me while I fucked this man's mouth.

"God, you're so hot. I've never been with a guy like you," he said, kissing my neck up to my ear.

"What do you mean? You're very attractive."

"Yeah, I'm attractive. You're *hot*." Pushing his hands

under my shirt, he clawed my skin. "I want my mouth all over you. How do you wanna do this?"

"Get on your knees."

"What, right here?"

"*Ja*, suck me."

He pulled away and looked at me. "Don't you wanna get a motel or, I don't know, climb into that fancy truck?"

I didn't reply. I looked in his eyes, placed my hands on his shoulders, and pushed him down.

"Damn, that's so hot."

While he knelt on the pavement, pawing at my pants to unzip them, all I could see was KC's face in my mind.

I thought sex was what I wanted—needed—but once I could see him, I couldn't get KC out of my head. I kept remembering him between my legs, looking up at me panicking, and his face in the bar. All that pain and defiance. And shame.

I knocked my head back against the truck's window and tried to wipe KC's face out of my mind. California What's-His-Name managed to get my pants open, and he thrust his hand inside, cupping my balls.

Holding my breath, I willed any other image besides KC's face into my head.

I looked down and saw this man with his mouth open, ready to suck away my sadness. "Ah. *Verdomme*." I covered myself with my hands.

I heard KC's voice. "You wanna fuck or not?"

"What? What did you say?"

"Nothing," California said. "It's just, if you're not up for it, that's cool."

I sighed. "Go back inside."

"You all right?" He stood, dusting the dirt off his suit pants.

"*Ja*," I said through my teeth, "I am fine. I'm sorry. I just can't."

He stumbled back inside and I drove. I thought sex would make me feel better. I should have known it would not. It never did. Now I was hard, pissed off, and I still had a three-hour drive home.

"Hello?" Brady's voice was loud in my truck, coming through the speaker through Bluetooth.

"Brady?"

"Luuk? That you?"

"*Ja.*" I released my breath. I felt relieved to talk to someone who could understand me.

"You alright? You sound weird." He yawned.

"I need to fuck."

"Oh." He laughed. "I'll be right there."

"No, I'm not— I couldn't do it."

"Couldn't do what? Where are you? What time is it?"

"Idaho. It's one in the morning."

"What're you doin' there?"

"I cannot talk to Carolina about this. She wouldn't understand."

"What's goin' on? Talk to me." I heard shuffling as Brady sat up in his bed. "You can trust me."

I took a deep breath. "When I feel… badly about myself, I fuck. It's what I do. It's what I've always done. And I thought — But I couldn't do it. I could not stop seeing his face."

"Whose face?"

I sighed. "KC. Kevin Cade."

Brady laughed. "Oh, man, one more sucker all jacked up over a Cade brother. Did you have sex with him?"

"No. Not… yet."

"Well, if you got that kinda hole to pound, why are you in Idaho?"

"You were right. He's not out. He might never be. I've been out my whole life. I don't know if I can deal with his… issues. He's screwed up. He threw himself all over a woman in the bar. He was trying to prove to me he's not gay. But since the first night I met him, I cannot stop thinking of him. Wanting him." I dragged my fingers through my hair. "Maybe I am the one who's screwed up. God, he's so rude. He acts like a child. What's wrong with me?"

"You said you've been out your whole life? Your parents were cool about it?"

"*Ja.* They just knew. It was never a thing."

"You know, I actually remember somethin' about him from when we were kids. You know his brothers, right? All four of his very *manly* brothers?"

"*Ja.*"

"Well, you never knew his dad. I did. Wisper's such a small town. Everybody knows everybody. I remember their mom used to take 'em everywhere with her. She'd play with 'em at the park, take 'em for walks along the river. I was jealous. My mom worked. I never got to spend time with her like that. But then Daisy Cade just disappeared, took off one night and never came back.

"It ruined their dad. He became an awful human bein'. He treated those boys like shit. One day, my dad and I were at the grocery store in town, and Kevin was there with his dad. We were in the checkout lines, and Kevin wanted his dad to buy him a pack of crayons or markers or somethin'. His dad just ignored him, but Kevin kept on.

"He bugged and begged his dad. I remember watchin' that man's face morph from irritated to irate. He whipped Kevin in the store. I don't mean swatted his butt for misbehavin'. I mean, that man took off his leather belt in the middle of the grocery store and *whipped* his kid with it. My dad had to step in, which then almost became a fight between his dad and mine."

"*Jezus.*"

"Yeah. I remember cryin' when we got home 'cause I felt so bad for him. All 'cause he wanted to color? I was probably eight, nine maybe. So Kevin had to have been seven, maybe six. But, Luuk, think about it. If that was Kevin's role model, a man like that? And now he's lookin' at his brothers? Comin' out is *hard*. Even when your parents are lovin' and supportive. Imagine the fear he must've felt."

My new furniture had been delivered almost two weeks ago, but it still sat in the garage, wrapped in plastic, waiting for me to get my ass out of my head. I'd thrown myself into work, planning and organizing a free spay and neuter clinic and taking most of the farm calls so Carolina could stay at All Animals during the day and go home at six o'clock every night.

She'd been so tired lately, falling asleep at Dr. Prittchard's desk during our lunch breaks. We went to Coffee Shot one afternoon to grab an espresso when it was slow at the clinic, and she nodded off right there at the table. It must have been nice to have someone to keep her awake, sexing her brains up all night long.

I didn't know anything about that, and it was starting to affect me.

After KC pulled his bullshit at my house and threw himself all over the woman at the bar, I was physically frustrated. And mentally. And emotionally. I wanted to scream at him for the way he'd treated me, for the way he'd treated himself. I wanted to hit him. He'd been trying to punish himself. I'd known that.

And since then, I'd felt this need to break something. I was so angry with myself. I knew I should not have gotten involved with him. I told myself not to do it, but I didn't listen. Not the day at Cade Ranch with Ma and her "gay is okay" campaign and not the day he came to my house, barging his way inside.

But I couldn't stop thinking about what Brady had said. About how afraid Kevin must feel.

I ran every day, sometimes twice a day. If I had free time, I worked out or ran, trying to exhaust myself so I could sleep. When I couldn't, I stayed up all night thinking about KC. Thinking about the look on his face in the bar and thinking about the inexplicable power he held over me. About touching him and kissing him. Tasting his skin. And then I would just have to get up and run again.

I was so tired, but Carolina had so much going on so I didn't complain.

"If you don't mind, I'm gonna take off early. Our last appointment is at four thirty, and then you just have a couple farm calls." She dropped a stack of patient files onto the desk in the office and flopped into the chair.

"*Ja*, sure. Is everything okay?"

"Ma's not doin' so well."

"Oh no. Why did you not say something earlier? I'm so sorry, Carolina." I felt awful that I hadn't noticed her mood.

"Thanks. The guys are so sad. I wish there was something I could do to help Dean feel better but— And Kevin's an absolute wreck."

"How do you mean?" I hoped she couldn't hear the desperate need in my voice for her to explain.

"He's, I mean, he's just so…" Carolina shook her head and sighed. "It's hard to watch."

I worried about him. I was afraid to see him because I didn't know if I would punch him or wrap my arms around him and never let go. I thought about KC and about what "absolute wreck" meant and about Ma and how much she would be missed while I drove to my last farm call of the day.

Philomena Beasley needed help with the piglets I'd delivered several weeks ago. They were all sick, passing some kind of disease back and forth between them. She was worried about E. coli, but I had a feeling she was dealing with rotavirus, given the litter's age and symptoms.

Mrs. Beasley waited for me in front of her barn, and as I stepped out of my truck, she reached over to shake my hand. "Hey, Doc. Thanks for comin' all the way out here again. I really 'preciate it."

"It's not a problem, Mrs. Beasley. How are you?"

"Oh, please, Doc, call me Phil. Everybody does."

A tall and striking woman probably in her mid-sixties, Phil had long, salt-and-pepper-gray hair (mostly salt) she wore in a braid to one side. She had purple reading glasses pushed up onto her head, and she wore a floral quilted jacket and denim overalls that had been folded several times up and over her black-and-white checkered muck boots.

Boscoe, Phil's gigantic, shaggy dog came running out from the woods behind the barn. The poor guy was covered in mud and burrs.

"*Hoi*, Boscoe." I reached down to pet the mongrel when he jumped up to lick my face. "*Hallo, hond*. How are you?"

"Isn't he the cutest? He's my little buddy."

Little? The dog was huge, probably eighty pounds, but he was a lover. He sat politely in front of me, leaning into my hand while I crouched to scratch his head.

"Well, Phil, how are our piglets?"

"I'm really worried. They're still scourin' all over the place. It smells awful."

"And how is the sow? Is she still nursing them?"

"No, she seems off somehow, but I dunno why."

"All right, let us have a look." I grabbed my pack, and we headed into Phil's barn with Boscoe heeling to my side.

When we finished with the sow and her piglets (Phil and I had both been wrong. The sow had mastitis and stopped nursing, causing the piglets to weaken and scour), Phil led me to her favorite horse, Rocky Balboa, who was lame in his right hind leg.

I jogged back to my truck to grab my head lamp, and when I turned back around, I saw the most amazing sunset over the mountains in the distance. The intense red and orange sky blazed like fire behind the blue and black mountain. My *mam* would have loved it. She would have painted it. She always noticed things like this. She was constantly distracted and would call me over to show me a sunset, a flower, a toad in the mud. I laughed out loud. What a thing to remember, a toad in the mud. Shaking my head, I fixed the lamp on my forehead and jogged back to examine Rocky.

After lightly anesthetizing the horse and shaving his hoof to release a potent abscess, I treated it with an iodine antiseptic, wrapped it, gave him a shot of antibiotics, and Phil walked me back to my truck.

"You know, I usually feed Doc P when he comes out. Lucinda tells me I can't do that anymore since he had his stroke, but you look fit and skinny enough to eat my food. Would you like a pie?"

"A pie?" I laughed. "No, *dank je,* ehh, but no. Please, do not go to any trouble for me."

Her whole face crumpled with disappointment. I'd offended her. I remembered Carolina telling me some of our clients paid in food and trade if they were struggling financially. They paid when they could, but Dr. Prittchard always accepted what they offered.

I looked behind Phil, to her old and weathered house, to her rundown black pickup truck that looked stuck in the mud, and to her barn with part of the roof caved in. *Ah, Luuk, jij idioot, why did you not just say yes?* "Em, well, what kind of pie?" I asked, flashing her a guilty smile, and her face lit up.

"Stay right here. I'm gonna go get it. You like lemon?"

I nodded. I didn't usually eat a lot of sweets, but I would take the pie and tell her I'd eaten it. She turned and hobbled through the muddy garden, back to her house, and while she was gone, I walked over to her truck to see if I could help her get it unstuck. Boscoe assisted.

"It won't start," she said, carrying the pie over to me. "It's been sittin' there for a few weeks. I dunno what's wrong with it. I was thinkin' of callin' the guy who gave it to me, but I don't wanna bother him."

"Someone gave you a truck? As a gift?" I asked, squatting to look at the tires.

"Yes, well, he sold it to me for a dollar. Do you know Kevin Cade? The Cade family?"

Whipping my head up to look at her, the expression on my face must have been ridiculous. "Kevin Cade gave you a truck?"

"Yes. His daddy and my husband were friends. They grew up together. My husband, Randall, that was his name, he passed 'bout a year ago."

"I'm so sorry for your loss, Phil," I said, but my mind was spinning.

"Thank you. Anyway, 'bout three weeks after he passed, my car died, and then Rand's old pickup died shortly thereafter. I didn't have a way to pull my trailer, and I couldn't afford to buy a new one, so Kevin gave me his."

She shrugged. "Wasn't that nice? That whole family is good stock. Those boys are all so kind. They raised themselves pretty much after their mama left and their grandmama was killed in that accident. And thank the good Lord for Sara Mitchum. She helped. I never woulda said it to Rand, but their daddy was no good. But they turned out to be good men, all of 'em."

My brains exploded in my head. This was the reason KC always borrowed Jack's truck?

I guess I just assumed he was… that he wasn't very responsible. That he was immature. But he—

Well, *verdomme.*

"Have you met them yet? The Cade brothers? Oh, I'm sure

you have. You've probably been out to treat their horses, huh?"

"*Ja*, I know them. Dr. Masterson is my best friend," I said and I stood. I thought if I used two blocks of wood under the tires, I might be able get her truck unstuck. Unfortunately, I was not so great with engines.

"Oh, that's right. I heard you went to school with Oly. I go to church with her mama. She's been pickin' me up on Wednesday evenin's and Sundays since my truck is outta commission. They're good people."

"Yes, I agree. Carolina called me to help her at the clinic when Dr. Prittchard became ill."

"And how do you like our little corner of the earth? Where you from, Doc?"

"I'm from the Netherlands. Yes, Wyoming is beautiful and I enjoy the work." I wondered if there was a way for me to get Finn or Dean out here to look at Phil's truck. I wouldn't want her to know I'd asked them to help—she seemed like a proud woman—and I wouldn't want Kevin to know I'd asked them or that I knew he'd given the truck to Phil. Maybe Carolina or Evvie could help me.

"The Netherlands?" she asked and laughed. "I'm not sure I know where that is. Geography never was my strong suit."

"It's next to Germany, north of Belgium and France. You've heard of Amsterdam, yes?"

"Oh yeah, where everybody takes marijuana."

"That's not all they do there." I laughed, rolling my eyes.

"Do you miss it? Miss your home?"

I hadn't been home in so long. Could I still consider it my home? My parents were gone, and my *omaatje* had passed years before they did, and I didn't have any other family I knew of. I was still in occasional contact with a couple of the kids I grew up with in Oudewater, and my friend Lissa still lived in Amsterdam, but those were the only ties I had to *Nederland*.

Actually, if I really thought about it, I didn't feel like I had a home, not since my parents died. When I had first come to Wisper, I thought it might be a place I could grow to consider home, especially because Carolina was here. She was the best friend I had ever had, and I absolutely adored her. But now, I wasn't so sure. I felt different in Wisper.

It wasn't something I wanted to look at too closely, and I wanted to tell myself I didn't know the reason why. But it was a lie. There was definitely a reason I felt different here. And I definitely knew what that reason was.

Or who.

Even though I knew it was absolutely ridiculous.

I shook my head. "Yes, I guess I do miss it sometimes. I haven't been there in a long time. I should probably take a trip back. But I love the States. I've been all over the US, and it always amazes me how much it can change from state to state. Wyoming has been one of my favorites."

"I'm happy to hear it. I was born and raised right here in Wisper. Rand and I both were. I've never wanted to be anywhere else." She tilted her head. "What about you? Do you have a special someone? Is there someone travelin' the world with you? You must have one, handsome as you are?"

"No, I'm afraid not." I smiled and thought maybe I should get a dog when Boscoe rubbed against my legs, looking up at me with his happy brown eyes. I'd wanted one since boarding school. Now that I was done with my studies, I could absolutely get a dog. Even if I left Wisper, he could come with me and be my traveling companion. *Ja*, I would get a dog.

"Oh, well now, I know a few single young ladies from church. Actually, I'm surprised Oly's mama hasn't tried to set you up already. Belinda Marsh is—"

"Thank you, Phil, but I'm not really marketed right now."

"In the market?" she teased. "Well, I can understand that,

but even if you just wanted someone to go to the movies with or dinner every now and then, Belinda is—"

"Really, Phil, thank you. You're very kind, but I doubt Belinda is my type," I said. "I'm gay." I hoped I wasn't being rude, but I had a feeling she wouldn't stop unless she had a good reason to. I knew there were a lot of people around Wisper who would have a problem—

"Oh, well, why didn't you just say so? It might not be a very popular opinion around here, but my nephew's gay. He invited me to his weddin' out east. It was beautiful. He married a man from Brazil. Very handsome. Now, lemme think. I don't know of any young men in Wisper that… hmm, but maybe in Jackson. I'll think on it."

Laughing, I placed my hand over my heart. "I think you might be what they call incorrigible. Really, thank you, but I'm not looking to date right now."

She smirked and raised her eyebrow. "You've already found someone, haven't you? Alright, you can try to keep your secrets, Doc, but don't forget, Wisper's a small town. I'll find out soon enough." She laughed, hooking her arm through mine. "Now, take this pie. It's a Lemon Chess Pie, an old recipe of my grandmama's. You'll love it."

"Thank you, Phil. Call me tomorrow and let me know how everyone's doing, yes?"

"You got it, Doc. Thanks again."

ELEVEN

KEVIN

"You ready, Prima Donna? Ugh, is *that* what you're wearin'?" Finn smarted when Jay came down the stairs, and Jack scolded him.

"Shut up, Finn. He's nervous enough as it is."

Mr. Burroughs was on his way to the ranch for the first meetin' about our equine therapy proposal, and Jay was *really* nervous. He'd gone over and over his business plan, tryin' to prepare himself and us. He worried what our brother's reactions would be to a stranger comin' in, wantin' a stake in our business.

I knew Jack would have somethin' more to say about it, but he promised Jay he'd listen first and at least attempt to keep an open mind. I knew he would, but he would also be protective of the ranch, the new business, our family, and Jay. The ranch was everything to Jack. He would defend it and protect it to the ground.

We'd never met this Burroughs guy, though Jay said he'd heard a lot about him. Mr. Markham at the bank talked a lot about him when Jay pitched his ideas, and Dean had contacted Billie and asked her to check him out, but she'd come back with nothin' but good things.

Theodore Burroughs was some sorta gazillionaire angel investor from Boston, lookin' for start-ups to invest in to help him get richer, and some just to satisfy his philanthropic wanderin's. I hoped his money would wander right onto our ranch.

Jay stood in the livin' room, lookin' like he might puke, and Finn winked at him, attemptin' to cut the tension with his wiseass jokes as usual.

"C'mon," Jack said. "Let's head out to the barn and at least act like we know what the fuck we're doin'."

When we got out to the porch, Jay took a deep breath. He'd been buggin' Jack for almost two years to take a chance like this. Jack had finally agreed, and Jay really didn't wanna fuck it up.

We made our way out to the barn and almost immediately heard a car comin' up the drive. Jay went to greet the guy, and I walked into the barn to find Dean. I was already over the meetin'. I knew it was important, but I just couldn't make myself give two shits. All I could think about was Ma lyin' upstairs in her bed, dyin'.

My mama had been stoppin' by to see her. They talked in Ma's room for hours one day. I had no idea what about, but it pissed me off. And it pissed me off that Ma still hadn't said a word about it. Well, maybe she'd tried, but I hadn't listened.

"Hey, you must be Jay," I heard the guy greetin' my brothers, but I found Dean in the barn and ran over to help him 'cause he had his arm up the ass-end of a mare, and he was covered in sweat and blood.

"Oh, Kev, get Jack. We might need Oly or Luuk to help if we can't get this foal out. He's comin' out breech."

"On it."

When I pulled Jack aside, I checked out the investor guy over his shoulder. He was pretty good lookin', about my height, dark hair, dark eyes, and his skin looked like somethin' out of a cosmetics commercial—light brown and dewy. I wondered if he used some kinda "make your skin glow" bull-shit or if he was just naturally that shiny. He eyed me up and down, too, and I looked away quickly, so my brothers wouldn't notice gay recognizin' gay.

Shit.

I kept my eyes square on Jack's. "We got a problem. Poppy's foal's comin' out breech. Dean needs you. Said we might need to call Oly."

"Shit. Okay. 'Scuse us, Mr. Burroughs. I'm gonna have our brother, Kevin, take you to the office. We got a bit of an emergency with one of our horses. I apologize, but we won't be too long."

Jay looked between Jack and me. He didn't seem excited for me to be the one to entertain Mr. Moneybags. "I'll take Theo. We can go over the business—"

"No, I need you, Jay. The foal is breech, and Kevin can't pull with his shoulder."

"Oh. Okay. Sorry, Mr. Burroughs. Please excuse us."

"No problem, guys. Take your time. And call me Theo. You say Mr. Burroughs and I look around for my dad." The guy laughed, and Jack nodded while Jay warned me with his eyes not to say anything stupid, and then they walked away, leavin' me alone with Theo.

"So, uh, the office is in the arena. This way." I turned to lead him in that direction.

"Can you give me a tour? This place is pretty magnificent. I'm kind of jealous you get to wake up to that view every morning."

Turnin' back, I saw him noddin' at our mountain. "Uh, yeah, sure."

I was pretty uncomfortable. This guy's money could make or break Jay's plans, and I didn't trust myself not to do or say somethin' to mess it up, but I also didn't wanna take him into the barn to get an eyeful of a big ol' bloody mess.

I showed him around the arena, showed him our foals

and yearlings, explained a few things, but the whole time, I was countin' down the seconds till my brothers would be done.

"So, what do you do around here for fun? Night life? Are there any good bars or..."

"Uh, there's Manny's in town. Pretty good country bar. Neighborhood bar. Whatever. Actually, on second thought, it's kind of a dive."

"No." He chuckled. "I meant somewhere I might find people like you and me."

"Oh, um, no, not around here. There's a few over in Idaho but..."

"So how do you meet people? I don't imagine there are very many options in this area."

"Yeah, I... don't."

"Oh, I'm sorry. I didn't mean to— I thought, I mean, you did 'the look.'"

"No, it's just— I don't—" I exhaled hard. *Fuck.* What was I supposed to say to the guy? I looked toward the arena entrance. Dammit. Where were my brothers?

Theo followed my line of sight and turned back to me. "I apologize. That wasn't very professional of me. Please, forget I said anything."

"Kev? Where are you?" I heard Jay callin' my name, and I sucked in a breath and held it.

Theo must've noticed the look of panic on my face. He shook his head a little. "I wouldn't," he whispered, and I released my breath.

"There you are. Sorry about that, Theo. My brothers will be right out. They just needed to clean up a little."

"Sure, no problem," Theo said, and I watched while his face changed from a regular guy to a businessman. "Thank you for the tour, Kevin. This place really is pretty cool."

"Yep," I said, and I followed 'em to the office, kickin' myself in the ass the entire way for not comin' up with anything better to say to the guy. Had I just ruined everything Jay had worked so hard on?

My brothers joined us in the office, and I sat there, tryin' to pay attention, but I wanted to scream. I felt like such a coward. I knew how Theo saw me. He saw a weak, scared little boy in a man's body.

It was how Luck saw me too.

Evvie knocked on the door, and the sound pulled me outta my head. "I'm sorry to interrupt, but there's a woman in the car out there. I just wondered if she'd like to come up to the house or to see the horses or something? She doesn't have to stay in the car."

"Theo, this is my wife, Evvie," Jack said.

"Hi, Evvie, nice to meet you." He stood, holdin' out his hand for Evvie to shake, and she walked over, shook it, and smiled. "That's my sister. I think she'd prefer to stay out there. I hope you won't be offended, but she's blind, and she has a hard time if she's in a new place, especially a place like this where it's really open. She can get overwhelmed. Unless I'm there and she can take her time to get familiar with her surroundings, she likes to stay where she has some control of her environment."

"Oh, okay. Well, if she needs anything, please just let me know. I'll be in the barn."

"Thank you. That's considerate of you. I appreciate it."

"Thank you, baby." Jack winked at her, and she smiled and shut the door behind her when she left the room.

"I apologize for dragging my sister along, but we're staying at a B&B in Jackson, and she really hates being cooped up there. I don't like leaving her alone too much."

"It's not a problem," Jack said. "You're both welcome here anytime." Theo had just won Jack over a little as his shoulders relaxed some and he smiled a bit easier. Knowin' Theo was the sole caregiver to his sister probably warmed Jack to Theo a ton.

I watched Theo then, as discreetly as I could. I wondered how he could have so much confidence, to just walk up to someone he'd never met before and start a conversation about bein' gay. Did people really do that? Was that normal? It had never happened to me before.

"Thank you. Actually, my sister is a big part of what drew me to your proposal. I'm always looking for new opportunities for her, to get her out of her comfort zone a little. She's pretty resistant, but it doesn't stop me from trying." He laughed. "But while researching these things, I've stumbled onto a few of the companies I've invested in."

He thought for a minute, then asked, "So the horses. How do you know if a horse is right for the job? I mean, animals are unpredictable. How can you be sure a horse will be cooperative? I guess I'm wondering how people don't get hurt if, for example, a horse kicks or jumps up?"

This was a question Jay had expected. He'd made me help him prepare, and I grilled him about his own damn business plan over and over. He answered this very question many times in our mock "meetin's." I watched a satisfied smile spread across his face before he answered.

"Well, Theo, that's part of what we do here. We train horses to behave the way we want. Jack has a knack for knowin' what to look for: their temperament, how they ride, how they're built, and how they move. Then, once we have the horse here, we train it, whether it's broke or not. So, for the purposes of equine therapy or an adaptive ridin' program, we would set out to find the right horses, buy 'em, bring 'em here, and train 'em."

"What do you mean if the horse is 'broke' or not?"

"If the horse has never been ridden, it needs to be broke," Jay said. "It needs to be trained for a saddle and to be ridden. That's Jack and Finn's specialty. They can break any horse you give 'em, and quick."

They spent the next hour talkin', and I zoned in and out.

After Theo had driven away and I released a gallon of breath, Jay turned to my brothers and me all standin' in front of the barn.

"Well?" he asked.

"Well, what?" Dean said, like he had no idea. A hint of a smile played across his face though.

"What'd you think of him?"

"Good job, Jay," Jack said. "I think that went pretty well."

"Yeah, *baby Jay*, you did a good job, yes you did, you cute little cowboy you," Finn cooed at Jay, like he was a toddler, smackin' Jay's back really hard, and Jay elbowed him in the ribs and stomped on Finn's overgrown foot.

"Oof! Oh, baby Jay, it's *on*."

"Finn, cut it out," Jack grumbled, walkin' back into the barn to find Evvie, probably. They hadn't had their allotted twenty-three out of twenty-four hours of the day together yet.

Finn tackled Jay and they fell to the ground, wrestlin'.

"I'm goin' for a ride," I mumbled.

"Don't be too long. We still have the whole day's work," Jack said, disappearin' into the tack room.

"Dammit, Finn. This is literally the only nice shirt I own anymore." Jay shoved Finn's head into the dirt, squishin' Finn's cheek with the back of his arm.

"Oh, baby Jay, don't hurt me," Finn mock-cried. "You know how sensitive my—"

Jay punched him in the nuts.

"Fuck, Jay. I did wanna have kids someday. Owww," Finn groaned. "You're gonna pay for that, you little shit."

I walked away when Jay laughed and stood while Finn writhed on the ground. He dusted himself off but ran for the house when he saw Finn chasin' after him.

Fuckin' brothers.

Ridin' hard, I took Classic out to the fields. I wasn't really goin' anywhere in particular, but I needed to be away from everyone. I needed space. I felt like I couldn't breathe, sittin' in that meetin'. Theo kept his word though. He hadn't said anything to my brothers, but I hated the way it made me feel to lie to 'em.

I hated that some stranger knew more about me than my own family did.

I felt like I couldn't breathe a lot lately. But bein' out in the meadow made it easier. I could be myself out here. I had a hard time makin' myself go home anymore. I'd never wanted to be the real me more than I did now.

The only reason I could force myself to go was to see Ma. She came closer and closer to death every day.

At this point, I was just waitin' for it.

I'd been sleepin' in the chair in her room every night for the last week. Sleepin was the wrong word. I sat there, listenin' to her breathin' and thinkin' about her. Thinkin' about what she'd done for us over the years, how she became our grandma, our mama, and my best friend. She'd become our compass. I thought about what I would do when she was gone, which direction I'd end up facin'.

I thought about Luuk. About that night in the bar, the look on his face. I owed him another apology. Ten times a day, I looked over at Jack's truck while I worked, wantin' to go to him. I wanted to tell him I was sorry for the way I'd acted, for the things I said to him at his house that mornin'. But I couldn't make myself go.

I saw in his eyes he knew what I was doin', throwin' myself all over a woman. He knew it and he knew why. He was hurt and pissed off, but also, he felt sorry for me. He pitied me. How could I go to him when I had no explanation other than that I was scared and weak?

And that I hated myself.

How could I tell him that?

The south mountain was black in shadow as the sun made its way across the late-mornin' sky, and I hopped down from Classic to shoot some pics with my phone. My mama's face kept poppin' into my head while I wandered around, and I remembered her voice from when I was a kid.

There was one memory I couldn't seem to shake. I'd been cryin' or whinin' about somethin'. I couldn't remember what, but I was mad she wasn't payin' attention to me. She was frustrated with me, too, and finally, she yelled, "Everything is not about *you*, Kevin!"

I had no idea how old I was at the time, but I remembered turnin' into myself when she yelled at me. I stopped cryin', stopped makin' any noise or movement at all, and I shut her out. Maybe that was when I shut everybody out.

I knew now she'd probably just been havin' a bad day. She was a young mom with five kids all under the age of seven or eight. She probably had a lot of bad days. I couldn't remember my dad ever helpin' her with us boys. Not like fathers today. You wouldn't have caught my dad wearin' a baby backpack, pushin' a stroller through town. No. She was on her own. She had my granny to help sometimes, but Granny worked the ranch just like Dad, Pops, and UJ before they died.

But when she left, I remembered thinkin' it was my fault. If I hadn't been so demandin', such a crybaby, if I hadn't pushed and frustrated her and been so defiant, if I'd been more like my brothers, maybe she wouldn't have left. I was too much. Too excitable, too colorful, too silly, too much to handle, too much…

To love.

As a kid, I *knew* that was why she left. I knew I had to hide that side of myself away. I couldn't risk pushin' my dad and my brothers away too. I needed 'em.

When I was older, it became a conscious choice sometimes, my behavior. Should I join the photography club or try out for football, even though I hated football? Should I apply to art school or stay home, work the ranch? What would my dad want me to do? What would Jack want? Should I be me, the guy who's silly and reflective and likes to take pictures, or should I chase the popular girls, party, and be obnoxious and loud?

The whole town knew our family. They knew our mama had left us, knew our ranch was failin', and I didn't want anyone to know I was the reason. If I'd been myself, they woulda known. So I wasn't. I became someone else. Someone who wasn't the reason his mama left.

Someone who hadn't failed his family.

I couldn't fail 'em in other ways.

I knew when I was probably thirteen years old what I was —that I was gay. I'd had glimpses before then. There'd been clues, but I ignored 'em 'cause they didn't fit the image I saw when I thought about what would be best for my family. When I went through puberty, though, there had been *no* doubt. It wasn't dreams of girls wakin' me up in sweats, makin' me jizz all over my bedsheets. But I saw how other kids reacted to such things and changed myself accordingly.

Every day when I got to school, I looked for Patrick Kessler, the other gay kid in Wisper, checkin' to make sure he was okay. I'd lay awake at night, worryin' he'd try to take his own life because of the way people treated him. So many times, I wished I'd had the courage to talk to him, to tell him he wasn't as alone as he thought.

I never did.

Now, as an adult, I knew I could have. I should have. I could've been Patrick's friend. I still wouldn't have told anyone else I was gay, but nothin' made my dad happy. I coulda been the real me, coulda pursued art the way I'd wanted. He probably wouldn't even have noticed. He threw a fit when Dean joined the football team 'cause it took too much of Dean's time away from the ranch, but by the time it was my and Jay's turn, the man barely knew we existed.

Except when I did somethin' he deemed unmanly. He noticed me then.

Like when I took pictures.

So instead, I chased women around like an idiot and acted like the consummate football playin', *extremely* heterosexual, cowboy asshole. But that was also when I first sought men out to have sex with. I knew I needed it, needed some kinda connection to who I really was. I needed *somethin'* to feel good.

Yellowstone was only a couple hours away, and there were a lot of tourists and not a few tree huggers who'd liked suckin' me off. I'd never let a man enter my body, but I'd screwed into a few of theirs.

After a couple bumblin' years of that, I gave up. I wanted to connect with a man so badly, but I knew I couldn't, so it just became another kinda torture. I went back to women, but I stopped havin' sex with 'em. I led 'em on, made 'em care about me so they'd baby me, mother me, and love me, and then I'd leave.

Thankfully, Finn led me back into takin' pictures. I shot a pic of a horse one day for him to post online, and it felt so damn good. I hadn't stopped since.

And now, with the changes goin' on with the ranch and with my brothers, I found myself back to where I was as a teenager. Did I do what was best for me, or did I do what I knew would be best for my family, for the ranch, for my brothers? Jack had hinted that he knew what I was, but did he really? Did he really want that? Didn't he know the kind of attention it would bring down on us? With the new business, I just couldn't risk—

"Kev! What the hell you doin'?" Finn called out to me, ridin' toward me on his mare. "You been gone for hours."

So lost inside myself, I hadn't realized it was evenin', and the sun had begun to set.

He jumped down from Gertie and walked over to me. "What's goin' on with you, brother? You disappeared."

I looked over at him and stared. He didn't know it, but I disappeared twenty-some years ago. "Sorry, guess I just got carried away."

"No, I don't mean today. I mean, where'd you go? Feels like you're gone. There's just a ghost of you where you used to be. You haven't cussed at me in days."

I laughed. There was no humor in it, and it reminded me of the night in the bar when Luuk laughed, when he saw what I was doin' to myself.

"I've never been here. Not for a long time, anyway."

Finn cocked his head a little, lookin' at me. Finally, he said, "So, why don'tcha show up? Introduce yourself."

Yeah, it was just that easy.

Shakin' myself mentally, I took a deep breath and plastered my usual persona back onto my body. "You're an idiot. C'mon, let's go. Jack's gonna kick my ass for stayin' out here all day."

"Idiot?" Finn mumbled. "I thought that was pretty fuckin' insightful." He mounted Gertie and I whistled, callin' Classic back from wherever the hell he'd got off to. When he came runnin' from the edge of the woods, I tightened my cinch and climbed on, turnin' him back east, to home.

"Kev?"

"What?" I didn't look at him.

"I know this is hard for you, with Ma and everything. You gonna be okay?"

"'Course I am. Why wouldn't I be?" I lied and took off, leadin' my horse into a gallop toward…

Back to black.

"Hey, Ma. How ya doin' tonight?" I asked, caressin' the backs of my fingers over her forehead. She was so cold.

"Kevin," she whispered, her voice like a wisp of wind. "Evvie said you were gone. I was worried." She reached her hand out for me, and it took all the strength she had to lift it, so I stepped forward, holdin' it, layin' both our hands down on the bed as I crouched next to her, tuckin' her blanket in tight to keep the heat in.

"Save your strength, Ma. I'm here. I just needed a minute. I'm not leavin' you. I won't ever."

"Okay, honey. That's good." She closed her eyes, fallin' back into sleep, and I lay down next to her as gently as I could, held her hand, and breathed her in.

I'd been so lucky to have her in my life, to have had her as my friend. I knew my behavior hadn't warranted the devotion she gave me, but just then, I was so glad she gave it. My life woulda been so much darker if she hadn't. Did she know that?

Did she know she'd saved me in so many ways?

Twelve

Ma died on a Thursday.

My brothers and I were all there with Evvie and Oly.

I held her hand, murmurin' to her that it was okay for her to go, that I'd be okay without her. I wouldn't. But I tried as hard as I could to lie convincingly. I wanted her to feel at peace about leavin'. I didn't want her to worry about me. She'd worried and fussed over me my whole life. She deserved to be done with that. She deserved for me to be an adult for once. For me to deal with her dyin' with some grace.

It was so hard, and I kept havin' to remind myself to breathe 'cause I held my breath every time sobs threatened to break free. *Boys don't cry.*

Half the town had shown up to pay their respects and to offer support, and occasionally, I heard Jack talkin' to people in the hallway. I thought I heard my mama's voice, but I hadn't left Ma's bedroom in days except to use the bathroom down the hall. I wouldn't leave her now. What if she was scared? She slept endlessly. Occasionally, though, she'd wake and look around, and I didn't want her to feel alone while she waited to go.

Doc and Mrs. Whitley stayed with us through it all. Doc had stopped all of Ma's medications almost a week before except for the morphine. She needed it 'cause she'd been in so much pain, and it helped her sleep and be still.

The guys had gone downstairs. I thought maybe to give me some time with Ma so I could say goodbye and cry without everybody breathin' down my neck. I didn't cry. It took everything I had in me, but I didn't.

Just once, I wanted to be strong for her.

I told her how much I loved her, how much I respected her, and how, even after all these years, she was still the most beautiful woman I had ever seen.

I thanked her for lovin' me even though I never deserved it. Even though all I'd ever done was make life harder. I thanked her for choosin' me. She loved me 'cause she wanted to. 'Cause that was what her heart told her to do.

She had the best heart of anybody in the world, and I told her that God or heaven or whatever was up there would be so goddamn lucky to have her with 'em.

I promised to try to be a good man. All she'd ever wanted for me was to love myself, and I told her I'd try so fuckin' hard.

She didn't hear me, but I told her I was gay. And that I was sorry. That I never meant to shame or embarrass her, but it was just who I was on the inside, and I hoped, once she'd had time to process it, she could forgive me from up above 'cause it was the real me. I needed her to understand. I needed her to know and to love me anyway.

A few hours later, she woke and asked for everybody.

When my brothers and the girls all stood around her, she looked at each of 'em and softly spoke their names. She told 'em how much she loved 'em, how much she would miss 'em, but that they were *not* to be sad. That she would be with her Mr. Mitchum, and they should be happy about that. And she said she'd be watchin' us from above, so we'd better not get outta line. She looked at Finn when she said it.

"And watch your language, Finnigan Cade." She tried to be stern with him, but she was so weak, and it came out as barely a whisper.

"Yes, ma'am. I will," he promised, nearly chokin' on his words.

And then she turned her head to me.

She pulled on my hand, and I leaned in close to hear her better 'cause her voice was just the barest hint of breath by then.

Whisperin' so only I could hear, she said, "Baby boy, I love you. Thank you for fillin' my life with such joy. I know you don't believe it, but you did. I admire you so much. Your talent, your love, and your courage. It's there, inside you.

"I know the thing you try to hide. I'm sorry I didn't talk to you about it. I didn't know how, but Kevin, there should be no shame when it comes to love. You have nothin' to be ashamed of, you hear me?"

"Mama," I whispered, and my tears broke free.

She knew? All this time?

Pullin' her hand to my face, I breathed her in, hidin' my eyes from hers. I didn't ever wanna forget how she smelled like sunshine.

"I love you and *they* will still love you. How could they not?" Takin' a labored breath, she said, "I want you to do somethin' for me. Will you?"

I nodded. Anything she asked of me, I'd do. Anything.

"Look at me."

Lookin' up, I saw all the love in the world in her eyes. How would I live without her?

"I want you to talk to your mama," she said. "I want you to listen to her."

Shakin' my head, I searched her eyes. There wasn't much life left, but she begged me with 'em.

"I will," I promised, even though I didn't want to.

"Now, I'm not gonna say goodbye to you 'cause I'm takin' you with me. How could I ever be without my best friend? And I'll be with you every day. Don't you ever forget I'm there."

"No, Mama." I sobbed. "I won't. How could I ever forget you?"

"Don't cry for me," she whispered, lookin' at the tears streamin' down my face. "You've had enough sadness in your life. I want you to be happy. I want you to let yourself love, sweet boy. You deserve it. You can *have* it."

I held her hand for the longest time, just lookin' in her pale blue eyes. She knew. And still, she loved me.

Liftin' her hand to my cheek, she swiped my tears away with her thumb, and she smiled so big for me, the same way she used to smile at Mr. Mitchum. Her face lit up like the sun for just a few seconds, and then her hand fell back down beside her on the bed, her breath escapin' in a long soft sigh.

I couldn't explain it, but I felt her go. I felt her leave her body, the room, the house. It was a rush in the air around me, like a quick gentle breeze, and it pulled at somethin' inside my chest as it passed and traveled out the bedroom window. It was so fast.

And that was it.

The person who loved me, no matter what she wanted, no matter what stupid thing I did, the person who *chose* to be my family, chose my brothers and me above anybody else, was gone.

Just gone.

I closed Ma's eyes so gently with my fingers, laid my head beside hers on the pillow, and cried like a baby. I heard my brothers movin' around, and Jay walked over behind me, wrapped his arms around me tight, and we both cried then, leanin' over the bed.

Our ma was gone.

Thirteen

Luuk

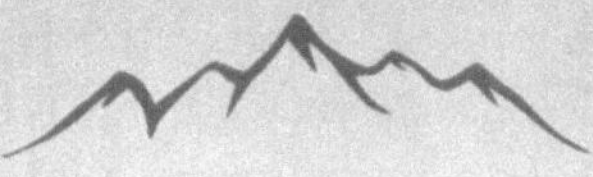

I'd been online for hours, checking animal shelter websites, looking for an adoptable mutt, when my phone pinged with a text. Larry, the wolfhound/corgi mix, couldn't have been any uglier, but his wide, wiry-haired face made him so adorable. I didn't think he'd be much of a runner, though, and with the amount of running I'd forced on myself in the last few weeks, I definitely needed a runner. Picking my phone up off the dining table, I read the text.

It had come from Carolina.

Ma is gone.

Ah. Verdomme.

I'd known it was coming, but still, it hurt. Thoughts of my parents tried to break through, but I'd become good at shutting them down. It took only two minutes for me to realize most of my sadness was for other people. I would miss Ma, though. She was probably the kindest person I'd ever met, but I hadn't known her long. Carolina, Evvie, Jack, and the others' lives revolved around her. They would be devastated.

But KC… His life would change. And probably not for the better.

I stood. I wanted to go to him, but how stupid would that

be? He didn't need me. I wasn't his family. The thought made my chest ache, and I clutched at it, looking around my little rented house. I paid five-hundred dollars a month to Jack and Ma to live in it. I'd tried to offer much more, but they wouldn't accept it.

This was her house, not mine. I walked from room to room, looking at all of Ma's personal things still left here.

There were a few photos of hers still, a few pieces of furniture, small things, ordinary things. But my eyes wouldn't focus on them. What I saw instead was a three-inch gash in the wooden frame of the bedroom door. I wondered what had made that mark. My eyes found a double line scratched on the wood floor. What had caused that?

Stopping in the middle of the hallway, I looked in the bathroom. It didn't have any evidence of life lived because it had been recently renovated, but I paused there anyway because, even though there wasn't a physical mark on the wall or the floor or the sink, the whole thing had been made by KC.

He was Ma's too.

What had caused him to be the way he was, who he was? Ma had had a big hand in it, and she made only good marks on him—I knew this for sure—but what else? Who else? Who else had marked him, dinged him, scratched him? Had Ma known about all of those dings? Was that why she loved him so much? Why she wanted me to be in his life?

But I'd failed her. I hadn't spoken to KC in weeks. I hadn't even tried, not once. I should have, if for no other reason than to please her. She deserved it.

I wasn't one to hurt myself purposely, not like KC. I didn't punish myself for the things I didn't like about myself, not anymore. But I knew being around him, being involved with him, would end up hurting me.

I wanted him anyway.

My *mam* had done that. Her whole life, she gave up what

she loved for other people, my father, me, my *omaatje*. She had been wholly unhappy because of it, though she loved me fiercely, but I didn't think she'd loved herself.

I didn't want to be like that.

I loved myself. I hadn't really ever thought much about it, but there were things I didn't like about myself, physical traits, personality things, like I wished I was funnier. I wished I wasn't so reserved. So... *voorzichtig*—careful. I didn't feel that way on the inside but... But overall, I thought I was a good person. I hated my hair. It was annoying.

But I didn't want to end up hating myself for giving so much to someone else, giving up what made me... me. I had to fight hard to become me as I was now. I didn't used to be this man.

Would that happen if I gave myself to KC? Because he was so... busted? Would he take the best of me and leave what was left?

Would I let him, like my *mam* had?

A knock on the back-porch door jerked me out of my thoughts, and I jumped, stubbing my toe on the corner of the wall.

What in hell? No one ever used that door. *I'd* never used the back door. I limped through the house, still seeing little marks here and there, proving a life had been lived here, more than one.

When I got to the door in the kitchen and placed my hand on the doorknob to open it, a weird sensation settled in my chest. In my body. It was like an energy in my limbs, a whisper in my blood running through my veins, and it traveled to my stomach, twisting and pulling me to open the door. The feeling quickly left, but I felt it all around me. And then it was gone, and the usual benign air and light and sound fell back in around me.

When I opened the door, KC stood beyond it on the back

porch, looking down at the floor with his hands holding him up on either side of the door frame.

I stopped breathing. I held my breath in my body so I could keep it, keep all of me from him. To protect myself. It had been an automatic response to seeing him. The other response was that all the blood in my head rushed down into my groin, and I lost the ability to think rationally.

He looked at me then, and all that breath rushed out.

"Will you let me in?"

The look on his face, in his eyes... Complete and utter despair. He'd been crying, his eyes rimmed red and watery still.

"Please?"

"*Het spijt me*—sorry. Please, come in. This is your house more than it is mine." Opening the door wider, I stepped back. He crossed the threshold and pulled the door closed softly behind him.

"No, I mean, will you let me *in*?" His voice was low and quiet, and he inched toward me, making me back up further until I felt the wall behind me. "Will you let me know you, *feel* you, in here?" Touching his fingers to my temple, he ran them through my hair, pulling gently and smoothing them down my neck to my chest. "In here? Stop bein' so polite and let me really know you?" He looked where he touched for a moment, then raised his head, whispering, "Please?"

I looked at him, too, examining him and the intent behind what he asked—what did he want from me? But did it really matter? I'd known, probably since the first moment I'd met him, I would give anything he asked of me.

Did that make me like my *mam*?

I didn't care. "Yes."

Leaning his forehead against mine, he closed his eyes. "I need— Luuk, I need you."

I wanted to touch him, to comfort him, but I was a little afraid. Would he run again? I brought my hand up slowly to touch his face with only my fingertips, and he leaned into them, wrapping his arms around me, holding his body tight against mine. He trembled.

"Come. Come with me." Taking his hand, I led him to my bedroom and my bed. "Lie down." He looked at me with doubt, asking with his eyes if I was sure I wanted this. Did I really want him? "Please, KC, lie down."

Finally, he did. He practically fell onto the bed, and I untied his boots and pulled them off, and he watched me as I did it, watched my eyes.

I was nervous. He was asking me to open myself to him, to be vulnerable, even though he hadn't offered anything of himself in return. I knew it could cause a lot of pain later. I knew it, but I wanted to ignore it.

I wanted nothing more than to hold him.

Never bothering to make my bed, a persisting rebellion from boarding school, my blanket lay in a lump by his feet, and I lifted it, pulling it over us when I climbed in on the other side. I wrapped my arms around him and pulled him close, holding him and waiting for him to talk.

A long time passed without either of us saying anything. He touched me, ran his hands all over my body, over my clothes and under. It felt good and I was aroused, but it wasn't about sex.

This was about intimacy.

He was desperate for it, and I wanted to give it to him. I pulled my fingers through his hair and over his cheekbones, his eyebrows, his nose, just watching his face while I touched him. He wouldn't look at me though. It seemed like he tried to when he peeked at my chin a thousand times, but he just wasn't there yet. He closed his eyes, and finally, we became still. He lay with his head on my chest, his hair brushing against my neck and jaw.

"What were you like as a boy?"

"I was—" I cleared the nervousness from my throat. "I was normal, I guess. A normal child."

"But you weren't normal."

"What do you mean? I was."

"No, you weren't, you were…"

"What, you mean because I'm gay?" I was a child. That hadn't mattered then.

"Yeah."

"KC, when you were six years old, were you worried you might be gay?"

"No, I guess not that young, though I knew I was different from my brothers."

"I didn't have any brothers or sisters, so I guess I didn't have anyone to compare myself to. The children at school were all different in their own ways, so I thought everyone was different in some way. I thought different was normal. I didn't know it mattered, although there was a kid that ate his own *snot*, like, all the time. This was not normal."

"He ate his own boogers? That's disgustin'!" He laughed, and hearing it, I did too. I couldn't help myself.

He was quiet for a while longer but then asked, "What were your parents like?"

Finally, he peeked up at me for just a second, and I smiled. I wanted to encourage him to let me in, and I wanted to see his eyes. He looked down, though, so after a moment, I moved onto my side so he would be forced to lie flat on his back or face me. Either way, I would be able to see them. He lay flat, looking up at the ceiling, and I lifted up onto my arm, caressing his cheek and jaw with my fingers while I spoke, and he closed his eyes and leaned into my touch.

I focused on answering his question. "Emm, they were… I don't know, they were quiet. My father was an incredibly quiet man. I barely remember him speaking, but he loved animals and farming, and he worked hard every day. That's why I became a vet, I think. This was how we spent time together. He showed me how to take care of all the animals on our farm. Now, it makes me feel... connected to him, even though he's gone."

"And your mama?"

I touched his bottom lip with just my fingertip, and *finally*, he looked into my eyes, and I lost my breath and all the thoughts in my head.

Did he have any idea just how beautiful he was?

His eyes were normally navy blue, but now, when he looked at me, they sparkled like *saffieren*. And then he smiled.

Fuck *mijn leven*! I could not have been more screwed.

In more ways than one.

"What did you ask me?"

"What was your mama like?"

"Oh, *ja*. She was, mm, my *mam* was complicated. She loved me. I never questioned it, but I'm not sure she loved herself. Or maybe she was just unhappy. Actually, I think if my parents hadn't died, they might have divorced. They rarely spoke, other than about our farm or to say, '*je eten staat op tafel.*' She was an artist, a painter. She saw the world very differently than my father and I did. I loved her for it, but I think my father... did not."

"Luuk?"

"Hmm?"

Closing his eyes, he said in the smallest whisper, "Ma's gone."

"I know." I kissed his forehead. "I am so sorry."

"You know?"

"Carolina texted. Before you arrived, I was walking through the house, looking at all of Ma's things. Remembering her." Thinking of him.

"I miss her already," he said and opened his eyes. Now he really looked at me, not blinking. "She was the only person who really ever knew me. Loved me."

"Your family loves you."

"Yeah, but they have to. She loved me 'cause she wanted to, 'cause she thought I was worth it. She's my— She was my best friend."

"*Ik weet.*" *I know.* He placed his hand on my stomach, caressing me over my shirt, taking the comfort he so desperately needed from my body.

"Will you talk to me in Dutch?"

"What would you like me to say?"

"Anything."

I smoothed his hair out of his eyes while he stared into mine. "*Het spijt me zo, mijn liefste, maar ik wil je leren kennen. Wanhopig. Mag ik?*"

"What'd you say?"

"I shall never tell." I smiled at him, watching how his eyes lit up when he saw it.

"How do you say 'will' in Dutch?"

"*Zou.*"

"How do you say 'you'?"

"*Je.*"

"How do you say… 'kiss'—" I leaned in to kiss him, and he laughed against my lips, mumbling, "Figured out what I was goin' for there, eh?"

"Next time say, *'wil je me kussen?'*"

And he kissed me hard. Grabbing my face with his hands, he held me still while he destroyed any resistance I'd had as protection against him. As if there had ever been any.

His kiss was slow and soft but so deep and demanding. He pushed me down onto my back with his hands on my chest, then sat up to pull the blanket away from us, watching as it slowly revealed my body.

Climbing over me, he straddled me and pushed my shirt up. I lifted my arms, and he leaned forward to pull it off, then sat back again and pulled his own shirt off, tossing both to the floor.

I wanted to be with him so badly, but what if this was just

in reaction to losing Ma? What if he regretted it later? I didn't want to be the cause of his regret. Again.

"KC…"

"Want me to stop?"

"No, but I think you will regret this tomorrow."

"I won't regret this *ever*," he said, leaning forward, resting his weight on his forearms beside my head, and his legs fell in between mine. "Luuk, I've dreamt about this," he whispered, stroking my jaw with his thumbs, "imagined it a million times." He kissed my bottom lip, but just on the edge, and very softly. If every nerve in my entire body hadn't been on fire, I might not have felt it. I lifted my hands and caressed his jaw, too, ran my fingers over his stubble, and lifted my head to kiss him.

I would worry later.

At first, it was just my lips on his, slowly and gently touching, looking into his eyes, and this time, he did not look away. But I sucked his lip, nipped it with my teeth, barely, and he moaned.

He tilted his head, licking and nipping me, too, begging entrance, and slowly, he entered my mouth when I gave it. He closed his eyes, but I did not. I pushed my fingers into his hair to pull him closer to me, and he thrust his tongue inside my mouth.

I had never experienced being kissed like this, the way KC kissed me.

It was hot. But also tender. He was insistent—dominant—but he begged and pleaded with his tongue.

It was consuming.

He plunged in and out of my mouth, a rhythmic rolling and sliding, matching the rhythm of his hips against mine, pressing his cock against mine, rubbing me through our clothes. His breath huffed out in short bursts, and I could feel him struggling to contain his desire.

Closing my eyes then, I gave him everything. Every time

I'd imagined kissing him, every time I'd imagined being with him, taking him into my mouth, taking him into my body, and entering his, fucking him—I put it all into the kiss. But this was not about fucking, at least not the kind I normally sought.

My hands shook from the overwhelming need I felt for him. I couldn't control it, and when he lowered his chest to mine, I groaned. I couldn't stop the noise when I felt the heat from his body on mine.

I'd wanted this man from the first time I saw him, but he'd denied me over and over. He'd been cruel. He'd denied himself, punished himself. And now, here he was, so... raw. He said he wanted this, said he'd dreamt of it and imagined it —and so had I—but had he thought about what would happen after?

I knew he would crush me. I knew it was coming.

"You're going to bust me, aren't you?" I whispered into his ear as he lowered his head to lick and suck my neck.

"Break you," he whispered against my cheek, running his nose from my chin up to my ear, inhaling, "and yes, probably."

But when he pressed his body against mine and pulled his head back to look at me, in that moment, I did not care.

FOURTEEN
KEVIN

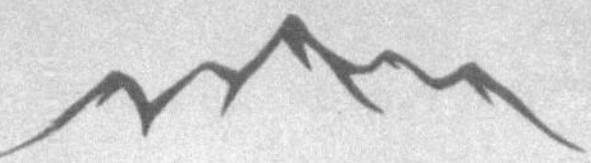

Luuk wrapped his legs around my ass and his arms around my back and rolled me, landin' on top of me, then slid down my body, kissin' and lickin' and suckin' as he went.

Everywhere his body touched mine felt like I'd been gently electrocuted. I'd never been touched by a man like that. Yes, men had touched me. Yes, they'd put their mouths on my body, but not because they knew me and wanted me to feel good. They'd just wanted to get off.

But Luuk knew me, as much as I'd let him, which, sadly, wasn't very much, but he knew me enough that he wanted to make me feel good. Could I make him feel good too? I had almost zero experience with actual sex. With a man.

Suddenly, I was so nervous, I felt my insides tremblin'.

Shit.

"Luuk?"

He froze. He probably thought I'd freak out like I had the last time we'd found ourselves in this kinda predicament. Raisin' his head, he looked up my body.

Holy fuck. He was so sexy lookin' up at me like that—skin flushed, lips swollen and wet, and his eyes, so intense and as blue-green as the shallow water in some exotic Caribbean ocean. Jesus Christ. My cock grew ten inches. I woulda sworn to it on a Bible.

I cleared my throat. "Um, I—" My breath puffed my cheeks as it tried to escape me—I was *so* nervous. "I dunno what to do. I mean, I do, I just don't have a lotta experience doin' it. And I wanna— You're makin' me feel so fuckin' good, but I-I don't know if I can… do that for you. But I want that. *So* bad."

Climbin' back up my body, he kissed my lips but didn't close his eyes. "You already make me feel good. Very good." He nipped my jaw with his teeth. "But that's part of the fun of sex, of getting to know someone, finding what your lover likes. I'll show you, and you will show me. Yes?"

"Oh, fuck yes," I breathed.

He chuckled. "I like kissing you. You are *very* good at it," he said, and he kissed me again, but deeper. His tongue was so slow and sensual in my mouth, and I groaned and breathed into him.

"I like that too." I mumbled it against his lips, shovin' my hands into his hair, pullin' a little. I didn't mean to; it was just what my body did.

Moanin', he said, "Do that again." His voice was that low, sexy hum I remembered from the first time I'd met him. I pulled again a little harder, and he groaned into my mouth, kissin' me so thoroughly that I was havin' a hard time breathin'. I pulled my head back to gasp for air, and he asked, "I want to taste your body. May I?"

Yes! I'll beg if you want me to!

I moaned and groaned too. In my head, I laughed at myself. I probably sounded like *Debbie Does Dallas*, but he didn't seem to mind. Shit, bein' the polite guy he was, he was still waitin' for me to answer.

"Luuk, you can do whatever the fuck you want to me. I

want it all." With just a little bit of an evil glint in his eye, he smiled and I swallowed. Loudly.

He worked his way back down my body with deliberate and unhurried movements. Maybe he wanted to take it slow, or maybe he was tryin' to kill me erotically, but he moved over every part of my upper body, my neck, my shoulders, my chest, up and down both my arms, my hands, even my fingertips, and he kissed and licked and sucked it all.

I lay there like some pillow princess, watchin' him, takin' him in. He was utterly beautiful. It almost hurt to look at him, and the sensations from his every touch paralyzed me. By the time he'd finished with one area, it went numb from all the nerve endin's just goddamn givin' up!

I panted, and my heart tried desperately to punch a hole through my chest by the time he made his way to the skin above my fly. *Oh, God, yes.* The anticipation of it all had me makin' noises I hadn't known men made until, finally, he unbuttoned my jeans and pulled 'em down my legs.

He'd removed my boots before crawlin' into his bed with me earlier, and thank fuck, 'cause if he had to stop now to remove 'em, I'd die from the lack of his tongue on my body. Pullin' my boxer briefs down and off, he let the fabric drag down the length of my dick, and he scraped his teeth over his bottom lip like he was starved and about to dig into a steak.

I reached for him—I needed that lip between my teeth— but he pushed me back down with his hands on my chest and scooted off the bed, standin' to shuck his sweatpants, but I threw my arm out and grabbed 'em, stoppin' him.

They looked like the same pair he'd worn before, the day I accosted him in his doorway then left him 'cause I'd been such a coward.

"I wanted to tell you I'm sorry. For last time. The things I said and how I acted. I'm sorry."

"I know." He leaned down to kiss me. *"Dank je wel."*

He pushed his sweatpants down his hips, and he was *not* wearin' boxers.

But then he turned and walked away from me!

"Where you goin'?" I lifted up onto my elbows. "Get back here."

Turnin' in the bedroom doorway, he commanded, "Stay," with heavy-lidded eyes, and he left the room. I saw the bathroom light come on and reflect off the wall in the hallway.

Oh my God, just rememberin' his long muscular legs and his ass walkin' away from me had me ready to explode. I fell back on the bed, strokin' my cock with my hand. "You better hurry up, or I'm doin' this without you."

Walkin' back into the bedroom, his eyes were glued to my hand on my dick, and my eyes glued themselves to his cock as it bobbed while he walked toward me. My mouth watered. He held somethin' in his hand, though, and when he stood next to the bed, he set it on the bedside table.

"Don't you fuckin' dare. That's mine," he growled, imitatin' me. The look on his face was carnal and pure sin when he made that growlin' noise.

I groaned. Oh, I *liked* him bossin' me, even if it was only to poke fun at me.

"Oh, you liked that?"

Slowly, I nodded, and he flashed the most seductive smile I had ever seen on another human bein'. His eyes literally twinkled behind his eyelashes.

"Yes," I rasped breathlessly, but whatever he'd set on the table occupied my mind, and I kept lookin' over at it till I realized what it was: condoms and... lube. I gulped. I actually *gulped.* "Aren't we 'sposed to have a conversation 'bout some things before we do this?" I asked, eyein' the bottle on the table again.

He sat on the bed next to me, and all I could think about was that his cock was at my eye level, my mouth level. Oh, I wanted it.

"Yes. We should," he said, and I sat up and dragged my eyes, kickin' and screamin', to his face. "I am tested every three months or so. My last test was a little over a month ago, but I haven't had sex of any kind since a few months before I left Denver."

"I haven't been."

"Haven't been what?"

"Tested," I admitted.

"Ever?"

"No. Wait, you were tested since you've been in Wisper?"

"*Ja*. The night we went to Dr. Whitley's clinic for my rib. I asked him to test me."

"Doc Whitley tested you? For— Really?"

"*Ja*. It's not a big deal. Usually, I use a home-test kit, but I was already there." He watched my face as I thought about the doctor I'd known my whole life knowin' about me bein' gay, if I just waltzed into his clinic and asked for an HIV test. "Have you had sex with a man before?"

"Um, yeah. I used protection, 'course, but I've never been…"

"You've penetrated a man but have never been yourself?"

I nodded.

"You've had sex with women?" he asked, lookin' a little confused.

"Yeah. Used to do it a lot, actually, but the last time was over three years ago."

"Are you bi-sexual?"

"Oh, no. I'm gay as the day is long, but I tried for a long time to make myself not… gay."

He thought for a minute. "But do you want that?"

"Want what?"

Pushin' me back down on the bed and leanin' over me, close, he spoke right next to my mouth. "Do you want my cock in your ass?"

"I-I dunno." I did know. Oh, I did.

He leaned back, dipped his head, and smiled. He knew I wasn't bein' honest. "KC, you know there's nothing wrong with what you want, yes? As long as it's consensual and physically safe, whatever you want is okay."

"Yeah, I know. But I, I'm—"

Terrified. I wasn't scared of the physical act. In fact, I wanted it so bad, I could barely breathe, but I was afraid of the power it would give him over me, the power to devastate me. And I was scared of what it would mean 'cause there would be no goin' back for me, I knew.

"It's okay. When you're ready for that, *if* you are, you can tell me. There are many ways for me to make you feel good. May I show you?"

I nodded 'cause my tongue was stuck to the roof of my mouth again. I couldn't think of any words to convey how much I wanted him to show me anything, everything, he wanted to.

He climbed over me, hoverin' above me, and leaned his face down next to mine to whisper in my ear. "And you may do anything you like to me. *Anything*."

Ohhh, fuck. My cock throbbed. He felt it against his belly, and he moaned in my ear, which just made it worse. He kissed me again, and we both got lost in it. He could kiss me for days, and I swore I'd never tire of it, but he pulled away finally, lookin' right in my eyes.

"I want to touch you. If I do something you don't like, or it doesn't feel good, tell me, yes?"

"Yes," I breathed, watchin' him as he looked down my body and back up again, like he couldn't decide where to start. I didn't care where! And I liked how he asked my permission by sayin' "yes?" It was sexy, like he had all the confidence I wouldn't say no.

If it were possible, it made me want him even more.

Movin' down my body again, slow, he rubbed every part of his body he could against every part of mine. He did that thing with both my nipples like he had before. Who knew a man's nipples could be so fuckin' sensitive? Jesus. I coulda come just from that and the sounds his mouth made on my body, the slow way his lips and tongue and teeth pushed and pulled my skin—all of it made more blood rush to my cock, and I didn't think I could take it much longer.

But I didn't need to worry 'cause he headed there next. He kneeled between my legs, and I watched as he caressed my inner thighs with his fingers, movin' closer and closer to where I wanted him.

I'd never been much for anticipation durin' sex. With women, I pretty much just got down to doin' the deed fast as I could so I could get it over with. And with the few men I'd been with, it was fast then, too, 'cause I'd wanted the release and nothin' else.

But with Luuk, even though I thought my cock would blow any second, I liked that he was slow with my body, deliberate and careful, not wantin' to push me too far, too fast. It made me feel... respected? Cared for? How fuckin' stupid did that sound? But that's how I felt with his hands slowly caressin' my body.

Grippin' the outside of my leg, he lifted it, bendin' my knee, and ran his tongue from the bend, down the very inside of my thigh, nuzzlin' his nose into the hair at the base of my dick. He inhaled and I growled. It sent this wave of primal need through my body, him bein' that close to me, inhalin' my scent.

"I have wanted you from the first moment I saw you," he said, lookin' up at me. "To touch you like this, to be with you..."

I pushed up onto my elbows, lookin' down at him between my legs, his mouth an inch away from the most private part of me, and I felt his breath on my skin. I was overwhelmed. It was what I wanted, this connection. The sex, yeah. I couldn't lie. I wanted sex with this man. I wanted hard, dirty, sticky fuckin' sex with him. I had to work really hard not to thrust my hips and shove my cock right down his throat.

I wanted to fuck his mouth more than I'd ever wanted *anything*. My breath came so fast, and I felt like I couldn't keep the air in my lungs long enough to benefit from the oxygen. My whole body strained. But… I wanted him to hold me. To know me. To—

He opened his mouth and sucked me inside him, and I thought I fuckin' died! *Oh God, fuck, fuck, fuck!* I watched as he bobbed his head up and down, his lips stretched wide over me, and I was ready to come just from the sight of his mouth workin' me.

"Luuk!" I barked his name, grabbin' his hair in my fist, and my head fell back in absolute ecstasy as I pumped my hips. I had to try *really hard* not to come the second his tongue touched my dick. This wasn't gonna take long; I'd waited so long to be with him like this, and it felt too good.

But it was more than just the physical sensations. It was such a turn-on that he knew who he was, what he wanted. He didn't give a shit what anybody thought of him.

He ran his hand up my body as he sucked me, up and over my ribs, my chest, my neck, my face. His fingers brushed over my lips, so I grabbed 'em with my teeth, pullin' 'em into my mouth, and he growled and rolled my balls in his other hand, sendin' vibrations through my body I hadn't even known were possible. He pulled the skin between 'em gently and… *oh, fuck.* And then he touched his finger to the skin behind 'em, pushin' as he drew me deep down his throat, and I came so fuckin' hard, I saw stars!

No woman had ever made me come like *that*.

I couldn't feel my body—I was floatin' at least two feet above the bed. He was talkin' to me, but I had no idea what he said. I just tried to breathe productively and make my body fall back to the earth.

"Whadidyasa?" I asked him, and he chuckled and kissed my hip, licked it, flicked it with his tongue.

"You are so sexy, KC. When you come, *mijn* God. So fucking sexy."

Finally, I could move my arms and legs again, so I trapped his body with my thighs and flipped him. He shuddered and gasped for air, and I was about to suck the sanity right outta him when his cell phone rang in the other room.

"Dear God, ignore it."

He groaned. "I cannot. It could be an emergency. I am on call tonight."

I nearly cried, but the phone stopped ringin', and I smiled like a deranged clown, raisin' my eyebrows to warn him of my devious intentions, but the damn phone rang again.

He rolled away from me, hopped up off the bed, and jogged for his phone. Well, at least I got to have a good gander at his backside as he went. I face-planted on the bed and waited, and thirty seconds later, he walked back into the bedroom, givin' me that sexy-as-fuck smile again. His dimples flashed like Christmas lights, and he answered his phone.

"This is Dr. van der Wouden." He listened for a few seconds. "Phil? Is that you? Phil, I cannot hear you." He closed his eyes, listenin' harder. "Yes, okay, Phil, try to calm down. I'm coming right now. Just hold on." He held his phone out to me and whispered, "Can you turn on the speaker? I need to get dressed."

Takin' the phone from him, I sat up on my knees. "Is that Phil Beasley?" I whispered and he nodded. I tapped the speaker icon on his phone.

"Phil, what has happened?"

"Oh God, Doc, Boscoe's been attacked. I nearly was too. A bear, a big one. I don't know where it went!"

Oh, shit.

"I'm on the way," he told her. "Phil, go inside."

"I can't. I can't leave Boscoe. Doc, he's hurt real bad. Oh, he's bleedin' so much!" Phil screeched and cried. She was panicking.

Okay, focus. I jumped up and threw some clothes on. I wasn't sure if they were mine or not, but they fit well enough.

"Phil, it's Kevin Cade. You still keep Rand's gun in the barn?"

"Oh, yes!"

"Run and get it. We'll be there fast as we can."

We both ran for Luuk's truck, but I remembered Jack kept his shotgun under the seat of his old Ford, so I grabbed it right quick, then threw myself into the front seat next to Luuk. We hauled ass down Route 20, and it felt like it only took us five minutes. Phil lived way out in the sticks. Normally, it would take twenty, at least, maybe twenty-five, but Luuk drove like a madman.

He stayed on the phone with her the whole way, askin' her questions about Boscoe and tellin' her to keep pressure on his wounds and to breathe, and I reminded her to look around for the bear.

Halfway through our country Indy 500 through Wisper, it occurred to me to text Carey to tell him to get to Phil's place and to call Game and Fish to meet us there to find the bear. I texted from my phone, and he replied instantly. He was probably still at my house, so he'd be closer to Phil's. Maybe he could get there faster.

He didn't though. Luuk and I were the first to arrive, but Carey, Dean, and Finn had only been a few minutes behind. Game and Fish didn't show up at all, so my brothers and Carey went out in search of the bear while I helped Luuk with Boscoe. He'd been tore up somethin' good. Luuk barked out commands, some in Dutch, and I did my best to figure out what he wanted.

"Get me feed bags. I cannot sew him in *de modder*!" Mud.

"Get me my... ahh, eh, *hoofdlamp*! Ehh, shit, lamp." He fumbled his words, then he smacked his forehead with the heel of his hand, coverin' himself in blood. "Ehh, head light. Headlamp. Get it!"

"Get me water. This is a *bloedbad*!" Puddle of blood?

Or maybe he was just cursin' in Dutch. I didn't know. He said, "*Hoe groot was die verdomde beer? Deze hond is de pineut!*"

He worked hard in almost complete darkness for twenty minutes, with Phil jumpin' outta her skin next to him, holdin' a flashlight and prayin', until, finally, he sat back on his heels.

"Phil, I am so sorry. He's gone," he said, clenchin' his bloody fingers into fists.

Ahh, shit. That dog had been a gift to Phil from her late husband, and they'd been two peas in a pod. She would take losin' Boscoe really hard. She sobbed, and I held onto her while Luuk covered Boscoe with one of the feed bags I'd grabbed from the barn.

After calmin' Phil down some, we took her into the house so she could clean up a little, but she shook and cried still, so Luuk scrubbed his hands in her sink and made her tea. Finally, she sat in her rockin' chair and took a couple deep breaths.

"Phil, what happened?" I asked.

"Oh, honey, it's all my fault. I was tendin' to the piglets, and I had my earbuds in. You know how I like my music. All of a sudden, I heard a roarin' noise and felt somethin' behind me. I turned around to see Boscoe goin' at a huge grizzly bear. He was in the barn. Boscoe was protectin' me. He jumped onto that thing, snarlin' and bitin'.

"I don't know exactly what happened 'cause I got the hell outta there. I came in here and watched from the window. I was so worried about the piglets and Boscoe, but then I saw the bear runnin' away, back into the woods, and Boscoe limped out and fell down in the mud. He saved my life." She cried again then, softly, and Luuk went to her, crouchin' down onto his knees in front of her chair. He held her hands.

"I am deeply sorry, Phil," he said. "I know how you loved Boscoe."

"Yes," she sniffled, "he was like a son to me." Reachin' out, she hugged Luuk to her chest. "Thank you, Doc. I know how hard you worked."

Somethin' flashed across Luuk's face when she thanked him. He looked angry, really angry, and I knew he wasn't mad at Phil for her words, so I figured it was himself he was angry with.

"How'd you get here so fast? And the sheriff? Thank God you did, but that was fast."

"I think Doc V mighta been a race car driver in another life, Phil. He drove like a bat outta hell. And I texted the sheriff on the way. He was at my place already with everyone, payin' his respects."

"Respects?"

Ahh, dammit. I hung my head. I hadn't meant to say anything. I didn't wanna talk about Ma. I was afraid I'd cry like a baby.

Luuk sat back, grabbin' Phil's hands again. "Mrs. Mitchum passed tonight."

"Oh no, oh Kevin." She looked up at me. "I'm so sorry. Here I am makin' such a commotion over a dog. And y'all came to help me. Oh, Sara. But she's with God now and her husband. That's somethin' to rejoice about." She sobbed then and Luuk soothed her, best he could.

I found it really hard, listenin' to someone else cry about Ma. It made me feel far away from my own sadness. I stood there, watchin' her fall to pieces and wonderin' why I wasn't. I felt... detached. The sadness and loss floated all around me, but I couldn't touch it. Couldn't reach it.

Luuk looked back at me while Phil's head was down as she wiped her nose on her sleeve, and the compassion he had for me showed all over his face. He knew what listenin' to Phil made me feel, and he hurt for me.

"We didn't find the bear, but he can't be far," Carey announced when he, Dean, and Finn walked in the front door of Phil's house, stompin' their boots on the rug there, shotguns and flashlights in their hands. "There's a lotta kicked up mud and blood in the woods. I think Boscoe interrupted his meal. I don't think he'll be back, but I'd like you to stay in town just in case."

"Pack an overnight bag, Phil," Dean said in his crisp military way. "You'll stay at the ranch."

"Oh, no, I'll be fine here. You boys are grievin'." She sniffled. "The last thing you need is a houseguest. No, thank you, Dean. I'll be okay."

"Then you shall stay with me," Luuk said. "I have extra rooms, and I need more of that cheese pie you make." He smiled up at her from where he still kneeled on the floor in front of her.

"Chess pie, honey. Really, I'm fine, y'all."

"Phil," Finn needled her, "you know we'll worry if you stay up here. And you shouldn't be alone. Go 'head and stay with the doc. Look at 'im, he's skinny. He needs to be fed. At least for a day or two, give Game and Fish some time to make sure that bear is caught."

"What about my animals, the piglets? Rocky can jump the fence if he's motivated far enough, but the piglets are defenseless."

"Now, Phil," Carey said, "the animals will be fine. Pigs have been takin' care of their own babies for all of time without your help. The sow will protect 'em, and I'll feed everybody and check on 'em when I meet Game and Fish up here tomorrow mornin'. Deal?"

"And I'll feed 'em tomorrow evenin', and we can go from there," Finn promised.

Phil looked around at all of us, considerin'. "Well, I guess if you're gonna make a fuss. But Doc, you got a TV? I need a TV. I gotta watch my shows and play my music."

Luuk laughed. "*Ja*, Phil, I have a gigantic television. Carolina and Evvie made me buy it. It's all yours."

I'd never noticed before, or maybe I hadn't ever heard him say Evvie's name before, but he pronounced it "Effie."

It was fuckin' adorable.

FIFTEEN

LUUK

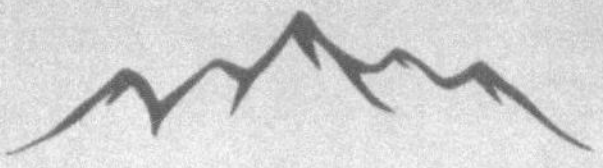

KC climbed into my truck next to Phil, and we brought her back to my house.

I wondered what he would say to his brothers, what excuse he would give to explain why he'd been with me when Phil called, but he didn't say a word, and they hadn't asked.

He had surprised me. I expected him to push me away again, but maybe he'd just been too distracted. Too sad. He rode back to my house in silence while she and I talked. She asked questions about Ma, but KC wasn't talking, and I didn't know the answers. I didn't think he heard anything she said.

"Have you boys talked about when the service might be?" she asked him. "Kevin?"

"Hm?"

"The funeral?"

"Oh, uh, I dunno. We haven't— I haven't—"

"Phil, what shows do you like?" I asked, trying to distract her.

"What?"

"What television shows do you like to watch? You said you need a TV."

"Oh, well, there's a few. I like *America's Got Talent* and *The Bachelor*. And, well, do you promise not to laugh?"

"Absolutely not," I said and laughed. If *The Bachelor* wasn't embarrassing to Phil, I was really curious to know what show she would be embarrassed of. KC looked behind Phil's head, and our eyes met as I peeked over at him for the millionth time, and he smiled, thanking me for distracting Phil.

Such a sad smile. The last hours had been so crazy, and he'd been forced out of his head for a moment. But now, he'd fallen back in. Back in the pain and sorrow. The grief.

Thinking about how I'd felt when my parents died, I remembered feeling relieved when I could escape the pain for a short time, but I also remembered missing it. The loss was a devastating feeling, but when I was without it, it felt wrong. I felt empty.

I wanted to reach over to grab his hand. But I couldn't. If we'd been alone, I would have tried, but we weren't alone, and I was certain he wasn't ready to announce to anyone that we were… whatever we were.

Had tonight been all about Ma? About his grief? Was that *all* it had been? I wanted to be more to him. I knew it was a bad idea. Every thought I'd ever had about KC had been a bad idea.

But I continued to think them.

"Okay, fine, I'll tell you. I absolutely have to watch—I mean, I'll cry if I miss it," Phil looked up at me, and I waited with bated breath, "*Dr. Pimple Popper*."

"I don't know what this means." There was a doctor to pop pimples? Was that a thing existing in actual reality? "Is it some kind of dermatologist?"

"You've never seen *Dr. Pimple Popper*? Oh, Doc, you're gonna love it. It's disturbin' and disgustingly addictive."

"I will take your word for it, Phil. I don't think I want to watch someone pooping pimples," I said. Then under my breath, I mumbled, "*Ik denk dat je gek bent geworden.*"

"What? Did you just call me a garden worm?"

A laugh escaped KC's mouth. And then another. He laughed so hard, he threw himself forward, clutching his stomach and hit his head on the dashboard, but that didn't stop him. He slid back in his seat, laughing more, snorting and stomping his boot on the floor.

"Okay, what have I said this time?"

"You called me a garden worm. That's what you said. That's not very nice, Doc." Phil crossed her arms over her chest.

"No, Phil, I said I think you have lost your mind."

"Oh, well, that's okay then."

More laughing and stomping, then leg slapping.

"Oh my God, lemme outta this truck. You're both nuts. This whole conversation is gonna kill me!" He laughed and laughed, and finally, Phil joined him.

"Seriously, what did I say?" I asked, trying not to smile. "Nothing I said sounded funny on the inside of my ears."

Phil fell over onto KC, and they laughed the rest of the way to my house. I pretended to be insulted, but inside, I smiled.

I'd distracted them both, and they didn't even know.

KC went home when we arrived at my house, and Phil fell asleep before I even had time to find pooping pimples on the television. I hadn't meant for her to sleep on my couch, but I didn't want to move her and risk waking her. I covered her with a blanket and pulled up a relaxing playlist on my laptop. Phil had mentioned she liked music, but I didn't know what kind. I decided "Chill as Folk" would be soothing enough.

Throwing my bloody clothes into a garbage bag, I stepped

into the shower. If I took them to a dry cleaner, they might have been salvageable, but I didn't want to bother with it. They were only a pair of jeans and a T-shirt.

Standing under the hot water, I thought back over the day. Carolina had taken the day off to be with Dean and Ma, and thank God she had. I was happy she had been able to be there when Ma passed. It was important to her to be there for Dean and his family. But because she took the day off, I'd been really busy.

I had no idea how many patients we saw, but I casted three legs on three different species, administered twenty-five various injections, de-wormed a litter of golden retriever puppies and three barn cats, and euthanized two extremely sick animals. There were no farm calls, thankfully, not until Phil called.

I worked through my lunch, just shoving a bite in my mouth here and there as I walked past Yola on my way to and from the exam rooms and lab. She held my sandwich up so I could take a bite as I hurried past her. I laughed when I remembered the look on her face as she lifted the lunch offering to my lips because my hands were dirty or filled with puppies. She rolled her eyes at me with one hand on her hip.

What would we do without Yola? What an amazing woman. If you needed help, if you didn't know what you were doing, if you needed your coveralls stitched or you needed to be fed, all you had to do was call for Yola. She had everything under control, and if something was *out* of control, Yola would make it her bitch until it cooperated. This applied to animals, computers, humans, and situations. If there was ever an apocalypse, it should be terrified of Yola.

On my way home, I picked up a salad from the diner and ate while I searched online for a dog to adopt. Then the day really got started. I got the text from Carolina about Ma, KC showed up and—

I shook my head. *Verdomme. Stop thinking about him.* His

body. The way his skin felt on my tongue. My fingers in his hair, his mouth, his thighs, his—

My phone pinged with a text on the sink, kicking me out of my nearly masturbatory shower session. I quickly washed and rinsed my hair and my body, trying really hard not to think about sucking KC off when I washed my—

My phone pinged again, and there was a third text as I stepped out of the shower.

Phil sleeping?

Quit jacking off. I wanna do it.

Get out of the fucking shower and unlock your bedroom window!

Shit! Wrapping a towel around my hips, I ran from the bathroom, trying to be quiet so I didn't wake my houseguest. I shut and locked my bedroom door and threw the window open.

I tried to whisper, "KC, what are you doing!"

"I didn't wanna break in through the front door and risk wakin' Phil," he whispered back. Grabbing the windowsill, he pulled himself up and through the window and fell to the floor. His boots hit the wall, making a loud banging noise, and we both froze, listening for any movement or sign Phil had woken.

After about thirty seconds of silence, he looked up at me and pulled the towel from my body.

"Oh God." He groaned when he saw my extremely solid erection. I was hard—of course I was, he was near, and I still hadn't recovered from my thoughts about him from the shower. He launched himself at me from the floor, tackling me and landing us on my bed. I tried to pull his shirt up, but he was everywhere, all at once, and I couldn't get a hold on it.

Touching me everywhere with his fingers and his mouth and tongue, he moved from my chest to my stomach, back up to my neck, scratched his fingers up my legs—it felt like he was trying to touch every inch of me.

But he stopped.

He became completely still for a moment, just breathing against my side.

"KC?" *Shit. Don't stop. Please don't stop.*

"I want you so much, I'm shakin'," he whispered.

My fingers found his hair in the dark, and I pulled his head up so I could see his eyes. "Then take me."

"Are you sure? 'Cause I don't think I'll ever recover from it."

I pulled him to my mouth by his hair and kissed him until he couldn't hold himself above me anymore, and he groaned.

"In the drawer," I said, nodding in the direction of my bedside table without looking away from his eyes.

Moving off of me and over to the edge of the bed, he stood and stepped to the side, closer to the drawer. He pulled it open and bent to reach into it, and all I could think was that I needed to see his body, his muscle, tendons, and skin.

I stood, too, and stepped in front of him. I was so close to him that I could feel the heat from his body and his breath on my face as he straightened. Holding his gaze, I pulled his shirt up and over his head as he gripped a condom and a small bottle of lube in his fist. I'd put them into the drawer before I took my shower, hoping desperately we'd end up in this exact situation. I never imagined it would be so soon.

Dropping his shirt to the floor, I kissed him, but I didn't close my eyes. He did, and I watched the lust and something else—relief?—on his face as I unbuttoned his jeans and pushed them down his legs. I couldn't look away as I crouched down to untie and remove his boots.

I pulled his jeans off of his thick, strong, and sexy legs, rubbing my cheek against the coarse hair on his thighs, and his whole body shivered. He looked down at me then, looked down his body, watching me as I took him inside my mouth again, bathing him with my tongue and saliva. His eyes burned dark blue fire.

Inhaling air between his teeth, his head fell back, and he grabbed my hair with one hand, pushing and pulling my head slowly back and forth along his cock.

He was so beautiful with his eyes closed and his head thrown back, every muscle flexed and hard, his jaw clenched, and his face washed in the moonlight coming in my window.

He was magnificent and lost in pleasure, and I was lost in watching him.

But I knew he wanted something more, so I released him and stood. Taking the condom from his hand, I tore the package open. My fingers shook and I nearly dropped it. It wasn't like me. I wasn't nervous—well, I was, but it wasn't like me to fumble and shake. I wasn't nervous about the sex. It had been so long for me, and I was hungry for it.

Looking at him, I was starved for it.

But it wasn't like me to let someone affect me like he had. To unnerve me, to… make me feel. I was self-conscious because he had watched me work on Boscoe. He watched me fail, and I tried hard not to let anyone see me fail.

But he had, and still, he came back.

I had to remind myself that, for him, it was maybe only about sex. Maybe he wanted comfort and I was there.

I trembled now as I rolled the condom onto him so, so slowly, and he opened his eyes to study me.

When the condom was in place, he leaned forward to kiss me, our lips and tongues the only things connecting our bodies for a moment—but only a moment because then he became frantic.

His breath shook and he lifted me, my whole body with just his hands on my hips. I felt… man-handled (this was a word, yes?) and so fucking turned on. He *threw* me back onto the bed, stepping between my legs hanging over the mattress. I sat up, touching his chest with the palms of my hands, wrapping them around his ribcage, and he pulled me against his body and held me there. It felt like he was hugging me, but he tensed, preparing to push me away.

He stepped back. "Turn over."

"No."

He blinked and he looked confused. "You don't want this?"

"No! No, I mean, yes, *fuck*, I do, but... *Ik wil je zien*—I want to see you."

He swallowed loudly. His Adam's apple jumped, and he stepped closer as I scooted back on the bed, leaning on my elbows.

"*Kom hier*. Come to me."

He did. He covered me with his body, crawling over me and releasing the death grip he had on the bottle in his hand, letting it fall beside me on the bed. I opened it, applying it liberally to my hand and working his cock with it, coating him and myself. He watched my hands, then looked up into my eyes.

"Are you sure? Please tell me yes 'cause I don't think I'll be able to stop if you change your mind."

"*Ja*." I wrapped my legs around his ass and my arms around his neck, gripping his hair in my fingers. "Yes."

He entered me slowly, moaning desperately and nuzzling his head into my neck, and waited for my body to adjust to him. He trembled and held his breath.

"KC. Look at me." Pulling back, he looked into my eyes. "Breathe." He took a deep breath and blew it out, and everything changed.

There was no more nervousness, no more uncertainty. There was only heat and sweat, arms, legs, lips, tongues, fingers, and hands.

His tongue was—*Jezus*. His kiss was so hot. Consuming, commanding, his tongue rolling and pushing and sliding against mine, inside my mouth, against my lips, over and under my jaw. My heart raced, and I moaned and panted and clawed at his skin.

And then… he began to move.

KC, as a lover, was intense, from the look on his face to the power of his movements. He was intentional—once I gave him permission, he never asked again. He took what he wanted. He was the sexiest man I'd ever been with, and I wanted just to watch his face, his eyes, as he fucked me.

He was so *in* it, the pleasure, the connection between us. I thought it might have been the opposite. I thought he would avoid the intimacy, that he would be afraid of it. And maybe he had been before, but not now.

"Fuck, Luuk, you feel so good," he whispered, his pelvis and abdomen stroking my cock every time he thrusted, making cum flow out of me, coating us both, making everything wet and slick and so, so hot.

In his ear, I whispered, "Harder, KC. *Laat me klaarkomen*—make me come."

He groaned. "You can't talk like that and expect me to last."

"Don't hold back. Come. I want you to— *Ja*, just like that. Oh fuck," I breathed, moaning when he grabbed my leg and held it against his shoulder, lifting it as his thrusts became hard and powerful, faster, and I couldn't take any more. I watched him above me, finding whatever he'd been looking for earlier when he'd shown up on my back porch.

I groaned and called out, forgetting to be quiet, and tried to keep up with him.

He was so *good*. My eyes rolled back into my head when he wrapped his fingers around my cock, pumping fast while he pounded into me. He leaned lower to kiss me again, and we both grunted and groaned and gasped for air.

Trapping my arms with his other hand, holding himself above me only with the power in his thighs, he held them against the bed as he thrust once more, hard, and came. He exhaled into my mouth, then hid his head in my neck, pressing his face to the mattress, shouting into it, "Luuk, fuck. Oh my God!"

And I came all over us both, the sounds of his release in my ear making it impossible not to.

He cried into my neck for the longest time.

I adjusted our bodies so we lay on our sides, and he tucked himself into me. I caressed him, rubbed his back, and held him while he cried, and eventually, he fell asleep in my arms, wrapped around me.

It was sad, and sexy, and exhilarating, and terrifying.

I lay there, thinking I had found myself in *big* trouble. I never wanted to move from this place, depleted, hot, wet, sweating, and surrounded by Kevin Cade.

Sixteen

Kevin

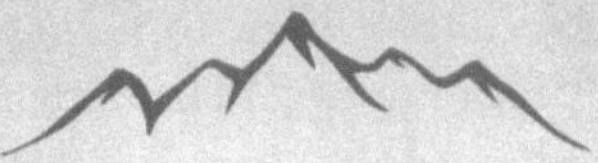

"Kevin, this is Isaac Markham and his father, Mr. Markham. From the bank?" Jack half said/half asked me. Like I was supposed to know who the hell they were. "Remember, I told you they'd be stoppin' by?"

"Right, yeah, good to meet you, Mr. Markham." I shook his hand and looked to Jack. No, I didn't remember. There'd kinda been a lot goin' on lately.

It had been ten days since Ma died.

Ten days since Luuk.

I'd left Luuk's house that mornin' through his bedroom window at the crack of dawn while he slept. He looked so peaceful, so beautiful, his lips open a little and his face relaxed as he lay wrapped around me.

Dressin' silently, I stood there, watchin' him breathe for the longest time. I saw a pen and a piece of paper sittin' on his nightstand, so I ripped a piece off and wrote the number one on it, then folded it up and shoved it into his dresser drawer.

One—for the first time I thought "I will fall in love with you." Maybe I already had. And then I took a picture of his beautiful face with my phone.

I'd imagined bein' with him so many times, but I'd never

imagined it would be so good. Well, okay, I imagined it bein' fuckin' amazin', physically, but bein' connected to him like that, the way he talked to me, held me, the way he looked at me—it was everything.

It felt so good, and I was desperate to see him again, but I hadn't called or even texted him. I was scared shitless. I didn't know what to say. What if he only took pity on me 'cause I'd been so screwed up over Ma—

"We're gonna be trainin' Isaac to volunteer with us when we start the new program. Mr. Markham would like him to start now. He don't have any experience with horses."

"Oh, uh, yeah, right." I shook my head, tryin' to dispel the image of Luuk naked underneath me outta my head and act like I knew what the hell was goin' on 'cause the expression on Jack's face told me he was gonna kick my ass if I didn't.

Mr. Markham looked like a stern motherfucker. He wasn't smilin', and I was pretty sure he knew I'd forgotten about his kid comin' to learn how to handle horses.

"So, we'll take it from here. Thank you, sir. He's in good hands," Jack said, and Mr. Markham looked at me, makin' a face indicatin' he didn't think that was the case, but then nodded.

"Isaac, you listen to Jack and put some effort into it, will ya? Those goddamn video games are gonna rot your brain." Isaac rolled his eyes and looked down at the floor but bobbed his head. "Good, I'll be back to pick him up after work."

"What? I have to stay here all *day*? It's Saturday!"

"Yes, young man. That's what happens when you use your mother's credit card to buy a thousand dollars-worth of video game bullshit without asking. You lose your freedom until you can prove that you're not a complete and utter moron. See you at six."

Mr. Markham shook Jack's hand and walked out the door, and Isaac groaned and fell into the chair across from the desk in the arena office.

"Sit there, kid. Enjoy the last few minutes of life without your back achin'. We'll be back shortly. Kev, a word?" Jack said, but it was an order to follow him, and he stomped outta the office. I followed, rollin' my eyes, and when we were far enough away that the kid couldn't hear us, he rounded on me.

"You forgot?"

"Yeah, so? There's been a lot goin' on."

"I reminded you last night, idiot."

"Whatever. Are we really doin' this? The kid ain't enthused, and I got better things to do with my time."

"Yeah, Kevin, we're doin' this. Mr. Markham's the guy who put us in touch with Theo. He runs the bank. He's some bigwig over there, so if he wants his kid to learn horses, we're gonna teach him. And you're just the man to do it."

"Why me? Finn's better at dealin' with people. Why can't he do it?"

"'Cause I said so."

"Dammit, Jack."

"Get over it. We'll all help, but he's gonna be your shadow."

"Fine."

Jack stared at me. "Well?"

"Well, what?"

"Get to it."

"What, now? It's seven in the mornin'."

He cocked his head. "There a better time?"

"I was gonna go for a ride."

"Tough shit."

"You know I can't teach him in a day."

"Yep," Jack nodded, "that's why he's gonna be here every Saturday and Sunday and three days a week after school till summer break starts. And then, who knows, maybe the kid'll move in. His dad ain't happy with him. Wants him to learn some responsibility and to 'grow up.'"

And he was expectin' *me* to accomplish that objective?
Shit.

"C'mon, kid. Hand it over."

"Screw you."

"No thanks, you ain't my type. Gimme that damn phone, or I'm gonna shove it up your pasty white ass."

"Seriously, man? This is literally the only thing keepin' me sane. Don'tcha have a heart?" Isaac begged me, holdin' his cell phone up in front of his chest in the middle of the barn.

"Nope."

"Come *on*. What if I promise not to use it till you tell me it's break time?"

"You don't get break time."

"Well, that's kinda my point. You're workin' me like a dog. This way, you can get a break from me, and I can get my tech fix. Like, maybe fifteen or twenty minutes every hour? That sounds reasonable."

"You're an idiot."

Jesus. It had only been one day dealin' with this kid, and already, I wanted to duct-tape his mouth shut and zip-tie him to a stall in the arena so I wouldn't have to listen to his incessant whinin'. I'd told him a hundred times to put his phone away and pay attention, but he kept whippin' it out, throwin' up peace signs in front of Mad Max through the stall bars, and snappin' pics of himself with the damn thing.

Snatchin' the phone from his hand, I shoved it into my back pocket. "Start down this aisle. Shit ain't gonna shovel itself."

"This is slave labor," he mumbled, but he walked back to start doin' what I told him.

My phone rang, and I grabbed his by mistake and couldn't figure out why the screen was blank, then laughed at myself. I pulled my own phone from my other back pocket, and Luuk's name flashed across the screen as RATM's "Killing in the Name" rang loud in my ears while my heart beat like a heavy metal base guitar.

"I'll be right back, get goin'." I walked outside and answered. "Hey."

"KC, *godzijdank*. Is Jack with you?" He sounded ruffled, a little frantic. "Evvie's here at the diner. Something is very wrong. Can you get Jack? I called him, but he does not answer."

"Hold on." I ran for the arena, yellin' for Jack. He was workin' with Ruby in the ring. "Jack! C'mon, Luuk's on the phone. He says somethin's wrong with Evvie. She's at the diner."

"Shit. Finn!"

"Got it." Finn jogged over to take Ruby's lead, and I put my phone on speaker and held it out so Jack could hear.

"Doc, what's goin' on?"

"I think she's in a panic attack. She's really upset and afraid, and we cannot calm her."

"Kevin, let's go. You drive. Luuk, put your phone on speaker so she can hear me."

"Hold on, she's in the kitchen. Okay, you're on speakerphone," Luuk said, and I heard shufflin' as Luuk held his phone out toward Evvie while Jack and I jogged for his truck.

"Evvie, I'm on my way. Everything's okay. Just breathe. Take a deep breath."

Evvie didn't respond. She was cryin' and freakin' out in the background. Her voice was muffled by somethin', and I assumed she'd hid her face in her shirt.

This was bad, that she lost her shit somewhere out in public like this? Not good. She hated these panic attacks. It was perfectly understandable given what she'd been through in her life, but she always felt bad when other people were around. She didn't like anybody havin' to deal with her problems. Nobody ever minded helpin' her, but I thought it was probably more about her not bein' able to control 'em and feelin' powerless over her fears.

"Hey! What the hell, man? You're just gonna leave me here?" Isaac hollered after me when Jack and I ran past him in the barn. "No way. You have my phone!" He followed us and threw himself into the bed of Jack's truck. I was about to turn to yank him back out, but Jack barked at me.

"Leave it. He's fine."

Danica Patrick had nothin' on me as I raced to town, checkin' on the kid every now and then in the rearview mirror to make sure he hadn't fallen out while Jack tried talkin' Evvie down over the phone.

When we got to José's diner, Jack didn't even wait for me to stop the truck. He jumped out, ran inside, and disappeared.

"Stay out here, kid. I'll be back in a minute."

Luuk stood behind the counter by the swingin' kitchen door in the diner, and when he saw me, he smiled that devastatin' sad smile of his.

"Hey."

"I think she's okay now. She calmed down as soon as Jack walked in," he said when I walked around the counter. I peeked in through the window in the door to see my mama and Jack on the floor with Evvie. There were pots and pans strewn all over the kitchen, and a big pot of some kinda steamin' brown liquid—chili?—had been overturned and dripped off the counter, poolin' on the floor underneath. *Damn.* This was a bad one.

"Hey, what's goin' on?"

Oh, good grief. I'd forgotten about my shadow.

"Dammit, I told you to wait outside."

"Yeah, but what's goin' on?" Isaac whined. "Something's goin' on. Everybody looks like the diner just got robbed."

I looked around at all the customers sittin' in the booths

and at the counter, and it looked like a few people had wandered in off the street to see what the commotion was all about. Isaac was right—they were all starin' at us, or they craned their necks, tryin' to see in through the pass-through window to the kitchen.

"Mind your business. There's nothin' to see here," Isaac ordered, like he was King of the World and not to be disobeyed, and Luuk and I looked at each other, tryin' not to laugh. What was wrong with this kid? He didn't even know what happened. But most people listened to him, duckin' their heads or lookin' to the person next to 'em, pretendin' to carry on an earlier conversation.

"Who's this?" Luuk asked.

"This is my new shadow. Isaac, meet Doc V."

"*Hallo*, Isaac," Luuk said, leanin' against the door frame, lookin' like a sex god with his thumbs hooked through the straps of his army-green work overalls, which he wore over a *very* nicely fitted gray T-shirt. He made my mouth water. His hair was messy, like he'd been pullin' his fingers through it. He'd probably been pretty nervous, watchin' Evvie freak out. "Shadow?"

"Yeah, apparently, we're the new Hogwarts for Horses."

"I don't know what this means."

Isaac and I both laughed. "Isaac's dad wants him to learn horses, and I'm the lucky S.O.B. who gets to teach his skinny ass."

"Kev?" Jack called my name, so I walked into the kitchen with Isaac followin' after me. Great. He was choosin' now to take this shadow crap seriously? "Can you pull the truck around back? I'm gonna take her over to see Doc Ross."

"Yeah, c'mon, kid."

My mama smiled weakly up at me, and I nodded. Looked like she'd been tryin' to help. Evvie still clutched my mama's shirt while Jack held her in his lap, talkin' low to her.

My shadow and I pulled Jack's truck around the back of

the diner, and I left the engine runnin' and went to help Jack with the door while he led Evvie outside. She climbed into the truck in a trance, and Jack looked at me.

"Can you—"

"Yeah, I'll find us a ride. No worries, brother. We'll help José clean up."

Jack and Evvie left, and we went back inside. Luuk had already begun to mop up the chili when we walked in.

"Oh, honey, what was that?" my mama asked. "What's wrong with Evvie? She was hysterical."

"She gonna be okay?" José asked, leanin' back against a stainless steel countertop.

"She had a panic attack. She gets 'em sometimes, though this one looked pretty bad. What happened? How'd she end up at the diner?"

"I don't know. I was walking back from the vegan market —José needed more peppers for his chili. But I saw Evvie sitting on the sidewalk, crying and hyperventilating. She kept saying 'I saw him! I saw him!' There was a man standing a few stores down the road, looking at her, but I think he was just trying to see if she was okay."

"A man? What'd he look like?"

"He was in the diner a few minutes ago. He came to help me with her, but Evvie just lost it then. But I think he stayed to make sure everything was okay."

"Show him to me?"

My mama pointed out the pass-through to a man standin' by the cash register. He was a little shorter than me and had cropped white-blonde hair and dark eyes. He looked worried, and he had his family with him.

"Does he look similar?" Luuk asked, and I looked over at him, wonderin' how he knew about Evvie's past. We'd never talked about it, but I guessed Oly'd probably told him.

"Yeah. He does."

"Kevin, please tell me what's going on. Is Evvie gonna be

okay?"

"Yeah," I turned back to my mama, "she'll be okay. Evvie's had a lotta bad shit happen to her, so this happens sometimes, but she's workin' with a doctor, tryin' to get 'hold of it."

"Yeah, there was this creepy dude from New York who tried to kill her, but Jack and the guys fought him and killed him!" Isaac gushed, like my brothers were superheroes or some shit.

I smacked the back of his head. "What do you know about it? Luuk, can you give us a ride? I need to dump my annoyin' shadow at home." I turned my head to look at him. "What're you doin' here anyway?"

"I was driving by and saw Daisy trying to pick Evvie up off of the sidewalk. I could see something was wrong, so I just thought I will try to help." He shrugged. "I shall drive your shadow home while you help here. I'll come back for you," Luuk said. He raised his eyebrows, looked over to my mama quickly, nodded in her direction, and looked back to me. I looked, too, and finally noticed she was really upset. She had tears in her eyes, and she looked shaken.

I nodded once, and he corralled Isaac outta the kitchen. "Come on, Shadow. Where do you live?"

They left, and José made a beeline for the swingin' door. "I'll just go help Mona with the customers. Don't worry about the rest of this mess. It's not a big deal. My kitchen's seen a lot worse."

"Thanks, man." When he was gone, I turned to my mama. "I promise. She'll be okay."

"I've just never seen anything like that. I was about to call nine-one-one, but Luuk showed up and said to call Jack. He checked her pulse and carried her in here. She was hitting him and kicking and screaming, and he didn't bat an eye," she said, and a tear fell down her cheek. "She didn't know where she was, Kevin."

"Got any alcohol around here? I think maybe we could use a drink."

"Oh, uh, no." She swiped her tear away with her knuckle. "José doesn't serve alcohol. I have a bottle upstairs. I'll go get it."

"Why don't we just go up there, and I'll fill you in. We could use the privacy."

I told my mama about Evvie's past, how we met her, and what happened in October. She'd read an article about it before she came back to Wisper, but she hadn't known any of the details. She was dumbfounded. She cried for Evvie, and I found myself comfortin' her. I even hugged her, and she held onto me like a cat in a bathtub, cryin' her guts out, though I thought it probably had more to do with me showin' her some compassion.

It felt really weird bein' in her space, seein' all the evidence of her livin' there above the café, although there wasn't much to her little apartment or much actual evidence of her life in it.

A small love seat was crowded into one corner, a small box TV with an old bent antenna sat on a wobbly side table next to it, and she had a boombox on the floor next to a little twin mattress by the window. Other than that, there was a kitchenette with a coffee mug in the sink and half a loaf of bread on the counter, a small bathroom with a standin' shower stall, and an exposed closet with a few items of clothin' hangin' up.

It looked sad and lonely. No photos or art hung on the walls. I didn't see a computer or laptop, and I wasn't even sure if she had a cell phone. The only personal things in the whole place were a couple piles of paperback books on the floor. They looked used and tattered.

I felt like a colossal douchebag, lookin' at her pathetic apartment. I'd been so angry at her, but seein' the dismal state of affairs surroundin' me might've thawed a little bit of the ice outta my heart. I thought about comin' to check on her the next day, but I kicked myself in the ass all the way back down the stairs to the diner. I was really confused about feelin' anything but hatred for her.

Luuk texted that he was waitin' in his truck for me out behind the diner while I cleaned and chatted with José, thankin' him for lookin' out for Evvie and for my mama.

"My shadow get home okay?" I asked him when I climbed into the passenger side of his big blue truck.

"Yes. He's, em, he's, what do you call it? Ehh—"

"He's a pain in my fuckin' ass, is what he is," I said while Luuk backed outta the alley.

"A pain in your fine 'fuckin' ass'," he said, flashin' me a smile, blindin' me with his dimples, "but I was going to say audacious."

"Phil still at your house?" His dimples equaled my hard dick, and we needed somewhere to be alone and fast.

"No." He laughed. "I was not sure I would ever get her out. I think she really missed having someone else around. All she does is cook. I think I gained twenty pounds in one week."

"Yeah? Well, if you take me there and strip off all your clothes, I'll let you know if you look fat."

"You are so rude sometimes, but… I like it," he said, lookin' over at me as he pressed a little harder on the gas pedal, "sometimes." He arched one sexy eyebrow to the sky.

"I'll be sure to watch my mouth. Just as long as you're watchin' it, too, while I suck your cock down my throat."

Thank *God* his house was only half a mile from the diner.

"Fuck," he whispered, nearly drivin' his truck through the garage door when he parked in the driveway.

Seventeen

Kevin

"What is this all over your body?"

"What?" I asked, lookin' down at myself while we lay on Luuk's livin' room floor, naked, sweatin', breathin' hard, and recoverin' from the best sex anyone has ever had —*ever*.

Apparently, my smart mouth really did turn him on.

When we were inside the house, he shut the front door softly behind me (well, as softly as you could shut that damn door. I really needed to fix it), and then we'd ripped at each other's clothes till they disappeared—my T-shirt was on the floor by the front door, and I coulda sworn it had a rip right up the middle. I would need to borrow one of his to wear home—and then he led me to his couch with his teeth on my lip and pushed me down.

When he came back from the bathroom with a condom, he tossed it onto the end table beside me and shoved his dick right in my face, with his foot up on the couch beside my leg.

He leaned in, holdin' onto the back of the couch with one hand, grippin' my hair by the root in his other, then fucked into my mouth like... I didn't even know! Like his very life depended on each and every thrust of his hips. And I sucked him down like he was providin' me with lifesavin' antibodies or some shit. And when he came, he roared.

I was so hard. I thought my cock would snap in half like a goddamn two-by-four if he touched it. His knees gave out, and he fell down onto me, straddlin' me, so I fucked him just like that, rubbin' him off while I did it. He came again right after I did.

He *was* a sex god.

I pushed him down onto the floor, and we made out slowly for a while, just kissin' and touchin' and feelin' each other.

"You have so many marks all over your body. What is this one?"

"Scars? Yeah, um, that one's from when Finn pushed me off a cliff into a lake. I fell onto a tree branch under the water, and it stabbed me." He licked the scar on my outer thigh.

"He pushed you off of a cliff?"

"Yeah, it wasn't very high. We were cliff jumpin'. It was supposed to be fun, but as per usual with Finn, things took a turn in a somewhat different direction."

"And this one?" He ran his hand down my forearm and threaded his fingers through mine, bringin' my arm up to his mouth to lick the burn there.

"My pops used to brand the horses." I shrugged one shoulder. "I got in the way. Jack put a stop to that shit. We tried freeze brandin' for a while, but it ain't really necessary for our purposes, so we just microchip and call it a day."

He sat up, lookin' over my body, and I felt the same burn I had before; everywhere he looked, my skin tingled and heated, and I watched his face, his eyes, while he looked me over.

"Did you have surgery on your leg? That one doesn't look very old." Touchin' his fingertips to my right shin, he ran his fingers up the inside of my leg and climbed on top of me, straddlin' me again.

"Yep. Broke it last fall. Ruby's mama decided she'd had enough of me. That was a *super* fun ride to the hospital."

"Hm, I think you are... emm, you're an eggshell." He smiled that devastatin' smile, the one that showed off his dimples and made his eyes light up.

I laughed. "What? Are you callin' me delicate?"

"*Ja*, you're very breakable," he joked. "You have so many marks, and I haven't even looked on the left side of your body yet. I must check."

"Yeah, just call me Humpty Dumpty," I mumbled against his lips when he leaned down to kiss me—his full, soft, plump lips.

"I don't know what this means." He kissed my chin and my jaw, rubbin' those lips against the stubble there, then licked down my neck to my left shoulder. "I know where you got this mark. It's weird to think I had my fingers in there. Does it hurt still?"

"No," I whispered when he licked my gunshot scar on my shoulder and kissed it, then kissed his way down my chest, my ribs, and back across my stomach, landin' on my *other* gunshot scar.

"What is this one for?" He kissed that, too, and sat back up, lookin' at me in question.

"That's from my gunslingin' days." I smiled and shot him with imaginary finger guns.

"What does this mean? It's from *another* gunshot?"

"Yeah, but it wasn't a big deal. It went right through, didn't hit nothin'."

"Who shot you?"

"The monster."

He blinked really fast, frownin', his forehead crumplin' into worried lines, and I reached up to smooth 'em away with my finger.

"*Wie is een* monster? *Wel verdomme*, KC?"

"Who?"

"Yes!"

"You know about Evvie's… history? I wondered earlier, when you asked if the man in the diner looked similar to the monster. His name was Paul, but it feels creepy to say it, like he was a normal person with a normal name. He wasn't."

"She told me about this monster. I knew he was bad, but— *Nondeju*. But how did *you* get shot?"

"It's a long story. I tried to protect her, but my leg was still in a cast. I was too slow." I gritted my teeth, rememberin'. Lettin' that douchebag get the better of me still pissed me off. He coulda killed Ma. He almost did kill Evvie. But then I remembered Ma's face that night, and I laughed as I said, "Ma took a good chunk outta him though."

"Ma shot him?"

"Oh yeah." I chuckled. "She saw me on the floor, bleedin', and I thought she'd freak and cry, but this rage flashed in her eyes, and she picked up my gun, aimed, and shot the fucker. He fell backward out the window, and I think it probably saved both our lives. I'm pretty sure he woulda killed us if he'd had the chance. Ma started flashin' the lights in the house, and she ran out to get my brothers."

"And then what happened?"

"I don't really know. I mean, I've heard the story, but I was only there for the gettin' shot part."

"*Jezus*." He rolled off of me, sittin' back against the couch, and I sat up too.

"I guess that's just more proof of your eggshell theory." How come I was the only one getting' shot around here? It reminded me of Ma, though, of how she conspired in the early days to get Jack and Evvie together. "Did you know they only knew each other a few weeks before they fell in love? Jack and Evvie? Crazy. But I knew, first time I saw her with him, everything was gonna change. And Ma knew it too." I laughed. "She knew before they ever even met. She kinda orchestrated the whole thing. She's a devious ol' lady. She... was."

Locatin' my jeans hangin' off a lampshade, I stood and pulled em on, facin' away from Luuk, and shook out my hands. I hadn't meant to talk about Ma. I didn't want to. I knew it would hurt.

"Hey," he said softly, reachin' up to brush his fingers down the back of my arm.

"The memorial is next Sunday. Did I mention that?"

"Carolina told me. Are you—"

"She bought me my very first camera. Ma did. I was fifteen. When I started high school, I had to take certain classes, electives they called 'em. The choices were art history, photography, or shop. I already knew how to build shit, and I figured art history would put me to sleep, so I took the photography class.

"I knew I liked it right away. The teacher would give us assignments over the weekends, and I'd spend all my free time lookin' for shit to shoot. Then, we'd all show our work at school on Mondays, and my stuff was always really different than anybody else's.

"The school's cameras were old and pretty basic, but I taught myself how to change the light, the shutter speed, aperture, whatever. It fascinated me, how I could control what people saw. I didn't want 'em to see me, but... if I changed the light, maybe they never would."

What in the world was comin' outta my mouth?

"You got anything to drink?"

"*Ja*. I'll get it," he said, and I turned to watch him walk naked to the kitchen and back, carryin' a bottle of—

"What is that?"

"*Jonge Jenever*. It's good." He took a swig from the bottle and passed it to me, and I gulped down a mouthful, thinkin' I liked my lips touchin' the same surface his had.

It tasted kinda like gin but stronger and with a heavy

smoky aftertaste. It wasn't bourbon, but it was pretty good—for gin. I chugged another mouthful.

"It's strong," he said, bendin' to retrieve his boxers from the floor.

"Good."

"Tell me more about your photographs. Do you sell them?"

I snorted. "Yeah, right. Nobody wants to see that shit." I turned away from him to find a shirt to wear, but he grabbed my arm to stop me.

"KC, don't say that. Your photographs are beautiful."

"What do you know about it?" I said, but inside, I swooned at the word.

"Well, I did learn art history, and I did not go to sleep." He took the bottle from my hand, took another swig, and set it on the coffee table. "Your composition is really interesting, and I don't know about light and shadow, but I know it's striking. It makes me… feel something."

"I gotta go." I didn't have a ride, but I figured walkin' might be good for me. This was all startin' to feel too good.

It scared me.

"Let me get dressed. I will drive you."

"No. I wanna walk."

"It's too far."

"Naw."

"Okay, but KC?" He pulled on my arm again, and I turned, fully, to face him. "I will be there Sunday."

"Yeah. Ma loved you, Alvie. You should be there."

"I will be there for you. If you need… anything. I'll be there."

Two. I will fall in love with you.

Cradlin' his face in my hands, I looked in his eyes, and all I could think was that I wasn't so fuckin' lucky. This man, this beautiful, smart, compassionate man—no way could I be lucky enough to have him.

This had to be just a severely anticipatory and prolonged hookup. Doc P would come back to the clinic full-time soon, and Luuk would leave and never look back. And what did it matter anyway? I couldn't have him. I couldn't be like Jack and Evvie and just decide to love him for all the world to see.

"I gotta go."

"Wait. Before you leave, I have an idea. I wondered what your opinion would be."

"What?"

"I was thinking we should get Phil a new dog. I've been looking online at shelter dogs. I found a couple I think she might like."

Oh. I thought he'd say somethin' about sex. Well, wasn't that just the cutest fuckin' thing.

Three.

"There's a shelter in Jackson and another close by in Idaho. I would like to see if I can get one of them to bring dogs to the spay and neuter clinic, to help get exposure for them. Maybe a few will get adopted, but, if not, will you come with me to look at the dogs? Maybe next week?"

"Yeah. I will." I leaned in and softly kissed his lips, inhalin' his breath.

"Dank je wel."

Four, five, six, seven, eight, nine, ten!

EIGHTEEN

LUUK

"Thanks for comin' to help me, Lookie Loo. There's no way I coulda handled both dogs by myself."

"*Ja*, they were a mess. You know, they never found the bear who attacked Phil and Boscoe. I wonder if this was the same one," I said to Carolina as I carried Boots, the Australian shepherd mix, to the recovery kennels in the back of the clinic. "I will call Game and Fish. He might still be near Mr. Bradley's property."

"I'm not too worried about Boots, but Jinxy is gonna need a lot of TLC. We should come back to check on him after the funeral today."

"How are you doing, Carolina? You haven't been feeling well, and now with Ma…"

"Oh, I—"

She became quiet for a moment, and I shut the kennel door, checking the flow on Jinxy's IV. I scratched his head and he tried to lick my arm, but his tongue hadn't quite recovered from anesthesia yet. It drooped out of the side of his mouth.

"Oh!"

"What?" I turned to look at her, and she had the weirdest

expression on her face. She was frozen and she looked terrified.

"Um, I think, I-I need to go to the pharmacy. Will you come with me?"

"*Ja, natuurlijk.* I'll drive. My suit is in my truck. Do you need medicine?" I asked, confused by the bizarre expression on her face. She looked a weird mixed shade of red and green.

"No. I— Let's just clean up and get outta here. I don't wanna be late." I followed her back to the surgery room, noticing her movements were off somehow. Stiff, like a robot.

"Are you okay? You look weird."

"I'm fine," she said, grabbing the disinfectant spray bottle and a roll of paper towels, then turned to clean the operating table, but she spun back around and blurted, "I think I might be pregnant."

"*Wat zei je?* Shit."

"I-I haven't had my period. There's been so much goin' on. We've been workin' so much and then Ma, and I-I didn't think about it. Dean's always jokin' around about havin' kids, and we use condoms, but there's been a couple times— Oh." She squeaked, clapping her hand over her mouth, looking at me, panic clear on her face. "Oh my God!"

"Carolina, breathe. Here, sit." I pulled a chair from the corner, holding it while she fell into it.

"Oh my God."

"You want children, yes?"

"Yes, I really do. I can picture it, a bunch of kids runnin' around, drivin' Dean and me nuts. But we're not even married yet. My house only has two bedrooms, and one of 'em is the size of a broom closet. I just started my career and— Oh, Luuk, the timing is so bad. Ma's funeral is today and—"

I laughed. I hadn't meant to, but I pictured Ma up in the clouds, making magic. Carolina glared at me, which only caused me to laugh more.

"What is so dang funny?"

"Sorry. I'm sorry." I laughed. "But I can picture Ma up there with the, like, magic, emm, what do you call it? *Toverstokjes*—magic sticks." I held my hand in the air to imitate a magician.

"A magic wand? Whaddya think, you're Hermione Granger? Swishin' and flickin'?"

I shook my head. "I don't know what this means, but yes. If you are pregnant, it's Ma's fault. She did this. I don't know how but"—I laughed so hard I snorted—"can you not see it?" Kneeling in front of her, I hugged her, laughing still. "Carolina, if you are pregnant, you will be the best *moeder* in the whole world. There is no one kinder and more patient than you. This will be the luckiest baby. And probably the most handsome. Look at his father."

"Hey. It could be a girl."

"Come, let's go get a… pee test?"

"I saw you translatin' that in your head. Your eyes crossed a little. How do you say pregnancy test in Dutch?"

"*Zwangerschaptest.*"

"We'll stick with pee test," she said, nodding and laughing.

My eyes found KC the second Carolina and I walked in the door of the funeral house. I didn't go to him. I wanted to. He looked like a sad, lost little boy, and I wanted to hold him in my arms, but instead, I squeezed my hands into fists and hid them in my pants pockets.

I hadn't been to a funeral since my parents'. It was difficult but I managed. There were many clinic clients in attendance, and everyone came to say hello. I couldn't appear… affected.

KC smiled discreetly when he saw me, and I held my breath.

People were hugging the Cade brothers and shaking their hands, but still, I didn't go to him. I knew if I did, I would out him. I wouldn't be able to stop myself from comforting him.

I loved him.

Releasing my breath, I held in another.

Klote.

Ma's funeral was really sad but also funny and warm, a celebration of her long and amazing life—a celebration of all the lives she touched, which had been many. Had Wisper, Wyoming ever seen so many people? The attendance was impressive.

Carolina's mom and Dr. Whitley's wife had taken care of everything, and they doted on KC and his brothers like they were little boys, bringing them food and drinks, hugging them, and helping them with conversation, as it had been easy to see they were uncomfortable with the overwhelming attention.

KC had provided a few of his photographs to display. There was a picture of Ma and Finn dancing at Jack and Evvie's wedding, another of Ma and Jay sitting in rocking chairs and laughing on the front porch at Cade Ranch, and several older photos of her as a younger woman with her husband and another woman, who I thought had probably been KC's grandmother.

My favorite photograph, though, was an old picture of Ma holding the hand of a young boy, walking away from whoever the photographer had been. It was KC in the photo. I knew by the stubborn wave of his brown hair. He looked up at Ma, smiling in adoration as they strolled off into the sunset.

No matter where I stood in the room or whom I spoke to, I was always aware of him. I felt a physical pull toward him. I watched him and I worried about him. About how he was handling his grief. How he handled all those people, no matter how well-intentioned they were. He struggled, and it was obvious.

Brady found me standing alone, spying on KC from across the room, and KC watched us the entire five minutes we spoke.

"Hey, Luuk. How ya doin?"

"*Ja*, I'm good. You?" I shook Brady's hand and peeked at KC.

"Yeah, good. Man, this is big deal, huh? I've never seen so many people. By the way, you look damn fine in a suit."

I chuckled. "*Dank je wel.* So do you. Yes, many people loved Ma. Did you know her?" I asked, but I looked at KC again. I couldn't keep my eyes off him.

"Yeah, she was my fifth grade— What're you lookin' at?" Brady followed my line of sight. He laughed under his breath when he found KC at the end of it and turned back to me. "So, looks like maybe there's been some new developments in your life since the last time we talked?"

"What? Oh. Sorry."

He smirked. "It's cool. I'd be starin' too. So, things are going well?"

I looked around. It felt so bizarre to be secretive, but I didn't want to cause trouble for KC. Especially not today.

"Right. I get it. Later," Brady guessed. He peeked back at KC. "Okay, well, I'm gonna head out. You okay though? Funerals are hard."

"I'm okay." I sighed. "Thank you for asking."

"Alright, man. I'll talk to you later. This whole thing's makin' me wanna spend some time with my dad." He smiled, squeezing my shoulder as he walked past me.

"*Tot ziens*, Brady."

I smiled at KC, but he looked away.

Finally, the guests had all started to depart, and I stood next to Carolina while she and Dean said goodbye to them. I thought I should probably leave. I'd obsessed about KC long enough. He needed his family, not me.

"Hey, guys." A short black man approached Dean and Carolina. He used forearm crutches, and his arms were built with muscle from the repetitive action. The woman with him was intensely beautiful, with dark skin and long braids. She stood almost a foot taller than the man, but it didn't seem to impede his loud presence at all.

He teetered forward, leaning on his crutches toward Carolina, and she reached out to hug him. "Thank you for comin', Bigsy. Annie, how are you?"

"We're okay, love," Annie said. "How are you holding up?"

Bigsy shook Dean's hand. "We're hangin' in," Dean said. "Oh, Bigs, Annie, this is Luuk van der Wouden. He works with Oly at the clinic. They went to school together."

"Pleasure to meet you," I said, shaking both their hands.

"Ooo, where are you from?" Annie asked. "Your accent is sexy."

"Sweet Jesus, woman." Bigsy groaned.

Carolina and Dean laughed, and I blushed. "I'm from the Netherlands."

"Oh, an international man of intrigue."

"Good grief." Bigsy shook his head, and Annie winked at me. I laughed under my breath. "A'right, well, we're outta here. Call me if you need anything, okay, cowboy?"

"I will, Bigs. See you Tuesday for your ridin' lesson, yeah?"

"Yep. I'll be there for my *torture* session." Bigsy rolled his eyes.

"Nice to meet you, Luuk," Annie said as they walked away, and I smiled.

"You as well."

Turning back, I reached for Carolina when she swayed a little on her feet.

"Duck, you're pale as a sheet. You okay?" Dean asked, and he reached for her too.

"I'm okay. I think I just need to eat." She hadn't yet talked to him about the pregnancy test she'd taken in the bathroom at the pharmacy in Jackson. She hadn't wanted to go to the one in Wisper because she said the gossip would "spread like wildfire."

"I'll go get somethin'," Dean said and kissed her cheek, then stalked off to find her food.

"Carolina, here, sit." I pulled her by the hand to a chair in front of a big row of windows. "I think I'm going to go home. Are you okay? Do you need anything?"

"No, thank you, Luuk. I'm oka—" she said, reaching to hug me, but stopped with her arms extended toward me in the air. She bent and clutched at her stomach, and a green sheen descended over her face again.

"Carolina?"

She took two deep breaths and yelped, "Bathroom!" and ran out of the corridor.

I followed after her and heard Dean behind me.

"Oly? What's wrong?"

She sprinted for the women's restroom, threw the door open, and launched herself into a stall. Dean followed us in and I heard retching. I wet several paper towels, handed them to Dean, and left the room.

Dean's brothers, Evvie, and Carolina's parents all stood outside the bathroom door.

"She's pregnant, isn't she? She never gets sick," Carolina's mother accused as I looked around at all the curious faces. I had just been about to pretend ignorance when my phone rang. *Godzijdank!* Saved at the bell.

I tried to arrange my face into a plain expression, but I couldn't help a smile from emerging, not while looking at Carolina's mother with so much hope in her eyes. She gasped and clapped her hands together, and I made my escape.

"*Pardon*. I must take this call."

Looking around, I did not see KC. I wanted to tell him I was leaving or at least get one last peek at him, but he wasn't with the mob of people standing outside the WC, waiting to accost Carolina and Dean.

"This is Dr. van der Wouden," I answered my call, pushing through the exit, and heard an explosion of celebration behind me. I thought I might've heard Dean whooping, but I stopped when I saw KC leaning against my truck in the parking lot.

"Emergency?" he whispered when I approached him, and I nodded.

"Okay, and how long ago did she go into labor?" Mr. Bourdain's cow had been in labor for four hours, but the calf was not coming on its own. "This is too long. I'm on the way."

I hung up and opened my truck, looking for the map Yola had made for me of all the farms and ranches in and around Wisper.

"Do you know the Bourdain farm? I cannot remember where to go."

"Yeah. It's northeast of town. I'll go with you."

"No, KC. Thank you, but you need to be with your family."

"Yeah, 'spose you're right. Here, is that a map? Lemme see." I handed him the hand-drawn map, and he squinted a little and snorted. "Who drew this, a three-year-old? Uh, here. It's up off Ranch Road." He pointed to show me where I could find Mr. Bourdain's farm, and I remembered then where it was.

"Thanks."

"But I'll see you later? I mean, we're all goin' back to the house. You could stop by after your call."

"You want me to? I don't want to… be in the way."

"Stop by. I'm sure there'll be plenty of food. Oly's mama'll be there so…"

"Okay. I will come."

He looked in my eyes, and I wanted to reach for him, to hug him, but he clenched his fists at his sides, and I watched his Adam's apple bob as he swallowed. He wanted me to reach for him, too, but as he looked around us, I knew he was afraid of who might see.

"So, you know Brady Douglas?"

"*Ja*, Carolina introduced us."

"Oh, like, for a date?"

"Well, I think she hoped we would date, but no, we are only friends. It's nice to have someone to talk to, yes? Someone who I have commonalities with." I saw something in his eyes that worried me. "I'm sorry, but I really must go. I will see you later?"

"Okay," he said, and he stepped back, but his face looked… blank.

"Okay. *Tot ziens.*"

Ahh. Verdomme.

NINETEEN
KEVIN

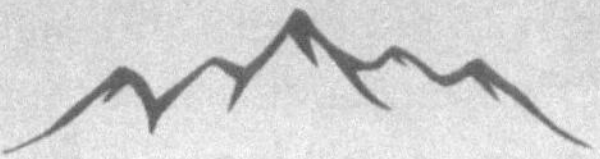

Everybody came back to the ranch to celebrate Ma's life and Oly and Dean's news. A baby? Ma woulda been jumpin' for joy. Dean strutted around like an idiot caveman with his chest puffed out. He might as well have been sayin', "Me make baby."

Finn sat next to me on the floor in the livin' room, laughin', watchin' Dean carry Oly all around, like she'd lost her legs.

The moron picked her up to carry her to the truck to come to the ranch. He picked her up to bring her into the house, and he carried her to the bathroom and back out to sit on the couch with the rest of us while everybody talked about Ma. Oly swatted him and rolled her eyes, but she swooned at just about everything he did.

"It was really nice of Theo and his sister to send that gorgeous arrangement to the service," Evvie mumbled while stuffin' cookies Phil had baked for us into her mouth.

"Yeah," Jay said, "and he was cool with pushin' our meetin' back. We postponed it a few weeks. Hopefully, next time, Finn won't talk about horse sperm, and Dean won't have to stick his hand up a horse's ass to impress the guy."

"Now, Jay," Finn said, "I just informed him of some of the procedures we implement here on the ranch. And there ain't nobody on this earth wouldn't be impressed with stud sperm collection, and ya know it." Was it impossible for the idiot to be serious? Ever?

"Shut up, Finn!" All three of my brothers yelled at him in unison.

"Yes, can we please stop talkin' about sperm?" Mrs. Masterson pleaded with red cheeks and ears.

"Ain't that all we been talkin' about tonight?" Finn said, and Jay chucked a couch cushion at him, but he rolled and dodged it as Carey walked in the kitchen door.

"I saw that. Things gettin' violent yet again around here? I'm not adverse to puttin' at least two of you in jail tonight," he joked and came to stand behind the couch, puttin' his hands on his hips, lookin' as stuffy as he could in his brown uniform and hat. He looked like Woody from *Toy Story*. "Did somebody order some kinda fancy feast from the city? 'Cause there's three guys standin' on your front porch with bags of some very tasty-smellin' food."

"What? No," Jack said, walkin' to the kitchen door, "we didn't order anything. Finn?"

"What're you lookin' at me for? I didn't order anything," Finn said, and Jack pushed the screen door open.

"Sorry, guys, we didn't order this. I think you have the wrong address."

"This is the Cade Ranch, right?" a polite male voice asked.

"Yeah, it is but—"

"Then we're in the right place. May I?" the guy asked, and everybody got up to see what the fuss was all about.

"Uh, sure." Jack looked confused, but he stepped back to allow the guy in.

"Is there a Jay Cade here?" the man asked, and he and two other servers came in the door, each carrying three or four huge bags of food. Finn perked up, sniffin' the air like a damn dog.

"Uh, yeah, that's me," Jay said, hurdlin' the couch, and he walked into the kitchen.

"For you, sir."

"Yeah," Finn laughed, "you definitely got the wrong house, man. He ain't no 'sir.'"

He slapped Jay on the back as the annoyingly polite server in his black pants, white shirt, and black apron handed Jay an envelope. When he opened it, his face did that "Tim the Tool Man Taylor" thing—"huu-uh?" (What? I watched re-runs just like everybody else. I was on couch rest for, like, a decade.)

"This is all from Theo and his sister. It's from that fancy fresh game restaurant in Jackson. This must've cost a fortune."

"What's on the menu?" Finn asked, edgin' closer to the food, and I coulda sworn I saw drool drippin' outta his mouth.

"Ah, well, we have ribeye, elk tenderloin, grilled buffalo, fresh-caught wild-stream salmon, and a variety of starters and sides," Mr. Stick-Up-Ass Server guy said.

Evvie and Oly mouthed the word "Buffalo?" to each other and made faces.

"And for dessert, we have tiramisu and crème brûlée with fresh berries and raspberry coulis. May we set up, sir? Then we'll leave you to it."

Jay chuckled. "Sure, thanks."

"Well, I guess you won't need my measly mostaccioli then," Mrs. Masterson said, lookin' a little hurt, and Finn draped his arm over her shoulder and sucked up nice and good.

"Mostaccioli pairs well with buffalo and salmon, Susan. Pile it on my plate. I'll eat your food any day."

She smiled and looked up at him, blushin' and battin' her

eyelashes, just like every other woman he ever met, and Oly's dad grumbled somethin' under his breath.

We sat at the kitchen table, eatin' the feast and talkin' about Ma. The food was probably good, but it tasted like cardboard to me. Everybody tried engagin' me in the conversation, but I had a hard time talkin' about Ma. Hearin' about her wasn't so easy either.

Luuk said he'd stop by, but he must've gotten busy with work. I'd just been about to wander up to my room to crash when he barreled in the kitchen door like he had the very first day he came to town.

Suddenly, I wasn't so tired.

"*Wat is dit*? Finn, have you cooked?" Funny how sometimes his Dutch sounded weirdly like English. Or maybe I'd just become so obsessed with him that I was startin' to understand him.

"No, Doc, though thanks for thinkin' I coulda cooked all this," Finn said. "This was a gift from our mysterious benefactor, the illustrious Theodore Burroughs and his beautiful sister."

"How do you know she's beautiful?" Jay demanded while he scooped more food onto his plate.

"Uh, 'cause I have eyes. And also, I looked 'em up."

"When did you see her?"

"When they were here," Finn said, like it was the most obvious thing in the world.

"She never got out of the car," Jay argued.

"You are aware that windows are transparent, aren't you, baby Jay?"

"Finn, don't you dare." Jay stomped his foot. "She's the younger sister of the guy who's gonna give us a small fortune. And she's blind. You leave her alone."

Luuk's head ping-ponged back and forth between my brothers while they bickered, and he smiled, laughin' under his breath. I supposed they could be pretty funny. Normally, I just thought they were annoyin'.

"Jeez, Jay. I saw her once. I was just curious."

"You know what they say about curiosity, don'tcha, dear?" Mrs. Masterson interjected as Luuk's cell phone rang. I'd just been about to make a wildly inappropriate pussy comment, as was my style, but Mrs. Masterson sat next to me. Snappin' my mouth shut, I pretended to be interested in the food in front of me.

"Finn," Jack commanded from on high, "I will wipe the barn floor with your ass. Leave it be."

"Excuse me, I must take this. *Hallo*, this is Dr. van der Wouden..."

Luuk walked into the livin' room to take his call, and Oly got up to follow him, but he threw me a sly smile as he passed. His lips didn't move, but his right dimple winked, and his eyes twinkled like stars.

"Guys, there's nothin' to worry about. It was just an observation. I will not debauch the little sister of our respected patron. I promise not to embarrass you or even flirt. There, how's that?" Finn said, smirkin'.

Everyone laughed and Mrs. Masterson snorted. "Yeah, that'll be the day," she said. "Let's take bets. How long till Finnigan here flirts with the pretty girl? And Jay, what does her bein' blind have to do with anything? Blind people can fall in love just as easily as anybody else."

"Whoa, whoa, now." Finn stiffened next to me. "Who said anything about love? All I said was she's good lookin'. Calm yourself there."

"Well, I think Susan is right," Evvie said, always the annoyin' optimist in the room, and the romantic. "Just because she's blind doesn't mean she can't tell what a great guy Finn is. I bet she flirts with him first. Everyone does."

"Evs, it's not me doin' the flirtin'. I am completely innocent."

"Yeah, but she has the distinct advantage of not knowin' what he looks like. I bet she can't stand him," Jay said with a smug smile.

"Jay!" Evvie scolded him.

"Baby Jay, I'm just as beautiful on the inside. Suck a"—he looked up to the ceilin', probably rememberin' what he'd promised Ma—"dandelion. That reminds me of a story," he mused with an index finger in the air, and everybody rolled their eyes and groaned. "Remember that time we were jumpin' on the bed in the front bedroom at Ma's house, and I pushed Kevin? Lil' Kev yelled, 'Finn, you dick!' and Ma came stormin' in." He turned to me, sniggerin'. "She grabbed your hand to hold you still so she could swat your butt, but you tripped over Jay's legs and fell, hit your head on the windowsill."

"Yeah," Jay said. "How many stitches did you need that time, Kev?"

"I dunno, maybe five," I said, reachin' up to touch the bump on my scalp left there after the bed-jumpin' incident. I didn't wanna smile, but I couldn't help myself. I remembered it clear as day. "She was so upset, blamed herself for my injury. She took me by myself to get ice cream, and I remember you two losers watchin' from Granny's truck when Ma helped me into her car. You knew I was gettin' special treatment, and it killed y'all."

"Yeah, well, she always did love you best. Besides, you laid the 'poor me' on real thick," Jay grumbled.

"I think he bribed her," Dean said.

"Nope. I'm just infinitely more loveable than all of you."

"I'm sorry to run," Luuk said, interruptin', "but there's another emergency." He led Oly by her hand to Dean, and I watched him walk. I watched his skin. His hair.

I wanted to be with him, but my entire family sat there, starin' at him. For just a second, I imagined what it would feel like if I held his hand in front of everybody. If I kissed him. Or even if I just sat next to him and looked at him as he spoke, as opposed to pretendin' he didn't exist, like I was now.

"Luuk, sit and eat. I'm goin'. You've already had two farm calls tonight," Oly said, cockin' a hip, and she stuck her hand on it.

"Strip her to her chair, Dean. She may try to hide in the bed of my truck."

"Strap, Doc, the word you're lookin' for is strap," Finn said, chucklin'.

"You know what I mean. She's trying to boss me over. She needs to sit there, eat, and relax."

"Luuk, you can't take all the farm calls for the next nine months. I refuse to be benched." Oly folded her arms over her chest, pushin' her nose in the air.

"Nobody's tryin' to bench you, duck, but it's been a long day, and you just finished pukin' your guts out. Let Luuk take the call. You can take 'em tomorrow," Dean said, tryin' to convince Oly. He pulled her into his lap, and she melted like a stick of butter in the microwave.

"Fine, but take someone to help. This is the fourth call of the day."

"I will be fine, Carolina. It's only a—"

"I'll go," I said way too easily. In my head, I winced. Yeah, that wasn't obvious. I cleared my throat and stood, then stomped to the door. "I'm tired of sittin' around here with you bitches, listenin' to you whine."

Mrs. Masterson clicked her tongue in disapproval of my language.

"Pass me that steak. If Kev's leavin', I'm eatin' his," Finn said, and outta the corner of my eye, I saw Luuk tryin' not to smile.

Twenty
Kevin

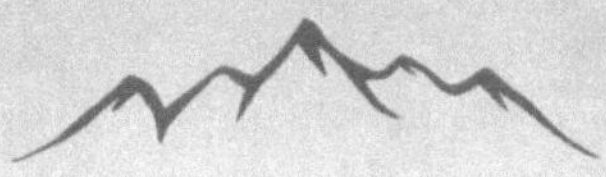

"**D**ank je wel."

"What for?"

"For helping me tonight. You have had a long day. You must be so tired." Luuk sat on the beat-up old loveseat in Doc P's office. He looked completely defeated. Exhausted

When he got the call tonight about an injured dog, he thought he was only dealin' with a broken leg—the dog had been hit on Route 20 by a truck—but by the time Doug Morris, his wife, and his daughter met us at the clinic, the black lab was already havin' a hard time breathin', and he had some massive internal injuries. Luuk did everything he could to save the dog—he worked so damn hard—but it hadn't been enough.

The clinic was deserted and dark except for the lights in the waitin' room and office. He leaned forward, restin' his elbows on his knees, and his head fell into his hands, and I sat next to him.

"I thought I could fix him."

"Hey now, you did everything you could. It ain't your fault."

"*Nee*? Did you see that little girl's face? I let her down. All of them. They asked me to save a member of their family, and I couldn't do it. I fucking failed. Again." The anger I'd seen in him before at Phil's house, it simmered just under the surface of his voice.

"Luuk, stop." I moved closer to him and wrapped my arm around his shoulders, pullin' him against my chest. "You didn't fail. You worked your ass off for that family. I watched you do it. The dog was hurt too bad. He was dyin' long before they got here."

I loved holdin' him against my body, like I was the only thing in the world keepin' him up, like he needed me, like I could comfort him and make him feel better. I'd never felt that way about anybody before.

He whispered, "I'm so tired of death."

Relaxin' back into the couch, I pulled him with me, and he turned and wrapped himself around me. He buried his nose in my neck and inhaled, and my whole body felt like a live wire. Leanin' back to look at me, he pushed my hair away from my face with his fingertips, lookin' in my eyes, and he kissed me. The kiss was deep but slow and quiet, and it filled up the room with us, makin' everything feel full and warm and perfect.

"I know."

"I'm sorry. I'm so selfish. Today was really hard for you, and I'm making this all about me. It's just that it's all around us. I don't want you to hurt, and I wish I could make you feel better. And then this dog tonight, that family…" He shook his head. "I keep failing in front of you." He sighed, huggin' me tight. "I don't want—"

I waited for him to finish his sentence, but when he didn't and he hugged me harder, I whispered, "You don't want what?"

"I don't want to disappoint you."

"Disappoint *me*? Are you kiddin'?"

What in the world was goin' through his head? He could

never disappoint me. I was the failure in this scenario. Didn't he know? I let everybody down. I'd let him down so many times already.

"Hey." I pulled my head back so I could see his face, his eyes. "What're you sayin'? You could never let me down. I'm the one. I've disappointed you so many times already. I disappoint everyone. I don't deserve you."

"What? No. You don't disappoint me. Why do you think that?" He touched his fingers to my cheek, rubbin' his hand back and forth over my jaw while he looked at me.

"Luuk, c'mon." I scoffed. "I'm a liar. I lie every day about who I am. I have my whole life. You… you deserve better than that. You deserve someone you can be with. You can't be with me, not without hidin' who you are and what you want. I'll let you down every day."

"Why must you hide? You're not hiding here with me now. You're not lying, not with me."

I laughed. It was a heavy, empty sound, and it made my stomach hurt. "Yeah, 'cause there's no one around to see." My heart plummeted into my boots. Maybe he didn't know yet how pathetic I was, how weak. I thought for sure, by now, I'd shown him. I didn't know why he still wanted to be with me, and *I'd* been so fuckin' selfish, hoggin' his attention, tryin' to soak up his goodness, even though I knew I couldn't give myself to him. I had nothin' good to give him, to replace what I took.

"KC, come home with me? You don't let me down. I don't want to let you go tonight. I like this. How you feel, how you make me feel. I don't want it to stop."

"I can't. I gotta work early tomorrow."

He kissed my neck, snugglin' as close as he could. "I wake early to run. I'll drive you home."

"Luuk—"

"*Godverdomme*, Kevin. Stop pushing me away. You are not

a bad person. You're not a liar. It's okay if you're not ready to—"

"It's okay?" I pulled my head back. "So then, you'd be okay with me *never* tellin' anyone I'm gay? You'd be okay lyin' to everyone too? 'Cause that's what you'd have to do to be with me, Luuk. You'd have to lie. Every fuckin' day."

"We don't have to lie. Your family knows who you are. They love you. You don't need to hide from them."

"What?" My family didn't know shit about me. He didn't either. I moved away from him. "What the fuck do *you* know about it?"

"KC—"

"No. Fuck you. Don't you get it? I'm not the guy you keep expectin' me to be. I'm *never* gonna be that guy." I stood and stepped away from the couch. "I can't be that guy."

I was terrified to be that guy.

"Go find Brady. He can give you everything you want. He's hot and successful. I bet he fucks like the devil. He's *out*." I raised my eyebrows, darin' him to argue with me, darin' him to deny that me not bein' out and proud mattered.

"I don't want Brady. I want you." He shook his head. "Kevin, you are precisely who I expect you to be. I haven't asked anything of you. I'm so confused. What is going on here? You're—"

"I'm what? Huh? Pathetic? Weak? Go ahead, say whatcha wanna say. It won't be news to me."

He stood and stepped toward me, grabbin' hold of my face. Leanin' in, he kissed me so gently, and I wanted to dive into him and barricade myself inside.

"You are so kind. Giving. Funny. Beautiful. I want you just like this. I want you how you are right now. You don't have to 'be' anyone. Just be you. I want *you*."

"No. You don't. You don't fuckin' know me. If you did, you'd run." I knocked his arms away from me and turned, and the wounded look on his face made me wanna slam my head into the wall. He was givin' me all of himself, offerin' everything I'd ever wanted, and all I could do was prove myself right. I was hurtin' him, lettin' him down.

"You *should* run, Luuk," I said, and the hollow sound of my voice scared me. "You shoulda already. I'll ruin you. You think you want me? Really? 'Cause I'm the guy who'll fuck you in the dark, but I won't even look at you in the light of day. Not when anyone else can see. I won't be the reason my family fails. The reason you fail. And I sure as fuck won't stand around waitin' for you to figure out just how much of a coward I am and then watch you run away when you do."

Fuck. Fuck. Fuck. Fuck. Fuck!

I forced my feet to carry me forward outta Doc P's office, out into the waitin' room, but my step faltered at the door. I wanted to run back to him and tell him I was sorry. I wanted to tell him I would try to be the man he deserved. That I could do better. *Be* better.

But I knew I couldn't. I would never be.

Listenin' for any sound he still moved, any sign that he existed, I waited, teeterin' in the open doorway.

I didn't exist. Not anymore. And there was no sound.

There was nothin'.

I couldn't go home. I didn't want to. I wanted to turn around and walk right back to Luuk.

But I didn't.

Instead, I walked a mile to the diner. I didn't know why I went there, but every time I thought to myself to stop and call Jay to come pick me up, I kept goin'.

When I got there, the diner was closed and locked up—it was nine at night on a Sunday. Duh. Of course the diner would be closed. I wasn't hungry anyway.

Lookin' up at the little window above the deserted restaurant, the one by the bed in my mama's apartment, I stood on the sidewalk, just starin' up there for the longest time. Why had I come here? She'd been at the funeral earlier in the day, but I hadn't talked to her. I said I'd look in on her after what happened with Evvie the other day, but it wasn't the reason I was lurkin' and pacin' in front of the diner.

I wanted answers. I wanted her to admit to what she'd done to my brothers and me. The longer I stood there lookin' up at her dark little window, the more I knew why I'd come. She owed me some goddamn answers, and I wasn't leavin' without 'em.

I *needed* 'em.

It was her fault. All of it. She was the reason I was such a disaster, the reason I couldn't have Luuk, the reason I was so devastated over losin' Ma. If she'd never left, Ma wouldn't have had to take care of us. I'd be sad Ma was gone, but I wouldn't feel so lost. So scared.

If she'd never left, she coulda protected me from my fuckin' father.

Lookin' around for somethin' to throw at her window to wake her ass up, I found a couple pebbles on the street and lobbed 'em up there, hittin' my mark and shoutin' her name.

"Daisy! Wake the fuck up!" I called out a few times, and finally, a light switched on in the little room. She peeked out at me, probably afraid—*good*—and lifted the window.

"Kevin? What's wrong?"

"I need to talk to you!"

"O-okay. Let me get dressed. I'll come down."

I paced while I waited for her to let me in, workin' myself into a ball of rage as the minutes ticked by. There wasn't anybody around, and the streetlights felt more like lonely stage spotlights shinin' down on me while I paced faster and faster.

When she finally opened the door, I stormed inside,

demandin' my answers. "Why did you leave? How could you leave your own fuckin' kids?"

She stood in the middle of the dark and empty diner, wearin' a pink fuzzy robe with some of those soft tan cowhide boots on her feet, but not the nice ones, the ones from the Thrift Mart, used and worn.

"I... I—"

"Well? What the fuck do you have to say for yourself?"

"You've had a long day. Why don't I make us some tea, and we can sit down and talk?"

"I don't wanna sit down. I wanna hear you admit it."

"Admit it? There are a lot of reasons I—"

"Just fess up, goddammit. I wanna hear you say it!"

"Kevin, please calm down. What's—"

"That you left because of me. You left 'cause of your annoyin', stupid, silly, *gay* son!" I couldn't believe what had just come outta my mouth, but I couldn't stop. I needed to hear her say it. I needed the goddamn validation. I needed there to be a reason I'd been so miserable my whole life. I needed there to be a reason I couldn't allow myself to be happy.

I was so fuckin' *terrified* to be happy.

Staggerin' back a couple steps, she clapped her hand over her mouth, suckin' in a breath through her fingers, and she whispered my name.

"Please. Don't look so shocked. You knew. Admit it. Admit that's why you left. It was my fault. I was too much to deal with. Too much to love." I sounded deranged, but there it was, the words out in front of me like a sickness between us. I couldn't take 'em back, and I didn't want to.

What did it matter? It was true whether she admitted to it or not. I couldn't be the person I wanted to be. I wouldn't be happy. And I couldn't ever be with Luuk. Not the way I wanted. I didn't deserve him. And he didn't deserve the damage I would inflict on his life. The kinda damage I'd inflicted on my own life, on my brother's lives. On her life.

"You don't need to say it. I know." I hung my head, acceptin' my misery, and turned to leave.

"Kevin. Stop!"

I froze at the door with my hand grippin' the handle so hard, the bones in my fingers felt like they would break.

She walked up behind me and wrapped her arms around me, huggin' me tight. I struggled to get away from her, but she wouldn't let go.

Like a caged lion, I snarled, "Let. Go. Of. Me."

Words rushed outta her, "Kevin, baby, I left because *I* was screwed up. Because I had so many issues, and I handled them so badly. It had *nothing* to do with you. Listen to me. There is nothing wrong with you. It was not your fault. You were not a bad kid. You were the kindest, most creative, most beautiful little boy. You were my best little buddy. You were always with me. You tried to take care of me.

"I-I was just so messed up. I was depressed, desperate. Almost suicidal. I needed help, but I didn't know how to ask for it. Your dad, sweetheart—we lived on two different planets. We didn't know how to talk to each other. There are so many other things that led me to making such a horrible decision, and I have regretted it every day since, but none of those things—*not one*—had anything to do with who you are.

"Kevin, I am so very proud of you, of the strong man and the brother you have become. I'm so proud of the way you cared for Sara, the way you look out for everyone around you. And I saw the pictures you took at the funeral today. I could tell they were yours just by looking at them. Baby, they're beautiful. I couldn't be any prouder of you. And who you love makes no difference to me. Luuk is a wonderful man. If he's who you want, then you should have him."

"What the fuck do you know about Luuk? I didn't say shit

about him." I rounded on her, knockin' her arms away, and she stumbled back.

"No, you didn't say anything, but I-I've seen you two together. It's obvious you care for each other."

I glared at her. I imagined glarin' her down to a puddle on the floor. The anger and hate fillin' my body in that moment took my breath away, and just hearin' her say Luuk's name made me wanna throttle her.

"Yeah? Well, it don't fuckin' matter. I can't have him. You oughta know that. You should know how the damage you inflicted affects me. Affects us all. You ripped us to shreds, lady. Dad? Jack? Dean. Finn. Jay. Me. Dad died when you left. His body still lived, but the man who loved us? He died. Disappeared. Somebody else occupied his body. Somebody hard and mean and absent. Pops too. Granny died and UJ, and we were left with two assholes occupyin' the bodies of the people who were supposed to love us. I was six *fuckin'* years old! All this time, I thought"—I sucked in a ragged breath—"I thought..." I turned and tried to open the door. I had to get away from her.

But I couldn't. My fingers refused to flex.

I'd never needed anyone more.

"Mama." Tears ran down my face, and I couldn't stop 'em. My legs gave way, and I fell to my knees. Everything I'd ever felt, all the years of hatin' myself, of wishin' I were different, it all came crashin' down on me.

I wanted so fuckin' bad to be better. To be good enough. For Luuk. For Ma. For my mama.

And for me.

"Oh, baby, I'm so sorry." She cried. I heard it in her broken breath. Droppin' down to her knees on the floor with me, she pulled me back against her. She held me and cried and said over and over and over, "I'm so sorry, my baby. My boy. I'm so sorry. I love you. It wasn't your fault. You didn't do anything wrong."

And I cried my guts out like the pussy crybaby I'd always been.

"Don't you remember? You told me it was my fault."

"What? No, Kevin. I never said that."

"You yelled at me. You said, 'It's not always about you, Kevin.' You were mad at me for being silly. I was drawin', and I wanted you to look at my picture. You were sittin' at the kitchen table with me, but you wouldn't talk to me, and I was tryin' so hard to make you happy. I danced around, bein' stupid and goofin' off. You told me to stop bein' such a bother. To stop bein' me. You said, 'Do you have to be so goddamn needy all the time?' And then you were just gone."

"Oh, God, I'm so sorry." She sobbed. "No, Kevin. It wasn't you. I couldn't deal with everything going on around me. I was a mess. I took it out on you. I shouldn't have done that. Please believe me, it wasn't your fault. I didn't want you to change. *I* wanted to change. I was failing at my own life, and I wanted to be different. I was desperate to be different, but I didn't know how. I was overwhelmed. I was— Kevin, I was just so *fucked up*."

I sat up, scootin' back to lean against the wall, tryin' to sop up the mess on my face with my T-shirt sleeve. "What do you mean 'fucked up,' 'messed up'? What does that mean?"

"Well… I was too young to have five babies for one thing. Please, don't misunderstand me, I was happy for each of you. I loved you all so much." She raised her hands to hold my face, and I shook her off, but she didn't let it stop her. "I *love* you."

"I was alone. I didn't have any help. My parents were angry with me for marrying your dad, and they wouldn't speak to me. They moved away, and then they both died a few months apart. I was completely alone. Granny didn't much like me, and Pops was a man to himself. All he ever cared about was Granny and you boys. He barely spoke to me.

"And your dad. He expected me to be someone I wasn't. He wanted an obedient wife who popped babies out one after the other. UJ tried to help me sometimes, but your dad didn't like that.

"I was so overwhelmed, and I wanted you to have fun and be kids, but your dad wanted you to work the ranch. He even tried to get me to homeschool you so you'd have more time to work. *All* he cared about was the ranch. The business. We argued about it all the time. We argued about a lot of things.

"And, well… there were just a lot of things. At the end, I felt like I was in a trance. I couldn't sleep or eat. I cried all the time. I thought you would be better off without me. I thought I was ruining everyone's lives."

"What things?"

"What?"

"You said, 'there were a lot of things.' You were about to say somethin' but you stopped. Tell me."

"It's not important." She shook her head. "I just remembered all the arguments your dad and I would get into, the awful things we'd say to each other. You don't wanna hear all that." Lookin' down at her hands, she clenched 'em into tight fists in her lap, and I knew she was lyin'. Tears streamed down her face, but she made no sound.

"Dammit, Mama, I'm here pourin' my heart out to you, and you're sittin' there sayin' how sorry you are, but you just lied to me. I wanna know what you were gonna say."

"It doesn't matter."

"Yeah, it does. Tell me. If it has somethin' to do with why you left, I deserve to know."

She exhaled loudly and closed her eyes, restin' her head back against the wall, but the tears kept comin'.

"I was… I," she took a deep breath, "I had another baby. You had a sister. But sh-she died. She died. In my arms."

Twenty-One
Luuk

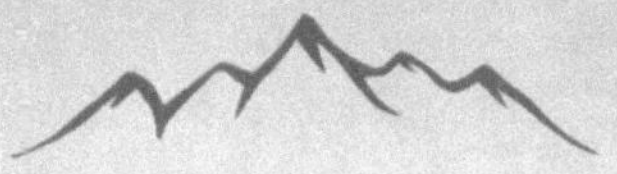

I'd been moping around the clinic all day. I had two farm calls before lunch, but they were quick and simple: a herd health check for a small organic llama farm and a horse who needed a few stitches because he'd had a little too much fun antagonizing a young Brahman bull. Carolina had been busy at the clinic while I was away, but I helped her catch up when I returned, and we took a break for lunch.

I'd been avoiding her a little so I didn't have to tell her I planned to leave Wisper. I knew she would be upset, and she would try to talk me out of going. But I had to go. To protect myself, I needed to get the hell out of Wyoming. I wasn't sure where I would go, but I'd already decided it didn't matter. Anywhere would be healthier for me than Wisper.

Anywhere Kevin Cade was not would be healthier for me.

He would not mean to do it, but he would destroy me, and the man I knew myself to be would disappear.

Because I loved him, and because he couldn't love me back.

"Luuk, you feelin' okay?" Carolina asked while she sat at Dr. Prittchard's desk, eating her veggie wrap. I stood, leaning against the wall, picking absently through my salad with my fork.

"Huh? Oh, *ja*, just tired. How are you? Very much happening lately."

"I'm okay. We have our first appointment with the doctor tomorrow. They should be able to tell us how far along I am. I'm so excited to find out."

"*Goed,*" I said and took a bite of my spinach salad. Not that spinach was ever flavorful, but it tasted like grass to me.

"Did I tell you Finn and Evvie are doin' a fundraiser, and they're gonna donate the money to a cancer charity? A concert. Isn't that cool?"

"Mmhm. *Dat is goed.*"

"Did I tell you I grew two new toes and wings, and the baby is an alligator?"

Huh? "What?"

"Luuk, what's goin' on with—"

Setting my salad on the desk before I lost my nerve, I said, "Carolina, please do not be angry with me, but I'm leaving."

"Leavin'?" Her eyebrows dropped and her eyes squinted in confusion, but then she shrugged. "You wanna go home and take a nap or somethin'? You do look tired. That's okay, I can cover—"

"No, I mean that I'm leaving Wyoming. I cannot stay."

"You're leavin' Wisper? Luuk, why?" And now her face showed nothing but hurt.

"I must."

"What's goin' on? You haven't been talkin' to me lately."

I shut the office door, and when I turned back to face Carolina, my eyes focused on the couch. I wanted to go back to that night with KC. I wanted to take back what I said to him. I wanted to take back the vulnerability I'd given him. He'd stomped all over it.

"I'm not going to leave you in the lunch. I will wait until

Dr. Prittchard comes back full-time or until we can find another vet to replace me. Don't worry."

"In the lurch. Luuk, c'mon, sit down. Talk to me. Tell me what's goin' on."

She pulled me by the hand to the couch, and I sat, then fell back, pulling my knees up to my chest. I closed my eyes and sighed, and she waited patiently while I tried to compose myself. Really, I was trying not to cry like a baby.

"I cannot stay."

"Did somethin' happen with Kevin?"

"Yes, and no. But it doesn't matter. Now, it's too late."

"What's too late?"

"I love him."

"You do? Luuk, I'm so happy for— Oh." I sat forward, dropping my head into my hands. "Did he say he doesn't love you? Maybe you just haven't given him enough time. You know he—"

"Time is not the issue. He doesn't love me. I don't think he can. He cannot love anything. He doesn't love himself. He doesn't know how."

"Did he say that?"

"No. He said, 'I'm the guy who will fuck you in the dark, but I won't even talk to you in the day, not when anyone can see.' He said something about failing his family and about making me fail. I don't know."

"That explains his mood the last few days. He screamed at Isaac all afternoon on Monday. Finn had to rescue the poor kid. And he didn't eat dinner with everyone the last two nights."

Everything inside me screamed to go to him when she said it, but I couldn't. I couldn't give any more of myself away.

"I cannot keep doing this. I cannot keep thinking about him. It's not good for me. This is why I have to go. If I stay, I will see him all the time. I cannot see him, Carolina. You understand?"

"Oh, Luuk, I'm so sorry." She grabbed my hand and squeezed. "He does love you. It's so obvious. Everyone can see it. Why can't he?"

"I'm so stupid. How did I think this could turn out any differently? I actually convinced myself I would be okay with — He's not out. He may never be. I don't know what he thinks. He thinks he lets me down. He thinks he lets everyone down, that he's not good."

I stood and paced the small office. "I know he has issues, but maybe this is more about me. Maybe he can see that *I* am not good enough. I fail all the time. And I live in fear all the time, afraid to take a chance because what if I do and then…"

"And then what? And you do not fail."

"It doesn't matter. None of it matters. I have to go."

"Where will you go?"

Good question.

There wasn't another place I wanted to be. The life I wanted, the person I wanted—the man I wanted—was in Wisper.

I'd thought about going back to the Netherlands. Connecting with my past. Seeing my parents' graves, our old home. Facing the loss of them. I'd been pushing it away for so long, pushing them away.

"I don't know. I haven't thought so far ahead. Maybe back to Denver? Or I was thinking I might go back to Amsterdam. Oudewater. I don't know. Maybe I will just drive until I cannot anymore. Like Evvie. See where I end out."

"Or maybe you could stay, but I could take all the calls out to the ranch and—"

"No. I cannot be so close to him, do you understand? If I stay, I won't get over him. You know I would still see him— Never mind. Can we stop talking about this? We have patients. Break is over."

I walked toward the door but stopped with my hand on the handle, facing away from her. "Are you angry with me?"

"Angry? No, Luuk." Carolina jumped up from the couch and launched herself at me, hugging me on her toes, "Whatever you need, I'll support you. You know that. I don't want you to go, but if you have to, then I'll just have to bring the baby to visit you, even if we have to go all the way to Amsterdam." She pulled back, holding my face in her hands. "Whatever you need, my beautiful friend. I love you."

"*Ik hou ook van jou, mijn beste vriend,*" I said and shook my head. "I'm sorry."

"Hey, we're still gonna do the spay and neuter clinic this weekend, right? It's your baby. You can't go before then."

"Of course. And I'm not going to abandon you. Let's talk to Dr. Prittchard. Lucinda keeps saying he's making her nuts. He might be ready to come back full-time now. And if not, I'm sure we can convince one of our classmates to help you. None of the large animal majors could pass up the opportunity to live and work in horse country. We'll call and see what people are into."

"Up to," she said, and she kissed my cheek and released me.

An hour later, I walked out to the waiting area to call my next patient back to an exam room and saw it was Mr. Morris and his wife. They had a new puppy, another lab, but this one was brown with green eyes. He was a happy little stinker, wagging his butt and pouncing on the gigantic mastiff next to him, and I was excited for puppy breath and licks, but when I called his name (Axle), Doug Morris stood up while his wife sat in a waiting room chair looking at the floor.

"We'd like to see the *other* vet."

Em... huh?

"Okay. You're very welcome to wait, Mr. Morris, but Dr. Masterson is quite busy. She's in surgery and will be until the end of the day." What in hell? Axle only needed a well-puppy exam and to be dewormed and vaccinated, certainly not rocket science, and it would take less than five minutes. Mr. Morris must've still been upset about losing Lucky. I felt awful that I was not able to save their dog, but I really had done everything I could.

"Where's Doc P?"

"I'm sorry, but Dr. Prittchard is not back full-time yet. He's not here today."

"Well, maybe I'll call him and tell him my concerns, let him know how you're treatin' people at his clinic."

Okay, now that made me angry. I had never been anything but kind and professional with this *kut*.

"I apologize if you feel you've been mistreated, Mr. Morris. Would you like to come back to the office, and we can discuss your concerns?" I wanted to get this ungrateful *klootzak* alone so I could tell him where to put his concerns. The waiting room was full of patients staring up at me, and Mrs. Morris looked mortified sitting in her chair, like she would disappear into the wall behind her if she could have. It was extremely difficult, but I knew I had to keep my composure.

"No. I don't wanna be alone with you. I know how you people are. I don't swing that way, and it's unprofessional of you to try to coerce me. It's disgustin'."

Oh. So, this was not about Lucky at all. I sighed, accepting the intolerance. It was nothing new to me. I hadn't been blatantly conspicuous, but I also hadn't been shy about my "lifestyle choices" since moving to Wisper. It just wasn't in me to hide.

Mrs. Morris pleaded under her breath, "Doug, *please*."

"Shut up, Fran. I'm callin' Doc P." He pulled his phone from his back pocket, holding it up to make a show in front of everyone, but Yola walked out from behind the counter and stood in front of him with her hands on her hips.

"I'm only gonna say this one time. Quit actin' like a moron, Dougie Morris, or I'll call your poor ol' mama. Now, you can see Doc V, or you can take your puppy and go elsewhere, but Doc P is not gonna drive all the way here for a five-minute exam just 'cause you have a hair up your butt. What's it gonna be?"

"You can't tell me what to do, Yolanda. I won't be pushed around and forced to deal with"—Mr. Morris hesitated, looking at me with clear disgust in his eyes—"his *kind*."

"His kind? Do you mean a Dutchman, or do you mean a very well-trained veterinarian who has only ever treated you with kindness and respect, even after your dog was hit by a truck because *you* weren't smart enough to keep him on a leash?" she said, looking down her nose at Mr. Morris even though he was taller than her. "Did you know Doc V left a very important family gatherin' to come here and help you that night? After a funeral? And this is how you treat him? I don't think so.

"Now, you can leave the puppy with Frannie to be treated, or you can take your business elsewhere, but either way, *Dougie*"—she squared her shoulders, staring him right in the eye—"I'm gonna have to insist you leave. You're disruptin' all the rest of these nice people's vet care, and you're wastin' their time, and mine, and Doc V's. So again, what's it gonna be?"

All eyes were on Mr. Morris and Yola, and there wasn't a person in the building who couldn't hear them. Carolina was probably dying to come out to see what was going on, but she couldn't leave her patient.

"You're gonna regret talkin' to me like this, Yolanda Perez. Fran, move it." He huffed out an indignant laugh. "What would Manny say about how you're actin'? Maybe I'll call him too."

"Ha! As soon as I tell him how you're actin', he'll say, 'You go, girl.' Now, take a hike."

Mr. Morris yanked his wife up by her arm and dragged his puppy by the leash. The poor dog was nervous, so he splayed his legs, and Mr. Morris pulled him through the clinic door like a sled on snow. He yelped when he was dragged over the threshold, then the door slammed shut and they were gone.

"Does anyone else around here have a problem with Doc V bein' a young and very good-lookin' *Dutch* guy?" Everyone shook their heads, and Yola nodded and stomped off behind the counter, probably to call Dr. Prittchard to warn him about the phone calls he would likely be receiving.

"Thank you, Yola. You're my knight in shining scrubs," I sang after her.

"Love ya, mean it," she called back.

"Okay, Mrs. Cahill, you and your adorable shih tzu, Bunco, are next." I bowed and swung my arm like a game-show hostess, pouring on my charm to disarm the tension in the waiting room and to show her the way to the exam room. She batted her eyelashes and smiled, holding Bunco out to me, and he licked my chin as I lifted him from her arms.

"I don't care what *country* you come from, honey, as long as I get to look atcha."

"Mrs. Cahill, you feisty minx. What's going on with Bunco? Is he still trying to eat *je ondergoed*—em, undergarments?"

Twenty-Two
Kevin

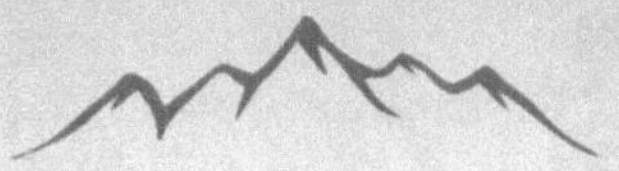

"He looks weird. What's wrong with him?" Isaac asked with his face all scrunched up when Dean walked down the hill to the barn.

"Isaac, mind your business. Jesus, kid, it's only seven in the mornin', and you're annoyin' me already. Save some for later, will ya?" I chugged the last of the coffee in my thermos, tryin' to arm myself for the day with the rugrat. "Remind me again, why you here so early on a Thursday?"

"Teacher workdays before the end of the school year today and tomorrow, and I get to spend 'em both with you." He mock-swooned, battin' his stupid eyelashes at me, then stood straight and rolled his eyes. "I'd rather be in a two-day-long STI-focused health class."

"Yeah, well, I'm *super* excited about it." I rolled my own eyes. "Now shut up and go finish waterin' the indoor stalls."

"Whatever. You know you love our daily chats," Isaac smarted, flippin' me off as he stalked toward the arena. Kid was a menace.

"Sounds like you and the kid are gettin' on like BFFs," Dean said, chucklin'.

"Oh yeah, you know me. I just love makin' friends. He's

right though. You do look weird. Somethin' wrong with the muscles in your face?" I cocked my head to one side, eyein' my brother. "Oh, that's just you smilin'. Got gas?" Clearly, he'd been properly laid this mornin'.

"Funny. But no, just plain happiness. Oly and I have our first doctor appointment today, and I'm excited about it, so bite me."

"Oh, right. Cool."

"You look like shit. What's goin' on with you?"

"Nothin'," I said, and I turned away, grabbin' a bale of hay from a wooden delivery pallet and tossin' it toward the barn.

It wasn't true. Everything was wrong. Everything felt wrong. Everything hurt.

"Still up for helpin' at the spay and neuter clinic Saturday?" Dean asked. "Oly mentioned somethin' about photos. There's supposed to be some people bringin' adoptable dogs in from a shelter. Luuk arranged it—"

"I said I would."

"Good. I think they're wantin' to post your pics online to try to drum up some homes for the mutts."

"Yup." I tossed another hay bale, and sweat dripped down between my shoulder blades.

"Okay, well, I'm headin' in for coffee. Want some?"

"No."

He spun on his heel to head up to the house, but I stopped him. I didn't turn though. "Dean?" I peeked over to the paddock where Jack and Finn were already working. What I wanted to say would be hard enough. I couldn't handle a whole family discussion on the subject of my sexuality. It seemed everyone had an inklin', but I hadn't said the words out loud.

I thought if I could say it to one of my brothers, just one, maybe… And there was all the shit with my mama. I didn't know what to do with it all. I needed to tell someone.

"Yeah?"

"Can I ask you somethin'?"

"Yeah." He stared at me, waitin' on me to say somethin', anything, but I didn't have a clue how to start. But I needed to get it outta me. I needed to be free from it. If I didn't, I couldn't have Luuk. And I wanted him.

I loved him.

And he deserved someone with courage.

"When, um, when Mama left, why did, back then, why do you think she did that? I mean, what'd you think was the reason?" I cleared my throat, bitin' the inside of my lip. Hard. I glanced at my brother, and he looked at me with confusion all over his face.

"Uh, I dunno. I guess I just thought she was selfish."

"Oh. Yeah. Right."

He walked over and sat on a bale of hay five feet from me.

"Why?"

"No reason." I shook my head.

"Kev."

Droppin' the bale in my hands, I wrung 'em together. I took a deep breath and turned toward him. I couldn't hide the look on my face. I was so nervous, I thought I might throw up. But more than that, I was so fuckin' sad. I was overwhelmed and vulnerable to the point of bein' busted and cracked in half, and I needed him to understand me.

"What did you think?" he asked.

"It's not— It don't matter." God. Why was it so hard? I wasn't ashamed of how I felt. Not anymore. But I didn't wanna lose my brothers. I didn't want 'em to look at me different. Pullin' my gloves off, I tossed 'em to the ground, and my eyes followed and stayed down on my boots for a minute. *Dammit. No. Just say it. Don't be a such a coward.* "I guess I thought, maybe I thought it was my fault," I finally admitted.

He didn't say anything right away. It took him a minute, but I waited. Could he understand? I'd held it in for so long that it just felt true, but when I said it out loud to Dean and the other night to my mama, it sounded ridiculous.

"I guess I used to think it was my fault, too, or I thought I coulda done more to stop her leavin'. But it wasn't your fault. It wasn't anybody's fault but hers. She *chose* to go."

"Maybe."

"Kev, what's goin' on inside your head? What could ever make you think she left because of you? C'mon, be honest. It's just you and me here."

I scoffed a laugh. "C'mon, Dean. I was different." I peeked over to the paddock again and to the arena. Nobody could hear us. They couldn't see me. "I thought she left 'cause she knew there was somethin' wrong with me. She was always so frustrated with me. I was a pain in the ass. I was loud and needy and… *different*… than the rest of you."

"Kev. It wouldn't have mattered if you'd been a goddamn alien. She's our mother. She was supposed to be here. She was supposed to take care of us and love us no matter what. She didn't. That's on her, not you."

"Yeah. I guess I know that now. But all this time, I thought… I thought I'd ruined everything. The way Dad was, how unhappy he was, all the problems we had with the ranch —I thought I'd caused it."

He blinked, shakin' his head. "I didn't know you felt that way." He stood, walkin' cautiously toward me, like I was the caged lion again. Like I'd swipe and maul him if he startled me. "I shoulda known. I'm sorry." Placin' his hand on my shoulder so slowly, it almost looked like he was movin' in slow-motion, but I stepped away from him, and he backed up a step, givin' me space. I hadn't said it yet, and if he touched me, I might lose my nerve.

"I went to see her the other night."

"You did? Why?"

"It ain't important, but I wanted answers. I was pissed off, and I wanted her to tell me why she left. I've been so fucked up over Ma. I blamed Mama for everything, and I needed her to tell me why."

"And did she?" he asked, the corners of his mouth turnin' down, and his face morphed into this doubt-colored mask. He didn't know.

"Did you know she lost a baby? After me but before Jay?"

His head snapped back like I'd decked him. "What?"

"Yeah. A little girl. Fiona."

"Fiona?" He closed his eyes, tiltin' his head to the side. "No, I— That name is familiar, but no. I didn't know that."

"She said she went into labor in the field over there"—I nodded to the field behind him—"by herself. The baby came early, and she wasn't breathin'. She died in Mama's arms. Right there." I pointed out past the front paddock to the northwest field, the same field we rode through every day.

He shivered.

"She said that's part of the reason she left. She couldn't deal with it. She said she tried, but Dad—well, you can imagine how Dad woulda dealt with it. She said he basically told her to get over it. But she couldn't. I think she was real depressed. I think she wanted to kill herself sometimes."

"Jesus."

"Yeah. But Dean"—I tried to swallow, but my mouth felt like it was filled with sand—"I-I know what that feels like." Forcin' the sand down my throat, I looked into his eyes. "I don't feel that way now, but there was a time when I was younger— I thought there was somethin' wrong with me. I thought what I wanted was wrong. *Who* I wanted. You understand?" I closed my eyes.

"Yeah," he whispered and took a deep breath, "I think I understand. You're sayin' you struggled with how you felt 'cause you… because you're gay?"

"Yes." I exhaled. It was loud and desperate, and I opened my eyes. "I'm gay."

"Kev. Brother," he said, shakin' his head, "there ain't

nothin' wrong with that. And I know you said Mama told you it wasn't true, but I wanna make sure you hear me. Her leavin' had nothin' to do with you. It was not your fault."

"Yeah, I know."

He put both of his hands on my shoulders, and this time, I didn't pull away.

"No, I need to know you *hear* what I'm sayin'."

"I heard ya." My heart beat so fast and my hands shook.

"Kev, your family loves you. *I* love you. There's nothin' you can say to make it not true." He pulled me against him, wrappin' his arms around me tight. "Nothin'."

Silently, I cried. I tried to hold it back, but I just couldn't. My whole body was racked with sobs, and after a minute, he was the only thing holdin' me up off the ground. He lowered us down to the dirt, and we sat there, stuck together while I cried out all the pain and shame I'd felt over the last twenty years.

I had no clue how long we stayed like that, but I cried till there wasn't nothin' in me left to leak. I'd figured things would change after I told him, but I thought it woulda been him who felt different.

But it was me.

I felt raw and exposed, but somehow, it felt good.

"Kev, Jack and Finn are headed over here. You okay to talk to 'em?" he asked, and I sniffled and pulled away. He cleared his throat nervously, but he didn't look away. He didn't get weird.

"I'm okay." I gulped down a few breaths, and we got up off the ground. "Dean?" I wiped my face clear of tears with the back of my hand real quick. Yeah, I was open—out—but I wasn't about to put on a show for the whole fuckin' world.

"Yeah, brother?"

"Thanks."

He ruffled my hair, tryin' to lighten the mood a little. "You're still a smartass, but I love ya."

"Fuck you. But… guess I love you too."

"Here ya go." Jack threw me his truck keys. "She's all yours."

"Huh?"

"Look outside."

Walkin' over to the kitchen door, I looked outside, and there, sittin' in our drive, sat a gigantic shinin' red Ford F350 Super Duty Pickup Truck. It faced west so I could see the passenger side, and it had a big ol' sign painted on it that said, "Cade Ranch Quarter Horses, Best in the West" with the same logo we had at the entrance to the property on the big iron arch.

"Holy shit, brother! That's a *fine* piece a' ass. Where'd it come from?"

"My wife bought it for me for my birthday. The dealership over in Jackson just delivered it."

Whippin' around, my eyebrows were probably poppin' off the top of my head, and he had the dorkiest, biggest, cheesiest smile on his face.

I snorted. "That's some birthday present. Ooo, can I drive it to the spay and neuter clinic?"

"No fuckin' way. That's why I gave you my keys. The rusty red beast is yours, Finn's, and Jay's. Fight amongst yourselves, or better yet, get that old junker out behind the arena runnin' and you got your own."

"Yeah, been thinkin' about that. Be nice to have my own wheels again. Oh, that reminds me, the truck I gave Phil is dead again. I been meanin' to get over to fix it up. Wanna help me? You're better with engines."

"Sure. We can run out there tomorrow. Evvie and Finn are gonna be rehearsin' for their benefit show. She doesn't want me listenin' while they practice. She's nervous, I think."

"Sounds good. Damn, that is a *nice* truck. Let's go see!"

We ran outside and climbed aboard the USS Jack Is A Lucky Motherfucker and took it for a spin around the ranch and out onto Route 20. Jack was like a kid in a candy store, laughin' and speedin' and revvin' the engine. Although all the tech new trucks came with nowadays annoyed the crap outta him, I figured Jay and Finn could teach him and get him drivin' hands-free in no time flat.

After we tested the four-by-four action on the new truck and muddied it up pretty good, Jack drove us home and got to work in the office, and I grabbed my camera gear and headed to the clinic. I parked my inherited red beast on the side of the road half a mile away 'cause there were a shit-ton of cars, and I couldn't get any closer. I flung my camera pack over my shoulder and hiked down the road the rest of the way.

I was really nervous to see Luuk. I wanted to see him—I was *desperate* to see him. I'd come to a decision after talkin' to my brothers. I hadn't talked much about me, but I told Jack and Finn I was gay. I just said it. "I'm gay." Finn snorted and said, "What took you so fuckin' long?" and Jack nodded and hugged me. I couldn't remember the last time that had happened, and it felt good.

Jay was outta town, in Seattle at some business shindig thingamajig, but I figured he knew already anyway. He'd probably guessed it years ago, but he loved me and never said a word. He let me come to it on my own.

I also told my brothers about our mama and what she'd told me. Talkin' to her had changed somethin' for me, and I wanted to tell Luuk about it. Which led me back to bein' nervous again 'cause, yeah, I was a verified fuckin' prodigy at talkin' about my feelin's.

But I'd come to the point of no return. I had to tell him how I felt. I needed to 'cause he was too important for me not to. If I didn't, I'd lose him.

Maybe I already had, but I had to try.

When I came upon the clinic, I was stupefied. Luuk had organized a small festival. There were little fenced pens all over the place filled with dogs, some with puppies, and screened-in ones with cats—all adoptable. A pettin' zoo took up half the parkin' lot with a llama, mini horse, some goats, rabbits, and a bunch of chickens and ducks runnin' around. I'd known Dean would be bringin' Sammy, but I hadn't had any idea just how big this thing would be.

Several open tents covered a makeshift operatin' room where Oly, Doc P, and Luuk had set up and were workin'. It looked kinda like a small assembly line, with Isaac leadin' the charge as head annoyin' volunteer. He directed all the rest of the high school kids preppin' animals for surgery and pettin' and snugglin' with 'em after they'd woken up from anesthesia. Amy Cline and Joe Jenkins supervised the kids, but they helped with the animals too. And Yola was the general, even bossin' the docs around.

There was a taco truck from Jackson, a smoothie truck, and some kinda fried veggie truck, too, like at the county fair. Luuk had even hired some arty teenagers to paint little kids' faces.

And bein' the brilliant and gorgeous guy he was, he had managed to secure some corporate sponsorship from a big online pet food retailer. There were big colorful banners everywhere and two booths at either end of the parkin' lot with free pet food, pet clothes, and toys, and the docs and all the volunteers wore blue T-shirts with the company's logo on 'em. On the back they said: All Animals, Wisper, Wyoming, Spay & Neuter or Get Bucked.

Luuk looked damn sexy in his fitted T-shirt and ass-huggin' jeans, and I was so damn proud of him for puttin' it all together. He would help so many people and animals. He looked like he was havin' a ball as he laughed and danced, shakin' his ass to music a little while he wiped down his fold-up operatin' table. He talked with Isaac, Isaac's sister, Jules, and Dean while they stood off to the side of the tent, watchin' the docs work.

Pullin' out my camera, I snapped photos as I sneaked closer. I knew I was supposed to be takin' pics of the animals, but I felt like I'd seen Luuk in *his* natural habitat, and I was mesmerized by him. I hid behind an SUV and stalked him for a while, just watchin' him move and work.

I'd never felt pride before like I did for him, seein' what he'd done, and I'd never, *ever* wanted to walk up to a man and kiss him in plain view of the whole wide world.

But I did now.

I was so in love with him.

My feet started walkin' toward him before I'd given my permission, but I stopped 'em. I'd hurt him the last time we talked, and if I waltzed up to him now and took him in my arms like I wanted to, I was likely to get knocked out by a stiff punch to my stupid fuckin' mouth.

"He likes you, too, you know."

Whippin' my head to the side, I found Isaac standin' next to me, peerin' out to see what I'd been starin' at. I didn't say anything. I was startled and stunned by the kid. I'd been so dazed by Luuk, I hadn't even seen Isaac comin'.

"What? It's so obvious. It's pretty painful to watch, actually. You love him. He loves you. Get over yourselves and do somethin' about it. It's the freakin' twenty-first century."

I raised my eyebrows at him.

"Yeah, I know there's a lotta hillbillies around here who probably don't agree, but who gives a shit? There's a ton of kids who support you here in Wisper. Half our school is on one end or the other of the LGBTQIA+ spectrum. Queer is cool now. I think I might be Questioning myself, especially after spendin' time with your brother. I totally get why everyone is so into Finn," he said and laughed. "But seriously, I'm an Ally."

"I don't have any clue what you're sayin'."

"I think *you* might need the Sex-Ed class. Look, it just means that if you love Doc V, that's okay. You have the right to love and screw whoever you want."

"Jesus, Isaac."

"What? Dude, I spend a great deal of time online. You think I don't know about sex? I may not have had any in real life yet, but gimme time. The girls around here don't get me, and I'm a late bloomer."

"Yeah? Well, if you don't get out from behind your computer sometimes, you're never gonna bloom. You need sunlight to grow, kid."

"Yeah, yeah, well, I'm sure after the millions of hours of slave labor you're makin' me work, I'll look just as good as you. Actually, I'm countin' on it. I'm tryin' to get a sponsor for the game I play. My dad doesn't believe me, but I can make a ton of money playin' that game and postin' videos of it. If I'm sexy and buff, I'll make more money."

"Aww, Isaac, you think I'm sexy?" I rolled my eyes.

"Well, your ass is pretty nonexistent, but your arms are dope. It's your face that messes it all up." He flashed me a shit-eatin' grin. "Seriously, boss, go for it. How often does happiness come around? You should grab it while you can. I gotta get back to my post, but I expect to see you over there soon, sexin' up the good doctor."

He jogged back to the surgery tents, and I stood there, watchin' for a few minutes longer. Isaac gave me a headache most of the time, but I imagined talkin' to him was a lot like how other people felt talkin' to me. He could be sarcastic as shit and pretty funny, if I was honest about it. I decided I liked Isaac, and admittedly, I kinda enjoyed havin' my own little smartass protégé. At the very least, I bet I could get some good material outta him to use on my brothers.

As much as I wanted to, I decided not to talk to Luuk right away. He looked pretty busy, and I still needed to shoot some film of all the animals available for adoption. I made my way to one of the little pens and got started, roundin' up some kids to play with the dogs, and then pulled 'em out, one by one, to get 'em calmed down and lookin' a little more photogenic. The puppies were cute and all, but I figured they'd be adopted pretty quick, so I focused mostly on the older shelter dogs.

Busy was my favorite, an Irish wolfhound mix, four years old and so docile. I thought about takin' her home myself, but I remembered Luuk wanted to find a dog for Phil. So I filled out the paperwork and left her with the shelter people while I finished takin' my pics.

The clinic wound down, and as people left and the staff packed and cleaned up, one of the dogs, a pit bull mix I'd mistaken for aggressive, broke outta his pen and took off runnin' toward Sammy. Yellin' over the crowd for Dean to intercept him, I thought he would attack the horse, but he didn't. He raced over and stood in front of Sammy, defendin' him and growlin' at some snotty kid chuckin' rocks from behind the clinic.

"Would you look at that," Doc P said. "He's protectin' that damn horse. I thought he was gonna rip Sammy to shreds."

I walked up behind the asshole kid, grabbin' hold of the neck of his shirt, and dragged him around the front of the clinic to find his parents. I didn't even need to look for his mama. She was already stormin' up to us.

"Dammit, Travis, what'd you do now?"

"Nothin'!"

Laughin' under my breath, I released the kid, and when I turned around to head back to get the dog, I ran right into Luuk. He steadied me with his hands on my arms, then took a big step backward, cuttin' off the contact I needed like air.

"I think that pit bull is Sammy's soulmate," he said in a quiet voice. "Maybe you should adopt him." He glanced over his shoulder, and we saw the dog sittin' at Sammy's feet, lookin' up as Sammy nudged the dog's back end with his nose. "I think his name is Tony Stark."

"Like the movie?"

"Probably. I thought he was mean, but it seems he's only really protective. There's another dog over there I hoped might be good for Phil. I thought, if no one adopted her by the end of the day, I would, and I would take her to Phil."

I smiled. I just knew he was gonna say Busy's name. "Oh yeah? What's her name?"

"Busy. She's a wolfhound mix, I think. She's ugly and scruffy as hell, but she's a lover."

Frownin', I tsked my tongue. "Oh, that's too bad. She's already been adopted."

"Oh. Really? *Verdomme, dat is waardeloos.*" He sighed. "She was perfect for Phil."

I took a leisurely breath, sighin' as I said, "Yeah, some asshole cowboy adopted her. Said he wanted to give her to a sweet ol' lady who bakes him cheese pies." I smiled. I wanted to grab him and suck his face!

"We chose the same dog?" he asked, smirkin' at me and lightin' his eyes on fire, but then he dropped his head, lookin' down at his runnin' sneakers.

"Sure did. I'm gonna take her out to Phil's tomorrow so I can fix her truck. It broke down again. I'm takin' him too"—I nodded over to the pit bull Dean was now carryin' back over to the pen like a baby—"for the ranch. Hopefully, he'll be as protective of all our horses as he was of Sammy. He can help scare off wolves and cougars and shit." I waited for him to look up at me again, but instead, he looked out over my shoulder. He wouldn't meet my eyes.

The whoop-whoopin' of a siren interrupted us, and I looked to my left. Carey was slowly makin' his way through the traffic around the clinic in his cruiser. He rolled down his window, hollerin' my name.

"Kev! I need you and Dean. I already called Jack. He and

Finn are meetin' us out at Cal Johnson's farm. We got some bear huntin' to do. Doc, I need you too. I'm hopin' we can dart the sucker, and I need someone with knowledge of sedatives."

"*Ja,* I'll meet you there," Luuk called back. "KC, my truck is behind the clinic."

"Yep, lemme just tell Dean."

I found Dean playin' with the pit bull, scratchin' his belly while he flopped on the ground, rollin' around like a goofball. I relayed Carey's message, and he said he'd meet us out at the Johnson's farm just as soon as he finished loadin' Sammy into the trailer. After explainin' the situation, the shelter lady said I could pick up my newly adopted dogs later, and she gave me her cell number, then Luuk and I set off. Boy, did I not have any fuckin' clue how the rest of my day would go.

We were quiet while we drove to the Johnson farm. There was so much I wanted to tell him, but it wasn't the right time. Also, I was *really* nervous. I didn't know exactly what I wanted to say, and I didn't know how to start talkin'.

But he beat me to it. "Did you get good photographs today?"

"Um, yeah, I think so. I had some of the little kids walk the dogs and play with 'em, and I think they were havin' a good time. I swear some of those dogs were actually smilin' at me."

"*Ja,* I watched you for a little while. This was a good idea, to have the children help."

"You were spyin' on me?" I grinned at him, but he turned away, lookin' back at the road as he drove. "Luuk, I wanted to talk to you—"

"Listen, KC," he interrupted, "I need to say… I'm going to leave Wisper."

"What?" My heart pounded in my ears. "But you're comin' back, right? You'll come back?"

"Em, no, I think not." The sound of his voice, his words—he was politely detached.

"Luuk, wait, before you say anything else, I need to tell you some—"

He slammed on the brakes, throwin' us both forward, and I caught myself from goin' through the windshield with my hands on the dashboard. "Shit!"

"We found the bear. He just ran in front of us." Yankin' the steerin' wheel, he parked his truck on the side of the road and jumped out, runnin' around to the back to rummage through his supplies.

"Shit. I don't have a gun."

"Here." He handed me a long dart rifle from the bed of his truck and loaded a huge needle with some kinda liquid. "Get the other dart gun. It's on the floor in the back seat. And call the sheriff with our location. That bear looked starved. It's probably why he's been a nuisance."

We took off on foot after the bear, and I thought to myself, here I go again. The stupid fuckin' situations I found myself in. But Luuk was calm and measured. Carey and Dean were trackin' in from the east, Luuk and I from the west, and Jack and Finn were posted at the Johnson Farm just in case.

"Where you gonna go?" I asked while we hiked through the woods, searchin' for the bear. We'd been walkin' in silence for probably twenty minutes, and I was five feet or so behind him, tryin' to see his face when he answered my question.

"Hm? Oh, I… I don't know yet. I cannot leave right away, at least not until I find someone to help Carolina. Dr. Prittchard is almost ready to come back to work full-time, or I should say, Lucinda is ready to release him full-time."

"Yeah, she's a battle-ax, for sure."

"I don't know what this means."

"I just meant she's a tough ol' lady. She runs the show at the Prittchard household."

He laughed but it was half-hearted. "*Ja.* She and Yola should rule the world."

"You got that right. There would be no hunger, no injustice, no bullyin', and no war. They'd put their collective foot down, and that'd be that… But, Luuk, *why* are you leavin'?"

"I, em, it's just… time for me to go. This was never meaning to be—*een vaste baan*—a permanent job. Wisper isn't my home," he lied, tryin' to avoid the him-and-me of it all. I could tell 'cause he messed up his words and hesitated a lot before speakin'.

"It could be."

"Could be what?"

"Wisper could be your home. This could be permanent."

He stopped walkin' but didn't turn to look at me. Sighin', he said, "KC. This is not— Please. Please don't make this harder for me. I know this thing between us is different for you than it is for me but…"

Walkin' forward, settin' the butt of the dart gun on the ground at my feet, I wrapped my arms around his chest from behind. I held on as tight as I could, and I braced myself against him, drawin' courage and strength from his body.

"I love you." All the breath rushed outta my body, and I was scared shitless of what he might say, but it felt so right to tell him I loved him. I felt relieved to tell him. But he didn't say a word. "I said some awful things last time we were together, and I'm so sorry, but I don't want you to go. I'm in love with you."

"Kevin," he whispered my name, hangin' his head, and his heart pounded in his chest. I felt it thumpin' away against my forearm.

"Hey." Liftin' my hand, I pushed on his jaw so he'd turn his head toward me, so I could see his eyes, but he didn't open 'em. "Luuk, please, will you look at me?" Finally, he did, but there was so much doubt. "I know what I want. It's what I've always wanted. I was just too scared and fucked up to admit to it. I'm sorry it took me so long. I know I messed this up, but I *love* you. Please, don't go." I kissed him, and he relaxed his body back against mine.

I knew it was an unbelievably bad time to be declarin' my love and feelin' him up, but I needed it. I couldn't even imagine him leavin' me and never lookin' back. It felt like someone was shovin' shards of glass through my gut when I tried to picture it in my mind.

He exhaled hard when I pushed my tongue inside his mouth, pressin' my lower body against his. I was desperate for him to know how much I wanted him.

But then I heard some twigs snappin' and a vaguely familiar voice.

"Well, well, well, what on God's green earth do we have here?"

Twenty-Three

Luuk

The thick twang of Mr. Morris' voice ripped through the air as KC held onto me, kissing me and proclaiming his love for me. If that wasn't a reason to leave Wyoming, I wasn't sure what would be. With people like this lurking around Wisper, Kevin would never come out. Although, maybe he was out now, whether he liked it or not.

Mr. Morris and two unfamiliar men armed with shotguns and dressed in dirty camouflage clothing walked into the small forest clearing we stood in. They stopped several meters away from us, looking like they were enjoying what they saw, but in a disturbed way.

"Never thought I'd find *you* with your tongue down a man's throat, Cade. That's… interestin'. I find myself wonderin' what your ol' man would say about it." Mr. Morris' eyes roamed all over my body, watching KC's movements closely.

"Well, he's dead, *Dougie*, so I guess it don't much matter, now does it?" KC's arm around my chest tightened, and his other hand landed low on my back, like he was preparing to pull me away from the moronic men, like he thought he needed to protect me.

"I reckon not. But what about your brothers? They know you're a fag?"

"They sure do, just like they know you're an insufferable moron. They been hip to that shit for years."

What? KC had come out to his brothers? Or maybe he was just saying that. I was so confused. And terrified. I had never been in such a situation, surrounded by overtly intolerant people armed with guns.

"You're still *so* funny. You know, I knew there was somethin' unnatural goin' on with you and him that night he killed my dog. I saw it in your eyes. The way you looked at him and talked to him, touched him." He shivered visibly, unable take his eyes off my body. "And then my wife—you remember her, don'tcha? She forgot her purse on the counter in the waitin' room, stupid fuckin' woman, so I came back in to get it. I saw you two wrapped around each other like a couple of fuckin' fairies. I nearly threw up." He nudged his friend in the ribs, and all three men laughed.

I tensed. "Mr. Morris—"

"No. *You* shut the fuck up. You killed my dog in front of my poor daughter. You don't get to talk to me."

"I'm so glad your powers of observation haven't waned with the rest of your intelligence, Dougie," KC drawled. "You know, I do remember your wife. Doc V and I may be a couple of fairies, but you oughta take notes. Don't forget, your wife seemed to like bein' screwed by one. It's been a while, but I bet she remembers it fondly. I recall her likin' it many times, actually, and loudly."

Oh shit. Kevin! Nondeju. Did he want to be shot? Again?

"What the fuck did you just say to me?"

Behind Mr. Morris and his charming friends stood a large grouping of tall bushes and young trees, and they shivered and shook. The bear we'd been looking for poked his nose around one of the bushes, sniffing the air in our direction. He made no sound but began his wobbly approach. Less than half a kilometer separated him from Mr. Morris, and I knew I only had a few seconds to act. If the bear decided to really run, maybe less.

My dart gun was still in my left hand, the butt resting on the ground, and my grip tightened around it. I knew KC had seen the bear. He breathed "shit" in my ear as I lifted the gun at the same time Mr. Morris took the first few steps toward us, most likely to punch KC's smart mouth.

Morris stopped. "What the fuck do you think you're doin?"

"Mr. Morris, do not move."

"Fuck you. You think you can threaten *me*?" His buddies must have heard the bear loping toward them because they both turned their heads, looking behind him at the same time, and they froze, neither one remembering the gun hanging off his shoulder.

"Doug—"

"Shut up, Vern."

"Don't. Fucking. Move," I said, and I quickly lifted my gun, aiming it at the bear's flank as he shuffled to the side. He was skin and bones and clearly unwell. Unfortunately, to get the shot, I would need to aim right past Morris' torso. But if I didn't, Mr. Morris might have become Mr. Bear Food.

"Put that gun down, asshole. You probably can't shoot right anyway. Limp wrists make for bad aim." He laughed, and I fired.

Several things happened at once. Mr. Morris' buddy pushed him out of the line of my sedating fire, and he tripped over his own legs and fell to the ground, landing on his back. My dart hit the bear where I intended, but he was not happy about being shot, and he charged. He must have been very, very ill—there was not a healthy animal alive who wouldn't perceive a shot to the ass as a threat and run.

KC yanked me behind him and raised the other dart gun I'd given him, firing at the bear and hitting him right in the middle of his chest. The bear let out a deafening roar, which fast became a wheezing groan as the second dart dispensed the sedative so close to his heart, and he collapsed, sliding forward in the dirt, landing face to face with Mr. Morris.

But the bear still moved. He raised his front paw, four-inch claws extended toward Morris, and Morris pissed his pants as KC planted his feet in front of me, like he would fight the bear if he didn't go down. But he did. The bear's arm fell, his paw landing on the middle of Morris' abdomen, and then the *klootzak*, Doug Morris, lost consciousness.

One of his friends vomited beside the bear and fell down onto his ass in the dirt. The other man kicked the bear a few times to make sure it was out and laughed.

"*Godverdomme!*" I dropped my dart gun and fell forward, holding myself up with my hands on my knees, my whole body shaking after the release of so much adrenaline.

"You okay, Doc?" KC turned and clapped his hand on my shoulder, massaging it with his thumb. I stood and took a deep breath, trying to regain composure and staring at him in complete and utter disbelief. My eyes must have been as big as baseballs, and he chuckled. He slid his hand to the back of my neck and pulled me toward him, kissing the edge of my mouth, making my lip tingle. "Good shot, Alvie," he whispered.

"Wake up, idiot." Mr. Morris' unconcerned friend tried to rouse him, and finally, after a few nudges from the man's boot, Morris woke and sat up, looking a little crazed as he pushed the humungous bear paw off of his stomach.

"C'mon, let's head back to the truck. I'm not gettin' a good signal out here, and we need to call the guys. 'Sides, I'm pretty sure Dougie wants to kill me after that comment about his wife. I never actually had sex with her, but he don't know that." He nodded in Mr. Morris' direction, wrapping his arm around my waist and dragging me along beside him.

"You shoulda seen ol' Dougie Morris." KC handed me a beer, sitting next to me at his kitchen table. "He pissed his pants!" He slapped the table and laughed so hard, he snorted.

Finn laughed too. "That guy's always been a douchebag. Sounds like he got what he deserved today."

"Yeah, he was in rare form, no joke. What was he doin' out there anyway?"

"Cal Johnson called him before he called me," Sheriff Carey said. "Doug's mama still lives next door to the Johnsons." He took a beer from the refrigerator, too, and sat on the other side of me. "So, Doc, whatcha think's wrong with the bear? He didn't look very good."

"Yes, I think he's starving. I don't know why, parasites maybe, or just habitat destruction. My guess is that he's been in town looking for food, and he's become immune to humans. I'm glad we were able to sedate him. I think Mr. Morris would have killed him. Now he can go to a sanctuary and get medical attention. He could not have survived much longer on his own. It was a little too close for comfortable, but it turned out okay."

"Well, I'm just glad no one was hurt," Carolina said with her mouth full of pizza. "I freaked out when Dean told me you were goin' after a rabid bear. I know you guys think you're all so tough, but you never know what can happen. We've got babies to think about."

"Sorry I scared you, duck." Dean leaned over to kiss Carolina's cheek. He flashed her a knowing smile, but it took everyone else a few minutes to catch on.

KC grabbed my hand under the table, and I looked at him when he smiled and squeezed. This felt different. Usually, he spent every minute we were in the same room with other people avoiding me; he wouldn't even look at me. But now he looked. A lot. But he still wouldn't touch me where his brothers could see. So, had he come out, or not?

"Oh, Kevin, Missy from Paws-R-Us told me to tell you to text her," Carolina said. "She took the dogs back with her after the clinic, but she said you can pick 'em up at the shelter."

"What *dogs*?" Jack growled. "Kevin, don't you dare tell me you adopted one."

"Umm, no?" He smiled a big silly grin. "I adopted two."

"Dammit, Kevin!"

"Two dogs?" Evvie asked. "I've never had a dog. What kind are they?"

"Okay, okay, everybody calm down." KC laughed. "One is for Phil. We thought she might like another dog after Boscoe. But there was this pit bull—"

"A pit bull? Are you outta your damn mind?"

"Jack, you shoulda seen him." Dean turned in his chair, raving about Tony. "The dog broke outta his pen and ran across the lot to where some jerk kid was throwin' rocks at Sammy. I hadn't even noticed, and I was ten feet away. He planted himself in front of Sammy and growled at the kid, like he was Sammy's bodyguard. Then he sat down next to the damn horse and made goo-goo eyes at him."

"Yeah," KC said, "and I talked to the shelter lady. She said if Tony don't work out, I can take him back. But I figure, if he helps protect all the horses like he did Sammy, he'll be an asset to us. Give him a chance, brother. I think you'll like him."

"One day, Kevin. I'll give you *one* day."

"Thanks."

"What kinda name is Tony? For a dog?" the sheriff asked.

"His name is Tony Stark," Carolina said. "I think it's cute. You guys got anything else to eat around here? I'm starvin'." She looked a little embarrassed, but she rubbed circles over her stomach. We'd just finished eating five extra-large pizzas between the eight of us. Everyone stared at her. "What? Don't look at me like that. I'm growin' human life. It takes calories."

"Want a veggie quesadilla? I'll make you one."

"Mmm, yeah. Thanks, Finn." She flashed him an innocent grin, and he got up to grab a sauté pan and placed it on the stove.

He bowed with a flourish of his arm. "Your culinary wish is my command."

"Oly, I can't believe I forgot to ask, but when am I gonna be an aunt?" Evvie asked. "How did your appointment go the other day?"

"The appointment went well. The babies are due in December."

"Wait a minute. Did you just say *babies*?"

Carolina smiled so big. "Yep! There's two in there. Jeez. It took you long enough. I've been hintin' all day!"

"Holy shit," KC said, and Carey slapped Dean on the back and shook his hand.

"Oh my God, oh my God, oh my God!" Evvie bounced in Jack's lap.

"The doctor thinks I'm almost fifteen weeks already. Apparently, I've been pretty unobservant, but everything looks good. We even have a picture." Carolina pulled her phone from her back pocket, tapping the screen several times, and reached across the table to hand it to Evvie.

"Oh my God! There are real babies in there. Look, Jack."

Jack laughed. "Yep, I see two lil' peanuts. This one looks like Oly, thank God." Jack winked at Carolina, and Finn whined.

"Lemme see, lemme *see*!" He stood behind Jack and Evvie, trying to see the picture, then swiped the phone from Evvie's hand, and she laughed. "Aww, he looks just like his Uncle Finn."

Carolina scoffed playfully. "You know, guys, they could be girls."

Jack, Finn, and Dean all became quiet, and KC fidgeted in his chair next to me. I knew I had to be missing something. I couldn't imagine they would be disappointed if Carolina gave birth to girls. Finn passed the phone to Sheriff Carey, and he laughed, breaking the uncomfortable silence.

"If this kid looks like you, Finn, it ain't somethin' I'd be braggin' about."

"Hey!"

"Sorry, Oly, but they look like a blob of goo. How can you tell those are babies?" Carey chuckled and passed the phone to me.

Carolina had shown me the picture before the clinic earlier in the day, but *ja*, the babies did look like a blob of goo, but they were Carolina's blob of goo, so I loved them already. KC leaned closer to me to see the picture too.

"Wanna get outta here?" he whispered. "I kinda hoped we could talk."

I felt awkward—perhaps that was the wrong word. I felt hesitant and nervous. Something had obviously changed for KC. He told me right before we were nearly killed by the bear that he loved me—he was *in* love with me—and didn't want me to leave Wisper, and he didn't try to hide or deny our connection when Mr. Morris and his cronies came upon us in the woods. In fact, he held me tighter.

But now, he seemed tentative and reserved, and I was too much of a coward to touch him and push the luck. And I was confused. I had already made the decision to leave, and I feared, if we were alone, I would allow him to convince me to stay with promises of love. A home. A family. I wanted it so much, but it was also my worst fear. To find love—real, soul-gripping, life-affirming, sick-in-my-stomach love—then lose it because he walked away.

Or worse.

I lost everything once. I didn't think I could survive losing it all over again.

But could I survive leaving KC? As stupid as the thought was to me—I was a grown, educated, and rational person—I knew walking away from him would *hurt*. In fact, I worried it might kill me.

Kevin stood, holding his hand out for me, and I raised my eyes, gaping up at him. I must have looked completely surprised because he breathed a laugh and grabbed my hand, pulling me out of my chair.

"'Scuse us. Luuk and I got some talkin' to do."

I glanced around the table. Sheriff Carey looked surprised to see KC holding my hand, and KC's brothers probably were, too, but they tried to look unaffected. Evvie smiled and pressed her lips together.

"Okay. *Pardon*," I said, and Carolina winked at me.

"Kev?" Jack asked.

"Yeah?"

"Got plans tomorrow?"

"Well, yeah, I thought we were goin' over to Phil's to work on her truck?"

"Right, yeah, we'll do that. But I meant for dinner?"

"Nothin' concrete."

"Okay, be here then. Luuk, you're welcome to join us. I was thinkin' of invitin'"—Jack paused, then sighed—"Daisy to dinner, but I wanted to wait for Jay to get back from his conference or whatever the hell he's off doin'. He'll be back in the mornin'. Dean's pickin' him up at the airport."

"Oh. Alright then. I'll be here."

"Good." Jack relaxed back against his chair, and Evvie kissed his cheek as KC pulled me out of the house, the wooden screen door slapping and clattering behind us.

Twenty-Four
Kevin

We drove from the ranch to Luuk's place in complete silence, and when we pulled into his driveway, I tried to start talkin', but he shut me down after I'd only managed to squeak out, "Luuk—"

"I need a drink," he grumbled, climbin' outta his truck and walkin' to the front door without me.

When we were in the house, we stood in his livin' room three feet apart. I stared at him, but he wouldn't look at me. He looked down at the floor, the bottle of Dutch gin danglin' from his right fist by his thigh.

"You're scared," I said.

"I need a shower. That bear incident made me sweat pigs."

"Sweat like a pig."

"*Tuurlijk joh*," he said, rollin' his eyes. That had to be Dutch for "whatever."

Strippin' outta his blue T-shirt, he dropped it to the floor as he walked into the little bathroom, and I stood there motionless, watchin' him go, watchin' the muscles in his arms flex and release as he squeezed and relaxed his fists over and

over. I knew he was strugglin' with me tellin' him I loved
him, and I didn't wanna push him but—

No, dammit.

This was not the time to be polite and careful. This was
not the time to be a coward. If I didn't do somethin', and
quick, he would leave.

And I didn't think I'd survive it.

When the faucet squeaked and I heard the spray of the
water hittin' the shower tiles, I waited a minute to give him
time to get in and get wet so he'd close his eyes, and he
wouldn't see me comin'. I stripped off my own shirt and
kicked my boots toward the front door, pulled my socks off,
and padded to the bathroom.

He'd left the door cracked, so I nudged it open and
stepped into the shower with him, still wearin' my jeans. His
eyes were closed, his head thrown back into the fallin' water,
and it darkened his hair. He was perfection. I'd never seen
anything so beautiful… but he looked sad. He was in pain.

"I heard you come in," he said, his voice a quiet rumble as
he opened his eyes. They tracked down my body and back
up. "What in hell are you doing?"

"I wanna talk to you."

"Kevin, we can have this conversation *out* of the shower."

"No. I wanna have it right now. I'm tired of holdin' back.
Ain't you? Never sayin' what I really wanna say. What I need
to say. I love you, and I know it scares you. It scares the fuck
outta me too. I've never loved anybody like this before. I
never even thought it was a possibility for me till I met you."

His face was blank, but his eyes searched mine. They dug
right into me, and it made my heart beat so fast, but I had so
much more to say. I couldn't lose my nerve now. Touchin' my
fingertips to his brow, I wiped away the water droplets about
to fall into his eyes and slid my hand slowly down his face
and neck and his shoulder to his heart.

I tried to memorize the texture of his skin. In case I never saw him like this again, I didn't wanna forget how he felt against the palm of my hand. He closed his eyes when I splayed my fingers and pressed against him, feelin' for his heartbeat. I found it, and it gave me the courage I needed to say more.

"I know what you're afraid of 'cause I'm afraid of it too. Your parents left you. They didn't mean to, but they did. My mama left me. She did mean to, but I learned recently that maybe she had a reason." He opened his eyes, scrunchin' his eyebrows in confusion, but didn't say anything.

"I'll tell you about it later. The point is, they were supposed to be here, to love us unconditionally. They weren't supposed to leave. My mama leavin' did somethin' to me. It... hurt me in ways I didn't even know. And I think your parents dyin' changed you, did somethin' to you too.

"And now, I'm fuckin' terrified. What if I give all of me to you and *you* leave? What if I show you everything about myself, and you don't like it? There's some good stuff about me, but there's a lot of bad shit too. I can get pretty dark in my thoughts, and I can be a dick. So, what if you stay and then find out that I'm... that it's... too much and you don't wanna deal with it?"

"Kevin—" He pushed his fingers through his hair, combin' it up and away from his face. I wanted my fingers in his hair, too, but I knew I couldn't touch him like that, or I'd pull him to me, to my mouth, and I'd never say what I needed to.

"Please, lemme finish."

He stood so still. The water ran down his body in tiny little rivers, and his eyes—they flickered and burned blue and green, like copper fire. Every muscle strained, like he was workin' hard to lock himself in place, almost like he was angry. Maybe he was. He hid so much emotion inside himself, but he wouldn't let it out. He wouldn't let me see.

I wanted to say the thing that would unleash him.

I wanted to be the man who could bust him open and allow him to be free.

"Where was I? Oh yeah, and what if I'm a terrible gay guy?"

He scoffed, shakin' his head.

"No, I'm serious. I dunno the first thing about bein' gay. Isn't there a whole culture out there? Isaac tells me there's, like, a whole language about it. Some kinda spectrum? I don't fuckin' know. I looked it up, but I'm more confused now than I was before.

"But you been livin' that way of life forever. I've only lived it for a couple days." His eyes snapped to mine, and I smiled a kinda half-smile. "Yeah. I told my brothers. But what if, a few months down the road, you want someone else? Someone who knows what they're doin'? Someone smarter, kinder, more successful, more like you. Someone… better?" I swallowed, and it felt like the sound echoed through the whole bathroom.

My tongue was stuck to the roof of my mouth again. Every thought I had was pourin' outta me, but I was still scared, afraid he didn't feel the same way. My heart was beating so fast, I thought I might have an actual heart attack. I bit down on the inside of my cheek to distract my brain from the pain in my chest.

"If you left— If you leave, I dunno what I'll do, Luuk. I can't even picture you drivin' outta town in your big blue truck. It feels like someone's stabbin' an ice pick into my heart when I think about it. It *hurts*"—guidin' his hand up to my chest, I held it there—"in here." He dug his fingertips into my skin, then flattened his palm above my heart.

"And I think that's what you're feelin' too. You're thinkin' about your parents and how bad it hurt to lose 'em. That's why you're always so formal, so self-contained. Like maybe, if you don't let anyone in, don't let anyone really know you deep inside, then maybe it won't hurt so much when they go.

Or they die. I can't promise that won't happen. I wish I could 'cause I wanna give you everything you want.

"I wanna give you all of me. I wanna be your family, and I want you to be mine. I wanna wake up next to you every mornin' and look at your face as I fall asleep every night. I know I'm askin' a lot. You'll have to be patient with me. I mean, I dunno what I'm doin'. I dunno *how* to love you. I just know I do. Do you want me to touch you? Do you want me to hold your hand or kiss you in front of other people?

"I been afraid of those people knowin' about me my whole life, but I ain't anymore. Well," I said, laughin' a little under my breath, "I'm still terrified, but I wanna kiss you and hold you and love you so everyone can see you're *mine*. I was so proud of you today at the clinic. What you did there, Luuk? You're amazin', and I wanted to wrap you up inside me, right there in the parkin' lot. I don't care what they think, what they say. The only opinion that matters to me anymore is yours.

"So, will you give me a chance? Let me prove to you that I won't push you away again? Will you let me love you? I promise there's more inside me than just smartass comments. I think the good stuff might be really good, and it's all yours… if you still want it. If you still want me. You can have it all."

I'd never spoken so many words in a row in my life—not about how I felt—and I held my breath, waitin' for him to say somethin'.

Anything.

He didn't. He just stood there, still as stone, lookin' at me for, like, two minutes. It felt like a day, and my heart raced faster and faster, but still, he said nothin', and finally, it clicked in my brain.

I was wrong.

I wasn't the guy who could open him up. I wasn't who he wanted. I hung my head, breakin' eye contact, and my breath tumbled and tore outta me. Even the air in my lungs wanted to flee.

In the quietest rumble of a voice, he said, "Get out."

But I didn't believe it. I *knew* he wanted me. I felt it. I knew he loved me, too, but he was fightin' with himself inside.

"Get out of the shower, Kevin." Still so afraid, he still wanted to go. To protect himself, he would leave, and I would be forced to watch. I would be forced to live without him. How could I do that when everything inside me had changed? How could I do that when everything inside me loved everything inside him? How would I get through that?

No.

I wouldn't let him do it. I would not let him run and break us both apart in the process.

I tried to turn to get out of the shower so I could pull him out and make love to him till he knew in every single cell inside his body that I loved him, and I wouldn't hurt him. Not ever again.

I tried to turn, but he pushed me up against the back wall of the shower, crowdin' in behind me.

"Luuk—"

"Shut your smart mouth. Just… *houd je kop*—shut up." He dropped his hands, and I wanted to push back to feel his skin against mine again, but I sensed he didn't want that. Not yet. "I wanted you the first time I saw you," he rasped in my ear. "You knew. Don't pretend you didn't. Do *not* ask me why. You are arrogant and rude, and you push me away. Over and over. Do you think it did not hurt?"

"I'm s—"

"Shut. Up."

Pressin' my lips together to try to stop myself from shovin' my foot in between 'em, I closed my eyes, and he stepped into me, his wet chest against my back and his stone-hard cock against my ass. Draggin' his hands down my arms from my shoulders to the tips of my fingers, he threaded his fingers through mine and yanked my arms up, slammin' my hands on the wall above my head.

His voice was low and quiet and edged with... I didn't know. It was lust and anger and fear all rolled into one sound. "You're right. I'm fucking terrified. You think you're the only one with self-doubt? Fuck you. I doubt myself every single day. I fail all the time. What if I fail at this? What if I fail you? What if people are cruel to you because I... because of me? It will be my fault that you hurt. All you have ever dreaded will happen, and it will be *my* fault. Will you forgive me after this?"

"Luuk—"

"I said shut up. *Voor één keer in je leven. Jezus.*" He pushed hard against me, holdin' me to the wall, and I couldn't move. I didn't want to. It made me so happy that he was gettin' angry and finally showin' it. "And what if you leave? What then? What will I do? Because I want you. I want you so much. *Soms denk ik dat...* Shit." He squeezed my fingers so hard, it hurt. "Sometimes, I think I cannot... that I cannot live without you. I cannot stop thinking about you, wanting you. I have tried!" He pressed his forehead to the back of my neck, strugglin' to catch his breath, and I felt him tremblin'. It felt like the air was vibratin' all around us.

"You think I don't understand? That I don't know this darkness inside you? You think I don't feel it too? Because I don't show it, because I don't walk around treating people like shit as you do, you think I don't feel? Fuck you, Kevin." He whispered in my ear, "Fuck you. *Ik. Voel. Alles.* Everything." Releasin' my fingers, he slid his wet hands down my back and over my ribs, grabbin' my hips hard, clutchin' at the wet loops in the waistband of my jeans to pull me back against him.

"I want to drown in your darkness. I want to *fuck* it. I want to wrap you up inside of me so hard that you cannot even breathe, and I will never let go. What I feel of you— I cannot even describe the things I want to do to you, the *way* I want to… be with you. You have not even met me yet. You have no fucking *idee*."

His chest heaved up and down against my back, and he shoved his nose into my neck, inhalin' and lickin' the skin there, a long, slow lap with his warm tongue. He growled into my skin, and he fuckin' bit me! He bit hard. It hurt, but I'd never been so turned on in my life. Blood pumped through my cock in pulses.

"Go ahead. Introduce yourself then." I remembered when Finn had said somethin' similar to me, and I smiled, thinkin' about the expression on his face if I was ever to tell him just how I used his line. Luuk didn't think it was so profound. He scoffed and reached around to rip my fly open. Crouchin' down behind me, he yanked my heavy soakin' wet jeans down my legs.

He slammed the shower door open, and it hit the wall, crackin' the glass pane, one long, thick chasm diagonally down the middle, but he didn't even acknowledge it. Steppin' one leg outta the shower, he reached across to a wooden box sittin' on the back of the toilet, opened it, tossed the lid to the floor, and when he stepped back in the shower, he grasped a condom and a small tube of lube in his hand.

Standin' behind me again, breathin' hard, he yanked me around to face him and slapped the condom into my hand. "Put it on me."

Rippin' the package open with my teeth and spittin' the paper out, I didn't dare look away from his eyes. I didn't need to. I felt the heat and blood pumpin' through his cock against mine when I rolled the condom on, and I let my hands fall to my sides.

I waited. I was desperate for what was comin'.

Desperate for him to fuck me. To be inside me.

My heart raced to a nearly cataclysmic pace, and I worried for a split second that I might pass out and miss the best thing to ever happen to me, but he pushed me back around to face the wall, and I heard the cap on the lube snap open. I felt him strokin' it onto himself, and he reached between my cheeks, rubbin' it onto me too.

When he touched me there, I grabbed the wall and tensed. I wanted it so goddamn bad, but I was a virgin, so to speak, and *so* nervous. I knew there could be pain. But even through the anxiety, his touch on the most private part of me felt so good.

He whispered, "*Ontspan.*"

Relax. I'd known what he meant by the gentle command of his voice in my ear and the soft way he caressed his thumbs along the small of my back as he held my hips. He lifted my knee with his fingers grippin' my thigh and stepped down on the fabric of my jeans pooled at my feet, freein' my leg and guidin' it up to the ledge of the shower.

His other hand moved up to my shoulder, and he pressed down hard as he pushed a finger inside my ass.

Oh.

My body resisted for a few seconds, but the desire for him to do to me what I'd dreamt of him doin' since the first time I saw him took over. I relaxed, and he slowly pushed in further, groanin' against my neck. It was the sexiest breathless rumble, and he fucked me with his finger for a few minutes while he kissed and bit and scraped his teeth over my shoulder, and slowly, he added another.

I moaned and my head fell forward, smackin' the hard-tiled shower wall as I gave in to the overwhelmin' sensation. I loved it 'cause it meant I had him—he was mine in a way no one had ever been before—and I was his. And I wanted more.

"Do it. Fuck me. I want your body inside mine." I could barely force the words outta my mouth. I was tremblin' so bad and my teeth chattered, and he was desperate to do it, his whole body vibratin' with need. He held back only for my safety, but I knew my body would accept his. There was no fuckin' way it wouldn't. "*Please*, Luuk."

He gasped at my beggin' but pulled his fingers out, spread me open and, so slowly, pushed his cock inside. My body bowed forward, and I grunted and hissed in a breath. He held still for a minute, lettin' me adjust again, grippin' my shoulder so hard—I knew I'd be bruised from his fingers in the mornin'.

I willed my body to relax, and one inch at a time, he pushed in further and slid back. Then he pulled out, coated himself in more lube, and his breath came out in tight huffs when he entered me again, slowly, gently, till he couldn't go any further, and then...

Finally...

I met Luuk van der Wouden.

Oh. Holy. Fuckin'. Christ!

He was unleashed.

It was all I could do to not fall down. He let out an anguished moan, almost a cry, and he bent his knees, fuckin' up into me with so much force and passion and... desperation.

He groaned and grunted and cursed, in Dutch and English. All the while, his hungry hands and fingers clutched and scraped and pulled at my skin. Suckin' in short little gasps of air, his lips kissed and bit and sucked the skin on my neck and my shoulders and arms.

It did hurt a little while his body stretched mine, but I liked the pain, and I was so hard and so ready to come just from hearin' his frantic breath in my ear.

Amazingly, I couldn't be bothered with my own pleasure, though it felt so goddamn good. I remembered bein' alone in my room, imaginin' this, thinkin' about bein' vulnerable with him like this. I knew it would be good, but I had no idea *how* good. It felt like we were on another planet, just him and me.

Nothin' had ever felt so right.

I lifted my arms above my head and reached behind me, grabbin' his hair, pullin' his face back into my neck and pushin' my ass back against him as he reached around with his hand to stroke my dick. I swore, it felt like it only took thirty seconds, and I was comin'.

He growled when he felt my cum all over his hand and whispered my name as he thrust up into me one last time and came. He huffed his release in my ear, and the sound reverberated around us in the shower, piercin' my eardrums, even though it was only a breath.

His legs gave out, and we slid down the shower wall, and I gasped for my own oxygen, my whole body shakin', and I rasped, "Nice to fuckin' meet ya."

Twenty-Five

Luuk

After we— After I fucked him in my shower, I couldn't breathe. The weight and importance of what he'd given me overtook everything, and I was unable to hold myself up any longer. I'd never felt anything like it, the way I felt when we were together, when I was inside him. It was powerful. Overwhelming.

I'd been afraid of hurting him physically before, afraid of frightening him with *my* darkness. But when I was inside him, something inside me clicked into place, and there was only my body and his. My ability to go slow, to be careful—it disappeared. I just fucked. It was primal. Animalistic. Base.

I didn't have to be drunk to do it.

And he took it all. Didn't run away screaming. He didn't fear me.

He liked it. All of it, all of me, even the bad parts I'd spent all my life since my parents died hiding.

He wanted it and he loved me.

And I loved him desperately, more than I had ever thought I could feel for another person, but I hadn't said it back. I wanted to, but my heart hurt every time I thought the words, and I failed. I was still so scared.

Tangled in my legs and arms, he held me on the shower floor and waited for me to recover. Then he pulled me up, and I watched his eyes while he cleansed every inch of my body.

We didn't speak, and he only looked away when he needed to reach for soap or shampoo or when he washed my hair. That had been amazing, his hands and fingers massaging my scalp, combing through my hair. It was intensely private, and I never wanted him to stop.

When he had finished and rinsed the soap away, I was grateful for the water running down my face because it hid the tears falling from my eyes.

Now, KC and I sat cross-legged in the middle of my bed, naked.

"Please explain how you think you will be an unacceptable gay man."

"Wait just a minute. I didn't say unacceptable. I said terrible." KC laughed. "Okay, for example, lemme tell you how much I didn't know I would ever enjoy what you just did to me. Does that make me your bitch?"

"No, it makes you the best lover I have ever had."

He smiled shyly and looked down at the bed, so I leaned in to kiss him. Now that he'd given himself permission to be with me, he didn't hold back. He had so much passion inside him. So much love. He was hard in some ways but soft in others. He was utterly attentive, listening and watching everything I said and did, what my body told him. Somehow, he knew what I needed already.

I wanted to open myself to him, the way he had with me. "You were vulnerable with me. You allowed me to dominate you. Sometimes, I need that but... I have never been able to ask for it, at least not without alcohol. I struggle with needing it. I like how it feels, but... I don't know how to explain. I think maybe I don't deserve to feel good. After my parents died, I thought I had to be perfect. I still think that. I cannot mess up, cannot fail. I have to make them proud. I have to do what they would want me to.

"When they died, I was still so young. I became… lost. I constantly searched for them in other people, boys, men. I took drugs. Drank a lot. I missed them so much, and I didn't know how to live without them. I didn't know where I belonged."

KC uncrossed his legs, extending them on either side of mine, trapping me between them. He didn't say anything, just scooted closer to hold my hands in his, stopping me from digging my fingers into my thighs, waiting for me to continue.

"At first, it was only stupid teenage things. My teachers didn't like it, but they allowed it, probably because of what I'd been through. But it quickly became a lot more than simple rebellion. I fucked every guy I met. I even had sex with one of my professors. He was very young for a teacher, but still. And I was not safe. I did everything I could to *not* be safe. I wanted to die, but I didn't have the courage to— I missed my parents so much. They'd loved and accepted who I was, and suddenly, I was thrown into this life, alone, where barely anyone accepted me. No one knew me."

I pulled my hands away from him, shaking and flexing them, and I tried to back away from him, trying to escape the intimacy between us. I didn't mean to pull away; it was instinct—the instinct to shut him out and protect myself. I hadn't talked about my parents like this in— I had never talked like this. Ever. I told Carolina about them when we became friends in grad school, but I didn't tell her everything. I didn't tell her how close I'd come to killing myself. Talking about it hurt, and I *never* let myself hurt.

But KC wouldn't let me escape. He moved behind me, wrapping his arms around me and holding me so close. He rested his chin on my shoulder, kissing it softly and scratching his jaw lightly over my skin.

"I was sixteen and about to be expelled from my school. I felt so filled of anger. So lost and alone. I couldn't take it anymore. I was at a party one night, being foolish. Unsafe. But my *mam* appeared in front of me—I was very drunk. And then I saw my father. He looked so real. He reached out to touch my hand and shook his head, and I *felt* him touch me. I was so messed up, KC. I threw myself at him—I wanted him to hold me—but, of course, he wasn't really there. I fell on my face on the floor, and then I ran. Back to school.

"We had a new science teacher, probably because I'd screwed the other one, and she took an interest in me. I don't know why. Maybe she knew what happened, but I was too messed up to care. She helped me catch up with my school-work—I had not been to class for many weeks. And then, somehow, she helped me focus, and a year later, I graduated with honors and went to university. But from that point out, I did not allow myself to make a mistake. Ever. I was top of my class in university and grad school. I went out but didn't make friends. It was only for sex. It was the only way for me to... deal. I was completely alone.

"This is when I met Carolina. She was hurting, too, and we became instantly inseparable. We spent our free time studying or wandering around Europe. She helped me to relax. It was easy to be myself around her. She felt like fami-ly." I turned my head to look at him, and he reached up to wipe the tears from my cheeks.

"But perfection is impossible. Sex, this is somewhere I can be in control, but I've never been with anyone like you, someone who cared enough about me to be vulnerable with me.

"KC, I *needed* what you gave me tonight." I pressed back against his body and felt when his breath quickened. "The first time I saw you in your living room, I wanted you. It scared me, but I wanted you to be the one to give me something no one else ever had." Pushing back against him, we lay back on my bed, and I adjusted our bodies so we were face to face. "I thought about you so many times."

KC smirked. "Mm, you have no idea how many times I made myself come thinkin' about you. I mean, I thought I was already a serial masturbator, but shit. I could compete in the fuckin' Olympics now." I laughed, and he reached up to hold my face in his hands. "Please don't be ashamed of what you've done in your past. Not with me. I know how that feels, to think you wanna die 'cause you just can't *feel* what you feel anymore. 'Cause what you feel seems wrong. That's how I felt my whole life. Remember I told you I learned somethin' about my mama?"

"*Ja.*"

"Well, the other night, after I left you at the clinic? The night dumbass Doug brought his dog in? After I stormed out like an asshole, I walked to the diner. I wanted to be with you so bad, but I just couldn't. I was so afraid. Of what comin' out would do to my family, to our business, but mostly, I was afraid to feel happy. I didn't think I deserved it. When my mama left, I was so young, and I thought it was my fault she went. I thought there was somethin' wrong with me, and she just couldn't stand to be with me.

"I know that's stupid," he said when I shook my head. "Trust me, I get it, but it's the way I've always felt. Anyway, that night, I went to see her, and I demanded she admit it, that it was my fault and that she left 'cause she was ashamed of me."

How could he think that? It explained so much about his behavior, about why he'd pushed me away.

"But that wasn't why. She told me she had another baby after she had me. She gave birth to a little girl out on the ranch one day, but the baby came too soon and she died. My mama couldn't handle it. She tried, and she had Jay after the baby. And there were other issues, too, but when she walked out on us, I thought it was my fault.

"But, Luuk, the other night, when I heard her say it wasn't true? It changed everything for me. Somethin' inside me shifted, and all of a sudden, all the roadblocks stoppin' me from gettin' to you disappeared.

"I talked to Dean too. I told him what my mama said and how bad I'd felt about myself, that I thought all this awful stuff that happened to us was my fault, and I wanted to hurt myself when I was younger 'cause I thought bein' myself, who I really was on the inside, was wrong. Other than when I told you, it's the first time I ever told anybody I'm gay. I'm pretty sure he knew already, but I'd never actually said it."

I nodded and smiled, thinking back to Ma's "gay is okay" campaign.

"What's that shit-eatin' grin for? What do you know?"

"They all knew. Ma knew you were gay."

"I know. She told me before she… died."

"She did?" I asked, and he smiled and nodded. "Remember the first night you brought me here? I'd driven Carolina's truck to the ranch, and we ate hamburgers at your house?"

"Yeah. I love the way you say hamburgers."

"What? It sounds the same as when you say it."

"Uh huh, sure." He smiled, pressing his lips together, trying not to laugh at me.

"Oh, shut up. Remember Ma wanted to talk to me?"

"Yeah, to tell you about rentin' the house."

"Yes, and she wanted to talk to me about you. She wanted me to try to convince you that it's okay to be yourself. She knew I wanted you, and she asked me to try to show you that it's okay to be, well, gay." I laughed. "I called it her 'gay is okay' campaign."

"Are you kiddin' me?"

I laughed. "Nope."

"That connivin' ol' lady!"

"In her defense, she was correct. And she loved you fiercely. She saw how much you were hurting."

"I had no idea she knew all this time. It explains so much. For a while, I thought she might be turnin' into a cougar. Every time we were out, like, at the store or somethin', she'd say, 'Whaddya think about him? He ain't bad lookin', eh?' or 'Ooo, get a load of the behind on that young man. He looks *good* in those britches.' I figured she was goin' through some kinda menopausal awakenin'."

"What is britches?"

He chuckled. "Pants."

"You have the weirdest names for things."

"Look who's talkin', Mr. Can't Decide If He's Speakin' English or Dutch."

"*Je vindt het geweldig als ik Nederlands spreek. Lieg niet.*"

"What was that?"

"I said you suck."

"Aww, you know me so well." He popped up over me, straddling me and pinning my wrists to the bed above my head. "I do suck. Here, lemme show ya."

Leaning down, he sucked my nipple into his mouth, flicking it with his tongue, then slid his body down and between my legs.

"Wait."

"What? Don't tell me I'm doin' it wrong already?" He looked up at me through his eyelashes. *Mijn God, those eyelashes.* His blue eyes danced behind them, like a secret peeking out from behind my own forbidden door.

Wait. I wanted to say something. What was it?

Oh, ja. "No, you do nothing wrong, but I want to ask you something."

"Okay." He sat up.

"*Kom hier.*" I patted the bed next to me, and he crawled up my body, lying beside me carefully.

"What's wrong? You look worried."

Turning onto my side, I smoothed my hand over his cheek and jaw, resting it on his neck. "We have not talked about Ma. Not really."

He inhaled a loud breath and sighed. I was worried. I didn't want to upset him, but I knew it must've been a big raw thing inside him. I wanted him to know I would listen. I wanted him to be able to open up about losing Ma.

"You were so close with her. I know it hurts, but I'm here. If you want to tell me, I will listen."

"Ain't it stupid? After what we just did and said to each other, my gut reaction is to say, 'I'm fine,' and stuff what I feel deep down inside."

"It's not stupid. We're men. This is what is expected of us. We're supposed to handle it and move on. I have a feeling that applies a hell of a lot more to you than it does to me. I've met your brothers. And don't forget, I had a front row chair to the Carolina and Dean show. Mr. and Mrs. Don't Tell Each Other What They Feel For Years. I think Dean eats the cake for most stoic man award."

He laughed and kissed my nose. "You're fuckin' adorable. I think you meant 'takes the cake.' And yeah, he'd win for sure. Or he woulda. Oly's opened him up. Funny how it just takes the right person. You're that guy for me, Alvie." He sighed again and closed his eyes. "I miss her so much. That never goes away, does it? And it hurts even worse now 'cause I wanna tell her about you.

"I put her through so much shit. She was always worried about me. I wish I could tell her somethin' good for once. She had so much faith in me, and for so long, I felt like I didn't deserve it. I didn't understand it, but I think I do now. And I don't think I'm the man you deserve."

I shifted up onto my elbow, preparing to argue, but he opened his eyes. "Hold on," he said, and he pulled me back down. "I don't think I'm that guy *yet*, but I wanna be. I'll do whatever it takes to be him. You deserve it."

"You are this guy, and you deserve this, too, yes?"

He smiled and scrunched his lips. "Maybe I do."

"No maybe."

Twenty-Six

Kevin

"Things went well with Daisy tonight?" Luuk asked. "You seemed okay when I came back inside with the girls to eat."

"Yeah," I said, thinkin' back over the long overdue conversation my brothers and I had earlier in the evenin' with our mama when she came to the ranch for dinner.

I lay across his back, caressin' his muscular thigh with my fingers and lookin' up at the side of his face all smushed into the pillow on his bed, his hair a delicious and tangled mess.

I was boneless and exhausted after he'd just done things to me I hadn't even known were possible. He showed more and more of himself to me every time we were together, and it was such a turn-on. He was so hot and passionate, and a little bit kinky if I was honest, and I loved it.

"Yeah." I cleared my throat. I figured now was as good a time as any to start bein' the "new me," openin' up, sharin' my feelin's. "She told us about little Fiona, about losin' her, and how she fell apart after that. How screwed up she was and how it made her feel like she had to get away from us. She thought she was hurtin' us, or she was afraid she would, 'specially when Jay was born. She said she saw a doctor later, and the doctor told her she'd probably been sufferin' from severe postpartum depression."

"But you're okay? *Ja?*"

"I'm okay. Well, okay ain't the right word. After what you just did to me, okay is the last word I'd use to describe how I feel."

He flipped over underneath me. "Don't joke, *schatje.* I'm serious."

"I ain't jokin'. What does 'scratchya' mean? Do I annoy you so much you wanna scratch my eyes out all the time?"

"What? Scratch you?" He laughed. "*Schatje, idioot.* There is no 'r.' 'Schot-ye.' It means— It's like when Jack calls Evvie 'baby.'"

"Am I your baby?" Crawlin' up his body, I lay next to him, and he turned onto his side. I smiled. I felt kinda silly, but I couldn't help myself. When I looked at him, I felt so happy.

He gasped softly and closed his eyes. "KC, *je bent zo mooi, maar als je zo naar me lacht, laat je me ademloos…* And *ja*, you are my baby." He whispered his words to me, and the sound of his voice all around me made my cock rock-hard and my heart full to burstin'. Plus, no one had ever called me their baby before, and I fuckin' loved it. I loved that he said it in Dutch so it could be our secret.

"Tell me what you said."

"*Nee.*"

"Yes." He kept his eyes closed, tryin' to hide his vulnerability from me, so I leaned in closer and kissed his lips. I whispered, "Please, baby?"

He moaned, and I hadn't even touched him, just my lips to his. I kept my eyes open, watchin' the pleasure overtake his face as I sucked his soft bottom lip just a little. Releasin' it, I bit it gently, then slid my tongue inside his mouth, and he groaned and mumbled against me.

"I said, 'You are so beautiful, but when you smile at me like that, you take my breath away.'"

Smilin' again, I made sure it was the sexiest, most seductive smile I could muster, and when he finally opened his eyes, he growled and attacked me! He pushed me down onto my back and kneeled between my spread legs, then held himself above me, rubbin' his cock against mine, and I realized that this was my life now. I could love the way I wanted to, fuck the way I wanted. I didn't have to pretend anymore. I didn't have to lie. I could have Luuk, and I could love him any way I wanted.

I stilled beneath him.

"What's wrong?"

"You freed me." I held his face between the palms of my hands, lookin' deep into his soul. "I don't want you to 'fuck' me— Well, now, yes I do." I chuckled and bent my knees, trappin' him between my legs. "But I've waited my whole life for you to make love to me. I love you. Make *love* to me."

He shuddered and his breath came out in a rush, caressin' my face. "*Ademloos, schatje,*" he whispered. "You leave me breathless."

I worked my ass off all week, lungin' horses, diggin' holes for fence posts, throwin' hay, whatever needed to be done around the ranch. My shoulder ached like a bitch, but I couldn't remember any of it come Saturday night. I'd had many conversations with my brothers and Isaac, but I couldn't remember what they said to me or what I said back to 'em.

Luuk dominated my thoughts all week, even in sleep. I dreamt of him every night, even though he lay right next to me. When I wasn't with him, when I couldn't be, he was the only thing I could focus on. I worked all day, every day, the whole time with his face, his body, his lips, and his voice in my mind. I replayed us bein' together over and over, workin' myself up into a bother. As soon as Finn called dinner, I showered and drove to Luuk's house, or I met him at the clinic and went with him on farm calls.

I spent every night in his bed, tangled up in his legs, his arms, his whole body. His mind. We talked all night, every night. Honestly, it was a wonder either one of us could function durin' the days. Lotsa coffee, that was for sure.

For that one week, we lived in a bubble. Our own private perfect bubble.

We had sex as many times, in as many places, as we could, and the connection between us was explosive every time. We'd fucked in his truck, in mine, in the woods, in the clinic, out behind his house. We went for a drive one evenin' when he wasn't on call, just talkin' and touchin' each other, lettin' the night air caress and warm us as it rushed in through the open windows of the truck, but we couldn't wait to get home, so I pulled off to the side of highway and sucked his cock like all life on earth depended on it. He lay across the bench seat of the old Ford with his leg propped over the steerin' wheel, his fist in my hair, and his head hangin' out the open passenger window.

I was drunk on him, couldn't get enough of him. I wanted him so much that it hurt inside my body. If I couldn't be with him, my chest felt tight and uneasy, and I was restless and jittery. As soon as we were together again, my whole body relaxed, and I felt an ease I didn't think I'd ever known before.

He hadn't told me he loved me. It wasn't somethin' I ever thought I'd find myself wantin', but I did. And I still worried. Maybe he didn't. Maybe for him, this was all just about the sex he'd said he needed. I thought he loved me. I hoped desperately that he did. I felt it in my body every time he touched me or looked at me. But he didn't say it.

We were up in the little room above my barn Saturday afternoon after goin' for a ride. I'd ridden Classic and he rode Tank. He really wanted to ride Mad Max, but when he saw Jack workin' with him, he admitted he didn't think he could handle the beast. He hadn't ridden a horse in a long time, so he agreed he'd wait till he had more confidence he wouldn't end up on his ass in the dirt.

He didn't know it then, but he was gonna end up that way, regardless.

I took him out onto my land and showed him all the places I'd loved growin' up. I felt *wild* out there, openin' myself up to him, showin' him all the places I'd gone when I was sad or scared or pissed off. Or happy. All the places I'd gone when I was thinkin' about him.

I felt raw and vulnerable, and normally, it woulda scared the shit outta me, but now, bein' connected the way we were, it became a kind of power inside me. A strength. And I needed him to feel it. I made love to him in the mud on the bank of the creek runnin' through the ranch, and then we washed off in a bend where the water ran deep but flowed lazy. But I wasn't done, so I took his cock in my mouth, and he fucked into it as he floated in the water, clutchin' a low hangin' tree branch with his hands.

We made our way back to the barn slowly and in silence, just regardin' each other from atop our horses. When we got back, I took him to the little room upstairs.

"What is this room?"

"I guess it's a foalin' room. I mean, I assume that's what my pops and his dad built it for, so they could stay out here comfortably if they needed to spend nights in the barn. I know we gotta get ready to go to the concert, but I don't wanna let you outta my sight just yet." Stalkin' up behind him while he looked out the little window, checkin' out the view of the mountain, I wrapped my arms around his chest, turnin' him around to me.

"Are you ever *not* hard?"

"Um, pot"—I pointed to the enormous hard-on behind his jeans then pointed to my own—"kettle."

"I don't know what this means." He tried not to smile.

"The pot callin' the kettle black?" He shook his head, so I grabbed hold of his cock, strokin' it the best I could through the denim, and shoved my nose into the crook of his neck, inhalin' his skin. "It ain't fair of you to accuse me of somethin' you're just as guilty of."

"Ohh, *ja*." He moaned. "*Je hebt me betrapt.* I am caught."

"Yeah, I did catch ya." I licked up his neck and rubbed my lips down his jaw to his mouth, kissin' him like it was the last thing I'd ever be allowed to do. "And now, you're mine. All mine." Tuggin' his zipper open, I shoved his jeans and boxers down his hips, grabbin' his dick in my hand and revelin' in the heat from his skin. "This is all mine," I whispered and flexed my fingers, squeezin' him, and his breath caught for a few seconds and came out on a groan. "Mine," I growled.

"*Je denk dat*… argh! You scribble my brains like eggs."

"Scramble your brain like an egg?" I laughed into his neck.

"You know what I mean. You think you own me? You can control my cock?" He grabbed both my biceps and whipped me around, pullin' me back against his body.

"Oh God, say that again with your sexy fuckin' accent, right in my ear. I could shoot my load just from the sound of it."

"Ach, you are so rude."

"You love it. Admit it."

I tried to turn back around to face him, but he shuffled forward, pushin' me, and I tripped my way to the little bed in front of us. We fell down onto it, and he ripped my shirt over my head, hittin' me in the face with his fists in the process.

"Ow!"

"Oh, *houd je kop,* you baby. You deserve it for correcting me every time and for trying to boss me over."

"Boss you around?" I pressed my lips together to keep from laughin', but then I realized we had a little problem. "Shit. I'm outta rubbers." I flipped beneath him. "Um, okay, hold that thought. I bet there's some around here somewhere or maybe out in the truck."

Graspin' my wrists, he pushed 'em hard into the bed. "Don't move. You think I need a condom to make you come? I don't even have to touch your cock or your ass, and I will make you come like a kid with his first water dream."

"Wet dream?" I giggled like a little girl.

"Just for that, I'm going to torture you. I'm going to fuck your mind slowly. You will beg me to make you come, to suck you"—he shook his head slowly—"but I will not."

"Prove it. You can't resist my cock, 'specially when it's hard and strainin' toward your wet mouth." *Damn.* I was nearly writhin' on the bed, my body beggin' him to do what he said he would.

He jumped up and stood just outta my reach to remove his clothes. So. Damn. Slowly. He was right; I already felt tortured. Grabbin' his dick at its base, he stroked it out a couple times, lookin' right in my eyes, but then he let go and stepped further down the side of the bed, and I groaned.

"*Wat was dat? Wat zei je?*"

"Nothin'."

"Oh, you know *Nederlands* now?"

"I think I might be catchin' on just a little," I said, smirkin' and flashin' the smile I knew he couldn't resist.

"Oh, okay, so then what does this mean: *Ik wilde je zo aanraken sinds de eerste keer dat ik je ontmoette. Net als dit.*"

"I dunno, but it sounded hot. Does it mean you wanna be my sex slave for the rest of time, lyin' at my feet for the sole purpose of pleasurin' me any time I want?"

"*Ja.* You wish." He shook his head but couldn't hide his smile.

Movin' down to the end of the bed to untie my boots slowly, he raked his eyes over my body, like he had X-ray vision and could see under my clothes. My every hair stood on end as I watched his eyes roam all over me.

His hard cock slapped against his stomach as he moved, and I took pictures in my mind. I wished I had my camera so I could capture the lust on his face and the strain in his body while he tortured me slowly. A whole series of photos of him flitted through my head. A study of the slow, raw, achin' beauty of a man.

Pullin' off my boots, he let 'em fall beside him and climbed onto the bed on his knees, up and over my body. He undid my fly and pulled my jeans and boxers down a centimeter at time, his fingers never touchin' my skin. I wanted to pull him up so I could assault him with my mouth, but when I touched his head, tryin' to twist my fingers into his hair, he smacked my hands away.

"Have I forgotten to tell you? You may *not* touch me."

"There are rules to your little game?"

"Little game? Like a child is playing? Oh, KC, no, no, no." He laughed deviously, a low, sexy, sinister chuckle, and looked around the room. "Emm, *ja.* This is what we need."

Climbin' off me, he walked across to the corner of the room, grabbin' a long length of rope that lay curled up on a wooden chair, and he locked the door. A rope? What kinda kinky fuckery were Jack and Evvie into? Or was it Oly and Dean? *Ugh,* I didn't wanna think about it, but I figured I was about to be into it too.

I swallowed hard when he turned, lookin' down at the rope in his hands, and he lifted his eyes back to mine. He looked a little evil, but *oh* so fuckin' sexy as he stalked back to the side of the bed and grabbed my right hand. He tied the rope around my wrist cow hitch style, pullin' hard, then crouched down and threw the bulk of the rope under the bed, and I heard it slide on the smooth wood floor beneath me.

Standin' again, his cock was inches from my face, and the sight of it, with its hard length and soft head, glistenin' with pre-cum at the tip, made my mouth water.

Even though I could still move, I didn't want to. He'd said before that sometimes, he needed this control, but he didn't feel comfortable askin' for it. I wanted to give it to him. It went against my every instinct to be held down, rendered immobile and unable to move or fight, unable to hide myself if I felt uncomfortable or scared or embarrassed, but I'd never wanted to give myself to another person so desperately. I'd never wanted to give away my control.

But when I gave it to Luuk, the power I felt inside myself, about myself, grew.

It, too, became a strength instead of a weakness.

Climbin' on top of me, he made sure to touch me with his body everywhere he could *except* for where I wanted. 'Course, I wanted his hands everywhere, so it didn't really matter. He splayed 'em on my ribs and lowered his body so his chest touched my stomach, and I thrust my hips, seekin' any kinda contact I could get, but he moved off to the side of me.

I felt his dick against my leg, the cum at his tip wettin' the outside of my thigh, but then, quick as lightnin', he rolled away from me, jumpin' up on the far side of the bed. He crouched down again, grabbed the rope, and brought it up to tie around my left wrist.

He wasn't screwin' around. He tied it tight, not enough to cut off circulation, but enough so I couldn't get out of it. Pullin' so my arms stretched straight out, perpendicular to my body, he fastened the rope to the bed.

I could move my arms up or down about two inches in either direction, but that was it. He made no sound. I couldn't even hear him breathin'.

When he finished tyin' my legs to the bed, I lay in the

middle, spread eagle, arms and legs out and open, and my cock was so fuckin' hard—it coulda knocked down a house!

I thought for a minute maybe he wasn't as affected as me, but I watched him gazin' at my body, watchin' my dick pulse and twitch, and a wistful look flashed across his face.

But then he got to work.

Over the next hour, at least, he touched my body every-where. He kissed, licked, sucked, bit, caressed, scratched, and pinched every inch of me. He tortured every nerve endin'.

It was impossible to stay still, but every time I tried to move, to rub against him or to reach for his lips with mine when he hovered an inch above my face, breathin' on me and rubbin' his cheek against mine, he stopped. He was so right. I begged! I moaned and groaned and whimpered for him to release me so I could touch him, but he didn't.

I trembled from head to toe and begged him to fuck me. I didn't care that we didn't have a condom.

"Luuk, stop screwin' around."

"You don't like my *little game* anymore?" Crawlin' up, he kneeled above my face. "Open."

When I didn't immediately open my mouth, he grabbed my face with one hand, pushin' on my jaw with his fingers and thumb, forcin' my mouth open as he looked deep in my eyes, and fed me his cock. He threaded his fingers through my hair and pulled my head up a little, then fucked into my mouth while he held himself still with one hand on the wall behind the bed, usin' the other to push and pull my head. Groanin', his head fell back.

Holy shit.

He watched my face while he fucked my mouth, and I choked and struggled to breathe, but I was so turned on. I thought my cock would explode just from air touchin' it. He was devastatin' and powerfully sexy above me, thrustin' into me. I'd never seen anything like him, and I've watched *a lot* of porn. His expression was pure sin, so dark and erotic and full of lust. It poured outta him and into me, and I wanted more. I sucked like my mouth was made of Hoover parts.

But he pulled out and away from me.

"Don't you dare stop." My words slurred 'cause I was drugged by the taste of him.

Smirkin', he cocked an eyebrow, and slid down my body, careful still not to make any motherfuckin' contact with my dick, and he straddled my legs and started jackin' off over me.

By himself!

Oh my God, I ached so hard for him to fuck me.

His whole body was hard, wet and glistenin' with sweat and strainin'. He worked his cock slow, lookin' down at me, and his eyes flashed with electricity. It burned through me while I watched him.

He threw his head back, moanin' and pantin' while he made himself come. Watchin' him, the expression on his face, his body hard like steel, I felt that electricity move through me, from my feet to my head—it made me dizzy—and it flowed back down through my blood to my cock.

When he was ready, breathin' hard and shakin', he looked at me again, pumped two more times, and came all over my chest. He shouted his release, and an orgasm was *ripped* from my body, and he watched my face as I came.

He rocked me to my soul!

I pulled so hard on the rope that the bed frame creaked and cracked. Tears fell from the corners of my eyes, and I barked out my release into the empty air 'cause he *still* wouldn't touch me.

And then he collapsed on top of me, touchin' me everywhere all at once. The contact burned my skin, and sweat dripped from every part of me. I gasped for air and melted into the bed.

Liftin' himself up onto his elbows, his arms shook from exhaustion, but he held himself above me and kissed me till he collapsed back down again, his body settlin' into every curve, crook, and corner of mine.

We became one person instead of two.

"Are you ready to go to the concert? I think we may need to have a shower first."

I snorted and laughed so hard, I thought it would literally kill me.

TWENTY-SEVEN

LUUK

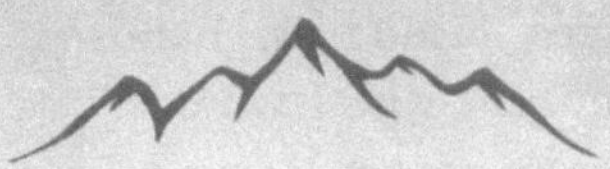

"You are very quiet. Have I frightened you? … KC?"

"Huh? Yeah. Huh?"

"We've been sitting in the parking lot for two minutes, and you haven't said a word."

"Oh. Sorry." KC opened the passenger-side door to my truck and stepped out. I followed, but before I could shut my door, he was around the truck and pushing me back inside, trapping me with his body. "I can't stop thinkin' about what you did to me today. I can still feel the rope around my wrists and your cock down my throat." Touching his lips to the sensitive skin behind my ear, he pressed his erection against my ass. "I need to be inside you. I want you. I want that feelin' again. I felt your soul inside my body. Do that again."

I moaned. "We cannot. Evvie and Finn are expecting us."

"I don't care."

"Also, you asked me to come with you. Do you really want to abandon our first date?"

"Is that what this is?"

Flipping around, I pressed my body to his. "Yes." I grabbed his face with both of my hands and kissed him hard. "You can fuck me later."

"I don't wanna fuck you," he breathed into my mouth. "I wanna *invade* you. Body and soul. Now."

"*In de parkeerplaats?*"

"Yes. Does that mean parkin' lot?"

I laughed. "*Ja.* Come, you can make me drunk, and I will lose my inhibitions."

He snorted. "Yeah, I don't think you need any help with *that.*"

I rolled my eyes, hiding my hands in my pockets so I couldn't touch him. If I did, I wouldn't be able to resist the urge to throw him in my truck and drive to my house so he could do to me what he wanted—invade my soul.

"Come."

"That's what I'm tryin' to do, but you keep tryin' to stop me." He bent his knees, lowering himself and pushing his arms through mine, and he grabbed my ass with both hands and kissed under my jaw. "This is gonna be torture."

"But you like when I torture you." I slid my hand down the back of his jeans, grabbing his ass, too, squeezing as hard as I could. So much for not touching him. I couldn't stop. "Let us go."

"Fine, but I'm goin' under protest. Mark that down somewhere."

"Are you nervous?"

"Yeah. I got bats in my belfry." He smiled up at me, a delicious and silly smile, and he laughed. It almost sounded like a giggle.

"What does this mean?"

He laughed again. He was being playful with me. I'd never seen this side of him. I'd seen him joke with his brothers but never with me, not like this. He was so free. So open. Almost like a child.

"Come on. What is bats in belfry?"

"I don't know what the fuck it means." He kissed my cheek. "Actually, I think it's akin to losin' your marbles."

"What. Are. You. Saying? Is this English you speak? I'm not joking. I need a Google Translator for KC speak." I turned my head, trying to see his eyes, but he burrowed into my neck, laughing more.

"I think so." He giggled again, choking in air through his laugh, and he snorted. It was infectious. He laughed so much, he had tears in his eyes, and I couldn't stop myself from laughing too, but he pulled away from me, straightening, shaking his head and looking at me with such an intense expression on his face.

"You are the most beautiful man on this earth when you laugh. I've never seen anything like it. You're gorgeous all the time, but you're always so serious. But when you laugh? That smile of yours lights some kinda fire inside me. I swear, it could swallow me whole. And those dimples? I haven't quite figured out how, but there's gotta be a way for me to fuck 'em."

He kissed me again, and it quickly changed from light and easy to deep and desperate. His hands moved up my back, pressing me close against him, and my hands found their way to his hips to pull his pelvis against mine. I wanted to be inside his soul.

It was difficult, but I pulled away. I had to stop it, or soon, I would be inside him, fucking into him in the open door of my truck, but he wouldn't release me. He followed my face with his lips, seeking more.

"Stop trying to distract me and answer my question."

"Want me to stop kissin' you?" He leaned back a little, looking in my eyes, but he kept kissing me slowly, licking me and dragging his open lips over my mouth.

"No, but if you do not, I think the sheriff may have to put us both in the jail." He chuckled, separating his body from mine, and he raised his hands into the air in surrender. "Tell me. Are you nervous?"

"Why would I be nervous?"

"You're walking into your neighborhood bar in the town you've lived in all of your life for the first time with a man."

"I always walk into Manny's with a man. Usually Jay."

"*Ja*, but Jay is not your date."

"You better hope not."

"KC, be serious."

"I can't. It goes against my DNA."

I rolled my eyes, and he led me by my hand toward the front of my truck, kicking the door closed with his boot on the way. Stopping in front of it, he turned toward me and pushed his fingers through my hair, messing it.

"Yes, Luuk. I'm nervous. I don't really care what they say about me anymore. I mean, I ain't lookin' forward to dealin' with it, but I'm just nervous about what people might do to cause a commotion and ruin Evvie's show. She's been freakin' out all week. They've put so much work into it, and I don't want anybody to screw it up. But I talked to her, and she practically begged me to bring you. She even told me I should push you onto the dance floor and kiss you for all the world to see."

I smiled, thinking about Evvie's face when she said it. She was ever the optimist. "Wait. You talked to her about this? About bringing me as your date?"

"Yeah."

I blushed a little. "So, you are going to dance with me? I have moves, you know."

"Oh, yeah, I *know*. But no. I don't dance." He pulled me along beside him as he walked toward the entrance to Manny's Bar, and I could hear the music starting.

"KC?" I stopped walking and waited for him to turn back to me. When he did, I said, "If you don't want to, if you don't think it's the right time or you are uncomfortable, it's okay. I don't need you to make a big show of this. I only want you to do what feels right for you."

"Fuck that. It's the right time, and you deserve it. You

deserve to be shown off. *We* deserve it. And, if you wanna know the truth, I wanna claim you. I want everyone to know you're mine, and they can't have you." He kissed my lips softly. "I ain't gonna bend you over a table and rim your ass in front of everyone but…"

"Wait. You know what this is?"

"Rimming? Mmm. Why yes, Luuk, I do. I told ya, *lots* of porn, remember?"

"*Verdomme.*"

Manny's had been opened up to the outdoors. A long bar made from planks of cheap wood stood just beyond a temporary fence surrounding the whole property. Manny headed the bar team, but there were a few young men and women actually pouring the drinks and filling red plastic cups with beer from a barrel keg.

Yola collected money at the entrance. She wrapped a red wristband around our wrists and winked at me when she noticed KC and me together. There were people inside and out. The turnout for the cancer benefit was impressive, three hundred people, at least, and over the sea of the crowd, stage lamps and thousands of colorful twinkling lights lit the night sky and a big banner that read "ED and the Man."

KC hadn't been joking when he said he wanted to claim me in front of everyone. We stood by the bar, watching the band as they played and listening to Evvie sing beautifully, and KC never stopped touching me. He rested his arm around my shoulder, slowly moving it down to circle my waist. And every few minutes, he would turn his head and whisper something into my ear. "Can we go home now?" Then, "Can we go home *now*?" And then, "Can we go home now? I wanna shove my—"

"Hey, guys! Aren't they amazing?" Carolina shouted over the music when she reached up to hug me then KC.

"Oly, what the fu— What's wrong with your stomach? Maybe you should be in bed."

Carolina giggled. "I'm fine, Kevin. The babies just decided to make their presence known. I popped." She rubbed her hands down her distended abdomen, and I saw the adoration in her eyes. Already, her little blobs of goo were so loved.

"Like a fuckin' popcorn kernel. Jesus."

I elbowed KC in his ribs.

"Sorry, it's just, I've seen you a lot lately, and I never noticed."

"It's okay. Scrubs hide a lot. C'mon, everybody's down in front of the stage." She grabbed our hands to pull us through the crowd, and KC looked at me behind Carolina's back. I couldn't help but laugh because his face resembled a sad puppy with his eyebrows pulled down over his eyes and his lips in a pout.

"Can we go home now?"

"Go home?" Carolina yelled over her shoulder, "They just started. Why would you go home now?" She was completely oblivious to KC's sexually devious intentions.

He raised an eyebrow, his pout turning into a wicked smile, and I shook my head.

"Is she singin' Metallica?" he asked, turning his head to the stage, recognizing the song. "Oh now, this is somethin' I can get into."

Finn played an electric guitar, and Evvie sang to a cover of Metallica's "Nothing Else Matters." Her voice was raspy and soft but powerful, and it made all the hair on my arms stand up. Another guitar player and a drummer crowded the small stage, and off to the side, a woman played a cello and a teenager played a violin. The song was slow and quiet, but when Finn wailed on his guitar and the drums kicked in while Evvie *sang,* the crowd went wild.

Finn began singing along with Evvie, lending his deeper voice, and KC grabbed my hand, pulling me to the front of the crowd. I kept checking the reactions of the people around us. He seemed oblivious, but I knew he wasn't. And I knew they were there—intolerant people. People who were afraid of seeing two men together. No matter where you went in the world, they were there. I saw a few dirty looks, several more curious looks, but no one said anything.

When the song ended, Evvie sat behind a keyboard, and the band transitioned into Bowie's "Heroes," which was possibly my favorite song ever, so I tried to relax and sang at the top of my out-of-tune lungs.

I was having so much fun, I hadn't even noticed KC staring at me until he pulled me to face him.

Time stood still as he looked in my eyes, and the music faded to a quiet lull while my heartbeat pounded in my ears. Finn and Evvie sang the kissing part, and KC brought his hands up to hold my face, stroking my jaw with his thumbs, and he leaned toward me to kiss me, just like Evvie had said —for all the world to see.

It was passionate—he was *in* it and I was… stunned. I hadn't thought he would really do it. The crowd roared, cheering us on, or maybe that had just been in my head and really they were cheering for the music, but I heard and felt acceptance, and I kissed him back.

I was in awe of his courage. Wrapping my arms around his back, I wound my hand around his neck, pulling his hair with my fingers a little, and I infused all the pride and love I felt for him into our kiss, so much so, when he pulled away to look at me again, I was completely breathless.

"*Now* can we go home?" He smiled and I melted.

"Breathless, *schatje*."

I led KC through the crowd to the parking lot so I could reward his courage, but we didn't get very far. I saw Brady, and he smiled and gave me "two thumbs up" as we passed him at the gate.

"Boss-man, that was epic." I heard a teenage voice, but I couldn't see Isaac until KC stepped to the side. Isaac stood behind him, grinning from ear to ear.

"Isaac, what the hell you doin' here? This is a bar."

"Whatever. Oh shit, here comes Manny. Gotta go, but glad you took my advice." Isaac turned to make his escape, and I saw Manny stomping through the fence past Yola at the gate with his fist in the air, but just like with the bear incident, the sound of Mr. Morris' voice ripped through all the emotion humming through me.

"Have fun tonight, Cade? You enjoyin' yourself, spreadin' your faggot filth all over this town?"

KC turned to the sound of Morris' voice and stumbled back when Morris punched him, right in his mouth, as he'd probably wanted to do for a long time. I steadied him, and he reached back to touch my stomach.

"Jesus Christ, Dougie. You really wanna do this at a cancer fundraiser?" KC touched the heel of his hand to his lip, then looked at the blood there. "Oww."

"Why not? Pretty sure you already ruined the festivities when you stuck your tongue down your girlfriend's throat. I had a front row seat to that. Fuckin' gross. What's it taste like? Ball sack?" Morris shuddered and made a disgusted face, nudging his friend, Vern (the guy who threw up in the forest), with his elbow, and Vern laughed.

"Are you okay?" I inched toward KC, placing my hand on the small of his back.

"I'm okay," he said. "You know what, Dougie? I'm gonna let you have that one. I figure I deserve it for all the shit I've given you over the years."

Isaac stepped in front of KC. "Leave him alone."

"Thanks for the backup, Shadow," KC said, but he pulled Isaac by his shoulder, steering him between us, "but this is between me and Doug, ain't it? This is about the thing I said about your wife. I shouldn't have said that. I'm sorry. But how long we known each other, since we were kids, right? I've always been a smartass. I never slept with her. I just said that to get your goat. Isn't that what this is all about? Or are you really threatened just 'cause I love somebody you don't approve of?"

"The world's changin'," Isaac said. "You better get used to it."

Morris rolled his eyes at Isaac. "Shut up, fag lover."

"Oh, well, hey now. We're not doin' that." Manny appeared and stepped in front of all of us. "He's just a kid, Doug. You leave him outta this."

Doug Morris looked up at Manny towering over him. "Really? That's all you have to say about this? You really gonna let this shit go down at your bar, on your property?"

"What shit would that be? Love? You got a problem with love, Doug? Freedom? 'Cause if you do, it's you I'm gonna ask to leave. You know I was military, right? I fought for both your freedoms. Yours and Cade's. What makes you think you deserve yours more'n he does?"

ED and The Man had stopped playing, and a small crowd of people quickly formed around us. The standoff between Manny and Doug Morris was obvious.

A female bartender walked up beside Manny, carrying a baseball bat. "Hey, boss." She held her bat up in front of Manny. "Have I introduced you to Wilma yet? This here's Wilma, gentlemen. She goes with me everywhere. Just a little informative aside for ya." She smirked and swung her bat beside her leg.

"But I was wondering," she said to Morris, "oh, so sorry, it's Doug, right? I haven't introduced myself yet. I've been here a few months. I'm Dede. I know you've checked out my ass, but it occurred to me you've never asked my name. Anyhoo, I was just wondering something. I saw you watching two women go down on each other on your phone the other night while you sat in the bar, drowning yourself in fifty cent beers 'cause your wife left you.

"So, tell me, what makes it okay for you to get off watching two women, but two men is what? Un-American? Now, don't get me wrong, I support two women going down on each other. I love it. I do it as often as I can, but I would really like to know. Why's that okay with you, but this"—she waved her arm behind her, toward KC and me—"isn't?"

Isaac harrumphed, and I wrapped my arm around his shoulder so I could stop him in case he planned to try to "fight" Mr. Morris in KC's honor.

"Ooo, good question," KC said and smiled. He looked back at me and grabbed my hand.

Morris didn't respond. He looked between Manny and Dede, his face turning red with anger.

"Thanks for that, Dede, but we won't be needin' Wilma tonight, will we, Doug?" Manny asked.

Morris grumbled something under his breath and looked at the ground.

"What was that?" Manny asked in a deceptively calm voice, but command and authority emanated out of his powerful and very large body.

Morris raised his head. "No, sir."

"Good. Glad that's settled. Now, everyone is welcome back to the show. Everyone is welcome at Manny's *anytime*. Manny's is a part of the Wisper community, as are you, Doug. You and Kevin have been a part of it your whole lives. And Doc V came here to help our community in its time of need, so he's welcome too. We can disagree about a lotta things, but we ain't gonna disagree about community."

Manny looked at Dede and nodded back toward the bar, and she shrugged and headed that way with her bat. Morris looked at KC and me one last time and glared but then he and Vern walked away to his truck. They climbed in and quietly drove out of the parking lot.

Staring at Isaac, Manny dipped his chin and raised his eyebrows. "Not until you're twenty-one, kid. Try it again, and I'll have you by your hairless peanuts."

"Yes, sir," Isaac conceded. Manny walked away, and Isaac smiled, batting his eyelashes at me. "Wanna drive me home? My dad's gonna hear about this, and it'll be better if I'm already there when he does. That way, he won't have to go out lookin' for me. It'll just make him madder, and I'll probably be indentured to the ranch till I'm seventy-five."

"*Ja*, come on, Shadow. Let's go." I smiled at KC, and he twined his fingers through mine.

"You know, Shadow is a perfect screen name for me. I'm kinda like a shadow ninja when I play my video game. I sneak up on the other players, then chop their heads off. I'm totally gonna trademark that shit. It'll go with my sexy new badass persona when I post my videos about the game and get rich."

KC snorted. "Whatever you say, pain in my ass. TM *that* shit."

Fifteen minutes later, we parked in front of José's Diner, and KC walked around to open my door. He pulled me out and shut it again with his boot.

"KC, the diner is closed, and stop kicking my truck," I said, looking at the dark and deserted restaurant. The whole street was dark except for the streetlamps. "You're going to make a dent in it."

"Sorry," he said, turning to kiss my cheek. "Yeah, I know it's closed."

"So what are we doing here?"

"I wanna introduce you to somebody."

He looked around on the ground and found a tiny rock, then threw it up at a window above the diner.

"What are you—"

"Kevin? Is everything okay?" Daisy poked her head out of the window, looking down at us with a worried expression.

"Yeah, everything's fine. Can you come down for a minute?"

"Okay. Be there in a sec," she said, closing the window, and she disappeared.

"I really need to get her cell number."

"KC, I have already met your mother. Several times."

"Just hold your horses," he said, pulling me to the diner door.

When Daisy opened it, he wrapped his arm around my shoulder and kissed my cheek. "Sorry to bother you so late. Again. But I wanted to introduce you to someone."

Daisy looked at me, confused, and I shrugged.

"Mama, this is Luuk, my… boyfriend." He looked at me and I at him. "Luuk, this is my mama." He smiled and his face was so open, so honest. He looked a little nervous, but he was determined to be brave.

Reaching up to hold his face in my hands, I kissed him. I breathed him in and reveled in the taste of his courage.

Daisy made some kind of squeaking noise. "Um, I'll just— It's nice to meet you, Luuk. Again." She giggled, but I didn't stop kissing KC. "I'll just see you two later. Sound good? Yeah? Okay. Goodnight then." The door closed, but then the bell on the handle jingled a little, and she said, "I love you, Kevin. I'm so proud of you." The lock clicked and the light under the awning went out.

He mumbled against my lips. "Okay, that was a little weirder than I thought it would be. I totally didn't mean for that to get all oedipal."

"What? What does this mean?"

"You know, Oedipus Complex? When a kid gets weird about his mom?"

"Do you ever shut up?"

"Fuck no."

"Kevin Christian Cade. Watch your mouth," I said, imitating Ma.

"You can watch it when you shove your—"

"Oh *mijn* God."

TWENTY-EIGHT
KEVIN

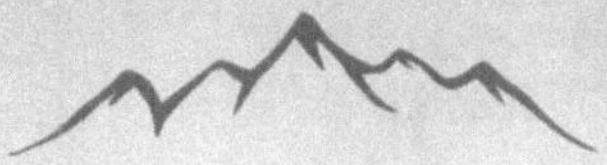

In the mornin', I woke to movement beside me in Luuk's bed when he answered his phone and snuck out to the kitchen to take the call. It was Sunday, so he didn't have to go into the clinic, and Oly was on call so I didn't know who it could be.

I closed my eyes and thought about my life. About how different it was now compared to six months ago when Luuk first came to Wisper, and I wondered, if the version of me from six months ago met the now-me, what would they say to each other? Would the then-me even believe what the now-me said? I doubted it. I probably woulda decked him.

Luuk crawled back into bed, and I turned to him. "Hi."

"Hi," he said, his eyes roamin' all over my face.

"I was missin' your blue eyes." I yawned. "They look like the sea in my dreams. You get a farm call?"

"Oh, no. That was Dr. Prittchard though. He offered me a permanent job. Officially. He's coming back full-time in two weeks, but he wants me to stay on. If I want to."

"Do you want to?"

Luuk shrugged. "I could learn a lot from him. He has so much field experience. I think he will be a good mentor."

"Oh, that's the reason you wanna stay?"

He still hadn't told me he loved me even though I told him, like, every five seconds. 'Cause I finally felt free enough to say it.

"*Het is een goede reden, ja?*"

"A good reason? Yeah, I guess it's a good one."

"How do you know what I'm saying?"

"I can read your mind," I said, closin' my eyes and rollin' onto my back. "I'm cool like that."

"It's not the only reason."

"No?"

He touched his finger to the crack in my lip. "How is your lip? Does it hurt?"

"I like the way it sounds when you say 'hurt.' Your vowels are sexy."

He snorted. "Well, does it hurt?"

"Nah, just a little sore."

His kiss on the edge of my lip was soft as air. "I think Mr. Morris is the one with limp wrists. This is not so bad." He kissed me harder.

"Ow," I said, laughin'.

He chuckled. "Don't laugh. I will laugh, then you will laugh, and it will hurt."

"Your laugh feeds my soul," I whispered. "Why should I try not to hear it?"

I opened my eyes and rolled, reachin' my head forward to kiss him this time. His hand found its way to the back of my neck, and he squeezed.

Poppin' up on top of him, I straddled him, and a devious smile spread across my lips when he pushed up, rubbin' his cock against mine. "C'mon. We need a shower. I'm fixin' to spend the day makin' you sticky and sweaty. I need a fresh palette."

"But I like when you are dirty and sweaty. It's sexy."

"Oh yeah?" Slidin' off him, I pulled him up and stood in

front of him, pushin' my boxers down my legs and off, lettin' 'em fall to the floor beside us.

"*Absoluut.*" His face was inches from my body, and I had an idea about what he might do with his proximity to my dick, but he smiled that smile, the flashy dimple one, and he stood, too, and pulled me by my hand to the bathroom.

"Ah shit, I keep forgettin' about this door. I'll see if I can find a replacement pane for it tomorrow," I said while he started the water, and we brushed our teeth. He watched me like he'd never seen anyone do it before, then stepped toward me and licked the frothy mess from the side of my lip.

Steppin' into the warm spray of the shower, I stuck my head under the water, and he wrapped his arms around me from behind and held on. We stood like that for the longest time, just breathin' and lettin' all the drama of the last few weeks wash away.

"So, you wanna teach me some Dutch? I figure I'm halfway fluent already since you can't decide which language to speak most the time."

Chucklin' into my neck, he said, "You want to learn—*Wil je het leren?*"

"*Ja.* I wanna know everything about you."

"Okay. *Hier is je eerste les*—your first lesson."

"Okay. I'm ready."

"*Ik hou van jou.*"

"Uhh, okay. I'm pretty sure '*ik*' means 'I.'"

"*Ja.*"

I turned to face him. "You're gonna have to help me. I was just screwin' with you. I have no idea what you're sayin'." I was lyin' though. I'd looked it up. "*Ik hou van jou*" meant 'I love you.' I tried not to smile, but my lips betrayed me hard.

"What is this smile for? I think you are into something."

"Who me?" I shook my head. "Nope. Please, continue." Archin' a brow, I couldn't stop the ridiculous grin on my face.

"You shit. You know what I'm saying?"

"Well, I couldn't find a Luuk van der Wouden translator app, but turns out, there's lotsa Dutch ones."

He smiled and kissed me, pressin' our wet bodies together. "*Ik hou van jou. Zo veel. Ik heb je altijd nodig.*"

I pulled my head back to look in his aqua eyes. "Oh, so you do love me? I was wonderin'. But what was the rest of that?"

"I said, 'I love you so much, and I need you always.'"

I kissed him so fast, I probably gave him whiplash. The kiss went on forever, and he held my face in his strong hands, breakin' me down and buildin' me back up with his mouth and tongue, while I touched and caressed and clawed at every inch of his body I could reach. He kissed away all my bluster, all my sarcasm, all my fear. With him, because of him, I knew I could be the man we both needed.

Finally, I pulled back to gasp for oxygen. "Luuk?"

"*Ja?*"

"What happens next?"

"What do you mean?"

"I mean for you and me. What happens next?"

Slidin' my hands up his arms, I felt the heat from his skin and the water slidin' down our bodies, his strong shoulders and his neck. I pushed my fingers into his hair, massagin' him with my thumbs.

"We can do anything we want to, but I was hoping we could just be together. No drama. Just us. Do normal things, eat dinner together, do the laundry, watch television. You know? But you will have to cook. I don't cook. Also, I never make my bed. You cannot force me." He smirked at me but tried to be serious. "Also, you will have to buy running shoes and run with me. It's good for you, and you must eat more salad."

Chucklin', I said, "Is that all?"

"You know what I would really like to do?" he asked, and I wrapped my arms around his back, pullin' him even closer.

"Hm?"

"I want to take you to the Badlands or Yosemite and follow you around while you take pictures."

"Oh, Doc, the dreamy things you say." I laughed into his neck. "That sounds like a date for Valentine's Day if I ever heard one."

"You're a sarcastic shit. It is romantic. I want to be inside your brain when you create your art. It's sexy to me. And we can rent a little cabin, somewhere out in the forest. No one around us for miles."

"Oh, well, now you're talkin'."

He whispered into my ear, "No one to hear us moaning and coming, over and over and over—"

"Let's go now," I growled, pushin' my hands down his back to his ass, squeezin' hard. I rolled my hips, rubbin' my cock against his, and he groaned.

"When Dr. Prittchard comes back to work, we will go. Can you take a few days off from the ranch?"

"Yeah, I'll talk Jack into it."

"Do you have a passport?"

"No. Why? We don't need a passport to go to South Dakota or California."

"No, but we will need them to go to the Netherlands. I want you to come with me. Will you? I want to go back for a few days. I think I need to."

"I'll go with you anywhere."

He kissed my neck, lickin' the water from my skin. "Really?"

"Yeah. Wanna go to the Netherlands? I'm totally there. Indonesia? Let's go. The Arctic Circle? Um, well, can we buy some serious thermal underwear first? But when do we leave? I love you. Take me anywhere. I'll go nuts if that's where you wanna go. Wherever you are is where I'm gonna be."

"You are already nuts."

"Yeah, for you."

"And you are a smartass."

"And you love it," I said, feelin' his smile against my neck. "Luuk?"

His slick hands traveled up my back and around to my ribs. "*Ja?*"

"Remember what I said last night? About invadin' you, body and soul?"

"*Ja.*"

"Feelin' up for that?" I captured his lip between my teeth.

"*Ja.*" He squeezed his hands on my ribs.

"I'm gonna do that now."

"*Ja,*" he exhaled, "okay."

Epilogue
LUUK

"You ready for this?" KC snapped a picture of my lips as I bit them. "I hope Tony's gonna be okay without us."

"He will be fine. Don't tell him I told you, but I caught Jack playing with him in the barn yesterday, feeding him bacon. And *spreek Nederlands.*"

"Aww, man. Okay, um, *Tony is een hond, en hij eet spek, en ben je…* uhh…" He winced. "C'mon, just tell me. I forget."

"*Ben je klaar? Klaar* means ready."

We sat huddled together on an airplane bound for Amsterdam. He'd been learning to speak Dutch from the internet. He wasn't very good at it, but he didn't give up. I tried teaching him myself, but that didn't go very well either. Every time I spoke in Dutch, he got this look in his beautiful blue eyes. They kind of glazed over, and I would find myself bent over the end of a bed, a couch, a table, desk, or kitchen counter. Or he would. Or one of us ended up on our knees.

The last two months had been amazing. I never knew two people could be *zich zo verbonden voelen*—so connected. Could know each other so completely. And I'd never felt more myself than the way I did with him. He accepted my moods and my negative self-talk, though he always tried to redirect my thoughts in positive or constructive ways. But he never became angry or frustrated with me.

We both had tendencies to disappear into a kind of darkness. I didn't go there very often anymore, not with him around, but I dealt with death a lot in my work, and sometimes, it got to me. He'd lay with me for hours, holding me, talking or joking if it helped me, or just in silence when there was nothing to be said. I'd told him everything. Every ridiculous thought and desire. Every fear.

And KC? He'd opened up to me so much. Sometimes, I couldn't believe he was the same man I met last December. Still the same sarcastic smartass I fell in love with, his mouth got dirtier the more I got to know him, but he didn't doubt himself anymore. He didn't hide. Not from me and not from anyone else.

He introduced me to people as his boyfriend. He was very proud of himself when he learned to say it in Dutch. He walked around all day saying, "*Dit is mijn vriendje.*" He kissed me in public, in front of his brothers. Honestly, sometimes, he couldn't keep his hands off of me.

Like now.

We were in the last row of first class, and the seats across the aisle were empty. It was night and dark on the plane, but still, we were on a freaking airplane. There were people everywhere.

"Just talk to me in Dutch. I'll pick up the words by osmosis," he said, and I rolled my eyes. "Tell me all the words to describe your body. I'll touch you, and whatever part I touch, tell me the word."

"You are so filled of it."

"Full of it? And no, I'm just wicked creative. C'mon. What's this called?" He touched the top of my head with his fingertip and pulled his fingers through my hair, messing it. He loved to mess my hair. I rolled my eyes again but gave in to his game.

"Dat is mijn hoofd. You know that one."

"Ah, but *wat is dit*?" Pushing my hair away from my forehead, he caressed my cheek.

"Dat is mijn haar, en dit is mijn gezicht—face." I held his hand to my cheek. *"En dit is mijn wang."*

"Umm, no." He chuckled. "I think you misspoke. I know you're the Dutch expert between the two of us, but I'm pretty sure *this* is your wang," he whispered in my ear, squeezing my cock through my joggers with his other hand.

"No, *dat is mijn lul*," I whispered back, "and you better take your hand off of it if you do not want me to push you between my legs right here on the middle of this airplane."

"Mmm, was that a challenge?" he teased, and I raised an eyebrow and leaned over to kiss him.

I pressed my hand over his and squeezed. "Don't tempt me, *schatje*."

Drawing back an inch, he held my gaze as he pulled my joggers away from my body and slid his fingers inside, grasping my dick in his hot hand, stroking me slowly.

"KC!" I whispered.

"That sounded like a dare to me, Doc," he said, pumping slowly, and when he smiled, I moaned. "And you know I *never* back down from a dare." Circling the head of my cock with his thumb, he collected the instant cum and rubbed it down my shaft. "I've been hard for you since you fucked me this mornin' before we left for the airport. We're gonna have to go directly to the hotel, or I ain't gonna be able to walk straight."

"*Jezus*, KC. Ung," I grunted when he twisted his fist.

"Shhh, don't want an audience, do ya?" he spoke against my jaw, licking there while he pushed my pants open further, pulling me free of them. Slowly and looking in my eyes, he leaned down to suck me into his mouth. My hips jumped up, and he moaned.

"KC, stop. We are going to be arrested… Oh *mijn God. Dat*

is zo goed." I relaxed into my seat as he pumped me with his hand and sucked with his mouth, fast, but it wouldn't take long anyway. I was so turned on by his brazenness and his willingness to embarrass the hell out of himself just to make me feel good. I hadn't been kidding though—we could totally be arrested for this!

I tried so hard to be still and silent, but it was nearly impossible. My breath came faster and faster, and I pressed my teeth into my bottom lip as hard as I could to stop myself from moaning.

He sucked harder, jerking me in fast little pumps, and I imagined us in the lavatory, with my cock in his ass and his in my hand, thrusting furiously into him, and that was it—I came in his mouth.

The ease traveled through my body as I stared at him in awe. He sucked me clean, stuffed me back into my sweatpants, and licked his lips, lifting his eyes back to mine.

Oh, those eyes. Dark blue heaven.

"Mmm, *lekker*. Now there's some Dutch for ya."

"Oh, you smartass."

The pilot's voice announced over the intercom that we were approaching our destination and should return our seats and tray-tables to their upright positions—we would be arriving in Amsterdam in thirty minutes, where the weather was a pleasant twenty-one degrees Celsius, or seventy-one degrees Fahrenheit.

I was nervous, uneasy, and afraid. Afraid of walking out of the airport and seeing the sky in the place that killed my parents. The place that betrayed me, but also the place that made me, shaped me to be who I was. I was afraid of how it would look to my eyes. Sound in my ears. The cars. I was afraid of the familiar scents.

Maybe KC had known this. Maybe it was what his little impromptu oral session had been about.

A distraction.

Grabbing his hand, I squeezed as he straightened in his chair, adjusting himself. He relaxed back against his seat and turned his head to look at me, reaching over to push my messy hair away from my eyes again.

I was sure he could feel my hand shaking and my heart pounding.

"Ik ben bij je, Luuk. Altijd."

I am with you. Always.

Het Einde.

If you liked the book (or loved it, I hope), please leave a review—even just a few words would help—on your favorite bookseller website, Goodreads, or Bookbub. We self-published indie authors rely heavily upon reviews to get our stories out to the masses. And thank you. I know it takes time to do this. I appreciate the time out of your day and the effort.

Dear Reader,

Ain't the special glossy cover pretty? Those colors were picked out especially for Kev and Luuk. The teal color is exactly what pops into my mind when I think of Luuk's eyes, and the orange represents the Western sunset and Kevin's angst. Lol.

Thank you for coming on their journey with me. This book came at a time when I desperately needed to get lost in something (even more than I was already lost in Cade Ranch ;)). These characters stole my heart, and it was my honor to tell their story. I'm a little obsessed with them, if I'm honest.

Luuk and Kev helped me through a trauma I was struggling to process, and I'll be forever grateful to them. It was so important to me to find LGBTQ input for this book because, obviously, I'm not a gay man, so I reached out to someone who does have that experience, and we worked closely to make sure this story was told right.

I also relearned a whole language for these guys! I'd taken a few Dutch courses in college and loved them, but it had been years and I didn't remember a lick of it. But when I started writing book two in The Cade Ranch Series, and Oly needed a best friend from vet school, Luuk introduced himself to me in all his Dutch glory. I contacted an acquaintance who was born and raised in the Netherlands and lives there still, and she helped me get the language right. She's become a dear friend, and often when we're emailing, she grades my Dutch! I rarely get an A. But I'm still taking my Dutch lesson every day, and someday, I hope to go to the Netherlands to hug her!

I'll admit, when I first wrote Kev's character, I didn't know him well. But as soon as I met Luuk, I knew Kevin down to his bones. Their love story ignited in my mind, and I've never had more fun getting to know two characters. If you've read this book through to the end, I'm pretty certain you've fallen in love with them too, so thank you. Thanks for being on their side!

Now, only two brothers' stories are left to tell…

I hope you're ready!

love always,
  greta

READ ON FOR AN EXCERPT FROM JAY'S BOOK,
BRAVED >>>>>

BRAVED

Ten Months Ago

"Jay!"

Jack yelled across the arena from the office doorway. It was a cold Monday mornin' in November. The day had just gotten started, and already, I was freezin' and miserable, workin' harder than I ever wanted to on my family's horse ranch. Every day, I had to convince myself I didn't hate bein' a horse rancher. Well, more like a shit shoveler. I'd never had the knack for horses, not like my brothers.

"Yeah?"

"C'mere for a sec."

Uh… okay. It wasn't very often my oldest brother, Jack, called me into the office. I kinda felt like I'd been summoned to the principal's office even though I claimed part ownership of said office just like the rest of my brothers.

I stopped what I was doin', set my shovel against a stall door, and headed over to where my brother had disappeared behind his big desk.

Knockin' on the doorframe, I looked in at him standin' there, waitin' for me.

"Jesus, Jay. You don't have to knock. This is your office too."

"Right." I stepped in, claspin' my hands behind my back.

"Well, sit down."

Like I said, called to the principal's office.

Jack sat in the computer chair behind the old dinged and weathered wooden desk, and I sat in the hard-backed chair opposite him. If I ran this office, the first thing I'd do would be to upgrade all this mish-mosh furniture. You can't have a respectable business without respectable surroundin's.

"We talked about your ideas for the ranch."

"Yeah?" I sat straighter in my chair. Really? He'd actually listened to me? He'd actually thought about my idea to grow our business and, hopefully, increase our profits? I couldn't believe it. Every time I'd brought it up, he dismissed it. Or me. Or just slammed a door in my face.

"You mentioned a dude ranch."

"Yeah?"

"Like I said, we ain't doin' that."

"Oh. Right."

I was sure he could read the disappointment on my face even though I tried hard not to show it. I hated showin' weakness in front of my oldest brother or any of my brothers—they were all older than me—but I knew I possessed the skills to make our business great. It was what I had gone to school for, but… I just couldn't find the courage to stand my ground.

Jack had held our business, and our family, together through thick and thin, bringin' it back from the brink of death more than once. How arrogant would it be for me to disregard all that?

"But…"

"But?"

"But I been thinkin' about what Mr. Williams said, about them therapy animals they got over in Jackson. A dude ranch just ain't us, Jay. Buncha rich people hangin' around here all the time, payin' us money to clean up after 'em and teach 'em how to ride for five minutes? Sure, we'd make money but we'd be miserable. I think we're better than that. I think we could do somethin' to make a little money and help people at the same time."

"Yeah. That's—yeah," I said, noddin'.

"You look surprised."

"No, I mean, I just didn't think you—"

"I looked it up. There's a shit-ton of information about it all. Many different kinds of therapy we could provide. But we couldn't do it by ourselves. We'd need therapists, doctors, equipment. We'd have to train the horses specifically for it. But"—he waved his hand at the computer screen on the desk —"it's all makin' my head hurt. So, you do it. Research it. Come up with a plan. Talk to whoever you need to. I dunno. Whoever. Do whatever it is we paid all that money to send you to that fancy school for."

"Really?"

"Yep."

"Okay," I said, shakin' my head in utter disbelief. "I'm on it. I'll start now." I jumped up and turned toward the door, ready to go. I already had a million ideas runnin' through my mind.

"But Jay?"

"Yeah?" I turned back around.

"I still expect you to do your work every day. You ain't gettin' off the hook. We still need your help around here."

"Right. I know. I'll work on this in the evenin's." *Ughhh. More horse shit.* Didn't my honors degree in business mean anything to my family?

"If you need time off to, I dunno, meet with people or whatever, schedule it. Just like you would any other job. I need to be able to depend on you bein' here."

"Right. Okay."

"Here," he said, holdin' out a stack of papers. "This is everything I found. It ain't much, but I printed it all out."

Huh. I hadn't thought Jack even knew how to use a printer.

"Thanks." I took the papers from him. "Can I ask, what changed your mind? I've been buggin' you about this for a while."

"Yeah, you have." He squinted, considerin' me. "I ain't adverse to makin' money, Jay, but the whole dude ranch thing just don't sit right with me. This does. And, I guess, Evvie."

"Evvie?" The woman who stole my brother's heart in a heartbeat.

"Yeah. She says I'm bein' a dick and I oughta give you a chance. I should trust you."

"Oh, well…" I laughed. "Okay."

"Go on then," he said, wavin' me off with a flick of his wrist and a nod.

I turned and headed toward the door but stopped at the threshold. "Jack?"

Sighin', he looked up from his messy desktop. "What?"

"Thanks. Thanks for trustin' me. I won't let you down."

"I know you won't," he said, and he actually smiled.

Walkin' slowly from the office, I tried not to grin like an idiot and to look professional, but as soon as I cleared his eyeline, I ran to find Evvie. She stood in the stall closest to the arena entrance, brushin' a horse and cooin' to her about fairy princesses in big country castles. I had no idea what in the world she was talkin' about.

"Evvie?"

"Oh!" Both she and Fancy jumped a little. "You scared me, Jay."

"Sorry." I stepped in front of her and reached out to pull her into a hug, careful not to squeeze too hard. She still had stitches, her whole body bruised and sore. She'd been through absolute hell, but still, here she was, workin' as best she could to help Jack. To help us all 'cause she loved him. She loved us.

"What's that for?"

"Just… for lovin' my brother. Thank you."

She giggled and hugged me back. "No thanks necessary. I couldn't stop if I wanted to."

Steppin' back, I leaned in to kiss her cheek. "Yeah, but still, thank you."

BE BRAVE. Read the next story in the Cade Ranch series, *Braved.*

Become a Wisperite!
Join my newsletter for a FREE short story, *Wild Heart: Welcome to Wisper*, Wisper news, and The Cade Ranch Sexcapades—
naughty little interludes for my subscribers ONLY!
Jack and Evvie's wedding scenes are there!
Sign up on my website: gretarosewest.com

Hang out with me in my Facebook group, Wisperites Unite.
facebook.com/groups/wisperitesunite

Join my Team!
Receive an advanced review copy of my next book. Join my ARC team, a wonderful group of people who help get the word out when I release a new book!
Sign up on my website
gretarosewest.com

Scan the QR code below to take you straight to my website.

About the Author

Greta Rose West was a floundering artsy flake until cowboy Jack Cade showed up, knocking on the door of her brain, pounding on it, and then he just plain kicked it down. She's a boy mom to a grown freakin' man, and she lives in NW Indiana with her husband and her two precocious kitties, Geoff Trouble and Sally Mae Midnight. When she's not writing, she's reading and devouring music. She enjoys indie films no one else likes, and her favorite food is Aver's Veggie Revival pizza.

You can find her on Instagram @gretarosewest, in her Facebook group, Wisperites Unite!, or on her website.

gretarosewest.com

facebook.com/gretarosewest

instagram.com/gretarosewest

bookbub.com/authors/greta-rose-west

goodreads.com/gretarosewest

www.ingramcontent.com/pod-product-compliance
Lightning Source LLC
Chambersburg PA
CBHW060749190726

48285CB00002B/361